SEVENFOLD SWORD: UNITY

JONATHAN MOELLER

DESCRIPTION

The quest of the Seven Swords will destroy kingdoms.

Ridmark Arban is the Shield Knight, questing to stop the rise of the evil New God. But Ridmark and his companions are caught in the war between the final remnant of the dying gray elves and the brutal muridach horde.

Unless Ridmark can save the gray elves, he and his friends will die, and the New God will rise in power to enslave the world...

LEGAL

A BRIEF AUTHOR'S NOTE

At the end of this book, you will find a Glossary of Characters and a Glossary of Locations listing all the major characters and locations in this book, along with a chart listing the nine cities & Kings of the realm of Owyllain, the bearers of the Seven Swords, and the seven high priests of the Maledicti.

A map of the realms of Owyllain and Andomhaim are available on the author's website at http://www.jonathanmoeller.com.

1

THE HOST OF CARRION

Eighty-six days after the quest of the Seven Swords began, eighty-six days after the day in the Year of Our Lord 1488 when the cloaked stranger came to the High King of Andomhaim's court, Ridmark Arban felt a growing sense of unease.

Perhaps even alarm.

It had become clear that he and his companions were not alone in the foothills of the Gray Mountains.

It was a cloudy day, the sky overhead like a hammered sheet of steel. Ridmark would have expected rain, but Magatai and Tamara Earthcaller agreed that the wind was the wrong direction for a storm. The rain came off the steppes, but it never came from the mountains. That was just as well because it was cooler in the foothills. Ridmark had spent enough days traveling under the blazing sun of Owyllain to appreciate the respite from the heat.

Right now, though, the weather was a distant concern.

The tracks in the valley held his full attention.

There were many shallow valleys in the lower foothills of the Gray Mountains, and Ridmark walked through one. A narrow creek wound its way through the center of the valley, fed by snowmelt from the mountains. The rocky valley was full of tough grasses.

All the grass had been trampled underfoot.

Ridmark took a few steps forward, examining the ground.

Everywhere he looked, on every inch of ground, he saw the tracks of muridachs.

Most of the ratmen wore boots, and he saw the distinctive nailed tracks their boots left on the earth. Other muridachs, usually their scouts and berserkers, preferred to travel barefoot, and they left clawed footprints. Ridmark had seen muridach tracks all over the foothills. According to the men of Kalimnos, the muridachs had been heading south in greater and greater numbers over the last year, marching to war against the weakened gray elves of the Illicaeryn Jungle. Tracks from muridach warbands were a frequent sight in the foothills near Kalimnos.

But an army had left this trail.

And unless Ridmark missed his guess, that army had passed this way recently. Maybe even yesterday.

He took an uneasy look around. Ridmark and his companions would make a tempting target for the muridachs. Of course, any muridach warband that attacked Ridmark and the others would regret it. Ridmark's wife was the Keeper of Andomhaim and a wielder of powerful magic. Kalussa Pendragon carried the Staff of Blades and could slaughter a troop of muridachs on her own. Tamlin, Krastikon, and Calem bore the Swords of Earth, Death, and Air between them.

And Ridmark could hold his own in a fight.

But could they stand against an entire army of muridachs? For that matter, if the muridachs realized that Ridmark and his companions had three of the Seven Swords, the ratmen might decide it worth the risk to claim weapons of such power.

A different kind of track caught Ridmark's eye.

It was about a handspan across and sunk deep into the earth as if something heavy had driven the track into the ground. Ridmark had traveled the length and breadth of the Wilderland in Andomhaim and had seen (and fought) many strange creatures, but he had never seen a track quite like this. It looked like the mark of a claw.

Or perhaps that of a giant insect.

It was past time that Ridmark got back to the others. If a muridach army was marching through the foothills of the mountains, they needed to change their route. Perhaps it would be better to swing north, as close to the mountains as they could manage. That would slow their journey, but better to delay a few days than to run into thousands of muridach warriors looking for a fight.

He took one step to the west and stopped.

A flicker of motion had caught his eye.

Ridmark turned in a circle, drawing Oathshield from its scabbard and sweeping his eyes over the valley. Dozens of boulders littered the landscape, dotting the trampled grass, and he glimpsed a moving shadow behind one.

His fingers tightened against Oathshield. Human armies, when they marched to war, always had stragglers, men delayed by ill fortune, or maybe by laziness. Perhaps muridach armies were no different. And perhaps the muridach stragglers, seeing Ridmark's dark elven armor and his gray elven cloak, had decided he would make an easy target.

He strode towards the boulder, Oathshield coming up in guard, and the muridachs came into sight.

There were four of the creatures. Muridachs tended to be shorter than humans but taller than halflings. These muridachs came to about five and a half feet in height, their bodies covered in brownish-black fur. They walked like humans and used weapons and tools as humans did, but they had the heads of giant rats, with beady black eyes and long, tufted ears pierced with earrings of bronze and copper. They also had giant, chisel-like teeth that could punch through flesh and bone and even armor without much difficulty. Pink tails curled behind them, as thick as Ridmark's arm. The musky stench of the muridachs' fur filled Ridmark's nostrils, and the ratmen advanced.

"This needn't end in a fight," said Ridmark in orcish, watching the muridachs. "But if you want a fight, I'll give you one."

The muridachs chittered with laughter. The voices of muridachs, at least male muridachs, were deep and raspy. But they all laughed with that same high-pitched, chittering laugh. Something about it grated on Ridmark's ears and made his skin crawl.

"Give us your sword and armor, human, and we shall let you go," said one of the muridachs.

Ridmark snorted. "Then you'll just kill me and eat me."

Again, the muridachs laughed.

"We can do this the easy way or the hard way," said the muridach leader, "and you have chosen the hard way."

Ridmark shrugged and took Oathshield in a two-handed grip. "As you wish, then."

He took one step to the left, and the muridachs hesitated, raising their bronze swords in guard. Strength surged into Ridmark through his bond with Oathshield, and he charged, moving faster than the muridachs would have thought possible. He swung Oathshield with all his strength and the soulblade's power driving his blow, and he took off the head of the muridach on the left. The rat-like head bounced away, the black eyes wide and staring with surprise, and the furred body fell to the ground, crimson blood spurting from the stump of the neck.

The remaining three muridachs whirled, trying to keep Ridmark in sight, and he drove Oathshield forward. The soulblade punched through the nearest muridach's leather armor and found its heart. The creature shrieked, and Ridmark ripped his sword free and stepped back.

The other two muridachs spread around him. Ridmark retreated, parried a slash with Oathshield, and then struck. His sword bit into the leg of the muridach on his right, and the creature stumbled. Ridmark backed away again as the muridach on his left attacked, and he parried three blows in rapid succession.

After the third attack, the muridach overbalanced, and Ridmark opened its throat with a quick slash of his soulblade. The final muridach howled and charged, and Ridmark parried, shoved, and sent the muridach stumbling back. The ratman's weight came down on his wounded leg, and the creature staggered.

Ridmark finished the muridach with a quick stab and looked around, but nothing else moved in the valley.

He cleaned the blood from Oathshield's blade, sheathed the sword, and headed to the west.

If there was a muridach horde loose in the hills, he needed to warn the others before it was too late.

~

CALLIANDE ARBAN RELEASED the Sight with a sigh of relief, rubbing her left temple with her free hand.

It was a morning ritual for her, one she had followed every morning since they had left Aenesium to travel to Kalimnos. Her sons were of her flesh and blood, which meant she could use the Sight to find them anywhere. They remained in Aenesium, in the care of Tamlin's master-at-arms Michael, and as far as Calliande could tell, they were safe and healthy.

That was a relief. Though it did little to assuage her guilt. She should have been with them, but her duties as Keeper demanded that she leave them in Aenesium. Did they resent her for that, she wondered? Did they feel that she had abandoned them? They had been glad to see her when she and Ridmark had returned to Aenesium after the defeat of the Necromancer, but Gareth and Joachim might have blamed her for leaving again.

Or maybe they wouldn't. Sometimes children were surprisingly resilient.

And sometimes they were not. King Hektor Pendragon had taken a new queen after the death of Queen Helen...and his eldest son Rypheus had never, ever forgiven him for that. Then again, Rypheus had grown into manhood with the Maledictus Khurazalin whispering poison into his ear.

Thinking of the Maledicti turned her thoughts to the Maledictus of Shadows and the trap at Kalimnos, and that turned Calliande's guilt into rage. The trap the Maledicti had prepared had thrown the death of Calliande's daughter into her face, had made her believe that

Joanna was alive and healthy. The delusion had shattered when Ridmark had beaten the Maledicti and Third had released Lord Amruthyr from his millennia-long torment.

Perhaps the Maledicti had thought the vision would break Calliande with guilt, as it almost had when Joanna had died.

It had only enraged her.

How dare they. How dare they throw her daughter's death in her face, use it as a weapon against her. The next time Calliande encountered one of the Maledicti, she would make them regret it.

Though the Maledicti had already heaped up a mountain of crimes, iniquities, and innocent blood in their service to their New God.

That thought reminded her to focus on the present. It would be an ill fate if the Keeper of Andomhaim were taken unawares and slain because she was brooding. Calliande took a deep breath, rolled her shoulders to ease the unaccustomed weight of her new armor, and looked back at the others.

It was a somber company that she and her husband led to the east.

Kalussa Pendragon walked behind Calliande, her face distant, her eyes hooded. Like Calliande, she wore a cuirass of overlapping plates of golden metal that hung to her knees, taken from the dungeons beneath the Tower of Nightmares. Sir Calem brought up the back of the line, his face blank, and he had not spoken a word save to answer a question since they had left Kalimnos. The mind-altering spell had removed Kalussa's and Calem's inhibitions, and they had spent that day acting on their attraction to each other. When the spell had broken, and clarity had returned, Kalussa had blamed herself for seducing Calem, and Calem blamed himself for taking advantage of Kalussa.

Calliande had to admit she thought the whole thing foolish, but she was not in the best mood.

Behind Kalussa came Third and Kyralion. Both were lost in thought. Kyralion wore the golden armor that Kolmyrion had given him in the Tower of Nightmares, a golden sword of gray elven steel at his belt. Lord Amruthyr had told Third and Kyralion that the fate of the gray elves lay in their hands. Calliande supposed that would give anyone cause to reflect.

Though she could not see how Third and Kyralion could decide the fate of the gray elves.

Prince Krastikon came next. Like the others, he had taken gray elven armor from the Tower of Nightmares before they had departed Kalimnos, and Calliande had to admit it suited him. Like the others, he looked distant. Perhaps he was thinking of his wife, far away in Trojas. Calliande felt a pang of sympathy for him. With her Sight, she could check on her children whenever she wished, and with her magic, she could find Ridmark anywhere. Krastikon enjoyed no such luxury.

After Krastikon came Tamlin and Tamara, and the two of them looked...

Happy. Unlike the others, they looked happy.

Tamara Earthcaller wore a long coat, a vest of scutian leather, trousers, and dusty boots, and she now carried Lord Amruthyr's staff in her right hand. She looked at Tamlin, and sometimes her mismatched eyes of purple and blue flashed with delight when she smiled. Tamlin had replaced the bronze armor of an Arcanius Knight with overlapping plates of gray elven steel taken from the Tower of Nightmares, and some of his old gallant manner had resurfaced. He played the courtly knight for Tamara, much to her amusement and pleasure.

Normally, Calliande would have said that it was obvious they were falling in love. Except that Tamara had also been both Tamlin's slain wife Tysia and Tirdua of Trojas. In a way, it was like a reunion. Calliande had been teaching Tamara to meditate and focus her mind, trying to draw out the memories that troubled her with nightmares, but so far it had not worked.

A squawk came to Calliande's ears, and she turned her head.

A struthian lizard loped towards them. The creature looked gangly and awkward, with a long neck, waving tail and spindly legs, yet she ran with fluid grace, her tail stretched stiff behind her for balance. Atop the struthian rode a Takai halfling in boots, trousers, and a vest of scutian hide, his muscled arms marked with swirling tattoos of blue and black. His green eyes remained ever watchful, and he had traded the practice of lacquering his hair into a horned shape for the simplicity of pulling it back into a tail. He carried a bow and a pair of javelins, and Kyralion's soulstone-empowered sword hung in its scabbard next to his saddle.

Calliande smiled as she saw him. Nothing seemed to dent Magatai's invincible self-confidence and cheerfulness. The Takai nomads seemed to regard facing death cheerfully as one of the highest virtues.

"Mighty Keeper," said Magatai, reining up Northwind. "Magatai has returned from scouting to the south."

"So the mighty Keeper has observed," said Calliande in a dry voice. Some quirk of the Takai language seemed to cause Magatai to refer to himself in the third person when speaking in Latin. "What have you seen?"

"There are no foes from here to the steppes proper," said Magatai. "Friend Ridmark has gone to scout to the east and the north, yes?"

"He has," said Calliande. Magatai was always polite, which seemed to be another trait of the Takai halflings, possibly to cut down on deaths from duels. Yet he always referred to Ridmark as "friend Ridmark," and he applied the same honorific to Kyralion and Third, but to no one else. It had taken Calliande about a day to figure out that Magatai only spoke that way about those who had accompanied him into the Tower of Nightmares to face the Maledicti and the Scythe. "I think he's coming back this way. He should be back soon."

Magatai frowned. "Magatai does not like this wind. It stinks of the ratmen."

"Do you think they are coming?" said Tamara.

Tamara and Tamlin had drawn closer. Kalussa tried to smile a little at Tamlin and didn't quite manage it.

"Magatai does not know, Tamara Earthcaller," said Magatai. He tapped his sword hilt a few times. "The ratmen are ever cunning and must travel in large groups to survive the journey across the Takai steppes, lest the warriors of the Takai destroy them. Magatai fears that we shall encounter such a large band in these hills." He snorted. "Though since friend Ridmark smote the Maledicti, and if you truly defeated the Necromancer and King Justin, then perhaps the muridachs shall be no threat at all."

"It is never wise to underestimate anyone," said Calliande. "I am surprised the Tumaks of the Takai have not allied with the gray elves against the muridachs. Surely you face a common foe."

Magatai snorted again. "The Tumaks would, but the gray elves are too haughty to accept aid." He glanced back at Kyralion. "Friend Kyralion is the first gray elf Magatai has met who is not ruled by his own arrogance. The Takai and the gray elves marched with many other kindreds to overthrow the Sovereign in his own citadel. But since that victory, the gray elves have withdrawn and only leave the Illicaeryn Jungle to raid the muridachs."

"The plague curse, probably," said Kalussa. Calliande felt a flicker of amusement. Even in her grim mood, Kalussa Pendragon still liked to have the last word. "The gray elves withdrew into the Illicaeryn Jungle after my uncle defeated the Sovereign. But now that Lord Kyralion has told of Qazaldhar's plague curse, we know the reason why."

"Magatai does not know why the gray elves do not seek aid against the muridachs," said Magatai. "The muridachs have many enemies."

"Pride can make men do strange things," said Calliande. She looked at Kalussa. "Like blaming themselves for something that isn't anyone's fault."

Kalussa looked away, her face coloring a little.

"You said you don't like the wind?" said Tamlin.

"It stinks of the muridachs," said Magatai.

"I cannot smell anything," said Tamara.

"That is because you are human," said Magatai. "Humans have weak noses."

Krastikon snorted. "Do we, now?"

"To be fair, so do the Takai, though we excel at all other things," said Magatai. He patted Northwind's neck, and the struthian let out an approving squawk. "But struthians, their noses are far keener than those of humans or halflings or elves. Or even whatever friend Third is. And Northwind does not like the smell of the wind from the mountains. It stinks of ratmen."

"Perhaps that is not surprising," said Tamara. "The muridachs have been crawling all over the hills for the last year. The men of Kalimnos had to fight them many times."

"Magatai is right," said Kyralion. "We may be in danger."

Calliande glanced back. Kyralion had come up in perfect silence. He was at least as stealthy as Third when he put his mind to it. He had the sharp, alien features of the elven kindreds, with golden eyes and pointed ears, and his skin was weathered and lined from years traveling under the harsh sun of Owyllain. Third followed him in silence, her face a calm mask.

"Why is that?" said Calliande.

"The muridachs have been sending more and more warbands against the Liberated as the plague curse worsened," said Kyralion. "There are no entrances to the Deeps in the Takai steppes..."

"There are multiple entrances to the Deeps in the steppes, friend Kyralion," said Magatai.

"True," said Kyralion. "Rather, there are no entrances to the Deeps in the southern parts of the steppes, near the Illicaeryn Jungle, and the northern entrances to the Deeps are watched closely by the Takai. The Takai kill anyone emerging from those entrances. If the muridachs want to bring a large force to the surface, they have to do it in the foothills of the Gray Mountains. And if they want to march an army to the Illicaeryn Jungle, the most direct path from the foothills to the jungle is here."

Calliande frowned. "Right here?"

Kyralion nodded. "This very valley, I believe."

Third frowned. "Perhaps we should change direction."

"Agreed. Wait a moment," said Calliande. She grasped the hilt of the dagger at her belt, the dagger that Ridmark had given her all those years ago outside of Dun Licinia. That dagger had a link back to Ridmark, and Calliande used that link to cast a spell, pinpointing his exact location. He was only a half-mile to the west, and she thought that he was moving quickly. "Ridmark's almost back. Let's halt here and wait for him to catch up to us, and then we can decide what to do."

"Sir Calem!" called Krastikon, walking back toward the line of pack scutians that bore their supplies. The big, placid lizards had bony shields covering their necks and sharp beaks. They didn't move all that fast, but they were strong and vigorous, and nothing seemed to bother them. Though when something did annoy the creatures, they could use their sharp beaks to make their displeasure known. "We'll halt here for a moment. I'll help you tend to the scutians."

Calem nodded, his expression unchanging. Calliande felt a pang for him. He had seemed dazed when she had suppressed the spell of dark magic that bound him into a brutal assassin, unsure of himself and uncertain of everything except combat. Then he had gotten to know Kalussa, and Calem had started to change, becoming something other than a killing machine.

Perhaps Kalussa blamed herself for seducing him, but there had been many other things in her life. Calem had known nothing but violence and torment and killing until Ridmark had defeated him and Calliande had suppressed the spell that bound him, and it was possible that his short time courting Kalussa had been the happiest that Calem had ever been. Calliande wished she could have done more for him or for Kalussa, but she had heard High King Arandar say often enough that not even a king could order a man's heart.

That was true of the Keeper of Andomhaim as well.

"If the muridachs are coming in force through this chain of valleys," said Third, "we ought not to linger here."

"No," said Calliande. "We should not. We'll move as soon as Ridmark returns."

"Perhaps it would be better to return to Kalimnos and the Pass of Ruins and approach the Monastery of St. James from the west, rather than the south," said Third. "If the gray elves and the Takai both are fighting the muridachs, we might walk into the war."

Calliande looked at Kyralion, unsure of how he would respond. The Augurs of his people had sent him to find the Shield Knight, the Keeper, and the woman of the blue fire, saying that only the woman of the blue fire could save the Liberated. Yet if Lord Amruthyr was right, the Augurs had lied to Kyralion, omitting the part that he had to play. It was hard to judge his emotions, but Calliande thought he felt betrayed.

Perhaps he wanted to return to the Illicaeryn Jungle. Maybe he did not.

"Agreed," said Kyralion. "The Takai steppes were dangerous when I traveled through them a year ago, and they have become only more dangerous since."

"Magatai fears not to kill muridachs," he announced. "Tens of thousands of them, though, might prove a challenge."

"Well," said Tamara with a smile. "You would want it to be a fair fight, wouldn't you?"

Magatai barked a laugh at that and then fell silent.

"Lord Ridmark comes," he said.

Calliande turned her head and saw her husband approaching at a jog from the far side of the valley and smiled.

Her smile faded when she saw his grim expression.

It seemed that he had already found the enemy.

TAMLIN COULD NOT RECALL EVER FEELING QUITE so uncertain of himself.

Strangely, he did not mind the feeling at all.

His life had been one of certainty for a long time. At first, as a child, he had been certain he would become a monk. Then he had devoted himself to escaping from Urd Maelwyn, then to avenging Tysia's death at Khurazalin's hands, and after his escape, to serving as an Arcanius and a Companion knight.

Then he had learned that his mother still lived.

And he had found Tysia again in the form of Tirdua in Trojas, and Khurazalin had killed her again.

Then he had met Tamara in the Pass of Ruins...and Tamlin found it hard not to stare at her.

Fortunately, she didn't seem to mind. And she spent as much time staring at Tamlin.

She was just like Tysia, and nothing at all like her. Tamara had Tysia's gentle nature, her thoughtfulness, her same smile and sly sense of humor. Unlike Tysia, she was far more confident, even brash at times. There was a wildness in her nature that Tamlin suspected she had learned from Magatai and the Takai nomads, and she was far more capable in battle than Tirdua had been. Calliande thought Tysia and Tirdua and Tamara and the four other shards had been pieces of the same woman split into different lives, and a woman raised in a palace would be quite different than one raised as a tavern keeper's daughter, even if her essential nature remained the same. Tamlin suspected he would have been a very different man if Justin had not destroyed the monastery, if he had followed his original plan and become a monk.

Maybe it was just as well, despite all the losses and pain. Tamlin suspected he would not have made a good monk. He liked the company of women too much. Certainly, during his time in King Hektor's service, he had experienced no difficulty in seducing female companions to his side, and that had been an enjoyable diversion.

But none of them had been Tysia.

In the end, they had only been distractions from the woman with the golden staff and the dusty coat standing next to him, and Tamlin found that he wanted her as much as he had ever wanted anything in his life.

He had to keep her safe, no matter what the risk to himself. No matter what the cost.

So, he cleared his mind for battle as Ridmark Arban jogged to join them.

The Shield Knight of Andomhaim was a grim-looking man of about forty, with black hair turning gray at the temples and hard blue eyes. Ridmark looked dangerous, but appearances were sometimes deceptive. In Ridmark's case, his appearance was deceptive because he was far more dangerous than he looked. The War of the Seven Swords had been stalemated for years between King Hektor, King Justin, the Confessor, and the Necromancer of Trojas, and in the space of a month, both King Justin and the Necromancer had been slain and their power broken. They had been defeated because they had challenged Ridmark and Calliande, and the Shield Knight and the Keeper had proven more than a match for their foes.

Even in Kalimnos, when the dark spell of the Tower of Nightmares had crippled the minds of the town, Ridmark had faced two of the seven high priests of the Maledicti, and he had fought them to a draw.

"Trouble?" said Calliande as Ridmark came to a stop.

"Yes," said Ridmark. From time to time, Ridmark complained that he was getting old, but Tamlin noted that the Shield Knight was not even breathing hard after his jog across the valley. "I saw the tracks from a vast army of muridachs, and I ran into four of their stragglers."

No need to ask what had happened to those stragglers.

"How recently had they passed?" said Third.

"Not long," said Ridmark. "Perhaps this very day. I'm not sure how many there were. Thousands, most likely."

Magatai grunted. "A great host went to make war upon the gray elves."

"The Keeper and I think it might be best to return to Owyllain through the Pass of Ruins and approach the Monastery of St. James from that direction," said Third.

Ridmark hesitated and then nodded. "Yes. Yes, I think you're right. We'll lose two days heading back to Kalimnos, and at least another week and a half circling around the northern flank of the Gray Mountains. But I don't see that we have any choice. If we run into a muridach army, we'll put up a good fight, but we'll get overwhelmed in the end. And if they catch us in the foothills, they might trap us in one of these valleys, or surround us if we're atop a hill." He let out a long breath. "No, better to backtrack and lose the extra days rather than to risk everything and get torn apart by the muridachs."

"The wise hunter does not pursue prey he cannot overcome, friend Ridmark," proclaimed Magatai. "Such is the wisdom of the Takai."

Ridmark snorted. "And who am I to question the wisdom of the Takai?"

"And if we return to Aenesium for supplies," said Kalussa, "you'll be able to see your sons again, Lady Calliande."

"Aye," said Calliande. "Aye, I would like that."

Calem stiffened. Perhaps he feared King Hektor's wrath for having seduced his daughter. Tamlin thought the strain between Kalussa and Calem ridiculous. Calem hadn't forced her, Kalussa had plainly wanted him, and the two of them were making themselves miserable over nothing. While Kalussa was his friend, Tamlin had thought she would benefit immensely from experiencing the embrace of a man, and Calem clearly adored her.

Well, perhaps Tamlin could talk some sense into her before they returned to Aenesium. Kalussa wanted a husband, and she could do far worse than Sir Calem. Maybe by then, the shock would have worn off, and Kalussa would be thinking clearly again. Tamlin knew the first time was often harder for a woman than for a man, though judging by the noises he remembered Kalussa making, it hadn't been that difficult for her.

He looked at Tamara and wondered what it would be like to kiss her, to experience other things. He wondered what it would be like to walk into his domus with her and to see Michael's reaction. That would...

A flicker of motion caught his eye, a golden-brown shape scrambling along the rocky slope of the valley.

"Something is coming," said Third, stepping to the side and drawing her swords.

Tamlin turned just in time to see a hideous creature scramble to the top of a nearby hill, a muridach warrior crouched atop its back.

2

THE INVASION

Ridmark had fought muridachs more times than he had wished, but he had never seen a creature like the one atop the hill.

It was as large as a wagon, its body a brownish-gold in color, its six legs braced against the earth, its antennae waving around its head. The creature looked like a giant cockroach, though Ridmark had never seen a cockroach with massive jagged pincers jutting from its head. A muridach warrior sat on the huge insect's back, a bronze-tipped wooden lance in his right hand. His left hand held a pair of leather reins, and Ridmark saw that the reins were tied to a pair of spikes that had been driven into the creature's head. The insect's head jerked left and right, the antennae waving and the pincers clacking.

"What the hell is that thing?" said Krastikon, drawing the Sword of Death.

"Kalocrypt," said Tamara and Magatai in unison.

They looked at each other, and Tamara gestured for Magatai to continue.

"The muridachs breed herds of them in the Deeps," said Magatai, "and as the Takai ride upon our struthians to battle, so do the muridachs ride their foul kalocrypts to war."

"Cavalry, then," said Ridmark. "And they must make for fearsome scouts."

"Aye," said Magatai.

"And they've seen us," said Calliande.

The muridach lancer raised a horn to his mouth and blew a long, ringing blast with the instrument. The echoes rang over the hills, and Ridmark heard a rustling, creaking noise.

A dozen more kalocrypts and their muridach riders came into sight, and the giant insects raced down the hillside, their pincers clacking. The damned things could move as fast as a charging horse.

"I don't think they're coming to greet us," said Tamlin, drawing the Sword of Earth from its scabbard.

"No," said Ridmark, lifting Oathshield. "Get ready. Keep them away from Calliande, Kalussa, and Tamara so they can cast spells."

The kalocrypts rushed into the valley, and Ridmark drew on Oathshield for strength and speed.

～

TAMARA TOOK a deep breath and then another, clearing her mind to work magic.

The staff of Lord Amruthyr felt cool and heavy in her right hand. The strange golden metal of the gray elves looked smooth, but it felt as if it had been wrapped in rough leather, and Tamara had no trouble keeping her grip on the weapon. The staff augmented and enhanced any spell cast through it, and Tamara suspected that was going to prove useful in a few moments.

She had fought kalocrypts before, and it never went well.

"My lady," said Tamara, holding her magic ready. "The spell to fold the earth will not hinder the kalocrypts."

Calliande nodded. "Too many legs for them to lose their balance, I expect. How do they fight?"

"They'll try to run right over us," said Tamara, watching the line of kalocrypts charge towards them. "The pincers can bite a man in half, and the muridachs will spear us as they run past."

"All right," said Calliande, grasping her staff in both hands. "We'll have to deal with them one by one. Kalussa?"

Kalussa Pendragon nodded and raised her dark staff, the crystal at the end shifting and writhing. Tamara had never met a king's daughter before, at least that she could remember, so she wasn't sure what to make of her. Kalussa had seemed so confident and sure of herself when she had come to Kalimnos, but now she seemed shaken.

But her hand did not shake as she leveled the Staff of Blades, and her eyes narrowed with concentration.

The crystal at the end of the Staff shivered and spat a fist-sphere of blue crystal. It hurtled across the valley and slammed into the head of the leading kalocrypt. There was a spray of green slime from the impact, and the creature went into a wild dance, throwing the muridach from its back. The huge insect shuddered once more and then curled into a ball.

Calliande struck next, and Tamara felt the surge of power from the Keeper. She conjured a column of acidic mist about two feet wide and twelve tall, and one of the kalocrypts ran right into it. The muridach on the creature's back screamed as it caught fire, and the kalocrypt went berserk with pain. The insect twisted and skittered away towards the hills, leaving the dying muridach to writhe upon the ground.

Tamara cast her own spell, raising her left hand and hooking her fingers into a claw. She didn't need the golden staff, not for this spell. A sphere of whirling mist appeared over her hand, and an effort of will sent it shooting across the valley. The sphere struck a muridach rider in the chest and exploded into a ragged cloud of acid, and the muridach fell from the back of its kalocrypt with a scream, the acid chewing into its flesh.

It was a horrible way to die, but Tamara knew exactly what the muridachs would do to them if they were victorious, and she felt no remorse.

Then the remaining kalocrypts drew close enough to strike, and

Ridmark, Tamlin, Calem, Krastikon, Third, Kyralion, and Magatai attacked.

The muridachs had no doubt thought to overwhelm them, tramping them beneath the kalocrypts' spiked legs and snapping pincers. It took only a second to see that the muridachs had miscalculated grievously. Ridmark dodged to the side at the last second, moving with the uncanny speed that his sword granted, and brought Oathshield hammering down in a two-handed blow. He hewed off the head of a kalocrypt, and the creature collapsed, its muridach rider catapulting out of his saddle with a shriek.

All her life, Tamara had heard tales of the terrible power of the Seven Swords. As Swordborn, Tamlin and Krastikon could not use the full power of their Swords, and Calem could only use the minor powers of his, lest he trigger the spell of dark magic that bound his mind. Yet the Swords' deadly edges cut through anything, passing through flesh and bone and armor as if they were not there, and the chitin of the kalocrypts proved no match for the Swords.

Prince Krastikon caught the pincers of a kalocrypt on his shield, the golden metal pulsing with purple light. Like the others, he had taken armor from the long-dead warriors of the Tower of Nightmares, but he had also taken a round shield, and the ancient metal fused with his earth magic proved strong enough to resist the pincers of the kalocrypt. The pincer rebounded from his shield, and Krastikon brought the dark blade of the Sword of Death up and then down in an overhand stroke. The Sword bisected the kalocrypt's head, and the big insect went into a jerking dance. Its muridach rider roared in fury and leaped from the saddle, spear raised to stab the Prince, but Krastikon stepped into the blow. The gray elven armor he wore turned aside the bronze point of the spear, and the Sword of Death opened the muridach rider from throat to navel.

Kyralion and Magatai hung back from the battle, bows in hand, and sent a steady stream of arrows at the enemy. Magatai bellowed imprecations in the Takai tongue as he loosed arrow after arrow, and Tamara knew just enough of the Takai language to recognize that Magatai challenged the morality of the muridachs' mothers, the faithfulness of their wives, the muridachs' ability to satisfy their wives, and the legitimacy of their children.

The Takai regarded battle insults as an art.

Tamara cast another spell, hurling a sphere of acidic mist at a muridach lancer atop a kalocrypt. The kalocrypt twisted aside at the last second, and the sphere of mist expanded across two of its right legs. The creature let out a clacking shriek and went into a mad dance as the acid burned into its carapace, and the rider fought to get its mount back under control.

Third seized the opportunity to attack. Tamara was a little frightened of her, though that had lessened after they had survived the Tower of Nightmares together. Nevertheless, there was no denying Third's skill. She moved with the speed and fluidity of a striking serpent, and her blows landed with the force of a hammer. Even with her ability to travel blocked by the three Swords, she was still a terror on a battlefield.

Which she proved by leaping onto the side of the kalocrypt, scrambling along its carapace, and killing the muridach rider before the ratman could draw his sword.

Tamara had always been able to handle herself in a fight, but she felt like a clumsy child next to Third.

She focused on another kalocrypt and cast a spell, engulfing the creature's head in a sphere of acidic mist. The kalocrypt went mad with pain and threw its rider. The muridach hit the ground with a thump and rolled to its feet, its sword flying from its scabbard, its beady eyes fixed on Tamara.

She started to work another spell, and Tamlin intercepted the creature.

The Sword of Earth was a green blur in his hand, and the muridach jumped back in time to avoid the blade. The creature snarled and came at Tamlin, chopping its bronze sword with a two-handed blow. Tamlin raised the Sword of Earth in a lazy, one-handed parry, and the bronze sword shattered against the mighty weapon. The muridach stumbled in surprise and Tamlin's movements became much less lazy as he whipped the Sword of Earth around and cut the muridach in half.

And as he did, two of the kalocrypts converged on him.

"Tamlin!" shouted Tamara, a surge of fear going through her, but he was too far away to hear her shout.

Fortunately, it didn't matter.

Tamlin moved at the last possible instant, his right hand sweeping the Sword of Earth before him. The blade sheared through the pincers of the kalocrypt on his right, and the pincers that would have bitten off his arm instead fell useless to the ground. He thrust his left hand, and a bolt of lightning arced from his fingers and slammed into the kalocrypt on his left. The lightning coiled around the creature like the lash of a whip, and it reared back, jerking and twitching.

Before either kalocrypt could recover, Tamlin moved. He chopped the Sword of Earth in two quick slashes, taking off the head of the kalocrypt he had wounded. The muridach rider howled in outrage and leaped from its saddle, and Tamlin dodged and took off the muridach's head. The second kalocrypt shook off the lightning attack, and Tamlin whirled and cast another spell. This was a spell of elemental air that let him leap higher and faster than the strength of his muscles would have allowed, and he soared through the air, swinging the Sword of Earth as he did.

The muridach rider's head rolled away, and the insect turned and skittered away from the battle, losing interest without its rider to guide it.

Tamlin had dealt with both kalocrypts in the space of about five seconds.

Tamara felt a surge of admiration. He was so quick and skilled. She knew his childhood had been a brutal torment of pain and fear, but it had made him into a ferocious warrior. And she had never seen him undressed, but she knew the body beneath the armor and clothing would be lean and scarred and heavy with muscle, and Tamara had a sudden, vivid memory of running her fingers down his back, feeling his skin beneath her hands...

She had never experienced that, but she remembered it as vividly as if she had done it this morning.

Tamara pushed the thought out of her head. A battle wasn't the time or the place for such musings, no matter how pleasant. Worse, another wave of kalocrypts rushed down the slope of the valley. Between the Shield Knight, the bearers of the Seven Swords, and the magic of Calliande and Kalussa, they had driven back most of the first wave of muridach riders, but the second one might prove more formidable.

And then a flare of blue light caught her eye.

On the hilltop overlooking the valley, where the first kalocrypt rider had sounded that horn, stood three muridachs. From this distance, Tamara could not make out details, but she saw that all three muridachs wore cowls and mantles the color of blood. They carried wooden staffs, and Tamara knew that those staffs would have been topped with the mummified heads of muridachs, or if the priest was particularly powerful, the mummified head of a human slave.

She knew that because the three muridachs were priests of the Lord of Carrion, the muridach god, and they would be powerful dark wizards. The muridachs had a natural inclination to dark magic, an inborn talent to it, and while their priests were never very skilled, they nonetheless had considerable raw magical strength.

Three would be enough to kill everyone in the valley.

The blue light brightened as the muridach priests worked their spell, joining their powers to strike.

"Lady Calliande!" called Tamara.

THIRD WHIRLED THROUGH THE BATTLEFIELD, killing at every opportunity.

She was at home in battle, almost at ease, or at least as close to it as she came. She did not discount the danger, nor was she foolish enough to think herself invincible. A warrior who failed to respect her foes would soon end up dead. A single misstep and not even Calliande's magic could save her.

But her father had bred her and shaped her for battle. The Traveler was dead now, and Queen Mara ruled over his realm, trying to teach his enslaved Anathgrimm warriors to live as free men. Third was no longer an urdhracos, no longer enslaved to the aura of a dark elven lord.

But she had still been made to fight and kill, and that was what she did best.

She scrambled up the side of another kalocrypt, her short swords drawn back to strike. The insects were fierce beasts, but Third suspected they only went to war when goaded by their muridach masters. Likely in the Deeps the kalocrypts lived on carrion and preferred to scavenge rather than risk a direct confrontation with prey that could fight back.

And it was far easier to kill a muridach warrior than a kalocrypt.

The muridach rider turned and tried to stab her with his spear. It was a clumsy thrust, and Third used her right-hand sword to beat it aside. Her left sword plunged into the muridach's throat, and she ripped it free, crimson blood glimmering on the blue dark elven steel of the blade. Without the muridach to guide it, the kalocrypt skittered away from the battle.

Third leaped from the creature's carapace and landed, her swords coming up in guard. She glanced at Kyralion, but he was safe, his face hard and focused as he sent burning arrows at the muridach riders. Third had to admit that she thought he looked splendid in the armor that Kolmyrion had given him, that she felt a flicker of pleasure as she looked at him.

It was a new feeling for her, one she had never experienced until she had met Kyralion, and she didn't know what to do about it.

But she did know what to do about the kalocrypts and the muridachs, and Third set to work.

She joined Ridmark as he carved his way through the foe, and they fell into their usual pattern of fighting, one that had served them well against the Frostborn and the Enlightened and so many other foes. Third was strong, but Ridmark was stronger even without Oathshield's power, and she distracted the kalocrypts, drawing the attention of their riders. And as the muridachs turned towards her, Ridmark delivered hammer blows with Oathshield, killing their mounts and letting Third deal with the riders.

A flare of blue light caught her eye, and Third looked up just in time to see the three muridach priests cast their spell. Something that looked like a whirling disk of shadow and blue fire shot across the valley. Third had seen spells like that before and knew it was an attack of dark magic designed to leach away the life of anyone it touched. But the Keeper of Andomhaim was ready, and Calliande's staff burned with white fire. She shouted and gestured, and a wall of translucent white light rose up from the ground. The muridachs' magic slammed into it with a thunderclap, but the will of the Keeper of Andomhaim proved the stronger.

Third looked at Ridmark. "I will deal with them."

Ridmark nodded. "Go."

He turned to face another kalocrypt before the word had even gotten all the way out of his mouth.

Third sprinted across the valley, leaving the melee behind. As she drew closer, she saw the red-mantled muridach priests focus on her, saw the grisly mummified heads hanging from their staffs. Their cowls turned in her direction. They saw her coming, and no doubt they would draw upon their magic to strike her dead.

It was a race, then.

Third ran faster, the blue light brightening around the muridach priests.

A faint pressure inside her skull vanished, one that she barely noticed unless she happened to look for it.

She had gotten far enough away from the Swords of Air, Death, and Earth that they would no longer block her ability to travel.

Third reached for the fiery song in her blood and traveled.

Blue fire swallowed the world, and when it cleared, she stood atop the hill. It had been a long jump, right at the edges of her ability, but she had done it. Third had reappeared behind the three muridach priests, who gaped at the battle in the valley, no doubt trying to figure out where she had gone.

Third raised her swords and started killing.

She plunged both blades into the back of the nearest muridach priest and then ripped them free in a single smooth motion. A quick step to the left, and she killed the second priest, driving her swords into the side of his furred neck. Blood sprayed from the wounds, the coppery smell overwhelming the musky odor of muridach fur, and the creature went down.

The final priest started a spell, pointing his staff at Third, the mummified muridach head bouncing as the priest gestured. Blue fire burned up the length of the staff, so Third hooked one of her swords behind the staff and yanked. The priest stumbled forward, still trying to work his spell, and the point of Third's second sword found his throat and ended his life.

She wrenched her blades free and looked around, but she had accounted for all three of the muridach priests, and there were no others nearby. For that matter, while Ridmark and the others still fought ten kalocrypts, Third did not see any more of the creatures in the distance.

But she saw something else from this height, something that disturbed her far more than more kalocrypts or even muridach priests.

Dust clouds.

The foothills of the Gray Mountains were dusty, but they supported many small trees and a large quantity of tough, resilient grass. For a dust cloud that large to rise into the air meant a large number of men were moving through the hills.

Men, or perhaps muridachs.

Even worse, Third saw the clouds to both the east and the west.

She drew on her power to travel and rushed to rejoin the fight.

RIDMARK DODGED TO THE SIDE, avoiding the snap of the kalocrypt's pincers. As he did, he slashed Oathshield, hammering the soulblade at the knobby joint in one of the kalocrypt's left legs. The legs, Ridmark had discovered, were the weak points of the giant insects. The chitinous carapaces that covered their bodies could take a pounding, and the pincers themselves seemed at least as hard as steel. But the joints in the legs were not nearly so well-protected, and Oathshield lopped off the limb. The kalocrypt shuddered and started to spin towards him, and Ridmark dodged and took off another leg. That was enough to make the creature lose its balance entirely, and its muridach rider shrieked as it lost its balance. The ratman recovered in time to get his bronze sword free of its scabbard and intercept Ridmark's first swing.

His next swing crunched into the muridach's neck, and the ratman went down, sword clattering away. The injured kalocrypt dragged itself towards Ridmark, pincers snapping. He dodged around the pincers and drove Oathshield into the creature's head. He didn't know if the kalocrypts had brains or not, but stabbing them through the head proved fatal. The kalocrypt collapsed as Ridmark ripped Oathshield free, its remaining legs curling up beneath it.

He stepped back, breathing hard, and looked for his next opponent, but couldn't find any left.

Dead muridachs lay on the ground, and the slain kalocrypts lay motionless. The creatures gave off a strange, greasy smell that reminded Ridmark of olive oil that had gone rancid. He looked to see if any of the others had been hurt. Calem and Krastikon had both taken minor wounds, but Calliande and Kalussa were already casting healing spells.

Kalussa was healing Krastikon, while Calliande healed Calem.

"God and the saints, but these things stink worse than the muridachs," said Tamlin.

"They do," said Tamara, staring at one of the dead kalocrypts.

"You've fought these things before?" said Ridmark.

Her mismatched eyes turned towards him. "Yes. But, Lord Ridmark...not that often. And I have never seen so many kalocrypts gathered in one place."

"Nor has Magatai," said Magatai, who had dismounted to retrieve his arrows from the dead muridachs. "From time to time Magatai has fought three or four muridachs riding kalocrypts, but never this many." He looked around and blinked. "How many did we kill? Magatai lost count."

"Seventeen," said Calliande, her voice grim as she straightened up. Calem followed her like a white shadow in his cloak. He seemed to be taking care not to look at Kalussa.

"Seventeen," repeated Kyralion. "The only time I have ever seen that many kalocrypts at once is when the muridachs gather together in an army."

"An army?" said Ridmark, remembering the tracks he had found.

"An army," repeated Third's voice, cold and controlled.

Ridmark turned his head as Third jogged to join them, her short swords in their sheaths at her belt.

"Any trouble with the priests?" said Ridmark.

"None," said Third. "They had clearly never dealt with someone like me before." Her black eyes met his. "I saw large dust clouds to the west and to the east."

"Dust clouds?" said Tamara.

"Such as the sort," said Tamlin, "raised by a large group of marching men?"

"Yes," said Third. "I fear that we are caught between two muridach armies marching south towards the Illicaeryn Jungle."

"Two?" said Tamlin, taken aback.

"Is Kalimnos in danger?" said Tamara.

"No," said Kyralion with a shake of his head. "If the muridachs have come forth in such numbers, they are marching to the Illicaeryn Jungle. My people were in dire straits when I left. It seems the situation has worsened since."

"If we cannot continue to the east and we cannot retreat to the west or the north," said Krastikon, "what shall we do?"

Ridmark looked around, thinking. "That hilltop where Third killed the priests? Head there, and we'll have a good vantage point. Third and I are going to scout to the east again, and Magatai and

Kyralion are going to go the west. Don't go more than five miles, and get back here as soon as you can. We'll decide how to proceed once we know more. Krastikon, you'd better get the scutians moving."

Krastikon nodded and used a spell of earth magic on the lizards, Calem aiding him.

"Ridmark," said Calliande. "The Sight...there is a lot of dark magic nearby, to both the east and the west."

Ridmark frowned. "Like the aura around the muridach priests?"

"Yes," she said. "But stronger. I think many muridach priests are moving through the nearby hills."

"I'm afraid you're right," said Ridmark. "Let's move."

AN HOUR later Third followed Ridmark as he climbed the slope of a hill.

This was something they had done many, many times before. The Shield Knight could move like a silent ghost through the wilderness, and the years since the defeat of the Frostborn had not taken his edge.

Certainly, his encounters with Justin Cyros and the Necromancer of Trojas and the Maledictus of Shadows proved that.

He was also Third's first and oldest friend, and she felt more comfortable around him than anyone else save her sister.

She felt more comfortable around Ridmark than she did around Kyralion. But Kyralion did not make her feel uncomfortable, not exactly. He just made her feel unsettled. She found her eyes drifting to him, her mind wondering what it would feel like to have him touch her, perhaps to kiss her, or even more...

Third was centuries old, and this was a new sensation to her.

In a way, she was almost grateful to find herself near a muridach army. Third knew how to fight and kill and win. What to do about unfamiliar emotions was something else entirely.

Ridmark came to a sudden stop, and Third halted as she saw what had caught his attention.

"Muridach scouts coming around the hill," he said.

Third heard the rasp of their boots against the rough ground, heard their deep voices as they argued in their own language. The scouts were not making any effort at stealth. That either meant that they were idiots, or...

"If there is a muridach army," said Third in a low voice, "likely the bulk of their forces are nearby."

The rasp of the boots got louder.

Ridmark sighed and rolled his shoulders. "We'll have to take them quickly."

Third nodded. "The usual tactic we employed against locusari warriors?"

Ridmark blinked. "The muridachs aren't nearly as fast as the locusari."

"All the better," said Third, drawing her short swords. "We can take them quicker, then."

"Well, you're usually right," said Ridmark, drawing Oathshield. The soulstones in the pommel and the tang flashed, and pale white fire glimmered around the blue blade. Likely the sword was reacting to the aura of dark magic around the muridach priests. "How many, do you think?"

"Four or five," said Third. She raised her blades. "Shall we?"

He snorted.

"What?" said Third.

"Just like old times, I suppose," said Ridmark.

"There are no frost drakes this time," said Third.

"That's an improvement, at least," said Ridmark, and he started forward, Third following.

The muridach scouts came into sight a moment later. As Third had guessed, there were four of the creatures. They wore leather armor reinforced with bronze studs, short swords at their belts and bronze-tipped spears in their hands. That was good. Third had been concerned they would have bows.

The muridachs froze when they saw Ridmark and Third.

"Greetings," called Ridmark in orcish. Third supposed his sense of justice compelled him to offer the muridachs a chance to depart. She would have just killed them all where they stood, but his conscience was sharper than hers. "If you…"

The muridachs charged, raising their spears. Likely they assumed that one human man and one woman would not put up much of a fight.

Or that they would make a fine meal.

Third stepped forward and drew on the fiery song in her blood, and blue fire swallowed the world. When the flames cleared, she was behind the muridachs, who had skidded to a halt in confusion at her disappearance.

She stepped forward and killed one with a quick stab from her swords. Third had hoped to kill the creature in silence, but she didn't quite manage it, and the ratman died with a gurgling croak. The other muridachs whirled to face her, and Third had to retreat, snapping her bloody blades right and left to deflect the spear thrusts aimed at her face and chest.

Of course, while she was doing that, Ridmark closed the distance.

Oathshield moved in a blur of blue metal and white flame, and Ridmark took off the head of a muridach warrior. The rat-like head rolled away, the expression frozen in astonishment, and the body fell with a spatter of blood. Third darted closer and stabbed, her swords finding the heart of another muridach, and the surviving ratman backed away, preparing to flee. If he escaped, he might warn the rest of the muridachs, but Ridmark finished the creature off before it made another three steps.

"Good work," said Ridmark, cleaning the muridach blood from Oathshield's blade.

"Thank you," said Third. She cocked her head to the side, trying to listen. "Do you hear that?"

Ridmark frowned and listened. "I don't, but you have better hearing."

"I think I can hear a marching army," said Third.

Ridmark looked around. "Let's head to the top of this hill. We'll get a better look from there."

Third nodded, stepped over a dead muridach, and followed Ridmark as he climbed up the hill. Perhaps a dozen yards from the crest, he sheathed Oathshield and dropped to a crawl, and Third followed suit. Reaching the top of a hill in hostile territory was always tricky business. Standing atop a hill was a superb way to let the enemy see you, but the vantage point offered a useful view of the surrounding countryside.

Ridmark came to a sudden halt as he reached the top of the hill, and Third hurried forward, wondering if he had seen enemies.

She joined him and froze in surprise.

Ridmark had indeed seen enemies.

The hill overlooked a broad, wide valley, and a horde of muridach warriors moved through it like a river in flood. There were thousands of the creatures. No, tens of thousands. Third saw muridach infantry in bronze ring mail and spiked caps marching in orderly lines, muridach berserkers stalking along the sides with their double-bladed axes. Here and there Third spotted the priests of the Lord of Carrion in their crimson cowls, and muridach lancers atop kalocrypts screened the flanks of the host. Creaking supply wagons were pulled by creatures that Third had never seen before, things that looked like glistening, hairless moles.

"There must be at least thirty-five thousand of them," whispered Ridmark.

"Maybe even forty," said Third.

"Sir Rion said that the muridachs breed like mice or rats," said Ridmark. "Most of the time, they're too busy fighting each other to threaten other kindreds and only come to the surface to scavenge. But when they're united against a foe..."

"Like the gray elves," said Third, thinking of Kyralion, of what Lord Amruthyr had told her in the final moment before his death.

"They can come forth in terrifying numbers," said Ridmark. "We need to get back to the others before the muridachs realized we've killed several of their scouting parties."

"Agreed," said Third.

RIDMARK SAW Calliande and the others waiting atop the crown of the hill and felt a surge of relief. So far, it seemed, the muridachs had not realized that any of their scout parties or kalocrypt patrols had been slain.

But the minute they did, the muridachs would attack in force, and Ridmark and the others would not survive that.

"You're back, thank God," said Calliande. "We need to move as soon as possible."

Ridmark spotted Kyralion and Magatai waiting near the scutians, and he suspected their news was bad.

"You've seen a muridach army, haven't you?" said Ridmark.

"A mighty host perhaps five miles west of here," said Magatai. "Magatai is uncertain of their numbers, but they were as numerous as the blades of grass upon the Takai steppes. All the tribes of the Takai would be needed to fight such a horde."

"At least forty-five thousand of them," said Kyralion. "Maybe as many as fifty. If there had been a single survivor from our fight with the kalocrypts, we would have hundreds of muridachs falling on us by now, maybe even thousands."

"It seems only the grace of God that they have not found us yet," said Krastikon.

"We can't go east or west," said Ridmark. "If we go north, we'll run right into the muridachs as well."

"What about the Deeps?" said Calliande. "Could we hide there until the muridachs pass?"

"I doubt it," said Kyralion. "The muridachs are issuing forth from their underground strongholds, and there will be stragglers."

"Another wave might be coming as well," said Third.

"Then it seems our only chance is to go south," said Ridmark.

Calliande frowned. "But the muridachs are marching south. If we had horses, we might be able to get ahead of them or loop around them to the east, but we don't. And once we're on the steppes, there will be no place to hide."

"There may be, my lady," said Magatai, "though the path is fraught with peril."

"Where?" said Ridmark.

"Cathair Avamyr," said Magatai.

Kyralion stirred at that.

"The ruined gray elven city," said Ridmark.

"It was to be the final refuge of my people, our last bastion," said Kyralion. "Most of our people would shelter within Cathair Avamyr, and the fortifications within the Pass of Ruins would hold the Sovereign's hordes at bay." He sighed. "But you all saw firsthand how that ended."

"Isn't Cathair Avamyr dangerous?" said Tamara. "You always talk about the Blood Quest to Cathair Avamyr."

"Cathair Avamyr is very dangerous," said Magatai. "Ruined it may be, but ancient guardian spirits guard its streets." He puffed up a little. "Magatai bested them in glorious battle, and the spirits granted him a boon." His left hand patted the spiraling tattoos on his right arm. "Hence he is resistant to magical forces. Not quite as resistant as friend Kyralion, of course, but enough to resist the insidious dream spell the wicked Maledicti used against us."

"Do the muridachs ever go to Cathair Avamyr?" said Calliande.

"Sometimes," said Magatai. "They never come out again. The guardian spirits slay them."

"And are the guardian spirits going to slay us?" said Krastikon.

Magatai laughed. "They will try! But we have the Shield Knight, the Keeper, Tamara Earthcaller, and three of the Seven Swords! And Magatai thinks that we shall have better odds against the guardian spirits of Cathair Avamyr than against a hundred thousand muridachs." He looked at Kyralion. "Perhaps the guardian spirits shall even let us pass without challenge since we are in the company of a gray elf."

"I doubt it," said Kyralion. "The guardians in Cathair Selenias attacked me before we approached Lord Amruthyr."

"Going to Cathair Avamyr will be a risk," said Calliande.

"Aye," said Ridmark, coming to a decision. "Going there will be a risk. But if we stay here, the muridachs will find us and overwhelm us. If we go in any other direction but south, the muridachs will kill us."

No one objected. That was a pity. Ridmark had rather hoped someone might have a better idea, but they had no other choice.

"If we are going to Cathair Avamyr," said Kyralion, "we need to move at once. The muridach scouts will reach this location at any moment."

"Then let's go," said Ridmark.

3

SCYTHE

The next two days were exhausting.

Tamlin was used to physical exertion. The dvargir gamemasters in the Ring of Blood had not been forgiving of weakness, and they had pushed him far past the bounds of his stamina. After he had escaped and joined King Hektor as an Arcanius Knight, Tamlin had gone on forced marches, had fought in battles and skirmishes where there was no choice but to fight or die.

War was also not forgiving of physical weakness.

Tamlin was used to this kind of thing, but Ridmark still set a hard pace.

They traveled for the rest of the day and well after sunset. It seemed that Third had some ability to see in the dark, and Northwind could smell the muridachs and the kalocrypts long before they drew near, which let them avoid the creatures.

They still had to fight roving groups of kalocrypts and muridach riders twice. Fortunately, both times the enemy consisted of only three kalocrypts and their riders, and they made short work of their foes. Once again, it seemed the muridachs had underestimated a group of humans on foot. Tamlin supposed that would last until some of the muridachs escaped to warn the others.

That would be bad. If the muridachs realized they could get their clawed hands on three of the Seven Swords, they would attack in force, hoping to claim the powerful weapons for themselves. Tamlin wondered if it would have been wiser to keep the Swords in Aenesium, but then the Swords might have been stolen, or Owyllain ripped apart in a new civil war as different lords and kings tried to claim the weapons.

In truth, there was no safe place for any of the Seven Swords. Perhaps the safest place was the hands of the Swordborn who could use the Swords as weapons but not draw upon their mighty magic. Anyone who could use the Swords' magic would be tempted to take up their power and try to claim the empty thrones of Justin Cyros and the Necromancer for themselves. Fighting one Necromancer of Trojas had been bad enough. Tamlin did not want to repeat the experience.

They continued traveling long after dark on the first day, and camped late and arose before the sun came up.

Towards the middle of the morning, they came to the Takai Steppes.

"That," said Krastikon, "is rather a lot of grass."

"Indeed," said Tamlin, who could think of nothing more profound to say.

He had glimpsed the steppes from the hilltops near Kalimnos, seeing them stretch away to the south. He had expected something like the moors near Trojas and the Cloak Mountains, a rolling plain dotted with rocky hills and small patches of trees.

The Takai Steppes were nothing like that.

It was like looking at a sea of waving greenish-gold grass, some of which was high enough to come to Tamlin's hips. The ground rolled in gentle swells, but none of those swells ever rose to the height of proper hills. For as far as the eye could see, there was not a tree in sight.

"Absolutely no cover in any direction," said Krastikon, scowling as he looked around.

"Fear not, Prince Krastikon," said Magatai, patting Northwind's neck. The struthian let out a squawk. "The high grasses shall provide ample cover. When the Takai wage honorable combat among ourselves, we conceal ourselves in the high grasses. Then when the enemy comes, we strike like lightning itself!"

"Like lions hiding in the grass to stalk their prey," said Tamlin, trying to keep the amusement out of his voice and not quite managing it. Magatai's relentless bombast would have been funny, except the halfling said it with such earnest seriousness. Tamlin had little experience of the Takai, but he suspected the halflings would regard insults (imagined or otherwise) as a deadly business.

And Magatai was as good of an archer as Kyralion, and somehow maintained that accuracy while his struthian mount ran circles around the enemy.

Fortunately, the amusement in Tamlin's tone sailed right over Magatai's head. It would take more than sarcasm to breach the fortress of the halfling's invincible self-confidence.

"Exactly like lions, Sir Tamlin!" said Magatai. "Exactly like lions. The Takai are the greatest warriors in all of Owyllain, and so should we not emulate the greatest hunters as well?"

"Concealment concerns me less," said Third, "than the trail we are leaving in this grass."

She had a point. Tamlin could see across the plains for miles in all directions, and as he looked north, he saw the trail they had left in the grasses, almost like a line of shadow drawn across the landscape.

"Fear not, friend Third," said Magatai. "As the sun goes down, the air grows cooler, which causes wind. That will flatten the grasses somewhat and obscure our trail."

"Not erase it entirely, though," said Third.

"No," said Magatai. "That is why we must be vigilant."

Fortunately, they saw no other enemies that day. Perhaps they had gotten far enough ahead of the muridach horde to avoid its outer patrols. Those damned kalocrypt things could move at least as fast as a charging struthian, but Magatai and Tamara agreed that the kalocrypts lacked the stamina of the struthians.

Towards the end of the day, something strange happened.

"Do you see it?" said Calliande.

To the north, outlined against the distant shapes of the Gray Mountains, Tamlin could just make out a dark speck. It looked like a flying creature, and he glimpsed the flex of vast wings.

"Aye, my lady," said Tamlin.

"I wish I had a damned telescope," said Ridmark.

"A...a telescope, Lord Ridmark?" said Kalussa, shaken out of her brooding by the strange word. Tamlin didn't know what it was either.

"A clever device some of the Magistri of Andomhaim built," said Calliande, shading her eyes as she watched the distant black speck. "As you know, the position of the thirteen moons can empower certain kinds of magic. One of the Magistri realized that by grinding glass to make a row of lenses in a metal tube, the image in the lenses could make distant objects look larger and clearer."

"Oh!" said Kalussa. "I can think of many times when that would have been useful."

"It would be a handy tool in warfare," said Tamlin.

"Magatai thinks it seems dishonest," said the halfling, squinting at the distant shape.

"More to the point," said Ridmark, "it would let us see what that flying creature is."

"Probably a fire drake," said Tamara.

Ridmark looked at her. "There are fire drakes this far south?"

"Oh, yes," said Tamara. "They attacked Kalimnos twice that I can remember. Once when I was a child, and once when I was old enough to fight."

"They are very dangerous to hunt, and they often attack our herds," said Magatai. "Fortunately, the Takai are superb hunters."

"Like lions," said Tamlin.

"Yes, exactly like lions."

The flying shape came no closer and vanished to the north, and they pressed on to the south.

They stopped for the night several hours after the sun had set, making a fireless camp. Eight of the thirteen moons were out, their mingled light turning a greenish-blue, which provided enough illumination to see. Tamlin feared that would make them more visible, but the muridachs and their pet kalocrypts hunted by scent as much as by sight.

Calem volunteered to take the first watch, and the others wrapped themselves in cloaks or blankets and went to sleep. Tamlin sat down with a sigh, his shoulders and knees aching from the long march. The gray elven armor he had taken from the Tower of Nightmares was far lighter and stronger than bronze, but it still had a weight to it, and that weight still dragged at him at the end of a long day.

He started to roll up his cloak to make a pillow, and Tamara sat next to him.

She looked beautiful in the dim moonlight, even with the sickly green tinge that light gave to everything. Suddenly, a memory flashed through Tamlin's mind of the first time he had taken Tysia in his arms, his body trembling with excitement and need.

She was frowning.

"What's wrong?" said Tamlin.

Tamara took a deep breath. "Can...I ask you a favor?"

"Yes," said Tamara. He hesitated, and then took her hand. "Anything."

Tamara took another deep breath and nodded. "Could you speak to Sir Calem?"

"Calem?" Tamlin looked to where Calem stood at the edge of the camp, a white shadow in his wraithcloak. He didn't think Calem had said more than two words over the last two days, and then Tamlin understood. "You want me to talk to him about Kalussa."

"Yes," said Tamara. "I know it is none of my business, but I'm afraid he might kill himself."

Tamlin frowned. "I...don't think he will. If fighting as a slave in Urd Maelwyn didn't break his spirits, then nothing will."

"Yes," said Tamara, "but losing...losing my other self, that almost broke you, didn't it?"

Tamlin said nothing, and she squeezed his hand.

"What happened to you in Urd Maelwyn was horrible, but Calem had it worse," said Tamara. "Calliande told me how someone wrote spells of dark magic upon him, used him as a mindless assassin." She gestured at the camp. "I think these are the first friends he's ever had. He might not know how to deal with a broken heart."

"Does anyone?" said Tamlin. "Perhaps you should speak to Lord Ridmark about this. Calem is more likely to listen to him than to me."

"I would," said Tamara, "but...I may be mistaken, but it seems like Lord Ridmark doesn't like Kalussa. He never talks to her, and she tries to avoid him."

"Ah," said Tamlin. He wasn't surprised Tamara had noticed that. "He doesn't dislike her. Else he wouldn't let her spend time near Calliande and his sons. No, it's a bit more complicated than that. When Rhodruthain brought Ridmark here, he happened to save Kalussa's life from the Confessor's orcs. Kalussa decided she wanted to be Ridmark's first concubine..."

"And Lady Calliande did not care for the idea?" said Tamara.

"She did not," said Tamlin. "And Ridmark did not care for the idea, either." He remembered Kalussa explaining her plan, how he had tried to warn her it was a bad idea. "Someone like Ridmark...his conscience is sterner than any king or magistrate. And the Shield Knight and the Keeper were both mourning their daughter. I think Ridmark did find Kalussa desirable, which probably didn't help, and she kept trying to seduce him. I'm not sure exactly what happened, but he finally lost his temper at her, and she's been frightened of him ever since."

"And then Sir Calem started courting her," said Tamara.

"Yes," said Tamlin. "I imagine Lord Ridmark was relieved."

"Calem and Kalussa are in love," said Tamara, "and what happened...I think it hurt both of them terribly. They both blame themselves."

"God," said Tamlin. He rubbed his face. "I don't understand it. They both obviously want each other. What's the harm?"

"I think they take a more rigid view of such things than you do, Sir Tamlin," said Tamara. Tamlin gave her a sharp look, fearing that he had insulted her, but she was smiling. "I'm not blind. I, ah...can guess how you dealt with your grief once you came back to Aenesium."

"Oh," said Tamlin.

Tamara shrugged. "It's not as if I can blame you. You did think your wife was dead." To his surprise, she smiled again. "You could hardly have known that she had six other lives."

"Then you are my wife, then?" said Tamlin. His voice was softer than he expected, with a rasp to it.

They stared at each other in silence.

"I don't know," said Tamara, a strange emotion going over her face. "Maybe I am. It doesn't make any sense. I've known you less than a week, but I know you better than I know anyone else. I've never done more than hold your hand, but I know exactly what it would feel like to kiss you."

"You make me wish," said Tamlin, "that we were alone. That we were not surrounded by companions who would overhear everything."

She smiled a little. "They're all asleep. Except for Calem."

"Third's probably awake," said Tamlin.

"Third would be too polite to say anything," said Tamara. She took a deep breath. "But do you remember the first time that you and Tysia...or you and me, maybe...slept together?"

"Yes."

"How would you have felt if I had panicked after?" said Tamara. "If I had said it was a terrible mistake and that we shouldn't ever see each other ever again?"

"Ah." Tamlin grimaced, looked at Kalussa's sleeping form, and then back to Tamara. "I think I see your point. I'll see if I can talk to him."

Tamara smiled and squeezed his hand. "Thank you."

"Though if I can ask...why do you care?" said Tamlin. "You've only just met Calem, and I don't think he's ever spoken to you."

Tamara sighed. "When the dream spell covered the town, we...er, walked in on him and Lady Kalussa. He looked at her...the way he looked at her was like the rest of the world had ceased to exist." She hesitated. "You look at me that way sometimes."

They stared at each other. Tamlin felt the pulse throbbing in her wrist. Something seemed to burn in his chest.

"Soon," said Tamlin.

"Yes," whispered Tamara. "Yes." She paused. "Just not in a field when we're surrounded by our friends."

Tamlin just managed to stop himself from bursting out laughing. "A good point." He released her hand and stood. "I'll hold you to that."

"We'll find out what else you have to hold against me," said Tamara, smiling up at him.

Tamlin's mouth went dry. He could think of any number of responses to that, both verbal and otherwise, but all of them were things he wanted to say or do while they were alone. So instead he offered a bow, straightened up, and walked to where Calem stood staring to the north, his wraithcloak rippling around him in the cool wind. He stood motionless, the greenish-blue light of the moons making him seem ghostly.

"Sir Tamlin," said Calem.

"Sir Calem," said Tamlin. He paused. "How are you?"

"All is well," said Calem. "I have seen no sign of enemies. Nor of any flying creatures."

"Good," said Tamlin. He hesitated, trying to decide what to say, and shrugged to himself. "But that's not what I meant."

Calem did not look at him. "Then what did you mean?"

"It was a hard business, what happened at Kalimnos," said Tamlin. "I saw the phantasms of my dead wife and Sir Aegeus, and I thought they were still alive."

"That was an ill thing," said Calem, his voice quiet. "Sir Aegeus was a valiant man, and he died bravely." He sighed. "I always wondered if he would ever make Lord Kyralion laugh."

"If anyone could have made Kyralion laugh, Sir Aegeus was the man," said Tamlin. He felt a pang as he remembered his friend, his companion in so many battles and more than a few drunken revels.

"It was an ill thing, and also that Lady Calliande thought that her daughter had returned from the grave."

The breath hissed through Calem's teeth. "That was especially evil. Lady Calliande is a great and noble woman. For the Maledictus of Shadows to use her grief as a weapon against her was unforgivable. If I ever lay eyes upon that evil creature, its remaining life will be measured in heartbeats."

"It was an evil thing," said Tamlin. "But we have gone into many battles together, so I should be blunt with you." Calem nodded. "Lady Calliande seems to be recovering more swiftly from her experience in Kalimnos than you are."

"Ah." Calem said nothing for a moment, his right hand flexing. "That is the difference, sir. The Maledictus's spell blurred the line between phantasm and reality. The Keeper thought she held her daughter. In reality, she sat on her bed and did nothing. The Maledictus made me think that Lady Kalussa and I were wed. In reality, I forced myself upon a brave and noble woman..."

"You didn't force her," said Tamlin.

"I did," said Calem. "Her judgment was impaired, and I took full advantage of..."

"Her judgment wasn't impaired, her inhibitions were," said Tamlin. "So were yours. Calliande said the spell probably couldn't force anyone to do something against their nature. The two of you had been spending a great deal of time together anyway, and if things had run their natural course, you probably would have asked for her hand in a year or so anyway."

"Nature," said Calem. "Yes. That proves that I am a monster."

A monster? For lying with a willing woman? For God's sake! Tamlin felt a wave of exasperation.

He wondered if this was how Ridmark felt most of the time.

"How does that prove you are a monster?" said Tamlin. "An unwed man taking an unwed woman to bed perhaps is not the most moral choice, but it happens quite often." Tamlin had done that himself more than once. "And we've faced men like the Necromancer and Khurazalin and Qazaldhar. Compared to them, how are you a monster?"

"I fear you do not understand," said Calem, his voice tight with pain. "We are very similar in many ways, Sir Tamlin. We were both gladiators in Urd Maelwyn." He took a deep breath. "But our paths diverged. You escaped and became an Arcanius Knight. My secret master took me and made me into an assassin. He made me into a monster." Calem bowed his head. "I can only remember my crimes as dreams, as fragments. But I know I have killed both men and women who did not deserve it. I would have killed the Shield Knight and the Keeper at the bidding of my secret master, had they not been the stronger."

"You cannot blame yourself for that," said Tamlin. "You were under the control of another."

"When Calliande suppressed the spell," said Calem, "I thought I could become something else. Something other than a murderous assassin. I wanted to be a knight as you are, as Lord Ridmark is."

"You are," said Tamlin. "You slew the High Warlock of Vhalorast. It would have taken a dozen Arcanius Knights to take him in a fight, and you killed him. We wouldn't have beaten my father or the Necromancer without your help."

"I thought I could change," said Calem. "Then we came to Kalimnos, and I understood the truth. I have always been a monster, Sir Tamlin, and I always will be. Else I would not have acted as I did."

"Tamara thinks you're going to kill yourself," said Tamlin.

"No," said Calem. "No, I will fulfill my oaths to Lady Calliande and Lord Ridmark as their vassal knight. But if I fall in battle, perhaps that would be for the best..."

"For a smart man," said Tamlin, "you're acting like a damned fool."

Calem gave him a sharp look, his green eyes flashing in the light of the moons.

"You're not a monster," said Tamlin. "If you had thrown Kalussa to the ground and ravaged her as she begged you to stop, that would be one thing, but that's not what happened, and you bloody well know it. And maybe the Maledicti or whoever your secret master is forced you to kill people, but that wasn't your fault. As well blame a man for walking behind you when you've got a chain around his neck. And you had better not get yourself killed."

"Would that not be better?" said Calem.

"No," said Tamlin. "If you're killed, who's going to carry the Sword of Air? And how do you think Kalussa will feel if you get killed?" Calem started to speak, but Tamlin talked right over him. "She blames herself, and if you go and get killed, she'll blame herself for that, too. Do you really want to do that to her?"

"No," said Calem. "No, I don't want to hurt her."

"Then listen to someone who knows what it feels like," said Tamlin. "You don't want to do that to her. I think you should just give her some time. Let her think about it. She wouldn't be so upset if she didn't care about you. She blames herself now, but eventually, she'll figure out that there's no one to blame, or if there's anyone to blame, it's the Maledictus of Shadows."

Calem sighed. "You speak sound counsel. I will think on what you have said." He shook his head. "It is...difficult. All my life, I was trained to fight and kill. Learning how to do other things, how to have friends, is challenging."

"If Third can do it, you can too," said Tamlin.

Calem blinked. "Third?"

"She was an urdhracos for a thousand years, and now she's not," said Tamlin. "You were an assassin for, what, ten years? If she can put a thousand years behind her, surely a veteran of the Ring of Blood can do the same with a mere ten."

Calem blinked a few times, and then let out a quiet laugh. "You are very persuasive, Sir Tamlin."

"One tries."

"All right," said Calem. "I will think on what you have said. And I will try not to get myself killed."

"Good," said Tamlin. "And even if you and Kalussa do not reconcile, consider Lady Calliande, and how disappointed she would be if you killed yourself."

"I do not wish to disappoint the Keeper," said Calem. "She is the only reason I have any freedom at all. Lord Ridmark would have been within his rights to kill me that day in the forest. But she took a chance and spared my life. I hope...I hope I can repay that kindness."

"It will be difficult to do that if you're dead," said Tamlin.

"That is so," said Calem. He snorted.

"What?" said Tamlin.

"You can go tell Tamara that I am not going to kill myself," said Calem.

"She will be pleased to hear it," said Tamlin.

"Have you bedded her yet?" said Calem.

Tamlin opened his mouth, closed it, settled on a response. "That's not..."

"Ah," said Calem. "You can ask cutting questions, but I cannot?"

"Well," said Tamlin. "Fair is fair, I suppose. And...no. But not yet. For God's sake, we're in the middle of a field getting chased by muridachs. And...no, I am not discussing this."

Calem smiled. "Good night, Sir Tamlin."

"Good night, Sir Calem," said Tamlin. "I am pleased that I helped you feel better."

"Albeit at your expense, of course," said Calem.

"If it helps," said Tamlin, "we are likely not the first men in the history of mankind to discuss their troubles with women."

"No," agreed Calem. "Though our troubles are likely stranger than most."

"That, sir, I cannot argue," said Tamlin.

He walked back to Tamara.

"How did it go?" said Tamara.

Tamlin sighed and sat down. "You were probably close enough to hear every word."

"Well, no," said Tamara. "I did see Calem smile, so that was probably a start."

"Probably," said Tamlin. He sighed and rubbed his face. "I don't know how helpful I was. It wasn't as if I could commiserate. My wife apparently lived seven different lives, and he blames himself for sleeping with Kalussa."

"It was good of you to try," said Tamara, and she leaned over and kissed his cheek. "Thank you."

He stared at her, and he wanted to pull her close and kiss her harder, witnesses be damned.

"Good night, Tamara," said Tamlin.

"Good night, Tamlin," she whispered.

She lay down in her cloak and went to sleep, and Tamlin lay down next to her. That felt so familiar, so comfortable, and he smiled at the thought.

He drifted to sleep, and in his sleep, he dreamed.

It was a strange dream, unlike anything he had dreamed before.

He saw a mist-choked forest, fog rolling past the barren branches. He glimpsed white ruins and towers, creatures with eyes like burning coals prowling through the trees. There was a ring of dark elven standing stones, the surfaces of the menhirs carved with disturbing scenes of torture and pain, their glyphs glowing with blue fire.

The Dark Lady swirled before his vision.

He had dreamed of her many times before, and she had warned him of dangers. For some reason, he could not hear her. He could see her just fine, and she looked as she always did – clad in wool and leather, a carved staff in her hand and a tattered cloak of brown and green and gray hanging from her shoulders. Her mouth was moving, her black eyes sharp with urgency, but for some reason, Tamlin could not hear her words.

"Tamlin?"

Tamlin blinked awake as Tamara shook him.

"Eh?" he said.

"It's time to go," she said. It was still dark out, but there was the faintest hint of light in the eastern sky.

"Aye," he said, trying to clear the confusion from his mind.

"Are you all right?" said Tamara, frowning. She, at least, seemed wide awake. Likely she was used to early mornings from her years working at her adoptive father's inn.

"I…think so," said Tamlin. "I had a strange dream. I'll tell you about it once we're moving."

Maybe she would know about the Dark Lady. Tamara had a surprising store of knowledge on a variety of subjects, knowledge she could not remember acquiring. Perhaps the Dark Lady was one of those subjects.

The Dark Lady…

Tamlin scowled as he sat up, trying to remember. The Dark Lady had appeared to him for years, giving him cryptic warnings of danger. Though come to think of it, she hadn't appeared in his dreams since before the battle with Taerdyn at Trojas, where she had warned Tamlin he would face an excruciating trial.

That had turned out to be all too accurate.

Yet she had not appeared in his dreams since. Not even to warn him about the trap at Kalimnos, which seemed odd. Something danced at the edge of Tamlin's thoughts, something that he had forgotten but could not quite grasp.

One of the pack scutians let out an angry croak.

"Yes, well, I'm not happy to be awake this early either, you damned lizard," said Krastikon, casting a spell of earth magic to sooth the annoyed scutian, "but if we don't get moving, you and I both are going to find ourselves in a muridach cookpot."

"Fear not, Prince Krastikon," said Magatai, checking the straps on his saddle. Northwind grazed placidly as he did so. "The muridachs will simply eat us raw. There will be no cookpots involved."

"You, sir," said Krastikon, "are a font of comfort."

There was work to be done. Tamlin rolled up his cloak, donned his pack, and followed the others south.

Soon the strange dream slipped from his mind entirely.

THE PLAINS STRETCHED in all directions, the grass rustling in the breeze.

It reminded Ridmark a little of the plains of Caertigris in eastern

Andomhaim, the outer march of the realm before the Lion Mountains and the kingdom of the proud manetaurs. Yet these plains seemed larger and wider, the grasses taller.

It was also hotter. It was almost always hot in Owyllain, but as they went south, the air grew more humid. Ridmark soon found himself sweating beneath his armor. Likely he would smell foul, but everyone else would as well. That and the smell of grass was near-overwhelming. There were blooms of purple flowers that grew on small bushes, and they put out a sweet scent that made Ridmark's nose itch and his eyes water. He hoped that the smell would throw off the noses of any muridach pursuers.

Somehow, he doubted they were that lucky.

"It is beautiful here," murmured Calliande.

"It is," agreed Ridmark. The grasslands gave the illusion of being alone on a vast green sea. "I'd prefer it to be cooler, though."

Calliande laughed. "I cannot argue." She brushed some dust from the golden armor she now wore. "The gray elves might have known the secret of making armor lighter and stronger than normal steel, but it still gets hot in the sun. Too much hotter and I'll be able to cook an egg on my chest."

"Your chest has better uses than that," said Ridmark.

She flashed a smile at him. "And what uses are those?"

He started to draw breath to flirt with her some more, but her blue eyes went wide, and her head snapped around to look to the north.

"What is it?" said Ridmark. He knew that expression. The Sight had risen within her in response to a nearby source of magical power.

"Dark magic," said Calliande. "A few miles to the north. And it's coming right at us."

"That's likely not a coincidence, is it?" said Ridmark, looking around. He didn't like what he saw. This land was too damned flat, and there was no defensible terrain within sight. The best they could do was a low swell a few hundred yards to the south.

"Probably not," said Calliande. "I'm not sure what kind of dark magic, either. It seems like the spells of blood sorcery that Mournacht used on that huge black axe of his." She hesitated. "And I think there is at least one urdhracos coming."

"An urdhracos?" said Ridmark. The Scythe had escaped from the Tower of Nightmares, but she had promised to come for Ridmark again. He had believed her, but he had not expected that she would return so soon.

"Yes," said Calliande. "I think we have perhaps a quarter of an hour before they find us."

"All right," said Ridmark, turning to look at the others.

"Trouble?" said Third, who had come up to join them.

"Yes," said Ridmark, raising his voice so the others could hear. "There's an urdhracos coming in our direction, along with either creatures or wielders of dark magic."

"Perhaps an advance party for the muridachs," said Magatai, raising his bow as if he expected enemies to erupt from the grass. Given how tall the damned grass was, it was a reasonable fear.

"Head for that swell," said Ridmark, pointing. "That's the closest thing to defensible ground that we're going to find. We'll wait for them there."

"Could we outrun them?" said Kalussa.

"I doubt it," said Calliande. "If an urdhracos is commanding them, it will be able to observe us from the air. No, better to stand and fight rather than having them harry us all the way to Cathair Avamyr."

"Cathair Avamyr is about a day away," said Kyralion. "Perhaps a day and a half."

"Maybe if we deal with the urdhracos and its minions now," said Tamlin, "we'll have a clear run to the ruins of Cathair Avamyr, and we can shelter there until the muridach horde passes."

"Aye," said Ridmark. "Let's move. Get the scutians on the hill. You all know what to do. Keep the enemy away from Calliande, Kalussa, and Tamara so they can work their spells."

"If that urdhracos was the flying creature we saw earlier," said Calliande, "it might have prepared to fight us. Be wary."

There was nothing Ridmark could say to that, so they hurried up the gentle swell. He looked around as they reached the top. It wasn't as high as he would have liked, but this was the closest thing they were going to get to high ground. There was also enough room for the scutians.

"Perhaps I should go and scout," said Third. "Once I am away from the Swords, I will be able to use my power to travel quickly and return."

Ridmark hesitated and then nodded. He didn't like to send her alone, but they needed more information about their enemies, and Third was the one best equipped to find it. For that matter, she would probably be a match for nearly anything the urdhracos could throw at them. Third left without another word, breaking into a jog. Once she was a hundred yards away, she flared with blue fire and vanished. Ridmark saw her reappear about a hundred yards away, run for another twelve yards, and vanish again.

"That always gives me chills," said Krastikon.

Ridmark snorted. "Given that you tried to kill us on the day we met, I can see why."

"Aye, and look how well that worked," said Krastikon.

"Lady Third is admirable in every way," said Kyralion. Ridmark looked at the gray elf. His expression was usually an unreadable mask, but a spasm of emotion went over his features. Longing, perhaps? Ridmark wasn't sure, and Kyralion's expression returned to its usual calm.

"I always thought so," said Ridmark, "and she tried to kill me the day she met me, too. So the two of you have that in common."

Tamara blinked. "Truly?"

"Yes," said Ridmark. "Long story."

Tamara frowned at him. "How many of your friends tried to kill you on the day you met?"

"Well," said Ridmark. He supposed it said something about the kind of life he had lived that he had to stop and think about it. "Prince Krastikon did, and Third, and Sir Calem..."

"Under duress," said Tamlin. Calem said nothing, his eyes on the plains to the north.

Tamara gave Tamlin a concerned look. "You didn't try to kill him, did you?"

"Certainly not," said Tamlin.

Tamara looked at Kalussa. "Did you, my lady?"

"Ah," said Kalussa. "No." Her face colored. "The circumstances of our meeting were rather different."

"She was tied up at the time," said Tamlin. "Also naked."

Kalussa gave Tamlin a glare that was just short of murderous. Ridmark wondered why Tamlin was teasing her, then supposed Tamlin was annoyed on Calem's behalf. Or perhaps Tamlin was trying to annoy Kalussa out of her self-imposed penance for the events at Kalimnos.

"Really," murmured Tamara. "What a strange way to meet someone."

"Perhaps," said Calliande. "On the other hand, that was how I met Ridmark, and we have been married for eight years. So maybe there are worse ways to meet people."

Tamara's dark eyebrows climbed halfway up her head. "Truly?"

"It is not the sort of day you forget," said Calliande.

"Many of Magatai's friends have tried to kill him," announced Magatai. "Of course, after they inevitably fail, Magatai forgives them, for he is magnanimous in victory. Then we get drunk together. Alas, Magatai has yet to rescue any beautiful women while they are naked, but evidently, this is a more common occurrence then he would have thought."

Ridmark let them banter. There were worse ways to let off pressure before a battle.

And he was certain that a battle was coming.

Blue fire flared at the base of the shallow hill, and Third reappeared, caught her balance, and jogged up to join them.

"What did you see?" said Ridmark.

"Thirty muridach warriors," said Third. "Large ones, each about seven feet tall. They are wearing crimson armor of a type that I have not seen before, and both their armor and their weapons are marked with sigils of blood sorcery."

"Did they see you?" said Ridmark.

"Yes, but that was inevitable," said Third. "They know where we are anyway." She took a deep breath. "The urdhracos is the Scythe."

"I see," said Ridmark. It seemed that the Scythe had indeed returned sooner than he had thought. He looked at Kyralion and Magatai. "These crimson-armored muridachs. Do you know what kind of soldiers they are?"

"Most probably the Throne Guards," said Kyralion.

"Magatai concurs."

"Just what are the Throne Guards?" said Ridmark.

"The best warriors and soldiers of the muridachs," said Magatai. "The muridach cities are ruled by a Great King, and as you can imagine, the Great King has many brothers, sisters, uncles, aunts, nephews, nieces, and cousins, all of whom would like to kill him and devour his corpse at his funeral feast." Calliande shuddered at that. "The Great King wishes to avoid that, and so every Great King forms his own Throne Guard. He feeds them alchemical elixirs to make them stronger and faster and hardier than normal muridachs, and they are fanatically loyal to him. Should the Great King fall to an assassin's blade or poison, the Throne Guards go berserk and slaughters every muridach of royal blood they can find until they are defeated."

"That seems like a good safeguard against assassination," said Kalussa, caught halfway between fascination and revulsion.

"Not really," said Magatai. "The muridach Great Kings are killed through assassination more often than not. The muridachs fight each other constantly due to their vast numbers. Yet the Windcallers of the Takai believe that the current Great King is a warlord of devilish cunning and iron resolve, and he has held the ratmen together. That is why they have been able to field such vast armies."

"This muridach Great King," said Ridmark. He saw red specks appear in the distance, a dark shape hovering over them. "I've heard rumors about a prophet of the Lord of Carrion who has appeared among the muridachs. I assume this prophet is helping the Great King to keep his throne?"

"So the muridachs claim," said Magatai. "They say this prophet is the voice of the Lord of Carrion. He has promised the world to the muridachs, and they think they will conquer all kindreds in the name of their god. It is all rubbish, of course. The Takai shall never be overcome."

"This prophet," said Ridmark, a dark idea occurring to him. "Is he a Maledictus?"

Third blinked. "I did not see a Maledictus with the Throne Guards."

"But the Maledicti command the Scythe," said Ridmark. "And a Maledictus advised King Justin, and another advised the Necromancer. I would not be surprised if this so-called prophet of the Great King turns out to be yet another of the Maledicti playing yet another of their damned games."

Yet based upon what Mhazhama had said in the Heart of the Nightmare, Ridmark knew that the Maledicti served the Masked One of Xenorium. It seemed that the Masked One saw himself as a herald or forerunner for the New God, just as John the Baptist had been the herald of the Dominus Christus upon Old Earth. Yet why would the Maledicti raise a horde of muridachs and turn them against the gray elves? The gray elves had held themselves aloof from the War of the Seven Swords. Did the Masked One intend to use the muridach horde against Owyllain? If so, why not let the gray elves hide in the Illicaeryn Jungle and instead march the muridachs to Owyllain proper?

It was yet another damned mystery.

Ridmark was getting sick of mysteries.

But as he watched the red specks draw closer, he realized there would not be time to worry about anything but survival in the next few moments.

The Throne Guards of the muridach Great King came into sight.

They were huge, just as Third had said, each creature standing seven or seven and a half feet tall. The muridachs wore crimson plate armor of a metal that Ridmark did not recognize, and blood sigils burned on the armor. The Throne Guards carried double-bladed axes of bronze, and more symbols of bloody fire burned upon the weapons. The muridachs were armored from head to foot, though none of them wore helmets. Their heads were oddly piebald, with patches of fur having fallen away to reveal skin covered with dark, lizard-like scales.

The Scythe of the Maledicti flew over them, her great black wings beating as they carried her through the air.

Like all the urdhracosi Ridmark had ever fought, black armor plating covered the Scythe's slim form, talon-tipped gauntlets concealing her hands. Leathery black wings rose behind her like a sail, and the darkness of the void filled her eyes. Her hair was an odd shade of silver, almost platinum, and it made for a marked contrast with her gaunt, pale face and its pointed elven ears.

Third shifted next to Ridmark, her grip tightening upon her short swords.

"Shield Knight!" called the Scythe, her voice ringing over the plains. "Did I not say that I would kill you one day? That day has arrived! You shall fall here, as you should have fallen in Cathair Selenias!" The void-filled eyes shifted to Tamara. "And I've killed you twice before, but I suppose I can do it again."

"Try it and see what happens," said Tamlin, his voice low and hard as he raised the Sword of Earth.

The Scythe blinked at him, and she let out a wild, cackling laugh. "I see. You love her? I have slain her twice, and you love her? Let us see if your love can survive a third death! Though I only think I will have to kill you once, Arcanius. Take them!" She rose higher into the air, a sword of dark elven steel in her right hand, blue fire and shadow crackling around her left hand. "Take them in the name of the prophet of the Lord of Carrion. Take them, and feast upon their flesh!"

"I'll deal with her," said Calliande, her voice low.

Ridmark nodded. "Wait until I give the word to strike."

The muridachs roared something in their tongue, and the creatures charged, raising their huge axes. The Scythe spun over them, dodging and darting like a butterfly in a breeze.

"Now!" said Ridmark, pointing Oathshield as the soulblade burned with white flames.

Calliande, Kalussa, Tamara, and Tamlin all cast spells at once.

Tamlin hurled a bolt of lightning that forked and struck two of the Throne Guards, throwing the muridachs to the grassy earth. Kalussa gestured with the Staff of Blades and flung a glittering sphere of crystal wreathed in elemental flame. It struck one of the muridachs in the forehead and exploded out the back of its skull in a spray of embers. Tamara hurled a sphere of mist that shot over the grass and wrapped one of the muridachs in a haze. The muridach fell screaming as the mist chewed into its flesh. Calliande struck the end of her staff against the ground and gestured, and the earth folded and rippled, knocking the Throne Guards from their feet.

Ridmark started to draw breath to instruct the others to attack, but they knew what to do. He charged forward, and Krastikon, Tamlin, Calem, Third, and Kyralion followed him, swords in hand, while Magatai hung back and sent arrow after arrow into the prone muridachs. One of the muridachs started to come to one knee, and Ridmark swung Oathshield with both hands. The soulblade took off the muridach's head, and it rolled away, black slime spurting from the stump of its neck.

Black slime? The muridachs Ridmark had fought earlier all bled red.

But there was no time to ponder the mystery as the others crashed into the muridachs. The Throne Guards roared and regained their feet as Calliande's white fire slashed at the Scythe, and they fought for their lives.

TAMLIN QUICKLY REALIZED that the Throne Guards were far more formidable than any of the other muridach soldiers he had faced.

They were bigger and stronger and faster, and their axes moved in a blur of bronze and blood-colored fire. For that matter, they were superbly trained and skilled, and it showed. A double-bladed axe was an unwieldy weapon in the hands of anyone but a master, and the Throne Guards knew how to use their axes as both weapons and shields. For that matter, they crawled with blood sorcery, and even without using the spell to sense the presence of magical forces, Tamlin felt the dark power radiating from the creatures.

That led to another problem.

The spells on their crimson armor were strong enough to deflect the edges of the Swords.

The Sword of Earth could cut through nearly anything, as could all the Seven Swords, but powerful magic blocked the cutting effect. When Ridmark had fought Calem and Justin Cyros and Taerdyn, Oathshield had resisted the cutting edge of the Swords of Air, Earth, and Death. Both the axes and the armor of the Throne Guards had the same power.

But Tamlin had not let the Sword of Earth make him complacent.

He retreated before the attacks of a towering muridach, the bronze axe rising and falling in wide, vicious arcs. Tamlin let the muridach's momentum play out, and then he struck, twisting to the side as he did. The muridach wore that strange red armor, but all armor had joints. The Sword of Earth bit into the back of the muridach's knee. The Sword passed through the leather backing the armor like it was made of wet cloth, and it did the same to the flesh and bone of the muridach's right leg. Tamlin yanked the Sword free as the muridach collapsed onto its left knee, and he swept the Sword around, taking off the muridach's head in a spray of black slime.

He whirled to face another foe. A second Throne Guard came at him, raising its axe for a massive overhand blow. Tamlin stabbed the Sword of Earth, and the point bit deep into the muridach's armpit. The Throne Guard came to a sudden halt, black eyes bulging, and Tamlin stepped back and whipped the Sword in a horizontal slash, beheading the muridach.

He turned, looking for another enemy.

"Tamlin!" screamed Tamara in warning.

He turned again and froze in surprise.

Because the first muridach he had beheaded was getting back up.

It shocked Tamlin less than he might have expected. Tamlin had fought numerous undead creatures in his life, most recently at Trojas, and he wasn't entirely surprised when the muridach started to get back up again. His first thought was that the Scythe had used a necromantic spell to raise the slain as undead. Magatai and Tamara had all said that the muridachs preferred to use their dead as dinner, but perhaps the creatures had taken a new tactic.

Then Tamlin realized two disturbing things.

First, the muridach wasn't dead. He had cut off its head and its right leg below the knee, but it was still alive.

Second, the muridach was growing a new head and leg.

Tamlin had thought that the muridachs looked ugly, but the new head that had sprouted from the muridach's neck looked worse than the first one. It was utterly hairless and glistening with slime, the skin a mixture of pink flesh and patches of grayish-black scales. The muridach loosed gurgling howl and charged at Tamlin, the bronze axe rising high.

He dodged to the side, and the axe missed him by inches, the heavy bronze blade sinking into the earth. Tamlin brought the Sword of Earth hammering down, and he severed both of the muridach's arms at the elbows, the blade sinking through the leather beneath the crimson plates.

The Throne Guard roared and stumbled back, black slime spurting from the stumps of its forearms, but already it was growing new arms. How could he kill creatures that could grow new limbs? He had taken off its head, and it had simply grown a new one. A quick glance around the battlefield showed that the others were facing the same difficulty. It jogged a memory in Tamlin's mind. He had seen something like this before, hadn't he? He had heard that the hydras in the marshes near Najaris could regenerate lost limbs and even heads. There had been rare creatures in the Ring of Blood who could do the same...

"Trolls!" shouted Ridmark, his hoarse voice ringing over the battle.

Tamlin cut off the muridach's head again. Once again it started to grow back.

"They're like trolls!" said Ridmark. "Kalussa, Tamara, Calliande! Wound them and then hit the wounds with fire or acid!"

"Tamlin!" Tamara's voice came to his ears, and he risked a glance back and saw her standing with Calliande and Kalussa. "Take its head!"

Tamlin nodded and cut off the muridach's head for a third time, and Tamara cast her spell. A sphere of acidic mist appeared over the spurting stump of the muridach's neck, and the mist sank into the torn flesh. There was a sizzling noise and a hideous stench, and the creature shuddered and collapsed to the ground.

And this time it did not get up again, and neither did it start growing a new head.

Tamlin rushed into the battle, targeting another muridach.

THIRD DODGED around the slash of a massive axe and attacked, plunging both of her short swords into the neck of a Throne Guard. The creature reeled, and Third chopped off its head with three heavy slashes of her right-hand blade.

She had fought trolls numerous times before and knew how to deal with the creatures. For those without magic, the only way to kill a troll and to make sure it stayed dead was to chop it into pieces and burn the pieces to ashes.

For those with magic, the process was rather simpler.

The muridach fell to its knees as its head rolled away, and one of Kalussa's spheres of elemental flame slammed into the stump of its neck. Kalussa's magic charred the flesh, and the Throne Guard fell to its back, the smoke rising from between its shoulders.

Third took a step back, raising her swords, and a scream filled her ears.

"You!"

She looked up just in time to see the Scythe fall towards her like a storm, her blue sword flashing. Third leaped back, and she dodged the blow aimed at her heart, but the Scythe's right wing caught her across the face. Third stumbled back, lost her balance, and fell hard.

The Scythe sprang after her with a shriek of rage, her sword stabbing forward.

Third slashed her right-hand sword, deflecting the Scythe's stab, and kicked with her left boot. Her boot hit the Scythe's right knee, and the urdhracos stumbled back. Third leaped back to her feet and went on the attack, her blue swords a whirlwind around her. But the Scythe was ready to meet the danger, her longsword and her clawed gauntlet weaving a wall of steel before her.

The urdhracos fought with icy, cool precision, but her face was a mask of insane fury, her lips peeled back from her teeth in a snarl, her void-filled eyes wide and glaring.

"You!" said the Scythe. "You came back! How did you survive?" Third parried, ducked under another swing, and slashed, but the Scythe danced around the blow. "You should have died in the Tower. You should have died!"

"You should have tried harder to kill me, then!" said Third.

"I hate you!" screamed the Scythe. "Why are you free? Why? Why? Why? I hate you! I hate you! Die with me. Die with me!"

Her attack redoubled, but the skill did not lessen. Third had centuries of experience with sword work, but the Scythe was her match, and it took all of Third's skill to keep the Scythe's sword and talons from finding her flesh.

"Die with me!" screamed the Scythe. "Die and..."

She staggered back, astonishment going over her face as an arrow sprouted from her side. Third risked a glance back and saw that Kyralion was running towards them. It was difficult to draw and release a bow of that size while running, but Kyralion did it, and a second arrow sprouted from the Scythe's stomach.

The urdhracos snarled in rage and leaped into the air, black wings beating, and Third looked around.

The battle was almost over. Once the weakness of the Throne Guards had been revealed, Ridmark and the others had gone about their work with methodical efficiency, cutting apart the muridachs and letting Calliande and Kalussa and Tamara strike with elemental magic to prevent the ratmen from regenerating their wounds. Only a few of the Throne Guards were still on their feet, and even as Third looked, Calem, Krastikon, and Tamlin drove them back, working in harmony to cut apart the creatures.

Ridmark ran towards Third, Oathshield burning in his fists, his eyes on the Scythe. Kyralion jogged to Third's side and loosed another arrow. This time the Scythe saw it coming, and she snapped her blue sword up, deflecting the shaft.

"Later, Shield Knight!" hissed the Scythe, her face twisted with hate. The arrows in her torso seemed to do no more than annoy her. "And you, false urdhracos!" Her eyes glared at Third. "We shall finish our business later!"

She started to turn, and then a strange, twisting spasm went over her face.

"Ridmark!" she said. "Go south! It is the only way you will survive! Go south!"

"What?" said Ridmark.

The urdhracos blinked. For an instant, she looked confused. Then Scythe banked, swooped over the trampled grass, and soared away to the north.

Where, Third supposed, she would report to her masters in the muridach host.

"Are you all right?" said Kyralion.

The last Throne Guard fell with a howl of pain, Tamara's acidic mist washing over it.

"I am well," said Third, though she was troubled. "Bruised and nothing more."

"Good," said Kyralion, and a flicker of emotion went over his face. "When you fell, I feared that you had been slain."

"Not yet," said Third, watching the black speck vanish to the north. She had once flown like that, she recalled, the horrible song of her father's aura filling her mind and soul, intent on venting her rage in killing and nothing more.

"I am glad," said Kyralion. He hesitated. "I am surprised the Scythe focused on you. I thought she would desire to avenge her defeat upon Lord Ridmark."

She and Ridmark shared a look. No, Ridmark understood. He had been there when Third had been freed, had been there when Mara had defeated the curse of her dark elven blood.

"The Scythe doesn't care about me," said Ridmark. "I'm just another human. If she waits another thirty or forty years, I'll die of old age anyway, and for an urdhracos, forty years isn't that long. But Third..." He shook his head. "She used to be an urdhracos."

"Imagine that you are dying of thirst," said Third, her voice quiet. "Imagine that you have been thirsty for so long that you have forgotten everything else, that there is nothing in the world but agony. Then you see a woman who has all the water she could ever want to drink. You would hate her for it and wish to see her dead."

"A grim fate," said Kyralion.

"Yes," said Third. "It was."

"Why do you think she said to go south?" said Ridmark.

"I have no idea," said Third with a shake of her head. "She is insane, that is clear. Perhaps she knows that south is the only clear path open to us, and she wants to keep us alive for the sport of it."

"We need to move," said Ridmark. "None of the Throne Guards got away, but the Scythe did. She'll tell her masters where we are, and they'll come for us in force."

"And I think we can assume," said Third, "that one or more of the Maledicti are with the muridach host."

"Yes," said Ridmark.

The others approached. Third turned a critical eye over them, checking for injuries, but it seemed they had come unscathed through the skirmish against the Throne Guards. Though Calliande had likely healed any wounds they had taken.

"We will need to move in haste, won't we?" said Krastikon.

"We shall," said Ridmark.

"If we do, we can reach Cathair Avamyr before sundown," said Kyralion.

"Magatai," said Ridmark. "Can Throne Guards usually regenerate like that?"

"They cannot, friend Ridmark," said Magatai. "Magatai has never seen a muridach that could heal itself in such a fashion. He has shot many muridachs through the eyes, but they never get up again." He spat upon the ground, and Northwind let out a disapproving squawk. "It is cheating. When Magatai kills a man, he should stay dead."

"I happen to agree," said Tamlin.

"This might solve the mystery," said Calliande, holding up a leather bottle. "Every single one of the Throne Guards carried one." She poured it out, and a thick black slime spattered against the ground. A few blades of the tall grass withered and turned black. "It's an alchemical elixir, but it seems the main ingredient is troll blood. That explains why their fur was falling out, and those scaly patches on their skin. Once the Throne Guards ingested enough of this, the only way to kill them is with fire or acid."

"Ratmen that regenerate," said Magatai. "While Magatai thrives on challenges, this is rather more challenge than he would prefer."

"Agreed," said Ridmark. "Let's get moving. I would prefer not to be here when the Scythe returns with friends."

Third nodded and sheathed her swords, and she glanced again to the north.

She suspected the Scythe would return sooner than she might wish.

"I am glad you are not hurt," said Kyralion, his voice quiet.

A shiver of emotion went through Third. She presented a calm mask to the world, and after nearly a thousand years of life, her emotions did not come and go quickly. To her, the emotions of someone like Kalussa Pendragon were like weather, come and gone in the blink of an eye. But within Third's mind, her emotions were like glaciers, huge and vast and implacable. She loved Mara and Ridmark and Calliande and their children, and she would slaughter nations before she let anyone hurt them.

Something similar shuddered through her ancient mind as she looked at Kyralion.

But there were no words in any of the languages she knew to describe the emotions.

"Thank you," said Third.

IN THE TWISTED world of the Durance that had once been constructed by the Sovereign, Morigna opened her eyes and let out a shuddering breath.

Not that she actually needed to breathe. Nor did she actually have a body that required air. But some memories were ingrained into her spirit, and she still took deep breaths when concentrating.

It would have been amusing, under other circumstances.

Right now, the circumstances were dire enough.

Morigna stood in the circle of black standing stones that imprisoned her within the Durance. In all directions stood the mist-choked forest, and in the distance, she saw jagged black mountains. From time to time Morigna glimpsed the creatures that dwelled in the forest, saw their glowing eyes staring at her.

She felt no fear of them. They couldn't hurt her.

Nor could the mad dwarven smith Irizidur who wandered endlessly through the forest, muttering to himself about how it had gone wrong, it all gone so wrong. Sometimes the creatures caught Irizidur and tore him apart, and his screams lasted for days.

But he always healed. That was the nature of the Durance, to ensure that its prisoners never, ever escaped their torment.

Morigna would have felt sorry for the wretched dwarf, but it was his pride and folly that had started the War of the Seven Swords, that had laid the path the servants of the New God now walked.

Well. She felt a little sorry for him. Mercy had never been Morigna's strong suit, but she was learning.

Right now, though, her whole attention was upon the Shield Knight and his companions.

Death was closing around them from all sides. Ridmark had escaped the trap the Maledicti had set for him in Kalimnos, but only barely. Now by ill chance, he and the Keeper and their allies had been drawn into the war between the muridachs and the gray elves.

That was another plot of the New God and its Maledicti minions, but Ridmark and Calliande might be slain in the impending downfall of the gray elves.

And if they were defeated, there would be no one to stop the rise of the New God, no one at all.

The Shield Knight and the Keeper were halfway to the answer. They had figured out some of the truth, had seen through the Masked One's veil of lies and shadows. They would figure it out in time, Morigna knew.

But they had to stay alive long enough to discover the truth, and if they died with the gray elves, the New God would rise unopposed to devour the world.

Morigna stared at the tapestry of fate, watching the shadows the past and the present cast upon the future.

In nearly every possible future, Ridmark, Calliande, and all their companions perished with the gray elves, and there was nothing Morigna could do to stop it.

Unless...

There was a potential future that did not end in defeat, a single path where they did not die.

Morigna's first attempt had worked. Even within her prison, she had been able to reach out and touch the mind of the Scythe, and the tormented soul of the urdhracos had repeated her message.

Perhaps now Morigna could reach the mind of the woman who stood at the heart of the storm.

For there was one potential future left where the Shield Knight and the Keeper did not die, and the woman Third was at the heart of that future.

"Third," said Morigna. "The hybrid. The lady of war. The former urdhracos."

She was the woman of flames the Augurs of the gray elves had seen in their vision, and that vision had terrified them.

For Third had the power to save the gray elves or to destroy them, and even Morigna did not know how Third would choose.

And Third was Morigna's last hope of saving the Shield Knight and the Keeper and stopping the rise of the New God.

She began the spell to reach beyond the walls of the Durance.

In the distance, Irizidur started screaming again.

4

CATHAIR AVAMYR

They pushed hard for the rest of the day, moving south as fast as they could manage.

Ridmark kept everyone close together. He was tempted to send Magatai and Kyralion and Third to scout, but he dismissed the idea. If another attack came, they had better odds if they were together. For that matter, if parties of muridach scouts were moving through the plains, anyone caught alone would be at risk. Third could hold her own against the Scythe, but Magatai and Kyralion would not. If the urdhracos caught them alone, she would kill them. For that matter, if the Scythe brought more Throne Guards to help her, not even Third could win against so many.

No, better to stay together.

And as the sun began to dip towards the horizon to the west, they caught their first sight of the ruins of Cathair Avamyr.

"Dear God," said Calliande, her amazement plain.

Ridmark agreed with the feeling.

To the south rose a broad, shield-like hill. The hill had been shaped into four terraces, making it look like a shallow step pyramid.

Upon the terraces rose the city.

It had once been huge, larger than Tarlion, larger than Aenesium, perhaps larger than both cities put together. Walls of white stone, each thirty feet high and ten thick, ringed each of the terraces, and domes and towers and spires rose within the walls. At the top of the hill stood a mighty citadel, bastions and towers rising high against the blue sky.

The city was beautiful, beautiful as the ruins of Cathair Selenias had been...and like the Tower of Nightmares, the city was a ruin.

Huge breaches had been blasted in the walls, and heaps of white rubble lay scattered in the plains around it. The gates had been smashed, and all the towers were crumbling, empty shells. The city still had grandeur to it, but it was the solemn grandeur of a tomb.

Ridmark knew that many, many gray elves had died here.

"I had no idea this place existed," said Tamara.

"Magatai has told you of the Blood Quest of Cathair Avamyr many times," said Magatai.

"Aye," said Tamara, "but hearing of a place and seeing it with your own eyes are two different things. Very different things. I never thought a city could be so large."

"Cathair Avamyr," said Kyralion, gazing at the ruins of his long-dead ancestors. "This was once the final refuge and fortress of my people. All the rest of our cities on this continent had fallen to the Sovereign and his hosts. We retreated here to build Cathair Avamyr as our last stronghold, and fortified the Pass of Ruins with towers and magic to keep the Sovereign's hordes at bay." His voice grew melancholy. "You all have seen the fate of the Pass of Ruins with your own eyes. The survivors fell back to Cathair Avamyr. The siege of the city lasted for decades. Tens of thousands of our enemies died, but in the end, we were overwhelmed. The survivors fled to the Illicaeryn Jungle and founded the Unity, and the remnant of my people has dwelled there ever since."

"Magatai spoke of guardians," said Ridmark, staring at the white ruins. Nothing seemed to be moving within the walls.

"When we fled, our wizards and nobles activated the remaining magical defenses," said Kyralion. "Likely the guardians are magical constructs similar to the ones we faced in Cathair Selenias."

"They were," said Magatai. "Suits of golden armor, animated by magic. Magatai challenged them and defeated them, and then they rewarded Magatai with a boon." He hesitated. "Some say there are great treasures within the ruins, but Magatai decided to exercise prudence and withdraw."

"Probably wise," said Ridmark. "We'll head through the northern gate and stay in the lowest tier of the city. We'll camp in one of the ruined towers, one high enough to look over the outer wall. From there we'll have a good view of the plains, and we'll be able to see any approaching foes. Once the muridach hosts pass, we'll continue to the east." He looked at Calliande. "Does the Sight show anything?"

"A lot," said Calliande, her voice faint, her eyes unfocused as she gazed at the ruined city. "There are many, many powerful warding spells in the ruins, Ridmark. All of them are damaged in some way. And the echoes...there were indeed terrible battles here, clashes between mighty wizards." She shivered, and her eyes came back into focus as she dismissed the Sight. "Cathair Avamyr will be a very dangerous place."

"Yes," said Ridmark. "Let us hope that the muridachs find it so as well."

Because they had no other option. They couldn't outrun the muridach hordes. If they stood and fought, they would raise a ring of slain foes around them, but they would still be killed. Their only remaining option was to withdraw into the ruins of Cathair Avamyr and hope that the muridachs bypassed the dangerous location.

Or that the ancient traps and wards in the city did not kill them.

"Come," said Ridmark. "Let's get inside the walls before dark."

He led the way toward the city's northern gate. Oathshield rested in its scabbard, but he kept his hand near the sword's hilt. The ruined city drew nearer, and at last, they approached the northern gate of Cathair Avamyr.

At least, what remained of the gate.

Once it had been a tall arch with doors fashioned from the golden metal the gray elves used for their armor and weapons. But the arch had been smashed into heaps of broken rubble, and the doors lay in twisted ruin upon the ground. Beyond the broken gate, Ridmark saw a broad square dotted with rubble and statues on their pedestals. Ruined houses of white stone ringed the square.

"Are there any wards upon the gate?" said Ridmark.

Calliande shook her head. "No. Old, broken ones, almost faded. They were probably ruined when the Sovereign broke the doors."

Ridmark nodded and led the way through the ruined gate, clambering over a pile of broken white stone and into the square. Utter silence reigned over the city, and Ridmark stopped just beyond the gate. The houses lining the square were empty stone shells, the roofs fallen in long ago. Here and there weeds and small trees poked up from the flagstones, their roots tangled and gnarled. Statues of gray elves in armor and robes stood on pedestals, and a large statue rose in the center of the square, showing a dozen armored elven warriors.

He turned, looking for danger, and blinked in astonishment.

"What is it?" said Calliande, and she turned and saw what had caught his attention.

Reliefs covered the inside of the city's wall, hundreds of colossal reliefs.

The reliefs reminded Ridmark of the scenes that he had seen on the walls of Cathair Valwyn below the city of Aenesium. Yet those reliefs had seemed full of hope, and had shown the gray elves coming to Owyllain and building their new civilization.

These reliefs were far grimmer.

They displayed the gray elves preparing for their last stand. One scene showed the gray elves battling against orcish hordes led by a dark elven lord in a winged helmet, who was almost certainly the Sovereign. Another relief showed the gray elves building fortresses in a mountain pass, likely the Pass of Ruins. Still another displayed Cathair Avamyr itself, strong and stalwart, with gray elven warriors standing resolute upon the outer wall. It looked like a strong fortress, unconquerable and invincible.

It was a far cry from the shattered, half-crumbling ruin that surrounded them now like a forest of bones.

"There are many such reliefs in this place," said Magatai. "They are everywhere. Your kindred, friend Kyralion, did like to make sculptures."

"They did," said Kyralion. He gazed at the images. "It is the story of the founding of Cathair Animus. The reliefs say that this city would be the final home of our people and that it would forever stand strong against the might of the Sovereign." He sighed. "But as with so many things, the Liberated were wrong."

"That is the Sovereign, I assume," said Kalussa, pointing at the dark elven lord. The image in the stone held a staff, and Ridmark realized that it was the Staff of Blades.

"It is," said Kyralion.

"The smaller dark elf next to him," said Calliande. "Is that the Confessor?"

"He is," said Kyralion. "He was the Sovereign's lieutenant and remained at the Sovereign's right hand for all his wars. Now he thinks to take the Sovereign's place and rebuild his empire."

"While the history is fascinating," said Krastikon, "I suggest we do not linger here. We will be plainly visible through the gate to anyone passing nearby, and our scent trails will lead right here."

"Agreed," said Ridmark. He looked around and then pointed. "That tower looks promising." It rose nearly two hundred feet into the air, its crown shattered, but it still looked sound.

"We might get caught and encircled there," said Tamara.

"Some of the windows open onto the nearby rooftops," said Ridmark. "If any attackers enter the tower, we can escape that way over the roofs."

"That tower would have belonged to one of the wizards," said Kyralion. "The purpose of the tower was to provide a clear place to observe the position and configuration of the thirteen moons."

"Are there any wards in the tower?" said Ridmark.

"There are some spells upon it," said Calliande, "yet nothing dangerous. I think it will be a good place to shelter for the night."

"Then let's make camp," said Ridmark.

He led the way down the street to the base of the tower. There was a long hall at the foot of the structure, and the tower itself was about two hundred feet tall and fifty across. The hall had no trace of life, and statues of gray elven warriors and wizards stood in niches along the walls. A flight of spiral stairs led to a round chamber that held stone shelves containing scrolls and books.

"A preservation spell," said Calliande, looking at the bookcases. "It's let these books and scrolls pass the centuries intact. A pity Antenora isn't here. She would insist we take all these back to the Tower of the Keeper in Tarlion."

"We'll make camp in here," said Ridmark, watching as Krastikon urged the scutians up the stairs. "If we get surrounded, we can escape through the windows between those bookcases." The roofs of the surrounding buildings were intact. "Third, Kyralion, let's check the upper floors."

Kyralion and Third followed him up the spiral stairs as Calliande and the others set up camp in the library. They passed through four empty rooms, and then came to the top of the tower. The rooftop had been torn away, and chunks of broken stone lay scattered around the floor. An enormous, intricate machine of golden metal sat in the center of the damaged room. It looked like a navigational instrument of some kind, with a dozen rings encircling a spherical core.

"Is that a magical device?" said Ridmark.

"It is not," said Kyralion. "It is a device used to calculate and predict the positions of the thirteen moons. It relies on metalworking and gears and mathematics, not magic."

"How does it work?" said Third.

"I confess I have no idea," said Kyralion. He shrugged. "I never bothered to learn. Most of the Liberated can use magic, though only some of us devote all their time to its study. Because I cannot join the Unity and am resistant to magic, there never seemed any point to learning."

Third hesitated, and then stepped closer. "Your kindred...they have not treated you well?"

"I would not say that," said Kyralion. "Rather, they find it difficult to understand me, as I find it difficult to understand them." He shook his head. "And if Lord Amruthyr was right, and they have lied to me... I have much to think on."

He shook his head once more and fell silent. Ridmark knew him well enough by now to realize he would say no more on the topic.

"We'll set a watch up here," Ridmark said, "and another at the foot of the stairs to guard the street."

"This plan seems sound to me," said Third.

"Aye," said Ridmark. "And we'll need to watch for these guardians Magatai mentioned."

"I suspect," said Kyralion, "they will only come out at night."

Ridmark did not like the sound of that.

THAT NIGHT CALLIANDE stood atop the ruined tower, gazing over the broken wall at the city and the surrounding plains.

The others slept in the library chamber, though Third kept watch on the tower's great hall and the entrance to the street. Only four of the thirteen moons were out tonight, painting the plains surrounding the ruined city in an ethereal silver glow.

That meant Calliande had no trouble seeing the lights flickering and dancing in the higher levels of Cathair Avamyr.

Blue and white and golden lights pulsed throughout the city's tiers, throwing eerie shadows in the gloom. Calliande kept the Sight in a loose grip, ready to warn her if any danger approached, and she saw the powerful wards gathered around the ruined fortress at the heart of the fallen city.

No sign of dark magic, though.

But the Sight showed her the power of the Staff of Blades ascending the stairs of the tower.

Calliande turned her head just as Kalussa climbed up to join her, the dark metal of the Staff rasping against the floor.

"Lady Calliande?" said Kalussa.

"I'm here," said Calliande, and Kalussa stepped to join her, the wind rustling past them. "Couldn't sleep?"

"No," said Kalussa, both hands wrapped around the dark length of the Staff of Blades. The wind tugged at her hair, and the sleeves of her crimson tunic rippled beneath her golden armor. "It's this place."

"Eerie, isn't it?" said Calliande.

"Aye," said Kalussa. "This must have been the largest city in the world once. Tens of thousands of gray elves must have lived here."

"Maybe even a quarter of a million," said Calliande. The thought of such numbers boggled the mind. Antenora had told her that on Old Earth there were cities where tens of millions of people lived, and Calliande could scarce imagine that. But she could imagine Cathair Avamyr as it had been in the days of its glory, tall and strong and proud, a shining bastion for the gray elves as they fled from the armies of the Sovereign.

"And now it is a tomb," said Kalussa.

"Yes," said Calliande. "It's like spending the night in a graveyard."

Though most graveyards were not dotted with ancient, lethal warding spells.

"It makes me think of Aenesium," said Kalussa in a soft voice. "Of what might happen to the city if we fail. Aenesium would have been destroyed if you and Lord Ridmark hadn't stopped Rypheus. Or if Justin had marched through the gates." She shivered. "It might still happen if we cannot stop the New God and the Maledicti."

"Perhaps," said Calliande. "But we are doing what we can. Which is why we're here, after all. Though I didn't expect we would have to take shelter in the ruins of the gray elves."

"No," said Kalussa. "I hope Tamlin's mother knows the answer."

"As do I," said Calliande.

"The things that Lord Ridmark told us, the things that the Maledictus of Air said to him." Kalussa shivered again. "How the Masked One has been using the Maledicti to orchestrate the War of the Seven Swords..."

"We've suspected as much since at least Trojas," said Calliande. "Maybe even before. It seemed odd that the Maledicti all claim to serve the coming of the New God, yet they somehow wound up assisting different sides of the war. No. What Mhazhama said to Ridmark only confirmed what we already suspected."

"Do you think the muridachs are another trap for us?" said Kalussa.

"I doubt it," said Calliande. "I think we've just walked into the war between the muridachs or the gray elves. Though I don't doubt that the Maledicti are behind this 'prophet' of the Lord of Carrion. The presence of the Scythe proves that."

"Kalimnos didn't look like a trap either," said Kalussa, "yet it was. The Maledicti went to great lengths to kill us. And it would have worked, too, if not for Lord Ridmark. We didn't have any defense against it. We..."

She fell silent, shaking her head as she stared at the ghostly ruins.

"Kalussa," said Calliande. "I don't think you want to talk about Cathair Avamyr."

Kalussa closed her eyes, swallowed, and nodded. The turmoil was obvious upon her face.

"Can I ask you something?" said Kalussa. "It...it might not be appropriate, but..."

"Go ahead," said Calliande. "I can guess what you want to ask."

Kalussa took a deep breath. "Were you...were you ever with a man? Before Lord Ridmark, I mean."

"No," said Calliande, watching the younger woman. "There was never time. My mother and father died when I was young, and if they had lived, they probably would have found a husband for me. But they died, and my magic manifested, so I was taken into the Order of the Magistri. Then I became the Keeper's apprentice, and then the Keeper in turn...there was always another battle to fight. Another wounded soldier to heal. I never even thought about a husband or even a casual lover...and then I met Ridmark."

Kalussa hesitated. "Did you...did you ever lie together before you were wed?"

"No," said Calliande. "I could claim heroic self-control, but that would be a lie. The truth is that we would have, but we kept getting interrupted."

Kalussa smiled a little. "Another battle to fight?"

"Something like that," said Calliande. "If you must know, the first time was about five minutes after we were married."

Kalussa turned a little red. "I am sorry to ask, but...but..."

"There's no one else to talk to about this, is there?" said Calliande, suspecting that Kalussa was at last ready to discuss what really bothered her.

"No," said Kalussa. "I wouldn't wish to speak to a man about it. There is Lady Third, and while she is valiant, I am frankly terrified of her. I would rather discuss such things with Tamlin than with her. I don't know Tamara very well." She blinked a few times. "And she wasn't affected by the dream spell. Which means...which means she probably saw..."

"You and Calem," said Calliande.

"Yes," whispered Kalussa, her anguish plain. "What am I going to do, my lady?"

"About Calem?" said Calliande.

"I was such a fool," said Kalussa. "I should have been stronger. I should have been able to resist the dream spell. I..."

"Kalussa," said Calliande. "I am far stronger than you with magic, and I still couldn't resist the dream spell. Ridmark likes to say that no matter how strong and how skilled a swordsman is, there is still always someone who is stronger and better. That is true for swordplay, and it is also true for magic."

"I should have had better self-control," said Kalussa. "Instead I threw myself at Calem like a drunken trollop, and..."

"Do you never want to see Calem again?" said Calliande.

Kalussa gave her a stricken look.

"I can't stop thinking about him," she whispered. "About him, and about what we did. I never knew anything could feel so wonderful. But I have the Staff of Blades. I have elemental magic, and I have the magic of the Well of Tarlion. I must exercise better self-control. I..."

"No one ever has perfect self-control," said Calliande. "No one is ever completely in control of their own lives."

"You have perfect self-control..." started Kalussa.

Calliande's laugh drowned the rest of her sentence.

"What?" said Kalussa, half-bewildered, half-offended.

"I have perfect self-control?" said Calliande. "That's very flattering, but it's also dead wrong. I just told you that Ridmark could have had me any time he wanted. And if I had control over my life, do you think I would be here? No. Ridmark and I would be at home in Tarlion...with all three of our children."

"Your daughter," said Kalussa.

"Yes," said Calliande. "Joanna." She took a ragged breath. "You can't control everything about your life, Kalussa. Sometimes bad things come into your life, like Joanna's death. But sometimes good things come into your life, and I think that Calem is one of those things. And I also think that you should talk to him soon, and if you don't, you'll regret it for a long time."

"I feel like such a fool," said Kalussa.

"Love can do that to you," said Calliande.

"I mean that it was worse for you," said Kalussa. Calliande noted that Kalussa did not argue that she wasn't in love with Calem. "I just...well, you know what the dream spell caused me to do. But it showed you Joanna. That must have been cruel."

"It was," agreed Calliande. "And I will always mourn for my daughter. But I have too much to do to let it paralyze me." Her eyes narrowed. "And the Maledicti will come for us again, I'm sure of it. When they do, I'm going to make them regret using that grief as a weapon."

"I imagine their regret will only last a short time," said Kalussa.

"One hopes."

Kalussa took a deep breath. "Thank you. I don't know if I feel better, but it was good to talk about it with someone. I...I should try to talk to Calem soon. Not yet, but soon. God, I don't even know what I'll say to him. I'll apologize for seducing him..."

Calliande raised her eyebrows. "He blames himself for seducing you."

"What? No. That is not how it happened," said Kalussa.

"Since you both blame each other," said Calliande, "perhaps you can forgive each other and start over. If you really want to have a husband and children, you'll have to learn to forgive each other at some point."

"Maybe you are right," said Kalussa. "I think..."

Calliande didn't hear the rest of the sentence.

The Sight surged through her, and she saw currents of magical power flowing through the lowest tier of the ruined city.

Something was waking up.

"Keeper?" said Kalussa.

Calliande leaned over the ruined wall and gazed at the street below, sending the Sight sweeping before her.

She found the currents of power at once. Dozens of concentrations of magical force moved through the street below, converging on the ruined tower where Calliande and the others sheltered. Each one of those concentrations of magical force was potent. They weren't things of dark magic, but rather warding magic. Likely these were the guardians that Magatai and Kyralion had mentioned.

And they were coming to confront the new intruders to their city.

"Lady Calliande," murmured Kalussa. "Those lights."

Calliande blinked. She had been so focused on the Sight that she had neglected what her physical eyes had been telling her. In the streets below, she saw dozens of pale white lights moving towards the tower, almost like men carrying lanterns of white glass.

"The guardians," said Calliande. "We had better join the others right now. We may have to fight."

Kalussa nodded and followed Calliande towards the stairs.

THIRD STOOD in the doorway of the great hall, watching the silent streets of Cathair Avamyr.

She supposed the sight would have put someone else into a melancholy mood. There was a solemn grandeur to the ruined city, an air of inevitable loss. The gray elves had put up such a fight to save their homes and families and civilization from the Sovereign's tide.

They had fought, and they had lost.

It was a sad thought, but Third was used to it. She had seen centuries of battle, had seen men die to defend their homes again and again. Sometimes their sacrifices saved their families.

Sometimes they did not.

That made her thoughts turn to Kyralion. The Augurs had sent him alone on his mission without adequate arms and armor, and they had lied about the vision they had seen. Yet he had never complained. He carried on, doing his duty. She wondered if he had family in the Illicaeryn Jungle. A father and a mother who were still alive? Brothers and sisters?

A wife?

It was such an absurd thing to think about, but her thoughts turned in that direction. It was such a useless fantasy. Third had no wish to settle in the Illicaeryn Jungle. She desired to fulfill her mission from Queen Mara and High King Arandar and return home to the Nightmane Forest. For that matter, she knew Kyralion had no desire to leave his kindred. A man who would undertake such an arduous mission to save his people would not abandon them. Certainly, he would not abandon them to run off with an ancient half-human, half dark elven hybrid...

Third's breath hissed through her teeth.

A flicker of light caught her eye. She had been brooding, but she was too experienced to let the brooding override her vigilance. Third took a cautious step forward, her hands dropping to her sword hilts.

A white light was moving through the street. More than one white light, come to think of it. And they were moving towards the ruined tower. Third took a step back, intending to go up and warn the others.

A glance back told her that was unnecessary. Ridmark and Calliande hurried down the stairs, Kalussa right behind them. Kyralion and the others came with them. Magatai came on foot, leaving Northwind in the library chamber with the scutians. It was a solid choice. The struthian's speed could not be put to proper use in the streets. For all his bravado, the Takai halfling had solid tactical sense.

"You saw the lights?" said Third.

"I did," said Calliande, coming to a halt near the doors. "With the Sight. They are concentrations of magical force. Guardian spirits, I think."

"The guardians of the city," said Magatai. "You remember the suits of gray elven armor we fought in the Tower of Nightmares, friend Third?"

"Hard thing to forget," said Third.

"These guardians are akin to them," said Magatai. "They are suits of armor with crystals in the chest. Soulstones, like the one in friend Kyralion's sword." He tapped the bronze sword that hung at his belt. "The only way to defeat them is by prying the soulstone free of their cuirasses. That is what Magatai did. When he defeated them, the spirits offered him a boon, and he departed with it, having completed his Blood Quest."

"Here they come," said Ridmark, lifting Oathshield.

Third waited as the guardians came into sight.

There were dozens of them, and they wore the armor of the gray elves, overlapping plates of golden metal upon a backing of chain mail. Swords rested in their gauntlets, and white crystals shone on their chests. They wore golden helms with T-shaped slits in the front, and glowing white mist swirled and danced within the helms.

"What are they?" murmured Tamara.

Third didn't expect anyone to answer, but Calliande spoke.

"Memories," she said, blinking as she drew on the Sight. "The memories of gray elven warriors, recorded in the soulstones. It is a weaker version of the spell used on the soulblades. They are constructions of magic, but they have the memories and skills of gray elven warriors."

"They must make formidable fighters," said Krastikon.

"They did," said Third, remembering the battle outside the Chamber of Meditation. "Focus upon the soulstones, as Magatai said. If we can knock them free, that will break the spells..."

She trailed off.

The armored forms went motionless, dozens of glowing helms staring at them.

"They appear to be waiting for something," said Tamlin. "Did they do this the last time you were here?"

"They did not, Sir Tamlin," said Magatai. The halfling sounded puzzled. "They attacked at once."

Then voices began speaking, dozens of them at once. They were deep and toneless but filled with authority nonetheless.

Third realized that the guardians were speaking.

"You are of our kindred."

"Magatai thinks they mean you, friend Kyralion," said Magatai.

"Yes," said Kyralion.

He stepped forward, golden sword in his right hand.

"Name yourself," said the chorus.

"I am Kyralion of the Illicaeryn Jungle," he said.

The golden figures considered him. "You are not of the Unity."

"No," said Kyralion.

"Then you are the one. You are the herald. The hour of doom has come."

"The herald?" said Kyralion. "The herald of what?"

"The doom of our kindred. Our doom, or our salvation. Is the woman of flames with you?"

Third shifted, the tension within her mind hardening. Kyralion looked at her.

"Yes, she is here," said Kyralion. "But she can speak for herself."

Third stepped forward, and she felt the attention of the guardians settle upon her like a physical weight.

"You are the woman of flames. You are the woman of blue fire. You are the lady of war."

"I do not know what any of that means," said Third. "I am Third of Nightmane Forest, sister of Queen Mara. I came here to bring the Shield Knight and Keeper back to Andomhaim. Until I came to Owyllain, I knew nothing of the gray elves or Cathair Avamyr or the Sovereign. How do you know who I am?"

"Our vision is unanchored in time," said the chorus. "We can see the tapestry of fate, and we have watched our kindred dwindle beneath the wrath of the Sovereign. At last the fate of the Liberated comes to its end, and we shall either meet our doom or we shall be saved."

"How?" said Kyralion.

"The woman of flames shall be the instrument of our destruction or our salvation," said the guardians.

"And how will I do that?" said Third. A mixture of irritation and confusion and growing anger went through her. "How can I possibly destroy you or save you? I am just one woman, and I know barely anything about you."

"We have seen you walk your path through the web of fate," said the chorus. "Your sister had and has a mighty destiny and decided the fate of nations. You, too, shall decide the fate of nations."

"Tell me how," said Third.

"We have seen you walk through the tapestry of time," said the guardians. "You were the daughter and slave of a mighty dark elven lord. Your sister slew him, and now you are free. The threads of many others wrap about your decisions."

"That does not answer the question!" said Third, her voice sharper than she intended.

"You and Lord Kyralion shall stand at the apex of fate," said the guardians. "The Kratomachar is rising, and its servants have come to destroy our kindred. You shall break the Unity, or reforge it. You shall save the Liberated or destroy them."

"Tell me more," said Third.

"We cannot, for the future is still in flux," said the guardians. "We shall allow you and your companions to depart in peace, for you are not the enemies of the Liberated. Yet you must beware. Your enemies come for you. Be on your guard. Kyralion of the Illicaeryn Jungle.

Guard well the woman of flames, for without her, our people are doomed."

With that, the guardians turned and walked away, dispersing back into the city.

No one spoke for a while.

"Well," said Magatai at last. "That was very strange."

5

FIREBOW

The next morning Ridmark and Third went to the great hall.

"I suggest that we ascend to the outer wall and make a circuit of it," said Third. Ridmark did not think she had slept at all last night. Her face was calm as ever, but the lines around her mouth and eyes seemed sharper, and there were dark circles under her black eyes. "From there we will overlook the surrounding plains. We will be able to see if anyone approaches."

"That is a good plan," said Ridmark. He wondered if she wanted to talk about what the guardians had said last night. Well, if she wanted to, she would bring it up.

Third glanced towards the higher tiers of the city and the towers of the ruined fortress at its heart. "Unless we wanted to go higher. We would have a better view from the top of the city." Her mouth twisted. "The guardians ought to let me pass. Since I am apparently their liberator or their destroyer."

"Perhaps not," said Ridmark. "We don't understand the ancient magic of the gray elves. Best not to take the risk. The view from the outer wall should be sufficient."

Third hesitated, and then nodded. "Yes. That is reasonable." Again, her mouth twisted. "Nothing about the magic of the gray elves makes any sense, so why should their guardians make any sense as well?"

She took two steps to the side, and then back again. Pacing was unlike her. She was far more agitated than she wanted to show.

"Why?" said Third. "Why did the guardians tell me these things? Why tell me that I could save or destroy them?"

"I don't know," said Ridmark.

"And Kyralion," said Third. "I..." She took a deep breath. "I owe you an apology."

Ridmark frowned. "I cannot possibly see how."

"When we fought the Frostborn," said Third, "and I met the Keeper for the first time. I could not understand why you were so conflicted. I do now."

"Because of Kyralion," said Ridmark.

"Yes," said Third. She gave an irritated shake of her head, the black tail of her hair slapping against her shoulders. "I do not..." She sighed. "I do not wish to discuss this further. Let us go scout."

"As you wish," said Ridmark.

Third took a step forward and then stopped. Ridmark wondered if she had changed her mind and wanted to talk, but instead, she turned towards the stairs.

Kyralion descended, hesitated, and then strode towards them.

"Lord Ridmark, Lady Third," said Kyralion. "It is good you are here. I need to speak with you both."

"What is it?" said Ridmark.

Kyralion stopped, took a deep breath, looked at Third, and then back at Ridmark.

"I think it is time that I return to the Illicaeryn Jungle," said Kyralion.

Third blinked, once. From her, that was like she had flinched.

"You feel that your people need you," said Ridmark.

"Yes," said Kyralion. "When I departed the Illicaeryn Jungle, the chief threat facing the Liberated was the plague curse that Qazaldhar had cast upon the Unity. That was something I was not equipped to fight, for I have no magic. Then the Augurs had their vision of the woman of flames and the Shield Knight and the Keeper, and I was sent to find you. I thought that perhaps if we were successful, if we defeated the New God and destroyed the Seven Swords, that might end the plague curse. But since we have come to Kalimnos, I have learned that the muridachs have moved against my people in far greater numbers than I thought. They have always been a threat to the Liberated of the Illicaeryn Jungle, but not like this." He took another deep breath.

"You cannot fight against the plague curse," said Ridmark, understanding, "but you can take up arms against the muridachs and fight to defend your people against them."

"Yes," said Kyralion. "I have a duty. The Augurs sent me to find the Shield Knight and the Keeper and the woman in flames, and I have done so. I thought this would save my people, but perhaps the Augurs were mistaken." He shrugged. "Or perhaps you will defeat the New God, and my intervention at the proper time ensured you will survive to be victorious."

"Perhaps," said Ridmark. He shook his head. "But you feel you must do this?"

Third said nothing, her eyes on Kyralion.

"I must," said Kyralion. "It is my duty. My conscience tells me this."

"We will miss your help," said Ridmark. "We wouldn't have won against Khurazalin or the Necromancer without your aid."

"And I will miss the company of you and the others," said Kyralion. "I have never felt...at home as I do now. But I have my duty, as you have yours."

"Kyralion," said Third, her face a mask.

Kyralion looked at her, and they stared at each other.

"You...could come with me, Lady Third," said Kyralion. Third swallowed, a muscle twitching near her eye. "The Unity needs warriors, and you are a great warrior. You would be welcome among us."

"As you are welcome among your kindred?" said Third. "You said yourself that you are an outcast, that you are not part of the Unity."

"Perhaps," said Kyralion, "but we are in no position to turn away help. And...I would like you to come with me."

They stared at each other. Ridmark felt like he was intruding on a private moment.

"Kyralion," said Third. She closed her eyes, opened them again. "I..."

Ridmark never did find out what she intended to say.

There was a flash of reddish-orange light to the south, and Ridmark looked in that direction just in time to see a fireball erupt over the crumbling towers, followed a half-second later by a ringing thunderclap.

CALLIANDE ROLLED HER SHOULDERS, adjusting the weight of the gray elven armor over her tunic and gambeson. She never liked wearing armor, though she recognized the necessity. Perhaps she ought not to complain. Men spent weeks at a time in armor while marching in the field. Then again, men generally did not have breasts that the armor always seemed to pinch.

She was walking in circles, trying to get the armor settled, so she was in front of the library's southern window when she saw the explosion.

Calliande froze as the thunderclap echoed through the chamber, and she reached for the Sight and sent it towards the flames. She saw the lingering currents of elemental magic that had produced the explosion, accompanied by the flare and flicker of a dozen spells. Half of them were elemental magic, and the other half were dark magic.

Dark magic? How had wielders of dark magic gotten past her? Alarmed, she sent the Sight sweeping towards the north, and she spotted a dozen wielders of dark magic moving through the city. They had the now-familiar aura of priests of the Lord of Carrion.

The Deeps, she realized. The subterranean levels of the city must extend to the Deeps, and the muridachs moved through the caverns of the Deeps with ease. Muridach warbands must have entered the subterranean levels of Cathair Avamyr through the night.

All this flashed through her mind in an instant.

"My lady?" said Kalussa, hurrying to her side. "Did you see that?"

"Yes," said Calliande, blinking as she concentrated on the Sight and their surroundings at the same time. "I'm not sure...but I think someone is fighting the muridachs."

She turned and looked back at the others. Most of them had been awake already, but the sound of the explosion had roused those who had still been sleeping. "We need to go. Krastikon, Calem, get the scutians ready to move. And make sure each of you is carrying a pack with food. If we're pursued, we might have to leave the scutians behind." Calliande would dislike leaving the pack scutians to be consumed by the muridachs, but the poor lizards could only move so fast.

The others scrambled to obey, and Ridmark ran up the stairs to the library, taking them two at a time, Third and Kyralion behind him.

"The explosion," said Ridmark. "Elemental magic?"

"Aye," said Calliande. "I think the muridachs are fighting someone. I don't know who."

"It is possible," said Kyralion, "that the muridachs are fighting the Liberated. Some of my kindred have the magical power to unleash an explosion of that size, and they might have sent scouts north to watch the progress of the muridach hosts."

"Should we aid them?" said Calliande.

"Maybe," said Ridmark. "How the devil did the muridachs get into the city? If they came through the northern gate, we should have seen them."

"Probably the Deeps," said Calliande. "We saw the underground galleries of Cathair Valwyn beneath Aenesium, and those opened to the Deeps..."

"And there were muridach warbands in there," said Ridmark, voice grim.

"Maybe we should withdraw through the northern gate and circle around the city," said Third. "If we are drawn into a fight in the streets, we could be surrounded and trapped."

"I think it's too late for that," said Tamlin, pointing out the northern window. "Look!"

Calliande crossed to the window. The library chamber was high enough to see over the city's northern wall. That meant she could see the dust cloud rising on the northern horizon, along with the dark mass drawing closer to the city.

"One of the muridach armies," said Ridmark.

"They will have kalocrypt scouts out," said Magatai. "We will not be able to leave the northern gate without drawing their attention."

"The southern gate, then?" said Tamlin.

Calliande didn't like that thought. They needed to go northeast, not south. Yet it seemed they had little choice. Trying to leave Cathair Avamyr through the northern gate would be suicide, as would attempting to leave the city through the caverns of the Deeps. Those tunnels would be swarming with muridachs, and the ratmen would have the advantage in the caverns.

It seemed their only option was to retreat through the city's southern gate.

"I don't think we have any other choice," said Calliande.

"Agreed," said Ridmark. "Let's move. And if Kyralion's kindred need aid, we'll help them. Perhaps we can fight our way out of the city together."

RIDMARK STEPPED into the street outside the tower, Third at his left and Tamlin at his right. There was another flash of red light to the south, followed by a thunderclap, and Ridmark heard the distant clang of sword against shield.

There was a battle raging on the streets nearby.

"We had better hurry," said Calliande, looking towards the square before the northern gate. "I think there are a group of muridach priests heading for the gate."

"They will almost certainly have a guard of soldiers, perhaps even berserkers," said Magatai.

"Then let's not wait here to meet them," said Ridmark, drawing Oathshield. A flicker of white fire ran up the blade. Ridmark wasn't sure if it was reacting to the dark magic of the muridach priests or the aura of ancient magical power around the ruined city in general. "Follow me."

He led the way from the tower, heading east around the base of the city's next tier. Ridmark's eyes swept over the crumbling towers and houses, but nothing moved in the ruins, though he knew that would not last. With a muridach army approaching from the north and fighting to the south, Ridmark and the others had found their way into the eye of the storm. It had happened by accident, but he feared that storm was about to wash over them.

Kyralion had been ready to depart to aid his kindred against the muridachs. Ridmark was beginning to fear they would have to go with him, simply because they could not withdraw in any other direction.

Ahead, the street turned south.

Ridmark went around the corner and found himself looking at a battle.

Nearly twenty men in either leather armor or the golden armor of the gray elves stood in the center of the square. The men were gray elves, with pointed ears and eyes of gold or silver or purple, and they wore gray cloaks identical to the one that hung from Ridmark's shoulders. The elves in leather armor carried bows, and the ones in metal armor bore swords. Both swords and bows were augmented with soulstones, whether they had been forged of bronze or of gray elven steel, and flames and lightning and icy mist crackled around the weapons.

Nearly two hundred muridachs surrounded the gray elves, attacking in waves. The gray elves fought back, unleashing burning arrows and attacking with their soulstone-augmented swords, cutting down any muridach that drew too close. One of the gray elves stepped forward. His armor was more elaborate than the others, and he wore a winged helm. The gray elf gestured, casting a spell, and a fireball exploded in the middle of the muridachs, throwing a dozen of them into the air.

Yet the creatures continued their attack, and Ridmark saw that the gray elves would soon be overwhelmed.

"Friends of yours?" said Ridmark.

"Yes," said Kyralion, though he did not elaborate. "We must aid them."

"We shall," said Ridmark.

"There are only a hundred and fifty of them," said Magatai, setting an arrow to his bowstring. "That will prove little challenge."

Krastikon snorted. "I would hate to see what you would find a challenge, sir."

"Let's see if Magatai is right," said Ridmark, and he strode forward, lifting Oathshield.

"YOU TAKE THE RIGHT," said Calliande, "and I'll take the left. You can avoid the gray elves?"

Tamara nodded, holding her golden staff with both hands as she drew upon her magic.

"What should I do?" said Kalussa.

"Kill as many of the muridachs as you can," said Calliande, purple fire starting to crackle down the length of her staff. "If you see any berserkers, priests, or Throne Guards, focus on them. They'll be the most dangerous."

Kalussa took a deep breath, the blue crystal at the end of the Staff of Blades shifting and crackling.

Tamara held her power ready as Ridmark, Tamlin, Calem, Krastikon, Kyralion, and Third walked towards the square. Magatai rode behind them on Northwind, his bow ready. For a moment neither the muridachs nor the gray elves noticed the newcomers, and then the muridachs started to turn in alarm.

"Now!" said Calliande, striking the end of her staff against the ground.

Tamara released her own spell a half-second later, forcing the earth magic through Lord Amruthyr's staff. Her magic was strong, though it wasn't anywhere near as strong as Calliande's. Yet with the staff to focus and augment her power, Tamara could affect nearly as large an area as Calliande.

That came in handy now.

Calliande's spell sent a distortion through the left side of the broad square, knocking the muridachs from their feet. Tamara's spell went through the right side, knocking over the ratmen but leaving the gray elves untouched. The gray elves hesitated in astonishment, and Ridmark and the others charged forward. The Shield Knight struck down two muridachs in rapid succession, and Tamlin and Calem and Krastikon and Third proved no less effective. Magatai started sending shafts into the ratmen, killing with every shot. Kalussa threw those deadly spheres of crystal from the Staff of Blades, the impact blasting apart muridach skulls.

Kyralion came to a stop, raised his bow, and loosed arrow after arrow, his hands a blur. He shot down muridach after muridach, sending the creatures dead to the ground. The gray elves gave a shout and charged into the fray, driving back the ratmen.

Tamara started casting a new spell. She sent another distortion through the ground, knocking the muridachs from their feet so the gray elves and her friends could strike. Then she conjured a brief curtain of acidic mist, wounding and stunning the ratmen.

"Firebow!"

Tamara blinked. One of the gray elves had shouted that, looking at Kyralion. For his part, Kyralion gave no response but kept loosing arrows into the muridachs. The gray elf in the winged helmet, the one who had cast the powerful fireballs, looked at Kyralion and grinned.

"Firebow!" he called, and he cast another spell. A sphere of fire shot from his armored hands and landed amid the muridachs. The sphere exploded in a bloom of flame, killing a half-dozen ratmen.

The gray elves cheered, shouting "Firebow," and charged into the battle. Tamara cast spell after spell, as did Calliande, and Ridmark and Tamlin and the others carved their way through the muridachs. In an instant, the defense of the muridachs collapsed, and the creatures whirled and began fleeing from the square, pouring down the street to the south.

"Should we pursue them?" called Krastikon, pulling the Sword of Death from a slain muridach.

"No!" said Ridmark. "No, hold! If we chase them, they'll lure us into an alley, and we'll be finished. No, let them go."

Tamara lowered her staff and caught her breath as the muridachs fled.

The gray elves looked at her and the others. Tamara had to admit that it was an unsettling feeling. The gray elves all had such intense eyes, gold and silver and purple. They weren't immortal, and to the best of Tamara's knowledge, the gray elves lived about a thousand years or so before death claimed them. Yet she felt the weight and age in their gaze, and she knew that the gray elves were far older than she was.

The gray elf leader pulled off his winged helm. He had brilliant silver eyes and thick black hair, his features sharp and alien. For all that, he looked harsh and grim, with deep lines cut into his face and dark shadows beneath his eyes. He took a few steps forward, staring at Kyralion.

Then the hard face relaxed in a smile.

"Kyralion Firebow," said the gray leader.

"Arliach," said Kyralion. "It has been a long time."

"Aye, too long, my friend," said Arliach. "It is good to see you, but I hope you have some good news for us."

Kyralion looked back at Ridmark and Third. "I might at that."

6

FALLBACK

Third looked at the gray elves, unable to contain her curiosity and seeing no reason to try. For all the time that she spent thinking about Kyralion, she knew little about the gray elves. The stories she had heard were contradictory, and Kyralion often had trouble articulating himself about his kindred. He always answered her questions, but some of the concepts of the Unity or the society of the gray elves did not translate into either the orcish or the Latin tongues.

But Third had centuries of experience assessing targets, and right away she noticed several strange things about Arliach and his gray elven warriors.

First, she was reasonably sure that they were all sick, every single one of them.

Kyralion was a vigorous man, able to travel and fight from dawn until dusk without stopping for a rest, and that strength showed in his face and his posture. The same could not be said of the rest of the gray elves. Kyralion's face was tanned and a little weathered. The gray elves looked pale, not from the lack of sun, but from exhaustion and illness. All of them had the same deep lines and dark shadows beneath their eyes as Arliach.

For that matter, as Arliach drew closer, Third noted the veins beneath his skin. They were turning black as if they were rotting, and many of the other gray elves had black veins visible on their faces and hands. Was that a sign of Qazaldhar's plague curse?

The second strange thing she noticed was the silent communication.

The gray elves kept glancing at each other as people did when having a conversation. Third recognized the familiar movements of face and eye, and the gray elves looked like men discussing momentous news. Yet they were utterly silent. Third was certain they were communicating without speech. Her first thought was that they were using some sort of hand code, yet their hands remained grasping their weapons.

Were they communicating through magic? The Magistri of Andomhaim could converse in silence and across long distances using their mindspeech spell. Were the gray elves doing something similar?

Third glanced at Calliande and saw the Keeper staring at the gray elves with a frown on her face. Calliande saw her looking, and Third walked to join her.

"Noticed it too?" murmured Calliande in a low voice.

"They are communicating without speech," said Third.

"They are," said Calliande. "There is a spell linking all of them. I've never seen anything quite like it before. It's like the mindspeech spell of the Magistri, but far, far more complex and profound. It's…" She frowned. "It would be almost like they share the same mind."

"Is this the Unity?" said Third.

"Perhaps," said Calliande. "But if it is, the spell has been twisted. There is a necromantic taint to it, one that is poisoning these gray elves."

"Qazaldhar's plague curse?" said Third.

"I don't know," said Calliande, "but it seems likely. Come. Perhaps we can learn more."

Third nodded and followed the Keeper as she walked to join Ridmark, who had come to stand next to Kyralion.

"You have found powerful friends, Firebow," said Arliach in accented Latin. He seemed genuinely glad to see Kyralion, a warrior pleased to have found a comrade in a dangerous place. Third had thought Kyralion a pariah or an outcast, yet given his skill and bravery, it would have been strange for the warriors of the gray elves to reject him. Perhaps it was the leaders of the gray elves who did not like Kyralion, while the warriors admired him.

"I have," said Kyralion.

"For unless I am wrong," said Arliach, "you have three of the Seven Swords with you."

"You are not wrong, my friend," said Kyralion. "This is Ridmark Arban, the Shield Knight of Andomhaim. His wife Calliande, the Keeper of Andomhaim. Sir Tamlin Thunderbolt, the bearer of the Sword of Earth. Sir Calem, the bearer of the Sword of Air. Prince Krastikon Cyros, the bearer of the Sword of Death. Lady Kalussa Pendragon, the bearer of the Staff of Blades. Tamara of Kalimnos. Magatai of the Takai nomads." Magatai offered a grand bow from Northwind's saddle. "And Lady Third of Nightmane Forest."

Third stepped closer, feeling Arliach's silver eyes upon her. The other gray elves remained silent, though they kept glancing at each other. Third suspected that Kyralion's introduction had stirred them up. Not surprising, given that the last time three of the Seven Swords had been in the same place had been before Kothlaric Pendragon's imprisonment at Cathair Animus.

"And this is Lord Arliach of the Illicaeryn Jungle," said Kyralion, "a wizard and a ranger of the Liberated."

"I am pleased to meet you all," said Arliach, his eyes upon Third. "But if you found the Shield Knight and the Keeper as the Augurs said...then is she..."

"Yes," said Kyralion. "Lady Third is the woman of blue flames from the vision. She is also a most brave and honorable woman."

Arliach glanced at the other gray elves. Again, Third had the impression of unseen communication passing between them.

"Perhaps in deference to the urgency of the situation, Lord Arliach," said Calliande, "we should restrict ourselves to the spoken word."

His eyes snapped to face her. "You can hear the Unity?"

"No," said Calliande. "But the Keepers of Andomhaim possess the gift of the Sight. I can see the links of magic that bind you together. All of you, that is, except Kyralion, who has always said that he is not part of the Unity."

Arliach let out a breath. "The Augurs said that the Keeper would be powerful. In truth, I feared that Lord Kyralion would never return from his task, that the Augurs had sent him away because he made them look..." He scowled and shook his head, perhaps in answer to an unseen question. "Regardless, we have more urgent matters to discuss."

"Yes," said Ridmark. "Such as what we should do next."

"Agreed," said Arliach. "But first...Lady Third is truly the woman in blue flames?"

"She is," said Kyralion. "She is the one from the vision."

"But she is not one of our kindred," said Arliach, his bafflement plain. "She is..."

"A dark elf," said Third, and she felt a little satisfaction as the gray elves blinked in unison. "Half human, half dark elf."

"A hybrid," said Arliach. "But that is impossible. If you were a hybrid of a human and a dark elf, you would have transformed into an urdhracos long ago."

"I did," said Third. "Long ago. Most likely before you were born, Lord Arliach."

"Impossible," said Arliach, suspicion coming over his lined face for the first time. "The dark elves have been our bitter enemies since before we came to this land. You cannot possibly be what you claim to be. And you cannot be the woman from the vision of the Augurs."

"As to the vision, I cannot say," said Calliande. She had slipped into the mien of the Keeper, cool and calm. She also seemed a little imperious, as she did when dealing with a lord or a nobleman who was refusing to see reason. Third appreciated the gesture. "But as for Third's history, it is entirely true. She was once an urdhracos, a daughter of the dark elven lord known as the Traveler. One of the Traveler's other daughters slew him, and Third was freed from his control. She confronted the dark power within her and subdued it, and became as she is now."

"I doubt not your word, Keeper of Andomhaim," said Arliach, eyeing Third. "Still, a dark elven hybrid. The Augurs will not be pleased..."

"I will speak for her before the Augurs, if necessary," said Kyralion. "She stood with us against King Justin Cyros and the Necromancer of Trojas. At Kalimnos, the Maledicti seized control of the ancient wards in Cathair Selenias and directed them against us. Third went into the ruins to help break the spell."

"No one who goes into the ruins of Cathair Selenias returns," said Arliach.

"We did," said Ridmark.

"Third is the woman in flames from the vision," said Kyralion. "What is more, she is a great warrior and a loyal friend. The Guardian Rhodruthain brought the Shield Knight and the Keeper here against their will. Third set out at once to find what had happened to them, and she crossed thirty-five hundred miles to come here."

Third said nothing, a flicker of pleasure mixing with her unease. She wasn't sure how she felt that Kyralion thought so highly of her. But whatever the emotion was, she found that she liked it.

"Perhaps we can discuss visions and prophecies later," said Ridmark. "Unless I miss my guess, those muridachs we defeated will be back with aid as soon as possible."

"Yes," said Arliach. "Yes, you speak wisdom, Shield Knight." His eyes flicked to Oathshield's burning blade. "I have no idea how a human became bonded to a high elven soulblade. But as you said, that is a tale for another time. Why did Rhodruthain bring you here?"

"You know of the New God?" said Ridmark. "The Kratomachar?"

A shadow went over Arliach's wan face, and the other gray elves flinched.

In perfect unison, Third noted.

"The dark power foreseen by the Augurs," said Arliach. "The defeat of the Sovereign was the herald of its coming."

"We are on a quest to stop its return," said Ridmark. "We are traveling to the ruins of the Monastery of St. James in the Tower Mountains to speak with someone who has knowledge of the New God. On the way, we were attacked by muridach scouts, and we had no choice but to withdraw to the south. We thought to take shelter within the walls of Cathair Avamyr until they passed, but it seems that is no longer an option."

Arliach blew out a long breath, glanced back at his warriors, and nodded.

"No," said Arliach, "no, it is not. I am afraid you and your companions are in great danger, Shield Knight."

"From the muridachs," said Ridmark.

"More than you know," said Arliach. "The muridachs have driven us to our final refuge in the Illicaeryn Jungle. We once maintained outposts on the borders of the jungle, and here in Cathair Avamyr, but all were destroyed. Never before in our history have the muridachs come forth in such numbers. Nerzamdrathus has..."

Ridmark frowned. "Who?"

"Nerzamdrathus," said Arliach. "The Great King of the muridachs. He has brought all the muridach cities of the Deeps under his control, and he is the greatest commander of the muridachs that we have ever faced." His mouth twisted. "But even Nerzamdrathus would not have been able to maintain his hold over the lords of the muridachs without the aid of that damned prophet."

"The prophet of the Lord of Carrion," said Ridmark.

"Yes," said Arliach. "He has fired the muridachs into a frenzy. He claims that the Lord of Carrion shall rise in power and that the muridachs will devour the world. Worse, he is a wizard of great strength, a match for any of the Liberated. He has been training the muridach priests, raising them to new heights of power and strength. With Nerzamdrathus directing the muridach armies, the prophet backing his rule with sorcery, and the plague sapping our strength, the muridachs have won victory after victory." His face was bleak. "We face total defeat, and soon. Perhaps before the year is out."

"I suspect that the prophet of the muridachs is the Maledictus Qazaldhar himself, or one of the other high priests of the Maledicti," said Kyralion. "On our way here, we were attacked by an urdhracos under the control of the Maledicti." He scowled. "Clearly the plague curse was the first step in a far larger plan."

"Weakening us so the muridachs could destroy us utterly," said Arliach. "Perhaps you are right, Firebow. But if you are, it is too late. We can do nothing to stop the muridachs, and there are too few of us to flee to another land, even if we had the strength for such a journey. The best we can hope is to stave off the inevitable for some time." He shook his head. "But our troubles are not yours, Shield Knight, though I fear you might have become trapped in them. What are your plans now?"

"To leave Cathair Avamyr through the southern gate," said Ridmark, "circle to the east, and continue to the Tower Mountains."

Arliach shared a look with his men, and again Third had the sense of unspoken communication between them.

"I fear it is too late for that," said Arliach. "Already two different muridach hosts are only a few miles north of Cathair Avamyr, and their kalocrypt scouts are circling around the western and eastern walls. Worse, a third muridach host is moving through the Deeps below our feet, and is using the cellars of the city to enter the surface."

"Why are you here, then?" said Ridmark. "If you know the muridachs are moving towards your final refuge in the jungle, why come all the way north to Cathair Avamyr?"

A faint grimace went over Arliach's face, the expression mirrored for an instant on the expressions of the other gray elven warriors. Third recognized the look of soldiers who were not happy with their orders but were attempting to carry them out anyway.

"The High Augur commanded it," said Arliach. "She did not believe that the muridachs had come south in such numbers, or that Nerzamdrathus had gathered so many different muridach lords under his command." He shook his head. "We have been harried by kalocrypt raiders the entire time and had to take refuge in Cathair Avamyr. The guardians of the city drove off our pursuers, but a large number of them escaped and followed us here, and you know the rest."

"I see," said Ridmark.

He looked grim. Third wondered if he had realized the truth of their danger. He probably had.

"Shield Knight," said Arliach. "May I be blunt?"

"Please," said Ridmark.

"I think you should come with us," said Arliach. "I think that if you go any other direction but south, you will be killed and bring disaster to all of Owyllain."

"Because of the Seven Swords," said Ridmark.

"Yes," said Arliach. "You have three of the Seven with you, do you not? The Swords of Death, Air, and Earth? The muridachs will recognize those Swords, and if any of them survived to report to their masters, they will realize that a tremendous opportunity has come their way. If they kill you, they can claim those Swords themselves."

"I know," said Ridmark. "That is why we have the Swords with us. There is no safe place to put them. Sir Tamlin and Prince Krastikon are Swordborn and can carry the Swords without suffering ill effect. Sir Calem cannot use the powers of the Sword of Air without suffering harm."

"But once the muridachs realize that you have the Swords, they will come for you in force," said Arliach. "You slew the Necromancer and King Justin. Both were evil men, but can you imagine how much worse a muridach bearing one of the Seven Swords would be? A muridach necromancer arising with the Sword of Death, or a muridach tyrant wielding the Sword of Earth? If Nerzamdrathus had one of the Seven Swords, he would have destroyed the Liberated years ago."

He was right, Third knew. If they went north, west, or east, they would run into the waiting claws of the muridachs. They would be overpowered and killed, and the muridachs would claim the three

Swords for themselves. King Hektor had reunified Owyllain save for Xenorium, but the realm might be destroyed by a muridach horde led by a wielder of one of the Seven Swords.

"Then you suggest we go south with you?" said Ridmark.

A strange sense of finality closed around Third, like the emotion she felt in the final moment before a battle. The Augurs and Lord Amruthyr both had foreseen that she was the woman in flames, that she would somehow save or destroy the gray elves. Third could not see how.

Yet it seemed they had no choice but to flee south with the gray elven patrol.

What else might happen that she had not foreseen?

"Very well," said Ridmark. "How shall we proceed?"

"We'll need to break out of the city first," said Arliach. "Likely the muridachs left a guard at the southern gate, and we will need to punch through it. Then we must make for the Illicaeryn Jungle itself. We still control large sections of it near our...our final refuge." He paused. "From there you can head northeast to the Tower Mountains and avoid the muridachs entirely."

"Very well," said Ridmark. "Let's move. The sooner we break out of Cathair Avamyr, the sooner we can speak more. I suspect we both shall have a great many more questions for each other."

"Yes," murmured Calliande, her eyes on the gray elven warriors. "Yes, we shall."

RIDMARK LED the way through the ancient street, the others following him, the gray elven warriors and scouts spreading out around them.

Watching them move was an uncanny experience.

Experienced warriors developed a rhythm as they worked together. Ridmark and Third had fought alongside each other so many times that he could tell what she was planning to do at a glance. For that matter, Ridmark and Calliande had been in so many battles together that he could guess what she would do in a dangerous situation – whether she would unleash earth magic or fire magic or use the power of the Well to augment his speed and strength.

But he had never seen anyone move with the eerie harmony of the gray elves.

They flowed around each other like water, never tripping, never stumbling. The gray elves covered each other as they jogged from ruined house to ruined house, moving with grace and speed. And through it all, they remained silent. They did not even use hand signals to communicate, though they glanced at each other from time to time.

That kind of coordination would make them lethal in battle. Even with their magic, Ridmark had wondered how the gray elven patrol had held off so many muridach warriors, and now he knew the answer.

He was certain that they were communicating with each other without speech.

Which, he suspected, explained a great deal about Kyralion.

He had spoken of the Unity, said that he was not part of it. Ridmark had wondered if the Unity was the government of the gray elves. Calliande had suspected that the Unity was some sort of warding or defensive spell. It seemed that she had been half-right. What if the Unity was a mighty spell that let the gray elves converse without speech, to link their minds and act in fluid harmony without the need for words?

Kyralion was resistant to magic. Perhaps that resistance to magic kept him from joining the Unity and communicating with the others without speech. Ridmark wondered if the gray elves were born as part of the Unity, or if they were joined to it as adults. If they were born to it, if Kyralion had always been cut off from the silent communication of his fellows...yes, that would explain a great deal. One of the gray elves, but not part of the Unity. One of the Liberated, but always an outsider, always alone. It also explained why he had such trouble with social graces. If most of the communication of the gray elves took place through the silent mental speech of the Unity,

Kyralion would have had to learn such things by rote and memorization, rather than mimicking his elders as children usually did.

Then they came into the square before the southern gate of Cathair Avamyr, and all speculation fled from Ridmark's mind.

It was time to fight.

The southern gate was in better repair than the northern one. The arch was still intact, though the doors had been shattered and thrown down long ago. There nearly a hundred muridach warriors milling through the square. Ridmark wondered why they had not set out scouts or put themselves into formation, and then a shrill scream rang out over the square.

The gray elves came to a sudden halt, rage flashing over their faces, and Ridmark saw what had drawn their attention.

The muridachs had gathered into a half-circle around four of their berserkers. The creatures held down a gray elven warrior, each one grasping one of the warrior's legs or arms. They had stripped the gray elf of his clothing and armor, and the warrior struggled naked in their grasp. His torso and legs were covered in blood, and Ridmark realized why a heartbeat later.

The muridachs were eating him alive.

The berserkers' heads stabbed down, again and again, their mouths yawning wide as they plunged their chisel-like teeth into the gray elf's body. They were tearing gobbets of flesh from the gray elf's legs and chunks of viscera from his belly. The gray elf's screams were raw and desperate and animal-like, his eyes bulging, his face a mask of pain. All the while the muridach soldiers hooted and cheered like men watching a show.

"Take them!" shouted Arliach, starting a spell, fires blazing around his free hand.

The four muridach berserkers looked up, snarling. One of them reached down and slashed the screaming gray elf's throat. The sheer pettiness of it enraged Ridmark. They had tormented the gray elf, and now the muridachs wanted to ensure that no one would ever rescue him.

The gray elven archers released their arrows, and the swordsmen cast their spells. Arliach's fireball exploded amid the berserkers crouched over the dead gray elf, flinging them to the ground as flames chewed into their fur. The archers sent a volley of arrows into the muridach warriors, and the swordsmen hurled fire and lightning and ice into the ratmen.

The spells and arrows killed a score of the creatures, and the rest charged in a screaming mass towards the gray elves.

There was no time for planning, no time for tactics. Ridmark raised Oathshield, drawing on the sword's power to strengthen and hasten him. Calliande and Tamara both cast spells, and the ground folded and heaved, throwing dozens of muridach warriors to the ground. The four berserkers howled in rage and charged, their fur still burning, and Kalussa hurled a crystalline sphere through the head of one.

Then the muridachs crashed into them, and there was no time for thought, no time for Ridmark to do anything but focus on his own defense.

He found himself facing one of the muridach berserkers, the stench of burned flesh and fur rolling off its body. The creature slashed its huge bronze axe at Ridmark, and he dodged, stepping into the attack. Before the enraged berserker could recover its balance, Ridmark stabbed, driving Oathshield through the damaged bronze armor and into its heart.

The berserker's roar of fury withered to a gurgle, and Ridmark ripped Oathshield free and turned to face a trio of muridach warriors who rushed him. Ridmark had to retreat, snapping his sword left and right to deflect their attacks. Something dark appeared behind the muridach on his left, and with a flash of a blue short sword, Third killed the warrior. The ratman fell with a screech, and the other two turned to face the new threat. Ridmark seized the opening and brought his soulblade hammering down, tearing open a warrior's neck. The final muridach tried to retreat, and Third stabbed her swords, her blades slicing open the back of the ratman's legs. The muridach bellowed, and Ridmark finished it off with a stab.

He raised Oathshield again, the crimson blood sliding off the white blade, and saw the gray elves tearing into the muridachs. Whatever else could be said about the Unity, whatever it really was, Ridmark had to admit that it made the gray elves into fearsome warriors. They were obviously ill, the strange plague draining their strength and stamina. Yet they fought in perfect, synchronized harmony, the swordsmen covering each other and stepping aside in time to let the archers shoot past them.

It helped that Tamlin, Calem, and Krastikon were ripping through the muridachs, the three Swords leaving dismembered pieces of ratmen in their wake. Kalussa kept up a steady volley of crystalline spheres and fire globes. Calliande used her magic to knock the muridachs off their feet, and Tamara summoned curtains of acidic mist.

Another pair of berserkers came at Ridmark and Third. She waited until the last minute and spun to the side, her blades flying around her. The first berserker stumbled as Third's swords sliced through its hamstrings, and the creature stumbled with a roar of pain and rage. Ridmark's chop to the neck killed the berserker, and he turned to face the second creature. It lunged at Third, and she dodged around the sweep of the blades of its axe, the movement almost dancelike. Ridmark took the opportunity to attack, using Oathshield to augment his speed. The soulblade found a gap in the armor, sliding into the muridach's chest and gashing its lungs. Ridmark wrenched the sword free as the berserker gurgled, and Third opened its throat with a quick slash.

The surviving muridachs had seen enough. The creatures whirled and fled. Ridmark expected them to retreat through the southern gate, but instead, they broke into a dozen smaller groups that scattered into the alleys and streets leading off the square.

The gray elves started to pursue them, rage on their faces. Likely they wanted to avenge the agonizing death of the gray elf the muridach berserkers had been using as a meal. But knowing the muridachs, they were retreating into the cellars of the city and would use that to return to the tunnels of the Deeps.

And if the gray elves followed, the muridachs would set an ambush and wait for their enemies to follow.

"Hold!" shouted Ridmark. "Hold! If you follow the muridachs, you will blunder into a trap!"

One of the gray elven archers glared at Ridmark. He looked thinner and sicker than Arliach, the black veins beneath his pale skin more prominent.

"We must avenge our fallen kin!" snarled the archer. "Humans understand nothing of this! Your lives are too short to understand our loss!"

"If you follow this muridachs, your life will be far shorter than you wish," said Ridmark.

The archer snarled again, but Kyralion stepped to Ridmark's side, bow in hand.

"He is right, Nilarion," said Kyralion. "If we chase the muridachs they will set an ambush for us and kill us all."

Nilarion grimaced, but nodded, visibly forcing back his anger. "As you say, Firebow."

"Lord Arliach," said Ridmark. He spotted the wizard gazing at the mutilated corpse of the dead gray elf.

"He was my nephew," said Arliach. "The last surviving son of my sister and her husband, all of whom fell fighting the muridachs or perished in the plague."

"We need to move," said Ridmark. "If we linger here, the muridachs will regroup and come for us."

"Or they shall gather Throne Guards and kalocrypt raiders," said Kyralion.

"You are right," said Arliach, pulling himself together. It seemed that Kyralion's word carried great weight. The Augurs might have lied to Kyralion about his vision, but it seemed the warriors of the gray elves held the Firebow in great regard. "Let us hasten, and be gone from this place at once."

They hurried through the gate, heading to the south across the plains before the muridachs could return.

7

THE ILLICAERYN JUNGLE

C alliande had taken many long and dangerous journeys in her life, some of them in desperate haste, enemies harrying her step every mile of the way.

The two days of their flight from Cathair Avamyr to the Illicaeryn Jungle wasn't the most harrowing journey she had ever endured, but it came close.

They had no choice but to leave the pack scutians behind. There was no way the poor lizards could maintain the necessary pace, and Calliande and Ridmark and the others stuffed extra supplies into their packs and let the beasts go. It saddened her to let the animals depart. Almost certainly the muridachs would eat them as they had done to that poor gray elf, but at least this way the scutians would have a chance to escape.

For the thousandth time since she had come to Owyllain, Calliande wished she had a horse. If they had horses, they could have outpaced the muridach footmen, and while the kalocrypts were fast, they did not have the stamina of horses. If Calliande had a thousand horses, they could have mounted the gray elves and smashed right through the host of the muridachs. For that matter, if she had the trisalians she had thrown against King Justin's host at the Battle of the

Plains, they could have crushed the muridachs and sent the creatures scurrying back to their warrens in the Deeps.

Calliande pushed aside the thoughts. Daydreaming would accomplish nothing. While she wished for things, she might as well wish for the Order of the Swordbearers and the Order of the Magistri to come to Andomhaim. With a thousand Knights of the Soulblade and a thousand Magistri, she could have driven back the muridachs, defeated the other bearers of the Seven Swords, and reunited Owyllain. Then Hektor Pendragon could have reigned over a realm at peace, and Tamlin could settle down with Tamara, Calem with Kalussa, and the New God would never rise to torment the world.

She gritted her teeth and forced herself onward, the weight of her armor and the straps of her back digging into her shoulders.

They were attacked four times in the first day from Cathair Avamyr, three times by muridach scouting parties on the backs of kalocrypts, and once by a troop of berserkers led by a pair of priests of the Lord of Carrion. Every time, Calliande and the others were victorious. The gray elves fought with uncanny harmony, and Calliande and Kalussa and Tamara loosed their magic while Ridmark and the others charged into battle, cutting down muridach after muridach.

They won all four fights, but five gray elves died. Two of them were killed the fighting, cut down before Calliande could heal their wounds. Three of them, as far as she could tell, died of exhaustion and the plague curse. Calliande did not know how much of the gray elves' stamina went to combating their plague curse, but it appeared the strain of resisting the illness coupled with the stress of battle finally overwhelmed their constitutions, their hearts giving out.

They passed on, leaving the dead behind.

On the second day, after a short and restless sleep, Third, Ridmark, and Kyralion ranged out to scout, and after Calliande had checked on Gareth and Joachim, she sent the Sight ranging around them. She saw no sign of dark magic or of any enemies, and Ridmark and Third thought they had gotten ahead of the muridach horde.

With luck, they would reach the Illicaeryn Jungle after another day and night.

Which meant they were safe enough for Calliande to start asking questions.

She could tell that Arliach and Nilarion and the other gray elves were uncomfortable with her questions. Or they were uncomfortable with speaking about the Unity to an outsider and a human.

Calliande didn't give a damn.

Like it or not, she and her husband and friends had gotten swept up in the muridach war against the gray elves, and if they had any hope of survival, she needed to understand everything she could. For that matter, Calliande wanted to discover how Qazaldhar had used the Unity to inflict his plague curse on the Liberated.

Third kept close as Calliande questioned the gray elves. She, too, had reason to learn everything she could about the Liberated and their Unity.

"Then the Unity is not just mindspeech?" said Calliande.

It was drawing closer to midday, the sun hot overhead, the air sticky and damp. Sweat dripped down Calliande's face and her back, and she frequently used the magic of elemental water to draw ice from the air to cool herself. The others marched south, pushing a path through the grass. The muridachs would have no trouble following their trail, but Calliande supposed it hardly mattered. All the muridachs were going south anyway.

"It is a more profound connection than that, my lady," said Arliach. "The Unity lets us communicate constantly. We share our emotions, our senses, our impressions and thoughts. Words are not required for this manner of communication. Indeed, words are cumbersome in the Unity. We can communicate so much more efficiently without the use of language." He smiled. "We mostly use speech for communicating with outsiders. The Unity is like the flight of an arrow, but the spoken word is a crawl by comparison."

"I see," said Calliande, remembering one of the things Kyralion had told her soon after she had met him. He had complained about the limitations of language, how a word that meant one thing to a man might mean something else to another. Since the gray elves seemed capable of communicating without speech, that explained why Kyralion found words cumbersome and clumsy to use. Especially since he was not part of the Unity.

She felt a flash of sympathy for Kyralion. It must have been a challenging way to grow up.

"It seems you do, my lady," said Arliach. "You possess the power of the Sight?" Calliande nodded. "In ancient days, many of our wizards possessed that power, though now only the Augurs wield it. I suppose you can see the Unity. It must be a wonderful thing to behold."

"It is indeed remarkable," said Calliande. That was true enough. As she focused the Sight on the gray elves, she saw the web of the Unity that bound them. The Sight interpreted it as thousands of threads of blazing blue light, linking together the gray elves in a mighty web. It was a powerful and potent work of magic, and the gray elves would be in constant communication, sharing thoughts and emotions and memories and images with the speed of thought.

A great feat of magic...and yet it disturbed Calliande.

Some things, she thought, ought to be private. She did not want anyone to watch or listen when she lay naked with Ridmark. And there were things in her mind she never wanted to share with anyone, things that shamed her. On the day of Rypheus's treachery, for a moment Calliande had considered letting Kalussa die of her wounds, enraged at the younger woman's attempted seduction of Ridmark. There was her lingering grief and guilt over the death of Joanna. It no longer dominated Calliande's thoughts, but it would always be a part of her. There were older emotions that she didn't want to share. She had been jealous of Morigna and angry at Ridmark when he had been with her, even if Calliande had kept those emotions walled away from her judgment. Sometimes she got exasperated with her children, and it was all she could do not to shout at them to shut up and stop fighting. For that matter, she missed her sons constantly and thought about them often.

Her mind was a stew of conflicting emotions, and Calliande knew she wasn't unique. It wasn't even a bad thing. It was simply how the human mind worked. She knew Ridmark would have thoughts and feelings he didn't want to share with anyone else, and that would be true of every living man and woman. Yet to be joined with everyone else, to constantly share thoughts and emotions, to be bombarded with their negative emotions even as they sensed hers...

If Calliande was honest with herself, it sounded nightmarish. Perhaps Kyralion was fortunate in more than one way that he could not be made part of the Unity.

She wondered why the gray elves had done this to themselves.

"Remarkable," said Calliande. "Tell me, can you communicate with the other gray elves scattered throughout the Illicaeryn Jungle? Or is there a...ah, limit to how far the Unity reaches?"

"There is," said Arliach. "The range varies by the individual gray elf in question, and larger groups of our people can communicate over further distances. For my patrol, the distance would be about five or six miles. Once we approach the final refuge of my people, we shall be able to speak with the other gray elves from about nine or ten miles away."

"A useful skill," said Calliande. A flash of insight came to her. "That's why no gray elf of the Unity can use one of the Seven Swords, isn't it? The power of the Sword would spread through the link of the Unity and overwhelm your kindred."

"That is correct," said Arliach. He smiled. "You need not fear that we shall try to take the three Swords from your companions. They would do us no good, and trying to use one of the Swords would injure the Liberated grievously."

"Have the gray elves always possessed the Unity?" said Calliande. "Or is it something that was created?"

"Not always," said Arliach. "When we came to this land, we built mighty cities and towers in imitation of the high elves from whom we descended. You traveled through the Pass of Ruins to come here, so you know how that portion of our history ended." Calliande nodded. "We made our last stand at Cathair Avamyr, and the Sovereign pursued us and destroyed the city. The survivors fled to the Illicaeryn Jungle, and there we founded the Unity."

"So the Unity is recent," said Calliande. "From the perspective of the gray elves, anyway. No more than a few thousand years old." For the gray elves, that would be only two or three generations.

"That is correct," said Arliach. "And it was the Unity that gave us the ability to defy the Sovereign. You saw us fight in Cathair Avamyr." Calliande nodded again. "The speed of our communication is a powerful advantage in a fight. Especially in a place like the Illicaeryn Jungle, where we can prepare ambushes and fade into the trees. Many times, the Sovereign sent armies into the Jungle to defeat us, but we whittled away those armies piece by piece and destroyed them."

"A powerful defense," said Third, who had been silent for the conversation so far.

"It is, my lady," said Arliach after a moment's hesitation. "Without the Unity, the Sovereign would have destroyed us before humans came to Owyllain."

"But it has some weaknesses, does it not?" said Third.

Arliach shrugged. "No method of defense is perfect."

"The plague curse, for one," said Calliande.

"That is the gravest weakness," said Arliach, looking at the other gray elves, "and if the muridachs had not come forth, the plague curse would still destroy us in time."

"How did the plague curse fall on the Unity?" said Calliande.

Arliach hesitated and looked at the gray elves again, no doubt communicating with them in silence.

"It was soon after the battles at Urd Maelwyn and Cathair Animus," said Arliach at last. "The Guardian Rhodruthain and the Master of the Arcanii Talitha betrayed and murdered High King Kothlaric Pendragon, and the Seven Swords were scattered. The Augurs were furious at Rhodruthain and refused to help any of the bearers of the Seven Swords, and the Liberated returned to the Illicaeryn Jungles. We hoped that with the Sovereign dead, we could rebuild our civilization, and perhaps in time we would return to our ancient heights."

"Then Qazaldhar found you," said Calliande.

"The Maledictus of Death appeared within our refuge," said Arliach. Again he hesitated, glancing at the other gray elves, and Calliande suspected they were deciding how much of the story to share. "He said that the Sovereign was dead, but that the Kratomachar would rise and conquer the world. In repayment for the defeat of the Sovereign, Qazaldhar pronounced a curse upon us. The plague curse spread through the Unity, and neither or Augurs nor our lorekeepers nor our wizards knew how to remove it. We have been slowly dying ever since, and now the muridachs have been roused to finish us."

"I am sorry," said Calliande. She had tried using the magic of the Well on Arliach twice, first to heal him of the plague curse, and then to attempt to break the necromantic aura of the plague. Both times she had failed. The plague was a magical disease, and the healing spell would not work upon it. For that matter, trying to dispel the necromantic magic of the disease had proven impossible. As soon as she attacked it, fresh dark power surged through the web of the Unity to renew it. Qazaldhar had woven the plague into the very fiber of the Unity itself, and the only way to break the plague would be to sever the individual gray elf's connection to the Unity.

That would be fatal.

"It is not your doing," said Arliach. "This battle has been underway since long before Connmar Pendragon founded the realm of Owyllain. Long before humans even came to this world, in truth." He sighed. "I fear you have come to see the dismal final chapter of our kindred. Once we ruled this entire continent, and our cities glittered like jewels in the sun. Now our final remnant awaits the end."

Third's face twitched and then settled back into its calm mask, and Calliande knew her well enough to realize that Third was hiding disdain. Arliach's attitude would be alien to Third. She would meet the end fighting, her blades covered with the blood of her foes, and would consider bemoaning the tragedy of her fate to be a waste of time.

Calliande wondered if that was Arliach's attitude, or if it was the opinion of the rest of the gray elves.

Perhaps it was the opinion of the Unity.

"Another question, my lord," said Calliande. "How did the Unity begin?"

"The Augurs founded the Unity when we fled to the Illicaeryn Jungle," said Arliach, repeating what he had said earlier.

"Yes, but...how exactly?" said Calliande. "It is a stupendous feat of magic. As the Keeper of Andomhaim, I am curious how it was done."

"I..." Arliach hesitated and looked at the other gray elves. "We are not permitted to speak of it to outsiders, by the decree of the High Augur. Perhaps when you meet the Augurs, my lady, they will tell you about our origins."

"Of course," said Calliande. "I look forward to it."

"If you will forgive me," said Arliach, "I would like to take a look around. We should be well away from the kalocrypt patrols, but I would prefer to verify that with my own eyes."

"Certainly," said Calliande. "Thank you for your time, Lord Arliach."

Arliach bowed and jogged away, three of the gray elven scouts falling in around their leader.

Calliande and Third shared a look.

"He didn't like that last question, did he?" said Calliande.

Third's mouth twisted. "No. It seems clear that while the Unity offers many advantages, it also exact a sharp price from its members."

"The advantages would be coordination and harmony and speed in battle," said Calliande.

"Aye," said Third. "During an ambush in a dense forest, that would be a fearsome advantage. But the disadvantages are sharp. Did you see how the gray elves all seem to agree with each other? It seems that the Unity enforces consensus. I doubt that any of them have had an original thought for centuries. For that matter, I wonder if Arliach's fatalism has spread through the Unity in the same way as Qazaldhar's plague."

It was one of the longest speeches that Calliande had ever heard from Third.

"That thought occurred to me as well," said Calliande. "I suppose there are worse things than consensus."

"It depends on the consensus," said Third. "In the scriptures, it was the consensus of the mob that Pilate should release the murderer Barabbas rather than the Dominus Christus."

"That is a good point," said Calliande.

"I wonder if the consensus of the Unity causes the gray elves to make similarly ill-founded decisions," said Third. "I can also see why the gray elven warriors admire Kyralion so much."

"Why is that?" said Calliande.

"Because he does not share their fatalism," said Third.

Calliande frowned. "Kyralion said several times that he fears the muridachs will destroy his kindred."

"That is simply a reasonable assessment," said Third, "and the most probable outcome. But he does not...wallow in despair the way the other gray elves do, probably because he is not linked to the Unity and so is not forced to join its consensus. When the Augurs had their vision of me, did they go to find me? No. Kyralion crossed half a continent to find you and Ridmark, and he has remained at your side ever since. Is that the act of a man who is given to despair?"

"It is not," said Calliande.

"And that is why Arliach and Nilarion and the others all heed Kyralion Firebow," said Third. "He acts. He leads. The others feel despair, but he does not. Perhaps he thinks his kindred are doomed, but he will not surrender."

"An admirable outlook," said Calliande.

"Yes." Third took a long breath. "He is." She shook her head. "But perhaps we can get far enough ahead of the muridach host that we can continue to the Monastery of St. James."

"I think it might be too late for that," said Calliande. "The muridach armies are too close. We might have become entangled in this war, no matter we do next."

Third said nothing for a long moment.

"I fear you are correct," she said at last.

THAT NIGHT, they stopped for a rest long after sundown.

Tomorrow morning, Arliach thought, they would reach the Illicaeryn Jungle.

Had she been alone, Third would have pressed on, hoping to reach the cover of the trees. But the gray elves were exhausted on their feet, their pallor increasing, the veins beneath their skin darkening. For that matter, her friends were tired as well.

And if Third was honest with herself, she felt exhaustion sinking into her bones. She required little rest, but even she had limits, and she would not object to sleep.

She lay down on the ground and fell asleep at once.

And in her sleep, she dreamed.

Third's dreams almost always recalled her centuries as an urdhracos, a long dark scream of blood and despair and death. She had been free for nine years, though that was a tiny span of time compared to the centuries she had been bound in the Traveler's service. She sometimes dreamed of his face, cruel and malignant and sneering, the eyes filled with shadow. Or she dreamed of killing, of the many foes she had slain during her enslavement.

But tonight, she dreamed of a place she had never seen before.

Third stood in a barren forest, the trees choked with mist. Far in the distance rose a range of dark mountains, stark against the gray sky. Eerie cries rang through the forest, and from time to time she glimpsed burning eyes in the mist. Her hands wanted to grasp her sword hilts, though she had the sense that nothing could harm her here.

A foolish sensation. No one was invincible. Her father had thought himself invincible and look what had happened to him.

Before Third rose one of the familiar rings of dark elven menhirs that her father and so many other dark elven nobles had created. Third had seen hundreds of them scattered across Andomhaim, so she recognized the familiar scenes of torture and murder carved into the black stones.

A woman stood just within the circle, watching her.

She was human and looked to be somewhere in her early twenties. She had black eyes and black hair bound in a braid, her face pale and sharp. The woman wore wool and leather and a peculiar cloak of tattered brown and green and gray strips that likely aided with concealment in a forest. A carved wooden staff rested in her right hand, the sigils sometimes flashing with white light. When they did, her eyes flashed with the same glow.

Third stopped at the edge of the circle and stared at the woman, her mind sorting through memories.

The woman stared back, head tilted to the side as she regarded Third.

"You do not know who I am," said the woman, "but..."

"No, I have deduced your identity," said Third.

The woman raised a black eyebrow. "Do elaborate."

"Before the end of the war with the Frostborn," said Third, "Ridmark was frequently visited by the spirit of his dead lover Morigna in his dreams. She tried to prepare him to wield the sword of the Dragon Knight. Before we left Aenesium, Tamlin Thunderbolt told Ridmark and Calliande of the 'Dark Lady' who appeared in his dreams and warned him of danger, and Kalussa mentioned that the same Dark Lady had appeared in her dreams before the battle at Trojas. Ridmark assumed that Morigna's spirit passed to its fate after the Frostborn, but I suspect that she instead has been offering guidance to Tamlin and Kalussa and possibly others."

The woman's thin mouth curled in a smile.

"My sister Mara described Morigna to me many times, for they were good friends. Based on your appearance, I suspect that you are the spirit of Morigna," said Third.

Morigna's smile widened. "A pity we never met in the flesh. You are very clever."

Third shrugged. "What I am is very, very old, and there are few things I have not seen before." She paused. "This is new, though."

"Nevertheless, your logic is entirely correct," said Morigna. "After the defeat of the Frostborn, the archmage Ardrhythain offered me a choice. I could continue to what awaits beyond the mortal world and trust to the mercy and forgiveness of God, or I could take up a mantle of duty here."

"And what mantle is that?" said Third.

"The Guardian of humanity," said Morigna. "For there are more dark powers in the world than the shadow of Incariel, as you well know, and more dangers than the dark elves. I cannot intervene directly, save for rare circumstances, but I can advise and warn."

"As you have been doing all of Tamlin's life," said Third.

"Half of Tamlin's life, anyway," said Morigna.

Third nodded, drew one of her short swords, and slashed it through the empty space between the menhirs. Or she tried to, anyway. The blade rebounded from the empty air with a flash of blue fire as if she had struck a stone wall.

"If you are the Guardian of humanity," said Third, sheathing her sword, "how did you end up trapped in this circle? Because I am reasonably sure that you are trapped."

Morigna grimaced. "I came to Tamlin's dreams to warn him of the trap that awaited you in Kalimnos. Unfortunately, five of the Maledicti and the Masked One himself projected themselves into the dream, and I was overpowered and imprisoned here. They erased Tamlin's memory of that dream."

"Which is why he woke up screaming that night, but could not recall why," said Third.

"Yes," said Morigna. "I have since tried to contact Tamlin or anyone else in their dreams, but I was unable to reach a human mind. However, I discovered that I was able to reach the mind of a hybrid."

"A hybrid," said Third. "The Scythe. Yes. That was why the Scythe told Ridmark to go south. You were speaking through her."

"Correct," said Morigna. "That was an experiment. Speaking with you is a more successful attempt. So here we are."

Third frowned. "Just where are we, anyway?"

"The Durance of the Sovereign," said Morigna. "A domain caught halfway between the material world and the threshold, anchored to a vessel in Urd Maelwyn. The Sovereign used this place to torment prisoners he did not yet wish to kill...or for prisoners like me, who are spirits and therefore cannot be slain."

Third let out a long breath. "It is a Tyrathstone, is it not?"

Morigna blinked. "It is. How did you know?"

"My father spent a great deal of time and effort trying to find one," said Third. "He thought that if he could retreat into the domain within a Tyrathstone, he could be safe against all his enemies. He never did find one and concluded that they had all been destroyed thousands of years ago."

"As it happens, he was wrong," said Morigna. "The Sovereign took one with him to Owyllain. There is one on the isle of Kordain, defended by another Guardian. I believe there is another within Urd Morlemoch. Fortunately, the Sovereign never found a use for his beyond employing it as a prison. Which, of course, is why we are here."

"Yes," said Third. "Though that does not explain why you have brought me here. I assume it is to give me a warning?"

"Again, you are correct," said Morigna. "Understand that I cannot tell you everything. You are not yet in the proper junction in time. Additionally, the nature of the Durance imposes limitations upon me..."

"And I will not remember most of this when I wake up?" said Third.

"No," said Morigna. "But some of it will linger in the depths of your mind. Perhaps it will aid you when the moment of crisis comes."

"Crisis," said Third.

"You are about to undergo a terrible challenge," said Morigna. "Ask me what you will, and I will answer what I can."

"Very well," said Third. She was unsurprised to hear that a deadly challenge awaited her. "A first question, then. I assume the Maledicti are behind the muridachs' attack on the gray elves?"

"You assume correctly," said Morigna. "Qazaldhar leveled the plague curse upon the Liberated, and now the Maledicti wish to finish off the gray elves. The gray elves have known of the coming of the Kratomachar, the New God, for some time, and the Maledicti feared that the Liberated might try to prevent its advent. So Qazaldhar created the plague curse to cripple them, and now the muridachs march to exterminate them utterly."

"The Augurs think that I can save or destroy them," said Third. "Why?"

"Because you can," said Morigna.

Third sighed. "If that is the quality of answers you gave to Tamlin Thunderbolt, I can see why he seems so exasperated."

"A better answer, then," said Morigna. "You can save or destroy the gray elves because you are like Tamlin and Kalussa and Krastikon."

Third frowned. "I am not Swordborn."

"No," said Morigna, "but you are an anomaly."

"Because of what I am," said Third. "A hybrid."

"Yes," said Morigna. "You were not supposed to exist, Third. Your father sired you to become his slave, his assassin and warrior, and you were an urdhracos for centuries. You were never to have been freed. Yet you were…and think of what you have done since. You saved the lives of both the Shield Knight and the Keeper, and if you had not, the shadow of Incariel would have devoured this world. Your father intended you only for evil, yet you have done great good, good that he never imagined. So is it with Tamlin and Kalussa and Krastikon and the other Swordborn. They were not included in the design of the New God and the Maledicti. The master of the Seven Swords never dreamed that any of the bearers of the Swords would have children because he does not understand love, only power and control. You and Mara were never supposed to exist, and yet you ripped a line of fire through the plans of the Warden and the Frostborn and the shadow of Incariel. And now you stand in the heart of the plans of the Maledicti, and you have the power to save the gray elves or to destroy them for their crimes and folly."

"I do not want to decide the fate of nations," said Third. "I want to fulfill my task from Queen Mara and High King Arandar, and bring the Shield Knight and the Keeper and their children back home to Andomhaim." She considered that. "If I save the gray elves, will that help the Shield Knight and his family? Or will it harm them?"

"The fate of the gray elves," said Morigna, "will decide the fate of the Shield Knight and his family. You shall stand at the eye of the storm, and you will choose in which direction it shall break."

Third shrugged. "Then I will choose as I think best at the time. My main objective is to return the Shield Knight and his family to their home."

Morigna smiled. "You never had a brother, Third, but if you did, I think you would love him as you love Ridmark."

Third shrugged again. "What of that? Perhaps I am too old for strong emotion."

"No," said Morigna. "The young have strong emotions. Yours are as deep as mountains."

"If you say so," said Third.

"What about Kyralion?" said Morigna.

Third opened her mouth, closed it. For the first time since this strange conversation had begun, she found herself at a loss for words.

"Perhaps I can guess," said Morigna. "You desire him, the first time you have ever desired anyone in all your long life. You admire his bravery, his devotion to his people despite his place outside their Unity. But you know that he loves his people and that you do not. You know that he would not return to Nightmane Forest with you, no more than you would stay in the Illicaeryn Jungle for him. A casual liaison is not part of your nature, nor is it of his. Yet you wonder what it would feel like nonetheless."

Third closed her eyes, opened them again.

"I can see why," she said, "Ridmark was so affected by your death."

Morigna inclined her head to acknowledge the compliment. "You know Kyralion is in love with someone else."

"Yes," said Third. "A gray elven woman. Likely one who has spurned him because he is not part of their precious Unity."

"You do not think highly of the Unity," said Morigna.

"I do not," said Third. "I do not yet know enough to make a final judgment. But what I have seen does not impress me. It makes a formidable weapon in battle, yes. But it also seems an instrument for enforcing consensus. A community can be a good thing, but it can also be a vile tyranny."

"You value freedom," said Morigna.

"I was a slave for fifty times longer than your mortal span," said Third. "Not even the Guardian of humanity can value freedom as I do."

"You are wise," said Morigna, "and there is one more piece of wisdom you will need to learn if you are to decide the fate of the gray elves, if you are to save the lives of the Shield Knight and the Keeper."

"What is that?" said Third.

"You must learn to forgive."

Third shrugged once more. "To forgive what? The gray elves have done nothing to me."

"Forgiveness is one part of empathy."

Third felt herself frown. "Empathy? Empathy for what?"

"Pain."

Third laughed in surprise. "Pain? No one understands pain better than I do, Guardian. No one."

"You have survived pain beyond the capacity of most humans to imagine," said Morigna, "and it has made you strong. Your entire mind was in pain for so long that you have forgotten what it was like not to feel pain."

Third shrugged. "Pain is to be endured. Anything else is a waste of time."

"Remember to have mercy on the pain of those weaker than yourself," said Morigna.

"Why?"

"Because you will choose whether or not the gray elves live or die," said Morigna, "but mercy is the only way you will survive that choice. Remember this."

The dream dissolved into nothingness.

Third's eyes blinked open, and she stared at the star-strewn sky overhead. Only two of the thirteen moons were out, which meant she could see countless thousands of stars. The elves, whether high, dark, or gray, had been born on this world, but Third knew that mankind came from another world, as had the orcs and the halflings and the muridachs. Third wondered if she was looking up at the light of humanity's ancient homeworld.

She wondered why she wondered that. Such philosophical musings did not come to her often.

Dreaming, she must have been dreaming. Odd that she could not remember the dream. When Third slept, she either had vivid nightmares or dreamed nothing at all. She frowned at that thought. Ridmark had sometimes suffered prophetic dreams, she knew, during the war with the Frostborn, and it seemed that Tamlin had been visited by a spirit called the Dark Lady in his dreams.

Had Third experienced a similar dream?

She searched her memory, trying to snatch any details from the mist of sleep.

Nothing came.

Well, if she couldn't remember the dream, then there was nothing to be done about it.

Third went back to sleep.

THE NEXT DAY they came to the northern edge of the Illicaeryn Jungle.

"Dear God," said Tamlin, wiping the sweat from his forehead. It had grown hotter with every step they took to the south, and now the air was so humid that Third felt like she was walking through a wet mist. "I've read about the Illicaeryn Jungle when I was a child, but to see it with my own eyes..."

Tamara came to a stop next to Tamlin. "I don't think I've ever seen so much green in my life."

The plains continued to the south, and then all at once, they just stopped. A huge wall of massive green trees rose before them, stretching to the east and to the west as far as Third could see. The trees were enormous, rising two hundred or three hundred feet tall, their massive branches spreading overhead like the ceiling of a cathedral. The branches threw the interior of the jungle into dim green shadow, and thousands of brilliant flowers of red and gold and blue covered the ground. Third saw dozens of birds fluttering overhead, their feathers of bright gold and blue and red, their harsh cawing echoing through the air.

"The Illicaeryn Jungle," said Arliach. "Our final refuge is two days to the south."

"A dangerous place," said Magatai, squinting into the jungle. Northwind squawked once, and then snatched an insect out of midair and swallowed it. "Good country for ambushes. It is not surprising that the gray elves have held out here for so long. You can hit your foes and then slip away into the trees."

"It is what we have done many, many times before," said Arliach. He smiled a little. "Surely you do not fear to enter the jungle, Takai?"

"Bah!" said Magatai. "Magatai fears nothing. And God, the ancestors, and random chance favor the bold. Better to act boldly than to fail timidly." He waved a hand in Kyralion's direction. "Look at friend Kyralion! He went in search of the woman of blue flames, and now he returns with mighty allies to aid you, Magatai himself not least among them. No, better to be bold."

With that, Magatai tapped his knees against Northwind, and the struthian squawked and ambled towards the waiting wall of the jungle.

"Well," said Krastikon, "far be it from me to argue with Magatai."

Ridmark looked at Arliach and Nilarion and the other gray elves. "Your kindred will let us pass? I would prefer not to have arrows shot at me from behind every tree and bush."

"We can continue unhindered," said Arliach. He hesitated and looked at the other gray elves. "We sense none of the other Liberated at this time. Likely they have all withdrawn further south. And the jungle no longer offers any protection. The muridachs have advanced in such numbers that they will flush out all our hiding places and hidden trails."

"Then let's not linger here," said Ridmark.

They continued into the jungle, following a trail that Arliach pointed out. The narrow trail and the thickness of the undergrowth forced them to go in pairs and single file. Third volunteered to bring up the back of the line, keeping watch for any muridachs that might have followed them from the steppes.

She remained vigilant as she followed the trail, watching the thick foliage around the path. It seemed a safe assumption that the brighter a plant was, the more poisonous it would be. Though Third suspected that any dangerous animals would be camouflaged and hide themselves in the trees. She would have to ask Kyralion about that.

As if her thoughts had summoned him, Kyralion came into sight and fell in alongside her.

"Lord Kyralion," said Third.

"Lady Third," he answered. "Lord Ridmark suggested we both keep watch. He thought that two pairs of eyes would have a better chance of spotting foes than just one."

"He is usually right about such things," said Third.

Kyralion smiled a little. "Then we can stride boldly into the jungle together, just as Magatai said."

"It is home for you, I think," said Third.

"I wonder," said Kyralion. "Magatai makes what I have done sound bolder than it really was."

"Does he?" said Third. "He did not speak falsehood. You did the things that he described." She hesitated. "And you seem bolder than your fellows who are part of the Unity."

"It is easy to be bold and act against the consensus of the Unity when you do not have the Unity inside of your head," said Kyralion. "I think..."

He fell silent and shook his head.

"What is it?" said Third.

Kyralion took a deep breath and took her hand.

A shock went through Third's nerves, but it was a pleasant shock. His hand felt hard and strong against hers, the fingers layered with calluses from bow and sword. She felt a sudden fluttering feeling in her stomach. Third had heard people describe butterflies in their stomach, but she had never experienced it before.

"Kyralion," said Third.

"If I was really a bold man," said Kyralion, "I would have done this long ago."

He leaned over and kissed her gently on the lips. She made no effort to stop him, and she found herself kissing him back a few heartbeats later, her free arm coiling around his back. At last Kyralion stepped back, and Third gazed at him, her heart racing.

"We," she said, trying to force moisture back into her throat. "We should keep walking."

"Yes," said Kyralion. He took a deep breath. "It would not be wise to become separated from the others here."

They walked in silence for a few moments.

"I...do not think it would work," said Third. "We are too different."

"I know," said Kyralion. "But we might die in the next few days. If I do die, I will die with one less regret." He blinked and then smiled. "And Magatai was right."

"About what?"

"It is indeed better to be bold."

The laugh burst from Third's throat before she could stop it.

For the rest of the day, she felt herself smiling from time to time for no reason.

8

CATHAIR CAEDYN

Two days after leaving the steppes, the jungles thinned, and Calliande saw the strange aura with the Sight.

She had traveled through many different forests over the years, but Calliande had never seen a forest quite like the Illicaeryn Jungle. The trees were huge, rising as tall as the great redwoods in the forest north of Aenesium, their branches spreading over the sky like the vaulted ceiling of a mighty cathedral. The thick canopy blocked the sun, and the floor of the jungle was always dim, the path surrounded by thick bushes and vines and brilliant flowers. The humidity never wavered, but at least they were out of the sun.

For two days they pushed south, the ground flat save for the tangles of the massive roots, and at last the earth began to slope upward. The trees grew thinner and smaller, and shafts of golden sunlight stabbed through the canopy, stark against the green background.

And Calliande saw the strange aura.

"Calliande?" said Ridmark.

She blinked at him and then realized that she had come to a stop in surprise.

"The aura," she said. "There's a magical aura ahead. It's huge and powerful, and I've never seen anything like it."

"A warding spell?" said Ridmark.

"No," said Calliande, trying to focus the Sight to make sense of it. "It's...I don't know, Ridmark. It's powerful, but it's not a ward. It's alien, but it's not dark magic. It's..."

She trailed off as the foliage rustled and Third and Kyralion came into sight along the trail. Third was staring to the south with a hard expression, her hands flexing as if she wanted to grasp the hilts of her swords.

"What is it?" said Ridmark.

"I can hear it," said Third.

"The aura," said Calliande, understanding. "You can hear the aura." Both Mara and Third had told Calliande that their minds interpreted the auras of powerful dark elven lords as songs, as beautiful, terrible, compelling songs.

"Yes," said Third.

"There's a dark elven lord ahead?" said Ridmark. He drew Oathshield a few inches from its scabbard and glanced at it, but no white fire danced around the blade.

"It is not the aura of a dark elven lord," said Third. She looked almost haunted. "I...do not know what it is. I have never encountered anything like it before."

"Does it have something to do with the Unity?" said Calliande to Kyralion.

The gray elf shrugged. "I do not know, Lady Calliande. I have never been part of the Unity and do not understand how it works. Yet we are nearly to the final refuge of my people. Perhaps you sense part of our magical defenses."

"In a way, Lady Calliande," said Arliach's voice.

She turned her head and saw Arliach and Nilarion approaching. The journey had worn hard upon the gray elves, their pale faces slick with sweat, their strange eyes bright and feverish. Yet they pressed ever onward without complaint.

"The aura," said Calliande. "It has something to do with the

Unity, doesn't it?" Already the Sight showed the web of connections between the gray elves shifting, strands moving to join the aura radiating from the south.

"It does," said Arliach. "What does the Sight show you, Keeper?"

Calliande considered the aura. The Sight interpreted it as a strange emerald-colored light. Yet there were sickly-looking yellow threads in the light, threads that wrapped into the taint she saw in the web of the Unity.

"Sick," she said at last. "The aura looks like it is sick and dying."

"Yes," said Third. "The song...it sounds like the final song of a dying man."

"That is because the Unity is dying, and the Liberated with it," said Arliach. "You are about to see the truth of us, Lady Calliande."

"Things that no human has ever seen, save for Kothlaric Pendragon when he came here to ask our aid against the Sovereign," said Nilarion. "Perhaps it would have been better if we had refused him."

"Or perhaps it would be worse," said Arliach. He took a deep breath and wiped the sweat from his eyes. "There are things that the Liberated are forbidden to speak of to outsiders, my lady, but you are about to see some of those things with your own eyes. We are approaching Cathair Caedyn, the final city of the Liberated."

"A city?" said Calliande. "I thought you lived in the Illicaeryn Jungle as nomads."

Nilarion smiled. "That is the impression we wished to give."

"Cathair Caedyn is our stronghold and our refuge," said Arliach, "and it is home to the heart of the Unity...the Sylmarus itself."

"What is the Sylmarus?" said Calliande.

"It is easier to show you," said Arliach. "Come."

THE JUNGLE GREW THINNER, the trees shorter and farther apart.

Then, at last, they came out of the jungle, and Ridmark looked upon the walls of Cathair Caedyn.

The jungle opened into a wide clearing, perhaps five or six miles across. A low hill took up the central half of that clearing, and the city rested atop the hill, surrounded by its tall wall of gleaming white stone. It looked like a smaller version of Cathair Avamyr, with the same style of towers and domes and houses, and Ridmark saw the similarity to the gray elven fortresses in the Pass of Ruins. Yet Cathair Caedyn was not yet ruined. It looked large enough to house twenty or thirty thousand gray elves, though Ridmark wondered how many actually lived in the city.

It was a beautiful place, and the solemn grandeur he had seen in gray elven ruins was reflected in the strong lines of the walls and towers. Yet that was not the most remarkable thing about the city.

The huge tree that rose from the heart of Cathair Caedyn drew the eye.

It was the single largest tree that Ridmark had ever seen. It had to stand at least a half a mile tall, higher than even the Tower of the Moon in Tarlion, and the base of the trunk was three hundred feet across. The branches soared overhead and covered the central third of city with their canopy. Veins of brilliant green light spread beneath the trunk, and the strange tree gave off a sense of power and strength and vitality.

Or, at least, it would have.

Because the great tree was obviously dying.

Half the branches had lost their leaves, and many of the remaining branches looked diseased, large patches of bark missing from the limbs. Scattered across the trunk and branches, Ridmark saw huge black growths that looked almost tumorous. It reminded him of the plague magic that Qazaldhar had unleashed in Trojas.

Behind Ridmark, the others came out of the trees and stared at the city. Tamlin, Tamara, Krastikon, and Magatai gazed at the city and the tree with obvious wonder on their expressions. Even Northwind somehow seemed impressed. Calem's expression was a blank mask, as always, and Kalussa held the Staff of Blades before her like a shield. Kyralion's face was hard, and Third's calm, but Ridmark knew her well enough to see the tension.

"Cathair Caedyn," said Arliach. "The last living city of the Liberated in this world."

Calliande nodded, her eyes on the enormous tree. "And that tree, I assume, is the Sylmarus?"

"Yes," said Arliach. "It is the heart of the Unity."

"It's alive," murmured Calliande, her eyes going hazy as she drew on the Sight.

Ridmark frowned. "Aren't trees usually alive?"

Though given the black growths and the dead branches, Ridmark wondered how long the Sylmarus would stay that way.

"Yes," said Calliande. "But not like this. That tree, Ridmark...it's awake. It's a thinking being. And old, so old. Maybe as old as this world." She shivered. "Maybe even older than the high elves." She shook her head, blinked her eyes back into focus, and looked at Arliach. "How is the Sylmarus the heart of the Unity, Lord Arliach? It has powerful magic, magic beyond anything that a human or a gray elf could wield."

"That is a question for the High Augur, my lady," said Arliach. He and Nilarion looked at the white walls of Cathair Caedyn, as did all the other gray elves in perfect unison.

"It is safe to assume that the High Augur knows we are here," said Ridmark.

Arliach blinked a few times and then nodded. "Yes. The High Augur requests our presence at once in the Court of the Sylmarus." He turned to Kyralion. "She wishes to speak with you immediately."

"I can imagine," said Kyralion. From time to time, Ridmark had seen a hint of bitterness on Kyralion's face, and that bitterness returned now. Kyralion had said that he was outcast from the Unity, and he was clearly not part of the harmony the other gray elves shared. Yet the gray elven warriors admired him, even seemed to hold him in awe at times. Perhaps Kyralion wasn't as outcast from the gray elves as he thought.

Or maybe this High Augur and the other Augurs did not care for Kyralion, and something of their dislike spread into the consensus of the Unity. Ridmark did not like that thought. He had assumed the

Unity joined all the gray elves equally together, but what if the Augurs had more power within that silent communion than the other gray elves? That kind of power could easily be abused.

"Then let's not keep the High Augur waiting," said Ridmark.

The gray elves fell in around them as they traversed the field towards the city and its hill.

"Lord Arliach," said Calliande, "what exactly are the duties of the Augurs?"

It seemed that some of Ridmark's suspicions had crossed his wife's mind as well.

"The Augurs are the leaders and guides of the Liberated," said Arliach. "We have had many different forms of government since the Liberated came to Owyllain – monarchs, republics, and elected councils of lords and wizards. The Unity makes such governments unnecessary. The Augurs are the closest to the Sylmarus, and they can use some of its power to glimpse the future."

"Such as the vision of the woman in flames," said Calliande. "The vision that sent Kyralion to find us."

"Yes," said Arliach. He hesitated a little. "There was some dissension among the Augurs over the vision, which was unusual. Most of the time they are in accord about the proper course of action, but..." Nilarion and several of the other gray elves looked at him. "But I should not speak of this now. The High Augur will speak of it with you if she wishes."

Magatai and Krastikon began questioning Arliach about the city's defenses, and the gray elven wizard proved less reticent on that topic. The outer wall stood thirty feet high and fifteen feet thick, with northern and southern gates. The watch towers held siege engines, both ballistae and catapults, along with crews of gray elves trained to use the weapons. Twenty-five thousand gray elves lived within the city's walls, with five thousand capable of wielding weapons and spells in defense of their people. Nearly all the gray elves had some magical ability, but only a few dedicated themselves to the study and mastery of magic as Arliach did.

Based on the city's size and the solemn looks the gray elves shared, Ridmark suspected that Cathair Caedyn had possessed a far larger population and more fighting men not all that long ago. Both Qazaldhar's plague curse and the muridach attacks had taken a bitter toll on the gray elves.

A short time later they climbed the slope to the gate. The doors of gleaming golden metal had swung open at their approach, and gray elven warriors watched from the ramparts overhead, armored in golden metal. Ridmark and the others walked through the gate and into a large square. It was a beautiful space, with three and four-story houses of white stone overlooking the square. A tree rose from a garden in the center of the square, covered in flowering blooms.

A small crowd had gathered to watch the patrol return and, no doubt, to get a look at the newcomers. The gray elven women wore sleeveless robes of blue and gold and green, their features sharp and alien. The children wore blue tunics and leather sandals, their faces solemn as they gazed at the humans.

On both the women and the children Ridmark saw the black veins of Qazaldhar's plague curse.

This was a city under siege. The gray elves were an alien kindred, but Ridmark recognized the signs. He saw the strain and fear in the faces of the women and children, fear that didn't come from just the plague curse. Every gray elven man Ridmark saw carried weapons and wore armor, and stacked against the walls were bundles of spears and quivers of arrows.

Cathair Avamyr had been a ruin, grim and solemn and tragic.

Cathair Caedyn had the air of a city waiting for its inevitable destruction.

"They are all staring," murmured Tamara.

"That is because they are impressed by Magatai's magnificence," said Magatai.

"They're not staring at us," said Tamlin. "They're staring at Third."

He was right. The gray elves, every single one of them, men, women, and children alike, stared at Third. She shifted a little, her face calm, but Ridmark saw her tense the way she did in the final moment before a battle.

"If the Unity links the gray elves," said Calliande, "and the Augurs truly saw her in their vision, they might recognize her on sight."

"We should continue," said Arliach. "Nilarion and I will escort you to the Court of the Sylmarus. Our soldiers and scouts will get some rest and return to their families."

"Yes, of course," said Ridmark. "Please, lead the way."

The rest of the gray elven soldiers broke off, some of them walking to join the women and the children. Ridmark supposed at least some of the women and children would be reunited with their husbands and fathers and brothers. Arliach and Nilarion led the way across the square. A street opened on the other end, leading in a straight line towards the massive trunk of the Sylmarus in the center of the city.

"You are the one."

Ridmark slowed as a gray elven woman approached them. She looked old, her hair turned to white, her sharp, alien features marked with faint lines. Age did not seem to lie as heavily upon the gray elves as it did upon humans, yet Ridmark had no doubt that this woman had seen centuries, perhaps even near the full millennia of life that came to the gray elves. She might have been older than Andomhaim itself.

The old woman stopped before Third.

"You are the one," said the old woman.

"I am sorry?" said Third.

"You are the one from the vision of the Augurs," said the old woman. "The one who will save us or destroy us."

Third opened her mouth, closed it, and found her voice. "I do not understand how. I do not desire to destroy anyone, but nor can I see how I can save you. Until an hour ago, I did not even know that this city existed."

"Have mercy upon us," said the old woman. "We do not deserve it, for we sought to become more than we are. But, please, remember us."

With that, she bowed and stepped back. Third stared at her for a moment, then shook her head and joined Ridmark.

"What do they expect of me?" whispered Third, her voice half-annoyed, half-bewildered. "What do they want of me? Calliande is the one who can heal people, not me."

"I don't know," said Ridmark. "Perhaps the High Augur will tell us more."

They left the square and entered the street. Ridmark suspected the Court of the Sylmarus would be a square at the foot of the mighty tree. As they drew closer, more details of the huge tree became apparent. It was a beautiful tree, tall and strong, and the light of the green veins shining beneath the bark seemed somehow calming, soothing. Yet the signs of blight grew more apparent with every step, the strange tumorous growths clinging to the trunk marring the beauty of the great tree. Had a forester of Andomhaim seen a tree with a blight that extensive, he would have recommended that his lord cut down the tree and use it for firewood.

"It is grievous, isn't it?" said Calliande in a quiet voice.

"Hmm?" said Ridmark, shaken out of his thoughts.

"Do you remember when we traveled through the redwood forest south of Castra Chaeldon for the first time?" said Calliande. Ridmark nodded. "I wondered why the road wound its way around the trees."

Ridmark shrugged. "Cutting down those trees would have been more work than just digging the road around them."

"Aye," said Calliande. "And it would have seemed...obscene, would it not? To kill something so old and beautiful and strong just for a road? I don't know what the Sylmarus is, Ridmark, but I think it is old. Maybe older than anything else in the world. And Qazaldhar blighted and poisoned it to strike at his enemies."

"Another crime to lay at his door," said Ridmark. "It..."

"Kyralion!"

It was a woman's voice, strong and musical, and it was filled with joy.

Ridmark turned his head as a gray elven woman emerged from one of the houses and ran towards them. She had thick golden hair and eyes the wrong shade of blue to be human. Like all the other gray elves, she had a sharp, alien face, with pointed upswept ears. She was wearing the golden armor of the gray elves, and Ridmark supposed she must have been a wizard with enough magical skill to be dangerous in battle.

She ran across the street and caught Kyralion in a tight embrace.

A brief look of resignation flickered over Third's face.

"I was so frightened," said the woman, stepping back as Kyralion eased out of her grasp. Ridmark could not quite read his expression, but he thought Kyralion looked regretful, perhaps even sad. "Mother said you would never return, but I knew better. I knew you would come back. And you found them, didn't you?" She beamed at him. "You found the Shield Knight and the Keeper and the woman in flames, didn't you? I knew you would."

"Yes," said Kyralion, gesturing. "This is Ridmark Arban the Shield Knight, and Calliande Arban the Keeper of Andomhaim." One by one he introduced the others. "And this is the woman in flames, Lady Third of Nightmane Forest."

The gray elven woman and Third looked at each other.

Then the gray elven woman smiled, though she looked a little frightened.

"My name...my name is Rilmeira," said the woman. "Thank you for helping Kyralion to come home. I...I was very frightened that he would not return."

It was difficult to gauge the age of gray elves, but Ridmark thought that Rilmeira was young, at least by the standards of the Liberated.

"He has been a great help to us," said Third. "I doubt we would have survived this long without his aid."

"I am glad, Lady Third," said Rilmeira. "I would have gone with him when the Augurs sent him to find you, but they forbade it..."

"Your mother also forbade you from speaking with me," said Kyralion. He took a deep breath. "It was for the best, Rilmeira. We both know it."

"I know," said Rilmeira. "I know." The sadness was obvious for a moment, and then she pulled herself together. "But a wizard of the Liberated may greet one of the scouts when he returns. And especially when the scout brings such illustrious guests."

Arliach and Nilarion looked at her, and Rilmeira scowled at them. Ridmark found it annoying to be surrounded by conversations he could not hear. No wonder Kyralion seemed so aloof at times. Though it was fascinating to watch the play of expressions on the faces of the three gray elves. They could communicate without speech, but their expressions reflected their emotions nonetheless.

"Is the High Augur your mother, Lady Rilmeira?" said Calliande.

Ridmark blinked in surprise, and the three gray elves broke off from their silent argument and looked at her.

"She is, my lady," said Rilmeira. "How did you know?"

"An intuition, let's say," said Calliande.

"And if your mother is the High Augur," said Ridmark, "perhaps we should not keep her waiting."

Arliach and Nilarion looked at Rilmeira again.

"I am accompanying them to the meeting," said Rilmeira, though she looked at Kyralion as she spoke. "It is my right."

"Perhaps we should not keep the Augurs waiting," said Ridmark.

Arliach took a deep breath. "Yes. Yes, you are right. This way, please."

9

UNITY

Calliande considered Kyralion, Rilmeira, Arliach, and Nilarion as they walked south, the white houses of Cathair Caedyn rising around them and the Sylvanus towering above like a living mountain.

She had been involved in many negotiations with numerous lords and knights and kings, and Calliande thought she saw the situation here. Rilmeira was in love with Kyralion. Even with the alien nature of the gray elves, Calliande had seen the adoration on Rilmeira's face, and a flicker of the same emotion on Kyralion's stoic features. Except the High Augur had forbidden her daughter from spending any time with Kyralion, and the High Augur had also apparently lied about the contents of her vision to Kyralion. Calliande wondered how close Kyralion and Rilmeira had been. Perhaps he had courted her, or whatever the equivalent custom was among the gray elves.

Had the High Augur sent Kyralion to pursue the vision of the woman in flames simply to get him away from Rilmeira? It seemed like a petty thing to do.

Calliande looked at Third, but her face gave away nothing.

A short time later they came to the Court of the Sylmarus.

It was a huge round plaza in the heart of the city, the ground unpaved and covered in grass. The massive bulk of the Sylmarus's trunk rose from the earth, as thick and as tall as the great towers of the Citadel itself in Tarlion. The green light shone over everything in a gentle glow, making the tumorous black growths all the more hideous by contrast.

At the edge of the roots stood six gray elves, one man and five women. The man looked older and wore elaborate golden armor, a sword at his belt, a winged helm tucked under his arm. His dark eyes roved over them, and he smiled when he saw Kyralion.

The five women did not smile.

All of them were in the gray elves' equivalent to late middle age, and all five of the women wore sleeveless blue robes, golden torques of rank wrapped around their left arms. Calliande's Sight flared to life, and she saw the intricate web of the Unity around the five women. Each of the gray elven women would be a powerful wizard.

The woman in the center wore a more elaborate robe than the others, and a golden chain of office hung around her neck. In her right hand, she carried a staff that looked like Tamara's, but far more ornate and topped with a round, jeweled headpiece. Her face was gaunt, even by the standards of the gray elves, and she had thick golden hair bound beneath a diadem and brilliant blue eyes. She looked like an older, harsher version of Rilmeira.

This, most likely, was the High Augur.

Her intense eyes met Calliande's, and the gray elven woman's lips thinned a little. Calliande had the overwhelming impression that the High Augur did not like her. No, that was too specific. Calliande suspected the High Augur did not like the presence of humans within Cathair Caedyn, and that she was unhappy about the return of Kyralion. Even as the thought crossed Calliande's mind, the High Augur glared at Rilmeira, who turned a defiant look toward her mother. Three of the other Augurs looked anxious. The fourth, an older woman with brilliant white hair, merely looked exasperated.

The gray elven man in golden armor approached, and Arliach and Nilarion offered him a bow.

"Lord Arliach," said the older man. His voice was hard and raspy. "You have news, I see."

"Aye, lord," said Arliach. "Lord Marshal Rhomathar, Kyralion has returned and fulfilled his charge from the Augurs. The Shield Knight and the Keeper are here, as is the woman of flames from the vision of the Sylmarus."

"I see," said Rhomathar. "Lord Kyralion?"

"Lord Marshal," said Kyralion, "I have the honor to present Ridmark Arban, the Shield Knight of Andomhaim. His wife Calliande Arban, the Keeper of Andomhaim. Sir Tamlin Thunderbolt, the bearer of the Sword of Earth. Lady Kalussa Pendragon, the bearer of the Sovereign's Staff of Blades." Some of the Augurs looked surprised at that, though the High Augur's gaze remained flinty. "Sir Calem, the bearer of the Sword of Air. Prince Consort Krastikon Cyros, the bearer of the Sword of Death. Magatai of the Takai halflings." Magatai offered a florid bow from Northwind's saddle. "Tamara Earthcaller of Kalimnos." Kyralion took a deep breath. "And Lady Third of Nightmane Forest, the woman from the vision. She is the woman of flames."

Neither the Augurs nor Rhomathar spoke.

"It has been my honor," said Kyralion, "to have been their companion in many adventures. They defeated Justin Cyros and took the Sword of Earth, and they also slew the Necromancer and stopped him from unleashing a plague of undead across the world."

The High Augur's lip twisted. "Human problems, created by humans." Her voice was musical and clear and cold as winter.

Again, the white-haired Augur rolled her eyes. The other three Augurs gaped at her in surprise.

"You have a thought, Seruna?" said the High Augur. "Please, by all means, share it with our guests."

"Only this," said Seruna. "The Sovereign created the Seven Swords, at least to the best of our knowledge. The Seven Swords will be instruments of the rise of the Kratomachar. The Sovereign was our problem long before the humans came to this world. Rather than bringing human problems to our doorstep, I rather think the humans have brought our problems home to us."

The two women stared at each other. Calliande had the impression they did not like each other very much.

"Well," said the High Augur, turning away from Seruna and the other Augurs, "let it not be said that the Liberated lack in courtesy. I am Athadira, and it is my honor to serve as the High Augur of the Unity of the Liberated. Seruna, it seems, has already introduced herself, as has our Lord Marshal." One by one she introduced the other three Augurs, who bobbed in quick, polite bows.

"Lady Third is the woman from the vision," said Kyralion. "I am certain of it. And Lord Ridmark is the Shield Knight and Lady Calliande is the Keeper."

"So I see," said Athadira, taking a step forward. "Yes. The Shield Knight bears a weapon of high elven power. A potent one. The Keeper is linked to one of the Wells, and...yes, she bears a mantle of alien magic, one inimical to this world. Likely it was fashioned upon the world humans originated from, this Old Earth."

"That is correct," said Calliande. "You possess the Sight, my lady?"

The High Augur's smile was condescending. "Of course I possess the Sight, Keeper. How else can the Augurs interpret the visions of the Sylmarus, the glimpses the Sylmarus gives us of the future?" She waved a hand at the city. "We are the heirs of fifteen thousand years of the tradition of the Liberated, and before that, one hundred thousand years of high elven history. You stand in an ancient civilization, Keeper of Andomhaim, one a thousand times older than your Andomhaim."

"Of course," said Calliande. Her initial reaction was amusement. She had been to Cathair Solas, the last city of the high elves, had seen the city soaring through the air at the command of its residents. She had spoken with Ardrhythain, the last archmage of the high elves, and had seen him unleash powers that could scatter armies and shatter mountains. Compared to that kind of power, that bombast of Athadira's boasts seemed comical.

But mockery and contempt rarely proved useful.

"Could you tell me more of the Unity, High Augur?" said Calliande. "I have rarely seen such a potent feat of magic."

"The Unity was the salvation of the Liberated," said Athadira. "If you have traveled through Owyllain, you have heard the history of it. No doubt Kyralion managed to relate some of that history to you in his clumsy and inept way." Third's eyes narrowed for just a moment, and Seruna rolled her eyes again. "But you will hear now the true history of the Liberated, Keeper of Andomhaim, the history of the kindred that your kind so ignorantly name the gray elves. And then you will understand that the elves of the Unity need no assistance."

"Of course, High Augur," said Calliande. "I am most interested in learning that history."

"You know we came to this land to escape from the urdmordar," said Athadira. "Once we cast off the restrictions of the threefold law of the high elves, we were free to grow in ways that the high elves could not. When we arrived in this land, we located the Well of Storms and built Cathair Animus to tap and control its magical power. Using that magic, we built mighty cities and raised tall towers, and built a civilization to exceed that which the high elves raised before the coming of the shadow of Incariel..."

"Pardon, High Augur," said Calliande, "but did not the archmage Ardrhythain of the high elves appoint Rhodruthain the Guardian of Cathair Animus?"

Athadira let out an irritated breath. "He did. More accurately, he named Rhodruthain the Guardian of the Well of Storms. The archmage Ardrhythain was too timid to cast aside the constraints of the threefold law, but he still wished to exert control over the Liberated, even as we left to create a new realm. Rhodruthain's task was to make sure that the power of the Well of Storms within Cathair Animus was never misused." She gave an annoyed shake of her head. "Rhodruthain was a fool. He still is a fool. If we had used the power of the Well as a weapon, we could have annihilated the Sovereign. Rhodruthain is the one who brought you here, is he not?"

"He is," said Calliande.

Athadira snorted. "He is mad. He brought you here as part of some scheme or another to defend the Well. Ridiculous. No mere humans can stand before the power of the Kratomachar. The elves of the Unity shall save the world, or it cannot be saved. It was a waste for Rhodruthain to bring you here."

"Before you can save the world," said Ridmark, "I suppose you will have to save yourselves."

Athadira smiled at him, like a teacher smiling at a slow pupil. "I do not expect you to understand. Humans are incapable of taking the view of the centuries as the Liberated can."

"You were telling me of the founding of the Unity?" said Calliande.

"Our civilization prospered and flourished," said the High Augur, turning her gaze back to Calliande, "but the Sovereign followed us, for he was jealous of our power. Our warriors were valiant, and our wizards powerful, but the Sovereign used treachery and trickery to overcome us. Finally, we lost control of Cathair Animus, and Rhodruthain refused to allow us to use the Well of Storms, the treacherous craven. At last, we were driven to the Illicaeryn Jungle, and here we found the Sylmarus." She gazed at the huge tree.

"What is the Sylmarus?" said Calliande. "I suspect it is rather more than a large tree."

"Obviously it is more than a large tree," said Athadira with asperity, "much, much more. It is an ancient and powerful being, the last of a kindred older than both the high elves and the dragons themselves. Once there were thousands of such trees, but now the Sylmarus is all that remains. When the surviving Liberated gathered in the Illicaeryn Jungle, we petitioned the Sylmarus for aid, and in its wisdom and mercy, it granted our petition. With the magic of the Sylmarus, we created the Unity, and raised the Liberated to new heights of strength and wisdom."

"What precisely is the Unity?" said Calliande.

Athadira's smile turned condescending once more. "Beyond human comprehension, I fear. It is the highest achievement of the Liberated, and the greatest feat of magic wrought in the history of this world."

"On the surface," said Calliande, "I would say that it is a shared mind, a link. I can see the web of power joining the gray elves to each other." Athadira's smile faded. "It must let you communicate without the need for speech or for even words. I saw Lord Arliach and his men fight. They moved in perfect speed and harmony. Little wonder you have held the Illicaeryn Jungle against all foes for so long."

"The harmony of the Unity makes our warriors into an unbeatable fighting force," said Athadira.

"It does," said Calliande, "but the Unity is also killing you."

Athadira smiled again. "I fear it is beyond your comprehension."

"It enforces a consensus," said Calliande. "It's hard for any gray elves to disagree from a course of action. You forbade your daughter from greeting us, and I saw how hard it was for her to challenge that." Rilmeira shifted.

"The Unity gives us harmony, order, and purpose," said Athadira, "something that humans plainly lack."

"Plainly," said Calliande. "The Unity also let the Maledictus of Death lay a plague curse upon you."

This time Athadira had no ready answer.

"The Sight shows me the aura of the Sylmarus, how it is the core of the Unity," said Calliande. "When Qazaldhar placed his plague curse upon the tree, that immediately meant the curse spread to every single gray elf connected to the Unity. It's been killing you ever since."

"It is a minor setback," said Athadira. "A cure shall be found. The Sylmarus itself..."

"A minor setback?" said Rhomathar. "Half our kindred have died of the plague curse since Qazaldhar leveled it upon us."

Athadira glared at him. "The Liberated have recovered from greater losses than that during our history. And it is ill-judged to show dissension in front of outsiders, Lord Marshal."

"Dissension is one matter," said Seruna, her exasperation plain, "but facing reality is another, High Augur."

"And what version of reality is that, Augur?" said Athadira.

"Unless something is done," said Seruna, "the Sylmarus will die, Cathair Caedyn will fall, and the Liberated will be utterly destroyed."

"That is poisonous talk," said Athadira, "and against the consensus of the Unity."

"The consensus, or your hopes?" said Seruna. "Because the reality is that the plague curse weakens us with every passing day. Even without the plague curse, we would have a hard time holding the city against Nerzamdrathus and his horde. With the plague curse, our defeat is all but guaranteed."

"Poisonous talk!" said Athadira, but Seruna kept speaking.

"We asked the Sylmarus for help," said Seruna, "and the Sylmarus gave us a vision of the woman in flames. It also showed us a vision of her and Lord Kyralion either saving or destroying the Liberated..."

Athadira's eyes all but flashed with anger. "The Augurs agreed to keep the entirety of the vision to ourselves, Seruna! You debase your office by speaking."

Seruna seemed indifferent to the High Augur's scorn. "And now Lord Kyralion has brought the woman in flames to us, along with the Shield Knight and the Keeper. Rather against your expectations, I might add. We face disaster on every front, High Augur. I think it is time we consider every option available to us, no matter how much you might dislike the prospect."

Athadira glared at Seruna, but the other Augur remained unmoved. For that matter, to judge from their expressions, the remaining three Augurs agreed with Seruna. Calliande wondered that she could read their expressions so easily, almost like reading the words written upon the pages of a book. Perhaps with the Unity constantly sharing their thoughts and emotions, the gray elves never bothered to guard their expressions.

Kyralion must have been in intractable riddle to them.

"Perhaps it is time for plain speaking, then," said Ridmark.

Athadira smirked at him. "Those of us in the Unity have no need of plain speaking, Shield Knight. The entire community of the gray elves knows itself, and consensus is reached at once."

"A notable achievement," said Ridmark. "Yet somehow, despite this lack of deception, we have heard differing versions of the vision that sent Kyralion to us. Kyralion said you bid him to find the woman in flames and the Shield Knight and the Keeper. Yet when against all odds he returns to you with the woman of the vision and the Shield Knight and the Keeper, you seem displeased. For that matter, when we spoke with Lord Amruthyr in the ruins of Cathair Selenias, he said that you told Kyralion an incomplete version of the vision, just as Augur Seruna just said."

"Impossible," said Athadira. "Lord Amruthyr died millennia ago, defending Cathair Selenias to the last against the hordes of the Sovereign."

"He did defend Cathair Selenias to the last against the Sovereign's armies," said Kyralion, "but he did not die. The Sovereign and the Maledicti twisted Lord Amruthyr's final spell, and trapped him within it, using his life to sustain the ward. When we came to Kalimnos, the Maledictus of Shadows and the Maledictus of Air warped the spell to use it as a weapon again us, and we had no choice but to enter the ruins and release Lord Amruthyr from his torment. Before he died, Lord Amruthyr bade Tamara to take his staff, and one of his knights gave me his sword and armor."

Athadira sniffed. "At least that explains how you and your companions came to be clothed in the steel of the gray elves. I should not be surprised that you would stoop to looting the graves of our kindred. But, then, you were never really one of us."

Again, Calliande saw Third's eyes narrow.

"Once again, High Augur, we stray from the point," said Seruna.

"You are right, honored Augur," said Ridmark. "Why did you not tell Kyralion the entire vision?"

"The role of the Augurs is to guide the Unity," said Athadira. "We help the Unity to achieve consensus and balance. We also must view the visions the Sylmarus grants us. For the Sylmarus possesses mighty magic, so powerful that it does not perceive linear time in the same way that we do. Often it has glimpses of the future, glimpses that we describe as visions. The Augurs must interpret these visions, for many of them do not make sense to mortal minds, even the minds of the Liberated."

"Alas, I am not one of the Liberated so this might be beyond my reach," said Ridmark. Calliande recognized the dangerous glint in his eyes. "The Sylmarus sent you a vision of the Shield Knight and the Keeper, and of Third and Kyralion standing together in a moment that would save or destroy the gray elves. Yet you only told Kyralion and the rest of the Unity of the woman of flames, not of his place in the vision. Perhaps you could explain this mystery to me."

Athadira drew herself up, gazing at Ridmark with hauteur. "It is the role of the Augurs to explain the Sylmarus's visions to the rest of the Unity. That was all we chose to share. Our decisions are not to be gainsaid by the rest of the Unity, or by outsiders."

"Because the vision was dangerous, or because you did not like its contents?" said Ridmark.

Seruna let out a short laugh. "I like him."

"Enough," said Athadira. "Whatever we might think of the vision, the Shield Knight and the Keeper and the woman in flames are here. Lady Third, step forward. I would speak with you."

Third did not move. Her face was cold.

"I can hear you perfectly well from right here," said Third.

Athadira let out an exasperated sigh. "Very well."

She strode forward a few paces, her staff tapping against the ground, and stared hard at Third. Third stared right back without blinking.

"You are a dark elf," said Athadira.

"Half," said Third.

"Why have you not transformed into an urdhracos yet?" said Athadira. "Whenever the dark elves lay with other kindred, the resultant hybrids inevitably succumbed to their dark elven blood, and were twisted into monsters."

"I was an urdhracos for nearly a thousand years," said Third. "Later I was freed of my dark elven blood and became what I am now."

"Impossible," said Athadira.

"Perhaps it was," said Calliande, "but it nonetheless happened."

Athadira shook her head and stepped back. "Perhaps it did, Lady Third, but you are nonetheless an abomination."

Third said nothing, but Ridmark tensed.

"You never should have existed," said Athadira.

"An anomaly?" murmured Third, frowning as if she tried to remember something.

"An elven man should never lie with a woman of lesser kindred," said Athadira, "and the dark elves were monstrous enough. You never should have been born. You should have been killed before you could become an urdhracos. Perhaps you have freed yourself as you claim, but..." Third remained indifferent, which only seemed to anger Athadira. "You should never have..."

"That is enough," said Ridmark, his voice cold. "Perhaps you did exceed the high elves in skill and power as you claimed, but you clearly fail to live up to them in courtesy. Even if you knew nothing of her, Third still helped Lord Arliach's patrol escape from the trap of Cathair Avamyr. If you have treated all those who helped you with such scorn, little wonder the gray elves are in such desperate straits..."

"Do not presume, Shield Knight, to speak of matters of which you know..." started Athadira.

"He is right."

Kyralion stalked forward to stand next to Third. His expression was usually impassive, but there was no mistaking the anger on his face now. Rilmeira looked at him, a strange mixture of longing and hurt on her features.

"Third is a valiant and brave woman," said Kyralion. "She crossed half the world to find her friends again. She fought King Justin and the Necromancer, the bearers of the Swords of Earth and Death, without flinching. She walked without hesitation into the trap of Cathair Selenias, and without her, we all would have died. For you to speak to her so brings shame upon the Liberated."

Athadira said nothing for a moment, her fingers tight against her golden staff. Her chest rose and fell with her breath, and the other Augurs, save for Seruna, shied away from her.

She hated Kyralion, Calliande realized, hated him with vicious intensity.

Had Kyralion done something to her? No, perhaps it was simpler than that. Kyralion was not part of the Unity, which meant Athadira could not read his mind and emotions, could not influence his will towards the consensus of the Unity. His very existence was a challenge to Athadira's authority as High Augur.

And that was an insult that a woman like Athadira would never forgive.

"Do not ever lecture me," said Athadira. "Third might be an abomination, but one cannot expect anything better from a creature of the dark elves. But you are a freak."

Kyralion said nothing, but he did not look away.

"All the other Liberated are joined in harmony within the Unity," said Athadira. "Not you, though. The greatest creation of our ancestors and you are unfit to become part of it. You should have never been born."

"Mother!" said Rilmeira, her dismay plain, but the High Augur kept talking.

"It is well that your mother and father died in battle when they did," said Athadira. "How it would have dismayed them to see what you have become, a constant flaw in the perfection of the Unity, a constant dissonant note in the harmony of our consensus. It would have been better if you had never been born."

"Mother, stop, please," said Rilmeira. "This is..."

Still the High Augur kept talking. "Thousands of years of the Unity, and you are the first flaw in it."

"Other than the plague curse," said Kyralion.

"As if a freak like you could understand the cost of that curse," said Athadira. "I had hoped you would die on your quest for the woman of flames. That seemed the kindest fate for something like you, someone who presumed to ask for the hand of the daughter of the High Augur. It would have been better if you had never returned here, if you had perished on your..."

Then Calliande saw something that she had never seen before.

She had known Third for nine years, ever since they had met in the Northerland during the war with the Frostborn. Calliande had seen Third in desperate battle, had seen her sit calmly at dinner, had even seen her smile and laugh a few times.

But she had never, ever seen Third lose her temper before.

It was terrifying. She did not scream or shout, not Third. But the veins throbbed in her temples, her dark eyes widening, and twin spots of color appeared on her usually pale face.

"That is enough," grated Third.

Her voice was as cold and harsh as the winter in the Northerland, and so threatening that Athadira broke off in mid-tirade.

"Do not interrupt," started Athadira.

"Be silent," snapped Third, stepping towards her. A flicker of fear went over the High Augur's face, as if she thought Third would strike her, and she moved her staff before her like a shield. "When I spoke with Lord Amruthyr, he said I would come to hate the gray elves. I could not imagine why but I understand now. Your Unity has made you into fools. You sit and wallow in the apathy of your despair, bemoaning the fate of your grand civilization rather than trying to save it. The Sylmarus offered you a chance to save your people, and Kyralion was the only one brave enough to take that chance. He crossed a continent and back again in the hopes of saving you, and this is how you greet his return? With scorn and mockery? I see now that Lord Amruthyr was right. Now that I have met you, I do have reason to find you contemptible. If you treat all your brave warriors this way, little wonder your kindred are about to perish from the face of the earth." Her scornful glare turned towards the other Augurs and Lord Rhomathar. "And you. You permit her to run roughshod over you? You know the one chance you have to save your people, but you stand there and do nothing?"

The Augurs and the Lord Marshal said nothing.

"You dare to..." started Athadira, her voice a little hoarse.

"We have nothing left to say to each other," said Third. She looked at Ridmark. "I suggest we leave at once and continue our task. There is nothing for us here. It was only ill chance that brought us to Cathair Caedyn. If the Augurs wish to stand and mourn as their final city burns, I so no reason we should stop them."

"Yes," said Ridmark. "If we leave now, we should be able to cross the eastern side of the Illicaeryn Jungle before the muridachs arrive."

"Third," said Kyralion, his voice soft.

She looked at him, some of the harsh anger fading from her face.

Athadira struck the end of her staff against the ground. The High Augur looked like she was about to explode with rage.

Calliande never did find out what she was going to say.

As one, Athadira, Seruna, Rhomathar, Rilmeira, Arliach, and Nilarion turned and looked to the north, identical expressions of alarm going over their faces.

"What is it?" said Kyralion.

"I fear we are too late," said Rhomathar. "The sentries upon the walls have just seen the muridach scouts emerge from the jungle."

10

RAIDERS

Ridmark had already made up his mind to leave Cathair Caedyn.

Arliach and Nilarion had claimed that the Unity joined the gray elves together in equal communication, but it was quite clear that the High Augur Athadira was the true ruler of the gray elves.

And she was clearly a fool.

She was not malicious, but he suspected that she was terrified, both for her people and for her daughter. Inexorable destruction was coming for the Liberated, whether in the form of the muridachs or Qazaldhar's plague curse, and she was powerless to stop it. So, the High Augur had retreated into brittle pride, reliving the past glories of the gray elves, exalting their achievements even as ruin closed around their final remnants.

He wasn't sure why she hated Kyralion so much. Perhaps she had been offended at Rilmeira's obvious love for him. Or maybe his inability to join the Unity was an affront to her pride and position. Perhaps it was simple jealousy – Kyralion Firebow obviously had the respect of the Lord Marshal and the warriors of Cathair Caedyn in a way that the High Augur herself never would.

But it was not Ridmark's problem to solve. He would help those who wanted aid against creatures of dark magic, but he could not help those who refused assistance. For that matter, he was disgusted by how Athadira had spoken to Kyralion and Third. Kyralion had done nothing to merit such contempt, and Third was a guest.

Ridmark wondered if he could persuade Kyralion to come with them, but he doubted it. Kyralion had undertaken his mission to find Third to save his people. He would not abandon them now, not in the hour of their final extremity. He would die with them, fighting under a leader who detested him.

Kyralion deserved better, but he had made his choice.

Then all the gray elves looked to the north with alarm, and a cold feeling closed around Ridmark.

Perhaps Kyralion would not be the only one to die in Cathair Caedyn.

If the muridachs moved fast enough and encircled the city, Ridmark and the others might find themselves trapped here.

"How many muridachs?" said Ridmark.

"We do not yet know," said Rhomathar. "The sentries upon the north wall have seen them..."

"And the western, eastern, and southern walls," said Seruna, her voice hard. "Scouts upon kalocrypts. They seem to be massing below the northern wall."

"They will try to strike at once, hope to take us off our guard," said Athadira. She looked at the other Augurs. "Come. Our spells will be needed in defense of the ramparts."

The other Augurs moved to follow Athadira as she strode from the Court of the Sylmarus. Arliach and Nilarion fell in behind the Augurs, but the Lord Marshal and Rilmeira remained behind

"Mother," said Rilmeira.

"Come, Rilmeira!" snapped Athadira, stopping to glare at her daughter.

Rilmeira planted her feet and did not move. Ridmark was reminded of a petulant daughter rebelling against her mother, but there was an echo of Athadira's steel in her face. The High Augur shook her head in irritation and stalked away, the other Augurs following.

Rilmeira and Rhomathar shared a look.

"Lord Ridmark," said Rilmeira. "I...I apologize for my mother's harshness. She bears a great burden of responsibility, and..."

"She does," said Kyralion, "but she had no right to speak that way to Third."

"She had no right to speak that way to you!" said Rilmeira.

Kyralion shook his head. "She has been speaking that way to me all my life. Shouting, usually."

"Rilmeira is right," said Third, her voice controlled again. "She has no right to speak to you that way."

Rilmeira and Third looked at each other, and some silent agreement seemed to pass between them.

"Perhaps we can discuss this later," said Rhomathar. "More urgent matters press."

"Yes, you are right, uncle," said Rilmeira. "Lord Ridmark...I have no right to ask this of you and your friends, not after my mother's behavior...but will you fight alongside us? Your friends have three of the Seven Swords, even if their bearers are Swordborn. If you have overcome Justin Cyros and the Necromancer, you must be warriors of great power."

"I don't think we have any other choice," said Ridmark. "We will fight alongside you. The muridachs will make no distinction between human and gray elf if they get inside the walls."

"And I do not think we can leave," said Calliande, her eyes going hazy. "There are surges of dark magic outside the walls. I think the muridachs have numbers enough to encircle the entire city."

"Whatever you decide, I must go," said Rhomathar. "I am needed on the walls."

"Then we shall come with you," said Ridmark.

Rhomathar and Rilmeira hurried north, and Ridmark and the others followed them.

He looked around the streets as they jogged towards the gates, and he saw Cathair Caedyn rousing itself for war. It was one of the stranger sights he had seen. Ridmark had been in numerous towns and castras that had come under enemy attack, and he saw many of the sights he expected to see. Warriors in golden armor rushed towards the walls, spears and swords in hand. Archers in leather armor followed, some of them equipped with soulstone-augmented bows like Kyralion's. Women carried bundles of arrows to the walls, or prepared buckets of water to douse fires. It seemed that the women of the gray elves did not fight as soldiers, save for those who had the magical power to be dangerous in battle. Rather like Kalussa and the Order of the Arcanii.

And all of it was done in perfect silence.

It was uncanny. Even in a well-commanded siege, the shouting was constant, with decurions bawling orders to their men and knights shouting commands. Yet the gray elves did everything in silence, and they moved in perfect, fluid harmony. There was no stumbling, no groups of soldiers getting in each other's way, no confusion. The gray elves moved with the harmony of a clockwork mechanism. Ridmark had to admit that the Unity would make a stupendous advantage in battle.

Though he had seen its disadvantage in how the gray elves were unwilling to stand up to the High Augur's rage.

And in the black veins beneath the pale skin of the gray elves, and the drawn exhaustion he saw in their faces.

They returned to the northern square, and Ridmark saw the gray elven warriors ascending the ramparts to line the walls. Lord Rhomathar and Rilmeira climbed to the rampart over the gates where the five Augurs stood. Seeing no reason to go elsewhere, Ridmark followed them, Calliande and the others close behind. Magatai dismounted from Northwind, spoke a few words to the struthian, and then followed them up.

The sight from the rampart was not reassuring.

Ridmark could see all the way to the green wall of the jungle itself, and the edges of the jungle seethed and crawled with muridach warriors. There were thousands of the creatures moving through the undergrowth beneath the huge trees. Ridmark saw the regular muridach foot soldiers in their leather and bronze ring mail, berserkers in their bronze plate, and Throne Guards in crimson armor.

There were also hundreds of kalocrypts skittering back and forth before the jungle, muridach riders on their backs.

"How the hell did so many of them get here so quickly?" said Tamlin.

The High Augur shot an irritated glance in his direction and then looked away.

"In jungle that thick," said Krastikon, "we could be half a mile from ten thousand muridachs, and we would never see them."

"That could be part of it," said Kyralion. "There are also entrances to the Deeps scattered nearby. Likely the muridach vanguard marched through the tunnels to arrive sooner than we thought." Athadira scowled at him and then looked away. "It is well that we arrived when we did. Any later, and we might have been outside the walls when the muridachs emerged from the tunnels of the Deeps."

"What are they doing?" said Kalussa, her voice uneasy. "It looks like they're just pouring from the jungle like water from a bucket."

"Probably they want to surround the city first," said Tamlin. "Make sure that no one can get in or out."

"Does Cathair Caedyn have an entrance to the Deeps?" said Ridmark as a dark thought occurred to him. The ruins of Cathair Avamyr had an entrance to the Deeps, and the muridachs had found their way inside. "The enemy might try to get inside the city that way."

"It does not, Shield Knight," said Rhomathar. "In ancient days, all our strongholds had entrances to the Deeps to guard against attacks from the dvargir, the kobolds, the muridachs, and the other kindreds of the Deeps." He did not look away from the field as he spoke. "But too often the Sovereign's armies forced open the gates through cunning stratagems. Cathair Caedyn has no entrances to the Deeps, and we would detect any tunneling attempt. This city contains the distilled knowledge of fifteen thousand years of Liberated siegecraft."

"We will likely need it," said Ridmark.

"Is it necessary for the outsiders to be here?" said Athadira. "The Liberated need no aid in our defense..."

"As Lord Marshal, the defense of the city is my responsibility," said Rhomathar. It was the first time that he had interrupted the High Augur. "We are in no position to turn away help."

Athadira scowled, no doubt unleashing a silent tirade at the Lord Marshal through the link of the Unity. Yet she did not protest, and her attention returned to the gathering muridachs.

"We may not face attack for a few days yet," said Krastikon. "It will take them time to move their siege machines into position."

Another dark thought occurred to Ridmark. The kalocrypts looked like giant cockroaches, and he had seen roaches in both Tarlion and Cintarra. The damned insects seemed capable of getting into anything...and several times he had observed them climbing up vertical surfaces.

"Can kalocrypts climb up walls?" said Ridmark.

"Yes," said Rhomathar, his voice grim.

"That's what they're doing," said Ridmark. "You can see...yes, there, there, and there?" He pointed. "The kalocrypts are forming up for a charge. They'll rush across the field, climb the wall, and try to open the gate."

"There are columns of infantry forming up behind the kalocrypts," said Third. Her anger had vanished, and she was all cool control once more. "I am not certain, but I think they have siege ladders."

"They do," said Kyralion. "I can see them as well."

Third nodded. "Some of the kalocrypts will try to open the northern gate. Others will attack the defenders on the walls, and while they are distracted, the muridach footmen will bring the ladders forward."

No sooner had she spoken the last word than the kalocrypts began moving forward in a line, nearly a hundred of the creatures. Ridmark knew the muridachs would keep their mounts at a walk until they came within arrow range of the walls, and then they would charge. And as they did, a dozen columns of muridachs would come up behind them, carrying siege ladders.

"A lightning thrust, then," said Kyralion. "A swift attempt to seize the city while we are off our guard."

"They will be disappointed, then," said Rhomathar.

"Lady Calliande," said Tamara. She had been quiet so far, holding the golden staff of Lord Amruthyr with both hands. Now her mismatched eyes were narrowed as she watched the kalocrypts. "The spell we used to control the scutians?"

"And the trisalians," said Tamlin.

"Aye, what about it?" said Calliande.

"Could we use it on the kalocrypts?"

Calliande blinked and looked at Tamara. "I hadn't thought of that. Yes, we might. At least, we could disrupt the control of the muridach riders. I don't think we could take command of the kalocrypts, but if the beasts break off their charge, or go entirely motionless..."

"They would be far easier targets for our archers," said Kyralion.

"Shield Knight," said Rhomathar. "It is clear you are an experienced warrior so I will ask you and your friends to go and strike where you see fit." Ridmark nodded. "Keeper, I will ask you, Lady Kalussa, and Tamara Earthcaller to remain here with the Augurs. They are the most powerful wielders of magic among our kindred, and you can direct your magic from here."

"Very well," said Ridmark, drawing Oathshield. All five of the Augurs looked at once. Likely they felt the aura of power around the weapon. He ignored them and looked at Calliande.

Once again, they were going into battle together.

It was possible this was the last time they would ever see each other.

A deep weariness went through him at the thought, and he pushed it aside. No one could see the future beyond all doubt.

Though he feared that this would end with their deaths and Cathair Caedyn reduced to ashes.

"I'll see you soon," said Calliande with a faint smile.

Ridmark nodded, took a deep breath, and turned to the others.

"Third, Tamlin, Calem, Krastikon, Kyralion, and Magatai, come with me."

Magatai grinned and drew his sword, lightning snarling up the blade. "It is time to teach the ratmen the folly of making war upon us."

"Let us hope they pay attention to the lesson," said Ridmark, watching as the enemy drew closer to the walls.

TAMLIN STARED OVER THE BATTLEMENTS, watching the kalocrypts.

The creatures had advanced at a slow, steady pace until they were at the base of the city's hill. Then one of the muridach riders blew a long blast on a war horn, and the riders shouted and cheered, brandishing spears over their heads. An answering cheer came from the thousands of muridach infantry gathered behind them, and the kalocrypts surged forward, their legs stabbing at the grass as the bulky creatures propelled themselves at the wall with terrible speed.

The gray elves answered at once, and they responded with terrifying skill and speed. Tamlin thought the Unity a strange and unnatural thing. He certainly did not want to share his inmost thoughts with anyone, let alone an entire city. Kyralion ought to be grateful he wasn't part of the damned thing.

Yet as he watched the gray elves respond to the muridach charge, Tamlin had to admit that the Unity offered deadly advantages.

The ballistae crews moved first, aiming their weapons and releasing. The bolts hammered home into the heads of the kalocrypts, the bronze shafts plunging deep into their bodies with a spray of green slime. The crews began reloading their weapons at once.

The archers attacked next, stepping forward and releasing. A storm of arrows hurtled towards the charging kalocrypts. The archers fired with uncanny accuracy, their shafts punching into the muridach riders and sending them tumbling to the ground. With their riders slain, the kalocrypts turned and raced off in random directions. No doubt the muridachs in the jungles would recapture the beasts.

The barrage of ballistae bolts and arrows stopped half of the kalocrypts before they reached the city.

The other half reached the wall, and just as Ridmark predicted, the creatures scrambled straight up the vertical surface, their serrated legs grasping the smooth white stone with ease.

The gray elves shifted formation to deal with the new threat. The swordsmen and spearmen rushed forward, trying to kill the kalocrypts as they scrambled onto the battlements. The archers stepped back and to the side, directing their fire towards the columns of muridach infantry charging towards the city.

"Get ready," said Ridmark, Oathshield's hilt in both hands. "If any of those things get on the wall, they'll have a foothold. We'll have the best chance of driving them back."

"We shall crush the kalocrypts like the insects that they are!" said Magatai.

"Big damned insects," muttered Krastikon.

Swords flashed, and spears stabbed. A nearby kalocrypt died, its head pierced by the swords of the gray elves. But another kalocrypt perched upon the battlements and leaped, and it landed with a crash, scattering both a group of swordsmen and archers. The creature started thrashing, spearing gray elves upon its legs and biting them with its pincers.

"Go!" said Ridmark.

Tamlin charged forward as the gray elves tried to recover their formation. The kalocrypt turned towards him, stabbing with a serrated limb. Tamlin whipped the Sword of Earth before him, severing the leg. It struck the ground next to him and bounced off the rampart to the city below. The muridach rider reeled as the kalocrypt lost its balance, fighting to keep his saddle, and Kyralion loosed an arrow that punched into the rider's throat. The muridach fell dead to the ground, and Calem leaped forward and took off the kalocrypt's head with a sweep of the Sword of Air.

A shout caught his attention, and Tamlin turned his head to see Ridmark and Third battling a half-dozen muridach foot soldiers. How the devil had the ratmen gotten on the wall so quickly? Tamlin saw that the muridachs had used the opening created by the kalocrypt to run their ladder to the wall, and now muridach foot soldiers were swarming up the rungs.

A muridach leaped at Tamlin, bronze sword drawn back to strike, jaws yawning wide to drivel the chisel-like teeth forward. Tamlin dodged and swung the Sword of Earth in a two-handed swing, and the mighty blade passed through the muridach's sword, the muridach's arm, and the muridach's torso without slowing in the slightest.

That made a mess, but it did stop the ratman.

Magatai boomed a laugh and leaped into the fray, slashing right and left with his lightning-wreathed sword. The jolts of lightning from the magical blade stunned the muridachs, and Tamlin and Calem killed the creatures before they could recover. As Ridmark and Third and Kyralion drove back the muridachs, Krastikon stepped to the battlements and began chopping with the Sword of Death. The muridachs' siege ladder had been built from thick wood and bound with bronze bands, but the Sword of Death cut through wood and metal alike with ease.

The siege ladder collapsed to the hill below, taking a few of the muridach soldiers with it.

Tamlin killed another muridach and turned. All along the wall, he saw fighting, the gray elves struggling against both kalocrypts and muridach foot soldiers. The gray elves moved in eerie harmony, but there were so damned many of the muridachs.

And many of the gray elves looked exhausted already, their stamina drained by the plague curse.

"Let's move," said Ridmark, and Tamlin followed him to attack the next kalocrypt.

~

TAMARA KNEW she ought to have been terrified.

She had been in many fights over the years at Kalimnos, but never in anything like this. The fight wasn't a skirmish between the hoplites of Kalimnos and a roving band of raiders, but a clash between armies.

Tamara had never seen so many muridachs in one place. It was like a sea of them poured out of the jungle, as if Cathair Caedyn was an island in a seething lake of muridach warriors.

She was frightened, of course, her heart hammering against her ribs, her fingers tight against the cool metal of her staff. Yet she was not terrified as she should have been.

Perhaps it was because she knew what the muridachs were doing.

Tamara looked at their formations, and they were familiar. Lord Ridmark's assessment was right. The muridachs would send the kalocrypts first and then follow with columns of infantry carrying ladders. Tamara could see that for herself with a glance, just as she could see that the gray elves were moving into the proper defensive formations to meet such an attack.

How did she know that? She had no experience of warfare on this scale.

Then again, no one had ever taught her how to use earth magic, but she could do that anyway. Perhaps the woman she had been, the woman who had asked Rhodruthain to split her into seven lives, had known how to use earth magic and had experience of battles like this.

What kind of woman had she been?

Tamara put aside the thought as the kalocrypts rushed towards the wall. She had, it seemed, already died six times. The memories of those deaths often filled her nightmares. Tamara had no wish to add a seventh death to that collection of bloody memories.

"Here they come," said Calliande in a soft voice. "Tamara, you and I will focus on disrupting the kalocrypts. Kalussa, when we distract them, strike with the Staff of Blades."

"I shall," said Kalussa, the crystal at the end of the dark staff shifting, her eyes as cold and hard as a blade as she gazed at their advancing enemies.

"You can use the Sovereign's Staff of Blades, Lady Kalussa?" said Lord Rhomathar, his voice distracted. Likely his full attention was going to directing the defenders through the Unity.

"Yes," said Kalussa. "Not as well as he did, but well enough."

"Here they come," said Tamara.

The surviving kalocrypts reached the wall and started to climb.

"Now!" said Calliande.

Tamara cast her spell, drawing on the magic of elemental earth and shaping it with her will. She reached out with her thoughts and touched the mind of the nearest kalocrypt. The huge insect's mind was a strange, alien thing, filled with instinct and hunger. Tamara could use earth magic to control scutians and other animals, but the kalocrypt's mind was too strange for her to influence.

She could, however, confuse the creature, and the kalocrypt came to a sudden halt, its antennae waving in bafflement. The muridach on its back let out a curse, and then Kalussa struck. A thumb-sized sphere of crystal shot from the end of the Staff of Blades and drilled through the kalocrypt's head in a spray of black slime.

Calliande cast her spell, purple fire dancing along her staff. She was far stronger than Tamara, and three of the kalocrypts went motionless. The High Augur shot a startled glance in Calliande's direction. The muridachs riding the kalocrypts lashed their reins in frustration, and Kalussa killed two of them before the final kalocrypt broke free of the spell and charged.

The battle settled into a pattern. Whenever kalocrypts drew near to the gate, Calliande and Tamara stunned the creatures, and Kalussa killed them with the Staff of Blades. From time to time a band of muridach soldiers rushed towards the gate, and Athadira and Seruna and the other Augurs responded, unleashing blasts of elemental lightning that killed the muridachs before they could open the gate for their comrades. All along the ramparts, Tamara saw fighting as kalocrypts scaled the wall and ladders slammed against the battlements. The defenders were holding at a high cost to the muridachs.

Yet for every muridach warrior the defenders killed, ten more could take its place. The gray elves had no such advantage. If the fighting lasted long enough, if the muridachs did not break, the enemy might win through sheer attrition.

Then Calliande looked skyward. Tamara followed her gaze and saw a winged shape circling high overhead.

"That's an urdhracos, isn't it?" said Tamara.

"Yes," said Calliande. "It's the Scythe."

"The Scythe of the Maledicti?" said Seruna, startled. "You have faced that creature?"

"Yes," said Calliande, voice distant.

Tamara thought about mentioning that the Scythe had apparently killed her several times and decided against it. "Could you use your magical lightning to blast her from the sky?"

"Not from this distance," said Athadira. For once, the High Augur did not sound condescending. "The Scythe is powerful enough to block anything I could throw at her from this far away."

"What is she doing?" said Kalussa.

"Scouting, obviously," said Calliande. "She can take to the air and report every detail of our defense to her masters...wait." Her gaze snapped across the field, behind the advancing column of muridach infantry.

There was a sudden flare of blue light behind the muridach lines.

"The muridach priests!" said Calliande, and her staff began to blaze with white fire. "They're casting a spell."

"We must move!" said Rhomathar. "If they strike the Augurs, we shall lose our strongest wizards!"

"No!" said Calliande. "I can ward you here. If you move, they'll kill you."

"Do not presume to command the Augurs of the Liberated!" snarled Athadira. "We..."

"Mother, she is right!" said Rilmeira, who had joined her magic to that of the Augurs during the attack, flinging blasts of lightning at any muridachs who drew too close. Despite her relative youth among the gray elves, Rilmeira seemed one of their stronger wizards, close in power to the Augurs themselves. "Mother, look!"

The blue light brightened, a vortex of shadow swirling around it. Tamara thought the blue light was at least a mile away, far enough that the muridach priests would not be within the range of the engines upon the towers. Yet even across that distance, she felt the immense dark power drawing together, grim and potent.

Calliande shouted and struck the end of her staff against the rampart. White fire blazed up its length and then exploded from its end to form into a shimmering dome of light. An instant later a howling lance of blue fire and shadow, as thick as one of the kalocrypts, screamed across the battlefield. It struck the dome of light with a thunderous crack, blue light and white fire flashing madly around them. Calliande stumbled back with a cry, her face a rigid mask of concentration, and Kalussa caught her elbow. But the Keeper stayed on her feet, and her concentration held against the storm of dark magic.

The blue fire winked out, and the Augurs struck back. All five of them cast a spell in unison, the power centering on Athadira. The High Augur thrust her glittering staff towards the sky with a scream, and a bolt of lightning howled down. It struck the staff and coiled around it, and Athadira pushed her free hand forward with a grimace of pain. A sphere of lightning a dozen feet across expanded from her hand and hurtled over the wall, across the battlefield, and towards where the muridach priests had cast their spell.

Even from a distance, the resultant explosion was impressive.

The muridach priests did not try to attack again, and Tamara, Calliande, and Kalussa turned their attention to the waves of kalocrypts and the muridach infantry.

RIDMARK STEPPED BACK, breathing hard, his shoulders and knees aching, sweat hot against his face and temples. His eyes swept the ramparts, looking for his next target, but he couldn't find one.

Nor could he see any additional fighting on the ramparts, though the archers were still sending flights of arrows over the battlements.

"I think," said Third, staring over the ramparts, "that the enemy is withdrawing."

She was right.

Ridmark looked over the wall. Hundreds of dead kalocrypts and thousands of slain muridachs littered the slope, blood and ichor seeping in the soil. In a few days, the stench would be intolerable.

Ruined and broken siege ladders lay scattered at the foot of the wall. The surviving muridachs from the most recent wave retreated in a mass towards the muridach army...

No. Not the muridach army.

The muridach siege camps.

Ridmark had not paid much attention to what was happening outside the walls while he and the others had fought for their lives against the muridach soldiers and the kalocrypts. The rest of the muridach hosts had been busy. Thousands of muridachs dug ditches, raising earthwork walls. Others assembled catapults and ballistae, and still others were busy on devices that looked like siege towers.

"Unless I miss my guess," said Krastikon, "they have numbers enough to surround the entire city while staying out of ballista and catapult range."

"You're not wrong," said Ridmark, staring at the vast host outside the walls.

The gray elves were trapped within their final city...and so were Ridmark and the others.

11

A YOUNGER WOMAN

Very little happened for the rest of that day and all that night.

Third listened with half an ear as the Augurs and the Lord Marshal talked about the city's defense. They had slain thousands of muridachs in the first attack, but over three hundred gray elves had been killed, some from wounds, others dying from the strain of fighting through the exhaustion of the plague curse. Third made a circuit of Cathair Caedyn's walls, taking a quick mental count of the muridach horde encircling the city.

There were at least a quarter of a million muridachs laying siege to Cathair Caedyn, maybe as many as three hundred thousand, and it was entirely possible there were more within the jungle or in the tunnels of the Deeps that she could not see. Third knew very little of muridachs, save what the Traveler had mentioned and what she had picked up during her travels, but she did know that the muridachs bred at a prodigious rate. It was not uncommon for a muridach woman to have between thirty to fifty children during her lifetime, born in litters of five or six. Frequently the muridach children killed and ate their weaker siblings, but many of them survived to adulthood.

The muridach population could grow to prodigious heights, contained only by their love of internecine warfare and the limits of the available food. Yet if a strong ruler could stop the feuding and direct the rapaciousness of the muridachs outward, they could become a force of terrible power.

It seemed that Great King Nerzamdrathus, backed by the power of this mysterious prophet, had done just that.

Third saw no way to stop the destruction of Cathair Caedyn and the annihilation of the gray elves.

What was worse, she saw no way to save Ridmark and Calliande and her friends, no way to fulfill her mission from Queen Mara and High King Arandar. Third wondered what she could have done differently. Every step since they had left Kalimnos had seemed to land them in deeper trouble. Should she have insisted they try to fight their way east through the foothills of the Gray Mountains? No, if they had tried, they would have been surrounded and over-whelmed. Or perhaps they should have avoided the ruins of Cathair Avamyr entirely. Yet if they had, no doubt the muridachs would have found them on the steppes. Maybe they should have refused to accompany Arliach's patrol to Cathair Caedyn. But the city was the closest thing they would find to a safe haven in the Illicaeryn Jungle, and if they had not come here, almost certainly the muridachs would have killed them.

In the end, Third supposed, it was simple ill fortune. They had been in the wrong place at the wrong time. If not for the trap of the Maledicti in the Tower of Nightmares, they would have left Kalimnos several days earlier and departed the foothills long before the muri-dach armies emerged. Third could not think of anything she could have done differently, anything that would have kept them from Cathair Caedyn.

It was as if the hand of fate was against them. Though Third did not believe in fate. She did believe in God, though. Perhaps the hand of God was against them.

That was an unsettling thought.

The woman in flames...

The Augurs said the Sylmarus showed them visions of the future. Had it showed them a vision of the inevitable destruction of the gray elves? Perhaps it was unavoidable.

But Third would not perish without a fight.

Neither would Ridmark and Calliande or the others.

She remained near Ridmark as the Augurs and the Lord Marshal discussed the defense of the city. Athadira was a pride-blinded fool, but fortunately, it seemed that while the High Augur led the city, the Lord Marshal had the final say over matters of defense, and Rhomathar was wise enough to listen to his guests. The Unity let the gray elves fight in perfect harmony, but they could not share experiences that none of them possessed, and Third suspected none of them had any experience in siege warfare of this scale. The gray elves were excellent skirmishers and ambushers, fighting and retreating into the depths of the jungle, but a siege like this was something else entirely.

Rhomathar drank up Ridmark's and Calliande's suggestions like a sponge, and even the High Augur remained silent, though she glowered often. Perhaps she realized that the Shield Knight's suggestions gave the Liberated a greater chance of survival.

Not much, but some.

As they talked, Third found her eyes drifting to Kyralion again and again. He didn't deserve this, either, to die fighting for a leader who clearly despised him as a threat to her authority. Still, at least the warriors of Cathair Caedyn respected Kyralion. She had seen that during the long, bloody afternoon upon the ramparts. Again and again, Kyralion had charged into the fray, and his presence had hardened the morale of the wavering, exhausted warriors. Third realized that the elves of the Unity could sense each other's fear in battle, but Kyralion's expression had remained impassive as he fought. To see one of their own charging so boldly into the fray stiffened their resolve, and Kyralion had rallied defenders that might otherwise have been overcome.

Third looked at him, and she saw Rilmeira staring at him as well.

Rilmeira...

Third found that she could not dislike the gray elven woman. She seemed impulsive and rash, and like so many of the gray elves, she wore her emotions upon her sleeve. Yet none of those emotions had the cruel arrogance of her mother.

And one of those emotions was that Rilmeira was in love with Kyralion. It was as evident as words upon the page of a book.

Third thought that Kyralion was in love with Rilmeira as well. Her mother had forbidden it, no doubt, but it was plain to see. Did that anger Third? No, it just made her weary. She hadn't asked for this. She had come to Owyllain to find her friends and bring them home again.

Not to meet a gray elven warrior who sometimes dominated her thoughts.

Rilmeira saw her gaze and flinched.

The next morning the muridachs still worked like a mound of ants, assembling catapults and siege engines. Third had not slept well, and she walked alone through the streets of the city, listening to the noise as the women and children brought more bundles of arrows to the wall, as the guard shift upon the ramparts changed. She found it easy to avoid the gray elves. They were all focused on their tasks, and there were many empty houses in Cathair Caedyn.

Third suspected Cathair Caedyn had housed a much larger population until recently.

At last, she came to a courtyard behind four houses. It had once contained a garden with a flowering tree, but no one had tended it for years. The garden was overgrown, but it was still a beautiful space. There was a stone bench beneath the tree, and Third sat down with a sigh.

The battle would begin soon enough, she knew. Ridmark said that the muridachs would likely launch another attack by noon, and Third saw no reason to disagree with him. Her instincts spoke of the coming battle as well. She had seen war, centuries of war, and she feared that the next attack might destroy Cathair Caedyn and everyone within its walls.

Third felt weary enough that she wanted to close her eyes, but if she did that she might dream, and she didn't want that. Instead, she gazed at the garden, letting her mind wander. It really was a beautiful place, and it was a beautiful city.

Her eyes drifted to the Sylmarus, the green glow shining beneath its bark despite the blights growing on its side. It was an ancient, strong thing, and it was sad to see it so sick, dying a lingering death. Third had never heard of such a creature, and she wondered where it had come from, if there were others of its kind somewhere in the world. Her mind interpreted its aura as a soaring song of beauty, but she heard the sickness in that song, the discord of illness...

A feeling of vertigo went through her.

She was looking at the Sylmarus...but she had the feeling that the huge tree was looking back at her, that she had the attention of that vast and ancient creature.

"My lady?"

Third blinked and turned her head.

The position of the shadows had shifted a little as the sun moved through the sky. Just how long had she been staring at the Sylmarus? It wasn't like Third for her attention to drift.

She had failed to notice that Rilmeira stood in the alley between two of the houses, staring at her.

The battle-hardened part of her mind (which was most of it, really) wondered if Rilmeira had come to dispose of a potential rival for Kyralion's affections, but one glance proved that idea ridiculous. Rilmeira looked nervous. She was wearing the golden armor of the gray elves, which should have made her look formidable, but Rilmeira looked as if she wanted to shrink inside it. She held her hands clasped in front of her chest, but they kept plucking at each other.

Third rose and offered a polite bow. "Lady Rilmeira." She decided to excuse herself. "I must..."

"Please," said Rilmeira. "Just call me Rilmeira. Mother is so insistent that we all use our ancient titles. But there are so few of us left. It seems ridiculous to care about such things now."

"I agree," said Third.

Nor, she feared, was there much time left to worry about such things.

"I wanted to talk to you, if that was all right," said Rilmeira. "I'm afraid I may not get a chance again. Lord Rhomathar and the Shield Knight think the muridachs will come in force today. If they are... repelling them will hold all our attention."

"As it should," said Third.

"May I ask...I wanted to ask you something," said Rilmeira.

Third nodded. "Go ahead."

"I wanted to ask...I think I would like to know," said Rilmeira. "I don't mean to be rude, but it...it I really wanted to know, and it's none of my business, but I have to ask, and..."

Third blinked. She didn't often feel pity, but she felt it now. Likely Rilmeira was accustomed to asking complex and difficult questions through the Unity. Articulating an unpleasant emotion was likely an alien experience to her. Perhaps that was why she had lost her temper at her mother earlier.

"I think I know what you are trying to say," said Third.

Rilmeira blinked, relief going over her face. "Oh?"

"You are in love with Kyralion and have been for years," said Third. "You have seen us together, and you are wondering if I am in love with him or if he is in love with me."

It was almost comical to see Rilmeira's relief turn to horrified dismay.

"I...I..." she started. "How did you know? Are you a sorceress?"

"What?" said Third.

"Did you read my mind?" said Rilmeira.

Third laughed despite herself. "No. I am just very old and very observant." She sighed. "Permit me to make another observation. You and Kyralion have been very close for a long time, but your mother has forbidden the two of you to marry."

"Yes," said Rilmeira. "Am I that transparent?"

"From someone who is part of the Unity, that is a strange question," said Third. "But to me, yes. I think the elves of the Unity are so used to reading each other's mind that you never learned to govern your expressions." She suddenly remembered something Jager had told her about the importance of keeping a straight face while playing dice games. "It is just as well you have never met my sister's husband. He would invite you to play a game of cards or dice, and he would walk away with every gold coin in the city."

"How would he carry them all?" said Rilmeira.

"Unimportant," said Third. Though knowing Jager, he would find a way. "But how long have you and Kyralion known each other?"

"All of our lives," said Rilmeira. "I confess I was a horrible child. I was the High Augur's daughter, and I could use that to get whatever I wanted. But Kyralion...I could never influence him or control him. At first, it enraged me. Then it baffled me. Then it intrigued me. I saw how hard he worked. He became one of our best swordsmen and archers. He could not use magic, but he was immune to it. That gave us an advantage in many fights with the dvargir and the muridachs."

"I imagine many a muridach priest died on the end of Kyralion's sword, wondering why his spell did not work," said Third.

"Yes," said Rilmeira. "My mother thinks he is a threat to the harmony and consensus of the Unity. His opinions were often at odds with hers. Mother would have us hide behind the walls of the city and hope the world passes us by. Kyralion thinks that we need to have friends among the Nine Cities and the orcish warlords, that if we do not have allies, we will inevitably fall."

"And you agree with Kyralion," said Third.

It was fascinating to watch the struggle go over Rilmeira's expression. She disagreed with the High Augur and the consensus of the Unity. It had to be a difficult challenge.

But she did it.

"Yes," said Rilmeira at last. "Given that a muridach host now surrounds the city, I think that is persuasive proof of Kyralion's argument."

Third nodded, thought about her next words. "When did Kyralion ask you to marry him?"

Rilmeira flinched. "You are indeed observant. It was about ten years ago, as the plague curse grew stronger. I would have said yes, but my mother was enraged. She...said many unkind things about Kyralion and forbade us from marrying. Then the Sylmarus sent the vision of you to the Augurs, and Kyralion volunteered to find you."

"And so he has," said Third.

Rilmeira hesitated, and then rallied her courage and plowed ahead. "Do you love him?"

Third thought about her answer, about that kiss in the jungle.

"Yes," she said.

Rilmeira wilted like a flower in autumn.

"But it does not matter," said Third. "You were his first love, Rilmeira. He does not speak much, but I understand him. And I understand him better, now that I have met you. He would have wed you, would still wed you, but your mother has forbidden it, and he is too dutiful to lead a rebellion. The only reason he was drawn to me was that he could not be with you."

"Do...do you really think so?" said Rilmeira. "Oh, it is a horrible thing to ask you, but..."

"I do think that," said Third. "And your mother was right about me."

"No!" said Rilmeira, anger flashing in her eyes. "No, she was not. She was wrong, and Kyralion was right about you. I saw you fight on the ramparts. The muridachs are dangerous fighters, but you were like a wolf among sheep. Perhaps you were an urdhracos, but now you are a warrior like the ones in the ancient histories of our people. No. My mother threw cruel lies in your face because she is afraid and because she does not like Kyralion."

"She wished to be cruel," said Third, "but she was not wrong. I may not be an abomination, but I am an aberration. I spent nearly a thousand years as an urdhracos, and as far as I know, I am the only urdhracos who was ever freed from the curse of dark elven blood. I..." She paused, trying to sort through her thoughts. "I admire Kyralion a great deal. But he loves his people, Rilmeira. I have no wish to stay in Cathair Caedyn, in the unlikely event we survive the new few days. Nor do I have any wish to take him away from his people. I am a hybrid and therefore cannot have children.

Unless I am wrong, you would very much like to have Kyralion's children."

Rilmeira blushed. She could do that prettily. No doubt she wanted both the children and the process of making them. "You...are not wrong."

"Kyralion was only drawn to me because he thinks he will never be with you," said Third. "Your mother is a fool."

Rilmeira flinched again. "She...is the High Augur of the Unity of the Liberated. It is a grave responsibility and one she takes most seriously. And she is afraid." Rilmeira looked at the ground. "She... knows, deep down, that we are likely doomed as you have said. Yet she refuses to acknowledge the depth of our peril, and speaks only of our inevitable victory."

Bitter resentment went over her face. Perhaps this was the first time she had ever spoken of it. Of course, likely everyone in the Unity knew of her resentment, but no one had ever acted on it. Maybe that was the price of the High Augur's consensus. The gray elves brooded upon their emotions but did not act on them.

"May I offer some advice?" said Third.

Rilmeira hesitated. "Of course."

"Never lie to yourself," said Third. "No matter how unpleasant the truth, no matter how much you wish to hide from it, never lie to yourself. I am what I am, and you are what you are. That was why I did not care when your mother called me an abomination."

"You didn't get angry until my mother started insulting Kyralion," said Rilmeira.

"Ridmark told me once that is how you know whether or not you really care about someone," said Third. "You get angry on their behalf. And you did not become angry until the High Augur started insulting him, either."

"I suppose not," said Rilmeira. "I am used to having Mother angry at me. But...but she should not talk to Kyralion that way."

"I suspect she is hearing everything we are saying right now," said Third.

"What?" said Rilmeira. "Oh, no, the Unity doesn't work like that.

We communicate without words. She cannot listen through my ears or see through my eyes, not unless I send the images and the sounds to her with my thoughts. She will know that I am talking with you and that I am annoyed with her, but that is all."

Third nodded. "I suppose the High Augur knows what I think of her, so it hardly matters."

"I am sorry," said Rilmeira.

"You are not responsible for your mother," said Third.

"No," said Rilmeira. "But...but I feel ridiculous. We're about to die, probably, and so I'm coming here and...and pouring all this on you..."

Third shrugged. "It is the truth, is it not?"

Rilmeira blinked and then smiled. "As you said. I do care about Kyralion. I was so worried about him when he left to find you and the Shield Knight and the Keeper. And then he returns with a woman who is prettier than me..."

Third blinked. "What?"

"Well, you are," said Rilmeira. "You said not to lie to myself. You are prettier than I am."

"What?" said Third again, baffled. Third knew she was not unattractive, but the harsh alien edge to her features was obvious. It was just as well that she did not desire human men, because humans always found her a little unsettling.

She had never contemplated the effect her appearance might have on elven men, though. Or that gray elven women might see her as a rival.

"I wish I had hair like yours," said Rilmeira. "It's so thick and black."

"I am a thousand years old," said Third, caught between amusement and bewilderment.

"And when I am a thousand years old," said Rilmeira, "I hope my hair is still that thick. And I never liked the color of my hair."

"Your hair is perfectly fine," said Third, bemused. In a thousand years, she had never had a conversation about the color of her hair. Or the color of anyone else's hair, for that matter.

Rilmeira tugged at a lock of her golden hair and sighed. "It's the color of our swords and armor. I always look like I'm wearing a helmet. Your hair is the color of the night in the jungle, and…"

"For God's sake!" said Third. Part of her mind was amused by how much she sounded like Ridmark. "I am a thousand years old, and we are in the middle of a siege. I am not comparing the color of my hair to yours."

"You do have nice hair," said Rilmeira. "You did just tell me to be honest."

Third laughed, and Rilmeira blinked, smiled, and then laughed as well.

"I…I hope you will not be offended," said Rilmeira, "but I hope we can be friends."

"I hope that, too," said Third. "I do not have many friends."

"Lord Ridmark is one," said Rilmeira, "is he not?"

"My oldest friend," said Third.

"I am surprised," said Rilmeira, "that you follow him, and not the other way around."

Third raised her eyebrows. "Why is that?"

"Because you are far older and far more experienced," said Rilmeira.

"In some ways," said Third. "I have only rarely led men in battle, and he has done that many times. A very different skill than killing, which I am very good at." She frowned. "There difference between us is that I will fight to the death."

Rilmeira frowned. "Would he not do the same?"

"He would," said Third. "He would fight to the death. But he would also win. I have seen it before. Battles we should have lost, but he won anyway. He will never, ever give up, not for anything. If there is a way to win this siege, he will find it."

"Maybe you will find a way to win the siege," said Rilmeira. "The Sylmarus sent the Augurs a vision of you."

"It also sent a vision of the Shield Knight and the Keeper," said Third. She shook her head. "Perhaps the Sylmarus should have a sent a vision of them and not of me."

"No," said Rilmeira. "But you give me hope. Maybe all is not yet lost."

Third looked at Rilmeira and felt regret. She looked so...young, so very young. Young enough that she had convinced herself that there was still hope, that this battle might have another outcome than the muridachs slaughtering the remaining gray elves in the smoking ashes of Cathair Caedyn.

But maybe Rilmeira would turn out to be right in the end.

"Maybe," said Third. "We..."

Rilmeira flinched and looked to the north.

"What is it?" said Third, getting to her feet, her hands going to her sword hilts.

"The sentries say the muridachs are moving," said Rilmeira.

"An attack?" said Third.

"I don't know," said Rilmeira. "Something strange. But we need to get to the ramparts."

Third nodded, and together they hurried towards the northern wall.

12

THE LORD OF CARRION

Ridmark stood on the battlements atop the northern gate and watched the muridachs.

The sun was rising over the jungle to the east, and in the morning light, he saw the muridachs working with the industriousness of an anthill. The vast horde encircled Cathair Caedyn, and he saw the muridachs assembling catapults and siege towers and other machines that Ridmark could not identify. The muridachs had fortified their camps as well, digging ditches and raising low earthwork walls.

Not that it mattered. On foot, the gray elves could not launch a sortie into the enemy lines. Had the gray elves possessed horses, they could have launched lightning raids into the muridach camps and returned to the safety of Cathair Caedyn's walls. If the gray elves had bound trisalians as war beasts the way that Calliande had taught the Arcanius Knights, they could have smashed the muridach lines. If they had a hundred Takai warriors riding struthians, they could have rained arrows down on the muridachs and then retreated to the city.

But the gray elves had no war beasts of any kind, and so they could do nothing but watch and wait as the muridachs prepared.

Ridmark did not like what he saw. There were at least three

hundred thousand muridach soldiers gathered below the city's hill, and they had numbers enough to attack from all four points of the compass at once. Yet based on their positions, Ridmark thought they would focus on the northern wall, throwing wave after wave of soldiers at the ramparts.

The casualties would be horrendous. Ridmark suspected nearly one hundred thousand muridach soldiers would die before the battle was over. But the muridachs placed little value on life, and Ridmark doubted the muridach lords or Great King Nerzamdrathus cared about the fates of their soldiers.

By the time the slaughter was over, a third of the muridach army would be dead, and Cathair Caedyn would be ashes.

Ridmark could not think of a way to prevent that outcome.

He heard a rasp of a boot against stone and turned to see Calliande climb up to the ramparts. She smiled at him, but he saw the weariness in her eyes. She had cast numerous spells yesterday and then devoted her strength to healing the wounded gray elves that she could save. Ridmark was glad that Kalussa had a link to the Well of Tarlion and had learned the healing spell since that meant she could bear part of the load.

"How are you?" said Ridmark.

"Tired," admitted Calliande, "but I'm not dead yet, so I shouldn't complain." She crossed to his side and gazed over the ramparts.

"How are the boys?" said Ridmark.

"They're well, as far as I can tell," said Calliande. Likely she had used the Sight to check on them as soon as she had awakened. "You know, I think this is the farthest I have ever been from them."

"Yes," said Ridmark. "But we're a long way from anywhere. I doubt many humans have ever come to the Illicaeryn Jungle."

"When we left Aenesium for Kalimnos," said Calliande, "I felt terrible. I kept trying to convince myself that there was a way we could have brought Gareth and Joachim with us, kept them safe with us." She sighed. "But as I look at the muridachs...I'm glad they're a long, long way from here. A muridach was the first creature I saw in

Owyllain. It wanted to take us as slaves and threatened to bite off Joachim's fingers if I didn't obey."

"I suppose the muridach regretted that," said Ridmark. Calliande was more forgiving than Ridmark was. But any threats to Gareth and Joachim switched off her conscience, and she became as implacable as the winter in the Northerland.

"Not for long," said Calliande. "It was dead before it hit the ground." She shook her head. "I'm rambling. It's bad, isn't it?"

"Yes," said Ridmark. She had seen just as many battles as he had.

"Well, we're not defeated yet," said Calliande. "A battle is never decided until it's over. Perhaps Nerzamdrathus will make a mistake, or whoever this prophet of the Lord of Carrion is will commit an error." She glanced back at the towering shape of the Sylmarus rising from the heart of the city. "And maybe Third will save the Unity."

"Maybe," said Ridmark, though he could not see how. "I would never bet against her." Though even if she saved the Unity, whatever that meant, in the next five minutes, they would still be surrounded by hundreds of thousands of muridachs.

"I feel sorry for her," said Calliande.

"Because of Kyralion and Rilmeira," said Ridmark. "She'll handle it."

"I know," said Calliande. "But Third has been such a good friend to us, Ridmark. I want her to be happy. Though I am not sure what happiness would be for her."

"Your matchmaking instincts are coming to the forefront," said Ridmark.

"I am quite good at arranging marriages, I'll have you know, Lord Ridmark," said Calliande with a smile. "The upside of gradually aging into a meddlesome old woman is that it's actually quite enjoyable to be a meddlesome old woman. I think I'll even be able to talk Kalussa and Calem back around. A brush with death is good for putting your priorities in order." She shook her head. "Assuming we live through this."

"Hard to play matchmaker for Third, I suppose," said Ridmark.

"Yes," said Calliande. "I..."

She trailed off, her eyes going hazy, and then her expression hardened.

"The muridachs are doing something," said Calliande. "Look."

She pointed at one of the siege camps, and Ridmark saw a troop of Throne Guards emerge in their crimson armor, escorting a dozen muridach priests in their red cowls and skull-topped staffs. Ridmark watched the creatures, wondering if they intended to cast a spell at the walls. There were ancient wards in the walls of Cathair Caedyn, strong enough to keep the muridach priests from blasting a breach, but perhaps the muridachs had found a way through that protection.

"They're casting a spell," said Calliande.

There was a flare of blue light from the priests, and then a voice boomed over the walls.

"Hear me!" said the deep voice of a muridach speaking the orcish tongue. The echoes rolled off the walls and the houses. "Nerzamdrathus, Great King of the muridachs, invites the gray elves to send forth an emissary to discuss the end of the siege! By the sworn word of the Great King, your emissary shall be permitted to meet with the Great King and return unharmed to your walls!"

Ridmark shared a look with Calliande.

"I wasn't expecting that," said Calliande.

THE MURIDACH HERALD repeated its invitation three more times, and Calliande watched as the gray elves responded in haste.

Warriors and archers rushed to the wall, ready to defend if the invitation was a ruse to cover an impending attack. Athadira and the other Augurs arrived on the rampart, along with Lord Rhomathar, Lord Arliach, and Kyralion. Third and Rilmeira arrived together, which Calliande thought odd, and Tamlin, Tamara, Calem, Magatai, Kalussa, and Krastikon joined them a few moments later.

"Why the devil would they ask for a parley?" said Rhomathar. "There is nothing to be gained from it."

Athadira let out a disdainful sniff. The High Augur looked

queenly in her robes, her jeweled staff flashing in the sunlight. "Perhaps the failure of their attack yesterday taught them the folly of opposing the might of the Liberated."

"I very much doubt that," said Seruna. "We could trade every one of our warriors for twenty of theirs, and they would still come out ahead."

"Likely they think to intimidate us and demand our surrender," said Kyralion.

Athadira glared at him. "We are the Liberated, Lord Kyralion. For fifteen thousand years we fought the Sovereign and his armies. We will never surrender, not ever."

"He wasn't saying that, Mother," said Rilmeira, her tone just on the edge of irritation. "He said the muridachs will demand our surrender, not that we should surrender."

Athadira turned her withering stare towards her daughter. "I know that, child. I..."

"The muridachs know you will not surrender so they will have three possible reasons for demanding a parley," said Ridmark before the argument could get up to full speed. Athadira and Rilmeira blinked at him, perhaps surprised that someone would dare to interrupt them. "First, to undermine your morale. Second, to buy time to prepare another plan. Third, as part of a clever stratagem that we cannot yet see."

"Another reason," said Third in a quiet voice. "Curiosity. Both the Shield Knight and the Keeper fought in the first attack, and the muridachs will not have encountered a threat of this nature before. The survivors from the previous attack will have told their lords and commanders about the Shield Knight and the Keeper. The muridachs want to assess this unknown threat."

"Perhaps we should decline the parley, then," said Rhomathar.

"Maybe not," said Ridmark. "The muridachs are dangerous, but it's Nerzamdrathus and the prophet of the Lord of Carrion who have made them so deadly. If we have a look at them, perhaps we can discern some of their weaknesses."

"Yes," murmured the High Augur. "Yes, the Sight could discern any weaknesses that they might possess. Very well."

"Will you accompany us, Lord Ridmark?" said Rhomathar. Athadira scowled but did not say anything. "Because another possible reason for the parley is to lure out the High Augur to kill her. They will find that harder if you are with us."

"Of course," said Ridmark. "But I suspect we've already fought against the prophet of the Lord of Carrion."

TAMARA TOOK a deep breath as she and Tamlin walked to the square with the others.

The High Augur had cast a spell to amplify her voice, and she and the muridach herald had negotiated for the better part of an hour. At last, Athadira had agreed to come out to speak with Great King Nerzamdrathus, accompanied by Ridmark, Calliande, Third, Kyralion, Rilmeira, Tamlin, and Tamara.

Tamara was slightly annoyed to realize that the High Augur was relying on the Shield Knight and his friends so as not to put any gray elves at risk.

Then again, the High Augur would be as safe with the Shield Knight and the Keeper as she could be.

Tamara came to a stop as the others waited before the gate. Lord Rhomathar would remain behind to command the defense in case the muridachs planned treachery. Tamara took a deep breath, her fingers tapping on the golden staff in her right hand.

"Are you ready?" said Tamlin, his voice quiet.

"Yes," said Tamara. "And no. I've fought muridachs most of my life. Just...not so many of them at once."

"I don't think anyone has ever fought so many muridachs at once," said Tamlin. "I read of the old High Kings' wars against the muridachs in the monastery library. They fought the muridachs often, but never in such numbers. The ratmen could never cooperate long enough to gather such a large army, and..."

He shook his head and laughed a little.

"What?" said Tamara, smiling. She didn't know what was funny, but she did like to see him laugh.

"You've probably fought muridachs more than I have, and I am lecturing you about it," said Tamlin.

Tamara shrugged. "You've read more than I have." She felt herself grow wistful. "I think I've seen five books in my life. Father Nathan had a copy of the scriptures in the church. I guess it came with the first settlers from Aenesium. Sir Rion had a few books on the history of Owyllain."

"I want a library one day," said Tamlin. He rolled his shoulders beneath his golden armor. "I have a room for one in my domus. I just haven't had time to find any books."

"I would like to read some books," said Tamara. "I do know how to read. There just hasn't been much opportunity for it."

And there might not be a chance for it. Not when the muridachs killed them all. Tamara supposed it was possible they might survive the siege, that they might yet be victorious against the muridachs, but she could not see how.

"Someday," said Tamlin. She saw the same realization on his face. He, too, knew that the odds were against them.

Tamara smiled, took his hand, and squeezed it. "Someday."

He smiled back. They were probably going to die in the next few days, she knew. According to her nightmares, she had died six times before. Tamlin had seen her die twice. Was he going to see her die again? Or was she going to see his death?

That thought distressed her as much as anything ever had.

Maybe there were some things she ought to do before it was too late.

"Ready?" said Ridmark.

"We shall meet with the muridach Great King, Shield Knight," said the High Augur, her tone aloof and frosty. Calliande had a knack for taking a calm, queenly mien when acting as the Keeper, but she lacked the arrogance of Athadira. "Take us there."

Ridmark looked at the gray elven warriors standing before the gate and nodded. The warriors opened a small postern gate, and he led the way outside the city.

The stench hit Tamara's nose at once, and her stomach clenched. Countless dead muridachs and kalocrypts lay scattered on the slope of the hill. The kalocrypts smelled bad when they were alive, but they smelled much worse once they were dead. With so many slain muridachs piled on the ground, the musky stink of muridach fur filled her nostrils. The odor of rotting flesh mingled with the musky reek, so strong that it made her eyes water.

They walked down the slope towards the waiting muridach embassy. The herald and the High Augur had bickered about the location and finally settled at a point halfway between the northern gate and the muridach siege camps. From here, they were out of arrow range of both the walls and the camps, and they could withdraw back to the city if the muridachs attempted treachery. Though Tamara supposed the kalocrypts could cover the distance, but they would come into arrow range if they chased anyone fleeing towards the city.

Her eyes fell on the muridach embassy. There were twenty hulking muridachs in the crimson armor of the Throne Guards, swords sheathed at their sides. Behind them stood a dozen priests of the Lord of Carrion, gaunt muridachs in their crimson cowls and mantles.

With them stood two figures, both grim and dangerous.

The first was a huge muridach, the single largest muridach man that Tamara had ever seen. He stood nearly nine feet tall, his rat-like head almost the size of a small boulder, his front teeth like swords. Blood sigils burned on his crimson armor, and in his right hand he carried a huge black sword longer than Tamara was tall, and more blood sigils blazed upon the dark blade. A twisted crown of gold and rubies rested on his head, and earrings of bronze and gold pierced his ears. This had to be Nerzamdrathus, the Great King of the muridachs, and power and malice rolled off him in waves.

Next to him stood a shorter figure draped in an elaborate black robe.

Or floated, rather, since the robed form hovered a few inches off the ground.

It was a Maledictus. Tamara recognized the design of the robe from the Tower of Nightmares. Mhazhama's robe had been silvery-gray, and the Maledictus of Shadows had worn a mist-colored robe, but this robe was black, so black it seemed like a hole in the air. Against the robed figure's chest hung a medallion of strange dark metal wrought in the shape of a double ring pierced by seven spikes. Tamara's skin crawled as she gazed at the Maledictus, and she felt the creature's attention as they approached.

"Damn it," muttered Tamlin. "I knew it. I knew it was him."

Behind the Maledictus waited the Scythe, her black wings folded and hanging behind her like a leather cloak. Her void-filled eyes turned towards Third, and her face twisted with hatred and loathing.

The High Augur hesitated for half a step when she saw the Maledictus and then lifted her chin and kept walking.

"You know that Maledictus?" whispered Tamara.

"Qazaldhar," said Tamlin, his voice hard. "The Maledictus of Death. We fought him in Cathair Valwyn and at Trojas. He helped kill Tirdua and Aegeus." Tamlin took a ragged breath. "He taught necromancy to Taerdyn...and he was the one who placed the plague curse on the Sylmarus."

The High Augur stopped a dozen paces from the muridach party, gazing at the ratmen with disdain, and Tamara and the others stopped around her.

They stared at each other for a long time.

Likely Athadira would wait for the Great King to speak first out of sheer arrogance.

The huge muridach took a step forward. Perhaps he was impatient for the killing to begin.

"So." Nerzamdrathus's voice was a deep rumble that made Tamara's teeth vibrate. "You are the High Augur of the last of the gray elves."

"I am," said Athadira, her glare unwavering. "And I assume you are the warlord commanding this rabble?"

The Throne Guards let out their chittering muridach laughs, their tails lashing with amusement. The Maledictus of Death shifted, his face still hidden beneath the deep black cowl. The Scythe opened and closed her right hand, her talons rasping against each other.

"I am Nerzamdrathus," said the huge creature, "Lord of the Warrens, master of the seven strongholds of our kindred, conqueror of the Deeps, and Great King of the muridachs. Soon I shall have an additional title."

"Oh?" said Athadira. "And what title is that?"

"The destroyer of the gray elves," said Nerzamdrathus. "I shall succeed where the Sovereign failed, and I shall exterminate the last remnant of your wretched kindred from the face of the earth."

"Hardly a convincing start to this parley," said Athadira.

"What is there to negotiate?" said Nerzamdrathus. "If you surrender now, we shall kill you painlessly. Our priests can prepare an elixir for you to drink, and it will slay your kindred swiftly and without pain. But if you resist, you shall suffer. We shall breach your walls and swarm your city. We shall devour your people alive, and rejoice in their screams. We will devour the children in front of their mothers and laugh as they beg for mercy. We shall consume the wives in front of their husbands. It will take weeks for the killing to end, and you shall be the last to die, High Augur, so you may hear every single member of your kindred perish before we at last grant you the mercy of death."

"By what right do you presume to make these threats?" said Athadira.

"I do not make threats, but promises," said Nerzamdrathus. "And I make them through the right of conquest. The muridachs hunger, High Augur, and your flesh is sweet to us. Once Cathair Caedyn falls, we shall continue our conquest. All Owyllain will belong to us. The Seven Swords of the Sovereign shall be ours. The Lord of Carrion has decreed it to be so. All that remains is for you to decide if you shall die in agony or in peace." His red-glazed eyes turned towards Tamara. "And to determine the nature of the strange companions you have convinced to die alongside you."

"There is no need, Great King," said the Maledictus.

Tamara flinched. The voice was horrible, a snarling wet gurgle that sounded as if had been forced through a dead throat. If disease and blight and illness could speak, they would sound like that.

She had never heard that voice before...but it had flickered through her nightmares.

One of her other lives had encountered this creature, maybe more than one.

"Prophet?" said Nerzamdrathus.

"The prophet of the Lord of Carrion," murmured Calliande. "Of course."

Qazaldhar lifted his cowled head and gazed at them.

His face was hideous. Both Mhazhama and the Maledictus of Shadows had been undead, but they had been mummified, withered husks. Qazaldhar was also undead, but his face was rotten and collapsing into itself. The green flesh of an orc had turned grayish-black and glistened with slime that dripped from the jaw and the ears and the nose. The eyes were black craters, and blue fire burned within them.

Yes. Tamara had seen that face in her nightmares.

"The human man is called the Shield Knight," said Qazaldhar, "and bears a weapon of high elven magic. The woman is the Keeper, a powerful sorceress. And unless I miss my guess, the Shield Knight's companions have three of the Seven Swords with them. The Lord of Carrion has indeed smiled upon you, Great King, and chosen you as his instrument. For soon three of the Seven Swords shall be yours."

"You have been deceived, Great King," said Calliande. "Qazaldhar is not a prophet of the Lord of Carrion but of the New God, the Kratomachar. He has been lying to you and manipulating you as a weapon against his enemies. He has no interest in the muridachs or the Lord of Carrion."

Qazaldhar loosed a gurgling laugh. "Heed not the words of this human sorceress, Great King. Have I not brought the word of the Lord of Carrion to you? Were you not chosen as his instrument and champion? And have you not risen high, far higher than any Great King before you? The entire muridach kindred bows before you. Soon you shall annihilate the gray elves, a feat that even the Sovereign could never achieve, and then you shall conquer the realm of the Nine Cities. What are these if not signs of the favor of the Lord of Carrion?"

Tamara felt a chill. Ridmark and Calliande had said that they suspected the Maledicti of manipulating the War of the Seven Swords, of orchestrating the battles behind the scenes in pursuit of their sinister goals, and watching Qazaldhar talk to Nerzamdrathus proved it. How long had Qazaldhar been manipulating the muridachs? How long had he been preparing Nerzamdrathus for this moment? How many different schemes and plots did the Maledicti have underway?

"It is curious," said Calliande, "that the Lord of Carrion would choose to speak through an undead orc who was once a priest of the Sovereign."

"The Sovereign has been dead for twenty-five years," said Qazaldhar. "A new order is coming. The time of the orcs and the humans is over. The hour of the muridachs has come. And you, Great King Nerzamdrathus, you shall be the one to spread the power of the Lord of Carrion across the face of the world."

"And once you are finished with the Great King," said Calliande, "you will cast him and the muridachs aside, just as you did with Prince Rypheus, Justin Cyros, and the Necromancer of Trojas." She pointed at Qazaldhar. "For I have seen him and his brother Maledicti serving the bearers of the Seven Swords, Great King Nerzamdrathus. He is playing you for a fool, just and he and the Maledicti did with King Justin and Lord Taerdyn."

"Behold the begging of the cornered prey," said Qazaldhar. "And her very presence here is a sign of the Lord of Carrion's favor. For the Keeper and the Shield Knight would have been your most dangerous foes, Great King, once you invaded Owyllain. Yet they will perish with the gray elves. Three of the Seven Swords shall be yours once Cathair Caedyn burns. They will..."

The glowing blue gaze passed over Tamara and then snapped back towards her with a sudden unnerving intensity.

Tamara stared back, refusing to show weakness before this creature.

"And behold!" said Qazaldhar. "Another sign of the favor of the Lord of Carrion! The seventh and final shard is here to die as well."

"Seventh shard?" said Nerzamdrathus, his beady eyes narrowing. "Seventh shard of what?"

"One of the most dangerous enemies of the Lord of Carrion," said Qazaldhar.

"And why am I dangerous, Maledictus?" said Tamara, hoping to goad him into an answer. Mhazhama and the Maledictus of Shadows had known who she really was, but they had refused to share any information. Perhaps Qazaldhar would be more talkative.

"Why is she dangerous, prophet?" said Nerzamdrathus. "She is a human female and a wizard of minor power. She is no threat to the children of the Lord of Carrion."

"Indeed not," said Qazaldhar, "but what she once was and what she might become are dangerous. Behold! Once there was a sorceress who fought against the rise of the Lord of Carrion. She failed and was mortally wounded, and fearing to fail in her duty, split her life and soul into seven shards. The seven shards were reborn as seven women, and one by one they struggled against the Lord of Carrion and perished. Now only the seventh shard remains, and when Cathair Caedyn falls, another foe of the Lord of Carrion will perish."

"The Lord of Carrion or the New God?" said Tamara.

Qazaldhar only smirked at her. Could not Nerzamdrathus and the other muridachs see how Qazaldhar had manipulated them, how he used them as his weapons? Perhaps they could not. Maybe Qazaldhar had told them what they wanted to hear, and they blinded themselves willfully. Perhaps Qazaldhar had manipulated Nerzamdrathus since childhood, twisting his mind as Tamlin had told her that Khurazalin had twisted Prince Rypheus Pendragon. With a chill, Tamara wondered if the Maledictus of Shadows had edited the memories of the muridachs, making them more susceptible to Qazaldhar's suggestions than they might have otherwise been.

Not that it mattered. The muridachs were here, and even if they realized that Qazaldhar had been manipulating them, they would not stop. No doubt Nerzamdrathus's desire to destroy the gray elves and conquer Owyllain was genuine. Perhaps Qazaldhar had simply given Nerzamdrathus and the muridachs the permission and the means to do what they wanted to do anyway.

"Enough," said Nerzamdrathus, his gaze swinging back to Athadira. "The time for talk is over, High Augur. Make your decision. You, your people, and your allies are doomed. All that is left is to decide whether you shall die without pain or after weeks of agony."

"I made my decision long ago, vermin," said Athadira, glaring at the Great King. The Throne Guards rumbled at the insult, but Nerzamdrathus lifted a clawed hand, and they fell silent. "Bring your hosts against the walls of Cathair Caedyn. The Sovereign failed to destroy us, and when you attack Cathair Caedyn, you shall meet his fate as well."

Nerzamdrathus loosed a chittering, high-pitched muridach laugh, and the Throne Guards and the carrion priests followed suit. It was disturbing to hear that sound coming from the hulking muridach king. Tamara remembered seeing that poor gray elven warrior getting eaten alive in Cathair Avamyr, and she had a sudden, vivid vision of Nerzamdrathus doing the same thing to her.

"So be it," said Nerzamdrathus. "We shall put the question to the test of arms, will we not? I gave my sworn word to allow you to return unharmed to the walls of your city, and the Great King of the muridachs keeps his word. So hear my word, High Augur of the gray elves. You shall see every last gray elf die. You shall be the final member of your kindred. Your death will take months, and you will beg for the end." He stepped back. "The attack will begin once I return to my lines. I suggest you be within your walls by then."

Nerzamdrathus turned and beckoned, and the Throne Guards and the carrion priests followed the Great King as he strode back to the siege camps. Qazaldhar gazed at Tamara for a moment longer, that smirk still on his rotting face.

Then he turned and glided after the muridachs, the black robes rippling around him. The Scythe snarled at Third one last time and followed the Maledictus.

"I know him," hissed Tamara, staring after the departing Maledictus of Death.

"He and Khurazalin killed Tirdua at the Blue Castra," said Tamlin, his green eyes hard and glittering as he watched the Maledictus.

"I know," murmured Tamara. "I dreamed of it in my nightmares. But I am sure I have seen that creature before. One of my other lives. Or maybe before I was sundered into seven..."

"We need to go," said Ridmark. "As soon as Nerzamdrathus gets back to his army, he's going to send the kalocrypts after to us."

"Your counsel is reasonable, Shield Knight," said Athadira. Somehow, she made it sound like agreeing with him was a favor. Tamara had to admire both Rilmeira's and Third's self-control for not slapping the High Augur. "Let us return to the city."

They turned and climbed the slope back to the gate of Cathair Caedyn.

And as they did, drums boomed from the siege camp, and the roar of tens of thousands of muridach voices filled the air.

The battle was about to begin.

13

SIEGE MACHINERY

The drums echoed over Cathair Caedyn as Ridmark and the others climbed to the rampart atop the northern gate.

"How did the parley go?" said Krastikon.

"A complete waste of time," said Ridmark, shaking his head.

"Was that Qazaldhar with the muridach embassy?" said Kalussa, the Staff of Blades grasped in both hands. "I saw a man in a black robe..."

"That was him," said Calliande, voice grim. "It was as we suspected. Qazaldhar has been masquerading as the prophet of the Lord of Carrion to the muridachs, just as he pretended to be Taerdyn's advisor and Khurazalin feigned friendship with Prince Rypheus."

"Why go to such lengths?" said Seruna. "Such an undertaking must have taken decades."

"It is how the Maledicti do their work," said Calliande. "Lies and trickery and subterfuge and pulling strings like puppeteers. Perhaps they thought the New God might require an army of muridachs. Or maybe they thought the muridachs would prove useful in disposing of their enemies." She blinked, her eyes going hazy as she looked at the muridach horde. "The gray elves knew of the Kratomachar, so perhaps they wanted to eliminate anyone who knew of the potential threat. Certainly, that matches with how the Masked One has acted within Owyllain."

"The Masked One of Xenorium?" said Athadira, startled. Ridmark half-expected her to claim that the Masked One of Xenorium was no threat to anyone. "What does he have to do with the Maledicti?"

"They seem to obey him," said Ridmark, gazing at the activity in the siege camps. "The Maledictus of Air said that the Masked One was an apostle or a forerunner of the New God, just as John the Baptist was the forerunner of the Dominus Christus." Belatedly he wondered if the High Augur had ever heard of John the Baptist.

"That is impossible," said Athadira. "The Masked One was once the Arcanius Knight Cavilius, was he not? The Maledicti would not obey a human wizard."

"Unless they were using him as a weapon," said Tamlin, "as they used my father and the Necromancer."

"It is not a mystery we can solve now," said Calliande. "Look there, and there, and there." She pointed in succession to the gaps between the muridach camps.

"Siege towers," said Ridmark. The muridachs had been busy assembling wooden siege towers, and now dozens of the things were finished. Each one stood forty feet tall, fronted with bronze plates to deflect arrows and ballista bolts. At the top of each tower was a raised ramp of wood and bronze. When the tower reached the walls, the ramp would fall, the bronze hooks at its end digging into the stonework, and the muridachs would swarm onto the ramparts.

"They will have a challenging time getting those damned things up the slope," said Krastikon. "Especially as it steepens towards the base of the wall. The gray elves should have ample time to hit them with catapult fire."

"They might not," said Calliande, blinking. "Look."

The siege towers started to move, slowly at first, and then faster. They had huge wheels studded with bronze nails. Ridmark's first thought was that they were being pushed, perhaps by muridach soldiers, or maybe by some kind of war beast.

His second thought was that the huge towers were moving a lot faster than they should.

He spotted the muridach soldiers pushing the towers.

The muridach engineers had fashioned a sort of wooden harness behind the base of the towers, almost like the handles of a plow. Nearly fifty muridach soldiers pushed each tower, and even from this distance, Ridmark saw the blue gleam of dark magic in their eyes.

The muridachs pushing the tower were undead. The muridachs usually ate their dead, but instead, they had collected the soldiers slain in the skirmishes. Likely Qazaldhar himself or the muridach priests had animated the slain, turning them into beasts of burden. The undead soldiers would not tire, and they would feel no fear as the gray elves rained missiles upon them. Come to think of it, arrows would not hinder the undead soldiers at all. Magic would be the only way to stop them.

"Are...are those undead pushing the towers?" said Rilmeira, shading her eyes.

"They are," said Calliande. "Lord Rhomathar, I suggest that you order any wizards with skill in fire magic to focus their attention on the undead muridachs. They will be vulnerable to elemental flame."

"And have the catapults target the towers," said Ridmark. "We can destroy as many undead creatures as we like, but it will be harder for the muridachs to repair their towers than it will be for the carrion priests to raise new undead."

"Your counsel is sound," said Rhomathar, and the gray elves began to move along the walls. Swordsmen and spearmen moved to await the arrival of the towers. Once the towers reached the walls, the muridachs could charge in a rush, and the archers would thin their numbers first.

It likely would not be enough.

Ridmark turned to the others. "We'll fight as before. Tamlin, Calem, Krastikon, Third, Kyralion, and Magatai, with me. We can be of the most use breaking up any footholds the muridachs carve out the walls. Calliande, Tamara, Kalussa. Stay here with the Augurs, and stop as many of the siege towers from reaching the walls as you can."

Calliande nodded and tried to smile at him. "Good luck."

Ridmark nodded back, and Calliande turned and started a spell.

THE TOWERS REACHED the base of the hill and rolled up the slope, and the gray elves struck.

Every catapult on the northern wall released at once, the clang of their gears echoing through the city. Dozens of white stones soared through the air and rained on the advancing siege towers. Most of the stones struck the bronze shields covering the front of the towers and bounced away, though they left dents. Several punched through the towers in a spray of twisted metal and shattered timber. One ripped through the top third of a tower, causing the metal ramp to fall to the ground and leaving the tower useless.

But the other towers continued their steady advance, wobbling a little as the undead muridachs kept pushing, and the gray elven wizards unleashed their attacks.

A dozen balls of fire hurtled down the slope, leaving trails of smoke in the air. Athadira herself cast the large and hottest of the spheres. They struck the undead muridachs and exploded in their midst, and the creatures went up like kindling, withering in the grips of the magical fires.

Calliande unleashed her own magic, drawing on the Well of Tarlion and fusing the magic to the mantle of the Keeper. A shaft of white fire swept from her hand, and she clenched her will and focused it. The magic swept across a group of the undead, and they fell like cut grass.

Yet more undead rushed to take their place, and the towers kept inching forward. Given the large number of muridach priests, Calliande feared that Nerzamdrathus and Qazaldhar might have thousands of the undead to throw against the walls.

They would have more than enough undead to get the siege towers to the city.

Kalussa started using the Staff of Blades, hurling fist-sized spheres of blue crystal at the advancing undead. One by one her spheres shot through the heads of the undead muridachs, sending their headless corpses rolling down the slope. Every one of the spheres destroyed an undead creature, but there were so many that it was like trying to empty a lake with a spoon.

"Lady Kalussa!" said Tamara. "Aim for the wheels! Aim for the wheels!"

Kalussa blinked, frowned, and then her eyes went wide with understanding. She adjusted the Staff and began flinging spheres of crystal at the front left wheel of the nearest siege tower. The crystalline globes could punch through bone and flesh and bronze without slowing, and even the heavy wooden wheels of the siege tower proved no barrier. Kalussa sent six spheres drilling through the tower's wheel in rapid succession. Before she could throw a seventh sphere, the wheel splintered beneath the massive weight of the tower. The siege tower leaned into the damaged corner, then toppled onto its side with a massive crash and began rolling down the slope. It rolled right over the undead muridachs and disintegrated into broken lumber at the foot of the hill.

A new plan came to Calliande. The wheels were the towers' weak points. Even with their skill and coordination, the gray elves could not aim their catapults accurately enough to target the wheels. But Calliande could direct her magic at the ground beneath the towers, and a wheel was only as good as the surface beneath it.

"Tamara," said Calliande. "Do you know a spell of earth magic to soften ground into mud?"

"Yes." Tamara blinked her mismatched eyes and then grinned. "I used it to help my father's pigs cool off in the summer."

"A good use for the spell," said Calliande. "Let's see if we can find another one." She pointed. "That tower. The front left wheel since the slope is sharper in that direction. On three. Ready?" Tamara nodded. "One, two...three!"

Calliande cast the spell of earth magic, driving the power through the mantle of the Keeper to strengthen it. Tamara cast a similar spell, forcing it through her golden staff. They released their spells in unison, and Calliande's will focused on the ground beneath the tower's wheels. At her command, the ground grew softer, shifting from packed earth to liquid mud. Tamara's spell hit a half-second later, and her magic added to the effect.

The tower's front left wheel suddenly sank halfway into the mud and got stuck. The undead muridachs kept pushing, heedless of the obstruction. The tower tilted further into the mud, and the undead pushed again. This time it overbalanced, leaned to the left, and fell upon its side with a booming crash. The tower started to roll down the hill, breaking apart as it did.

Tamara whooped. "Let's do that again!"

"A good idea," said Calliande, and they focused their magic upon another tower while Kalussa hammered away with volleys from the Staff of Blades.

Yet there were too many towers. The gray elves unleashed magical firestorms, Kalussa smashed wheels, and Calliande and Tamara turned the ground into mud. Yet fully half the towers struggled up the slopes and reached the battlements. Behind them, columns of muridach infantry advanced, shields raised to ward off arrows from the archers.

The towers' ramps fell onto the battlements with a mighty crash, and the fighting began in earnest.

AS IT HAPPENED, Ridmark and the others were standing not far from one of the towers when the ramp fell upon the battlements with a crash. A mob of muridach berserkers charged out, howling at the top of their lungs. The berserkers had abandoned their double-bladed battle axes, likely because there would not be space to swing the enormous weapons. Instead, they carried one-handed war axes with long crescent blades. The axes would be vicious in the hand-to-hand fighting atop the walls.

Kyralion snapped off two arrows, killing a pair of the berserkers and sending their bodies falling off the ramp to join the dead below the walls. The rest of the creatures did not even seem to notice. Howling, they leaped off the ramp and threw themselves into the gray elves. The golden steel of the gray elves was stronger than the bronze blades of the axes, but the berserkers' heavy blows punched through gaps in the gray elves' armor and carved wounds.

Ridmark, Third, Tamlin, Krastikon, Calem, Magatai, and Kyralion raced to meet them.

Oathshield's power surged through Ridmark, giving him strength and speed. He slashed the soulblade before the nearest muridach could react, and he took off the berserker's head. Next to him, Third stabbed at a muridach, and the creature stumbled as her blades bit into flesh. Ridmark ripped Oathshield across the muridach's throat.

Krastikon leaped into the battle, purple lighting flickering up and down his armor as he drew on the magic of elemental earth. He had once been an Ironcoat, one of Justin Cyros's elite soldiers, and the Ironcoats had taken their name from the ability to sheathe themselves in spells of earth magic so thoroughly that no blade could touch them. Krastikon used that power now, making no effort to shield himself as he waded into the berserkers. The muridachs launched blow after blow that rebounded from his head and torso without leaving a scratch, and all the while Krastikon swung the Sword of Death with mighty two-handed blows. The dark blade passed through the muridachs, sending them in pieces to the ground.

Tamlin, Calem, Magatai, and Kyralion fought alongside each other. Magatai used his lightning-wreathed sword to stun the muridachs, and Kyralion's golden blade licked out and wounded them. Before their opponents could recover, Tamlin and Calem attacked with devastating blows from the Swords of Earth and Air. Nothing could resist the deadly edge of the Seven Swords, and pieces of muridachs fell to the ground, the stones of the battlements turning red with their blood.

Then they had cleared the muridachs away from the battlements, but more ratmen rushed up the ladders inside the tower.

"The ramp!" said Ridmark. "Tamlin, the ramp! Quickly!"

Tamlin and Krastikon answered his call, the Swords of Earth and Death rising and falling. The two swords slashed through the bronze ramp, and it fell loose and clattered against the ground. Yet the tower was close enough to the wall that the muridachs could leap from its top to the ramparts, and they did so, though both Krastikon and Tamlin slashed the creatures out of the air with their Swords.

"We've got to get that damned tower away from the wall!" said Krastikon, grimacing. "We...wait, what the hell are you doing?"

Calem ran past him and vaulted over the battlements, his white wraithcloak billowing behind him. As he had during the battle against the Necromancer, he used the wraithcloak's magic to become immaterial, landing on the ground below the wall without harm. He became solid once more and sprinted in a circle around the base of the tower, the Sword of Air slicing through the timbers. There were cracking and splintering sounds, and the muridach soldiers who had been running towards Calem began to flee.

The tower fell backward, and Calem leaped, becoming a wraith once more. The apex of his leap took him two-thirds of the way back up the wall, and he materialized long enough to kick off the wall. His momentum carried him the rest of the way up, and he solidified, vaulted over the railing, and landed on his feet.

"Well," said Krastikon. "That is one way to dispose of a siege tower."

"A mighty strike, Sir Calem!" said Magatai. "Magatai enjoyed the befuddled expressions on the faces of the enemy."

"Let's see if we can befuddle them some more," said Ridmark.

He jogged to the west, heading for the next siege tower.

THE BATTLE RAGED AROUND TAMARA.

Up and down the wall the fighting grew fierce. Over half the siege towers had been destroyed, and the Shield Knight and Tamlin had destroyed more, but enough towers remained intact for the muridachs to rush the ramparts. And the muridachs did, charging up the hill with shields raised over their heads. The gray elven archers cut them down like wheat, but there were so many of the creatures that the archers could not shoot them all.

And there were so many ratmen that some of them reached the ramparts and rushed towards the Augurs. The Keeper and the Augurs were clearly the most powerful wizards in Cathair Caedyn, and therefore the muridachs needed to kill them. Calliande, Kalussa, and the five Augurs kept throwing their spells at the towers.

It fell to Tamara and Rilmeira to keep the muridachs at bay.

A troop of muridach soldiers rushed towards them, and Rilmeira shouted and thrust out her hands. A cone of lightning burst from her fingers and swept across the muridachs, the arcs harsh and dazzling. The stench of burned muridach flesh filled Tamara's nostrils, but she ignored the odor and cast a spell of her own. A wave of acidic mist washed over the muridachs, and Rilmeira's lightning set it aflame. It burned off quickly, but that was enough to finish the muridachs, and their charred corpses fell smoking to the rampart, stark against the white stone.

"Good timing!" said Rilmeira, flashing a smile at Tamara. She smiled back at the gray elf. Tamara could see why Kyralion had fallen in love with her. She was pretty by the standards of the gray elven kindred, and she was brave in battle and skilled with magic. Pity that Kyralion had also fallen in love with Third.

Another pair of muridach berserkers charged, and Tamara cast another spell. Her golden staff flashed with purple light, and she took the weapon in both hands as her magic charged it with the essence of granite. She swung the staff, and the muridach raised its bronze axe with a lazy, contemptuous parry.

The creature's shock was absolute when the staff shattered the axe and struck with enough force to cave in its chest. The spell had given the staff the power of a striking boulder. The second muridach raised its sword, but Lord Rhomathar was faster. His golden sword blurred with the speed of an insect's wings, and the muridach fell dead off the ramparts and landed in the square below.

Quite a few muridach corpses were piling up down there.

Tamara looked around, trying to spot another foe, and Calliande's voice rang out.

"Be ready!" said the Keeper, her staff glowing with white light in her hand. "Qazaldhar and the muridach priests are getting ready to strike. Can you see them?"

"The Sight has shown me," said Athadira, keeping her haughty mien despite the battle, flickers of lightning dancing up and down her jeweled staff. "There, just beyond the foot of the hill."

"I can shield us from their attack," said Calliande, the white fire glowing brighter around her staff, "but you will need to hit them."

"The Augurs of the Unity of the Liberated," said Athadira, "are more than capable of..."

"The High Augur agrees," snapped Seruna. Athadira glared at her. "We will strike with elemental spells if your wards can turn aside their attacks."

"Lord Rhomathar will guard us against the foot soldiers while we work our spells," said Athadira, turning her gaze to the Lord Marshal. A troop of gray elven soldiers hurried closer, muridach blood glistening upon the blades of their swords. "Rilmeira will assist."

"Tamara, help them," said Calliande, taking her staff in both hands. "Kalussa, keep breaking as many wheels as you can."

Tamara started to agree, and then blue light blazed at the foot of the hill.

The Maledictus and the muridachs were casting their spell.

The blue light shone brighter and began to spin. Shadows flowed and twisted through the blue glow, and soon a vortex of shadow and blue fire whirled below. Tamara shivered at the sight of it. She did not have the Sight as Calliande and the Augurs did, but nonetheless, she felt the terrible power radiating from the dark magic below.

"It's awful," whispered Rilmeira. Tamara barely heard her over the howl of the battle.

Then the muridach priests struck.

A lance of shadow and blue fire, as large as one of the siege towers, screamed up the slope towards them. Tamara flinched, but Calliande shouted and struck the end of her staff against the ground, thrusting her free hand before her. A wall of white light rose up from the rampart, shimmering and translucent, and the lance of dark magic hammered into it.

There was a brilliant white flash, followed by a thunderclap. A gust of hot wind blew past Tamara, tugging at her coat and hair, and for an awful instant, she feared the force of the wind would blow her right off the rampart and to the square below. In all the ways she had died in her nightmares, she had yet to die of falling from a great height. But the wind faded away, and she saw blue-white light playing around the Augurs as they cast their spell. Tamara sensed the currents of power snarling around them, the magic centering on the High Augur's staff. Lightning crawled up and down the staff, and Athadira shouted and raised the weapon.

A lightning bolt screamed out of the cloudless sky and landed at the foot of the hill with an explosion. Two more lightning bolts fell in rapid succession, and Tamara saw the sudden consternation among the muridach priests. She wondered if the Augurs' lightning had destroyed Qazaldhar, but doubted it.

Another lance of dark magic shot up the hill, and Calliande recast her warding spell, raising the wall of pale light to defeat the attack.

The clang of metal against metal came to Tamara's ears, and she turned to the east. A mob of muridach soldiers had broken free from one of the siege towers and rushed towards the gate. Likely they had orders to open the gate, but they would also kill the Keeper and the Augurs if they could get away with it.

Tamara struck first, unleashing a wave of acidic mist that washed over the muridachs. The creatures staggered, screaming their rage and thrashing as the mist burned into them. Rilmeira raised her hand and cast a spell, and she called another of those cones of lightning that ripped into the muridachs. It also set Tamara's acidic mist ablaze, and the creatures screamed again. The combination of lightning and acid killed about half of them, and the rest were wounded.

Lord Rhomathar and the swordsmen charged into the fray, blades rising and falling, and finished off the muridachs.

There was another exchange of white light and blue fire, and then Calliande lowered her staff with a shuddering breath.

"The power is dissipating," she said, her voice hoarse with strain and fatigue. "I think you killed about a dozen of the muridach priests."

"Perhaps they have decided to conserve their strength," said Seruna. The old woman looked tired, and the black veins beneath her pale skin had grown starker. Tamara hoped the strain would not kill her. She seemed a voice of reason compared to Athadira's arrogance. A pity she was not the High Augur.

"Perhaps," said Calliande. She grimaced and shook her head. "Or they're preparing a second wave of siege towers, and they want to hold their powers in reserve."

Tamara looked up and down the walls and saw that all but four of the siege towers had been destroyed. Yet there was another wave of towers inching forward in the camps below, pushed by more undead muridachs.

"Perhaps we should follow their example," said Calliande.

The towers began rolling forward, and Tamara felt cold dread settle around her.

They had nearly repulsed the first wave of attack, but Tamara suspected the second would be even stronger.

As the sun dipped over the jungle to the west, Ridmark lowered Oathshield, breathing hard. His eyes burned with sweat and smoke, and his shoulders and knees throbbed with dull pain. His armor and clothes were spattered with blood, both muridach and gray elven, though as usual nothing stained his gray cloak.

Below the wall lay the smashed wreckage of the muridach assaults. Broken timbers and shattered stumps remained of the siege towers, and thousands of dead muridachs carpeted the slopes. The mingled stench of blood, muridach fur, and burned wood was hideous. At the edge of the jungle, the muridach siege camps seethed like an anthill. Ridmark saw them assembling more siege towers and some other machines that he did not recognize, and he had no doubt that the muridachs would launch another attack as soon as they were ready.

But for now, the first two waves had been repulsed.

Ridmark had come through the fighting unscathed, as had his companions. But nearly five hundred gray elves had fallen. Some had perished on the blades of muridach swords and axes. Many others had collapsed from exhaustion, overcome by the plague curse. Physical exhaustion lowered the gray elves' resistance to the curse, and many had collapsed in the middle of the fighting.

The gray elves had lost a tenth of their fighting force in the first day of fighting. In exchange, they had killed thousands of muridachs, maybe over ten thousand of the creatures, but that barely made a dent in the vast host of Nerzamdrathus.

Ridmark had been in many battles, had been on both sides of a siege.

But as he looked at the muridach siege camps, he realized that he saw no chance of victory for the gray elves.

14

REGRETS

Two days later, Calliande slept the sleep of utter exhaustion. Twice more the muridachs had thrown massive attacks at the walls of Cathair Caedyn, and twice more they had been repulsed at high cost. The gray elves had held beneath the storm of Nerzamdrathus's horde, though Calliande did not think they could last much longer. Too many gray elven warriors had been killed in the fighting, and there had not been enough defenders to begin with. So far, the muridachs had been content to launch their attacks against the northern wall. Had they attacked all four sides of the city at once, Cathair Caedyn would have fallen in a day. But perhaps not even the muridachs had enough workers and lumber to construct that many siege towers.

The magic and valor of the gray elves had held. And, Calliande had to admit, without her husband and her friends, the gray elves would not have held for nearly as long. Without the Shield Knight to rally them, the defense would have collapsed, and the muridachs would have gained a hold on the wall. Without the Swords of Earth, Air, and Death to break the towers' ramps, it would have cost far more lives to destroy the towers. Without Kyralion Firebow to rally the defenders again and again, to inspire the gray elves to follow him into the fighting, the muridachs might have swept the city's ramparts clean of gray elven warriors.

And without Calliande and Kalussa, many more gray elves would have died.

Calliande and Kalussa were the only people in Cathair Caedyn who could use the healing magic of the Well of Tarlion. There had been many gray elven wounded, but Calliande and her apprentice had focused on the mortally wounded gray elves, those would have died without assistance. Calliande was used to this kind of work, was used to pulling the agony of mortal wounds into herself again and again.

Kalussa was not. Yet the girl threw herself into the task, her face growing tight and strained and pale, her eyes glittering with exhaustion. Perhaps she did it as a distraction from her fears over Calem. For his part, Calem flung himself into the battle with grim efficiency, leaving hundreds of butchered muridachs in his wake, and he single-handedly destroyed nearly a score of the siege towers. It had likely taken thousands of muridach warriors and laborers to assemble the siege towers, and Calem alone had destroyed their work.

But for every muridach they killed, more and more seemed to take their place.

Calliande grabbed what few snatches of sleep she could in the moments between attacks. After they repulsed another wave of towers and she had healed several dozen warriors, Calliande had been so weary she could barely keep her feet. Ridmark had taken her to one of the empty houses near the northern square, and she had lain down and intended to rest for only a few moments.

Instead, she had fallen into a deep sleep, too exhausted even to dream.

When Calliande awoke, morning sunlight leaked through the windows. The room of white stone was empty, the furniture long ago removed, and she lay on a blanket against the wall.

There were no sounds of alarm, at least not yet, though the faint odor of rotting flesh from outside the walls came to her nostrils. For a moment Calliande lay motionless, fighting the bone-deep fatigue that lay upon her like an iron weight. Then she closed her eyes, took a deep breath, and reached for the Sight.

She sent it spinning north, seeking for her sons, and found them. Gareth and Joachim were still in Aenesium. Both sleeping, she thought. Still healthy, she could tell that much. She hoped Michael and Father Clement were looking after them. Gareth ought to be a page in the royal court by now. King Hektor would have marched against the Confessor, but he would have left a regent in command of Aenesium, and the Palace of the High Kings would continue the government of Owyllain.

Calliande hoped her children would stay safe.

She hoped they would forgive her for leaving them orphaned.

Because she saw no other outcome to this siege.

With her eyes closed, Calliande prayed to God, asking for guidance, asking for his protection over the city and the gray elves. She asked for protection for both Owyllain and Andomhaim.

And most of all, she prayed for her sons.

At last Calliande opened her eyes and sat up, thirst clawing at her throat and hunger twisting at her belly. At least the danger of starvation was remote. The gray elves' skill with both the elemental magic of earth and water gave them the ability to call forth fruits and vegetables from the ground with ease, and Calliande herself could summon enough ice to keep the city from dying of thirst.

The city would fall long before thirst or starvation became a problem.

She turned her head and saw Ridmark sitting next to her, back propped against the wall, eyes closed.

Calliande gazed at her husband. She thought he was sleeping, and the harsh lines of his face had relaxed somewhat, his blue eyes closed. Had there always been so much gray at his temples, the lines in his face so deep? Maybe they had, and she hadn't noticed. In so many ways, he looked no different than when he had charged through the fire to rescue her from that dark elven altar on the Black Mountain ten years ago.

But he was different now. They both were. Ten years ago,

Calliande hadn't known who she was, her memory lost behind a veil of her own magic. Ten years ago, Ridmark had been a grimmer and angrier man, determined to get himself killed in atonement for his wife's murder. It had only been ten years ago, but it seemed so much longer.

She wondered if Ridmark had ever imagined that their lives would end here, far from home in a land they had never heard of until a few months ago. Though given how he had spent years wandering the Wilderland in search of the Frostborn, perhaps he had always known he would die in battle.

Calliande had thought that he had been sleeping, but his eyes opened, and he smiled a little.

"How are the children?" he said in a quiet voice.

"Well, as far as I can tell," said Calliande. "I think they're both sleeping."

"A good idea, truth be told," said Ridmark.

Calliande shook her head. "I'm more hungry than tired."

"Thought you might be," said Ridmark. He reached to the side and picked up a wooden plate. On it lay several slices of bread and sausage and cheese, and he also had a wineskin. "I've never been a wizard, but you keep telling me that magic is hungry work."

"It is," said Calliande. The hunger pangs in her stomach got worse as she looked at the food, and she reached over and took a slice of bread and several pieces of sausage. "How many fat Magistri have you ever seen?"

Ridmark snorted. "About as many fat Swordbearers. Which is to say, none." Ridmark shook his head, took a bite of bread, and swallowed. "Not that Swordbearers tend to live long enough to get fat."

"No." Calliande took the wineskin, had a drink, and passed it to him. The strange gray elven wine burned against her tongue, but it wasn't strong enough to make her woozy, and it did quench her thirst. "And I suppose neither shall we." She sighed. "I wonder if Gareth and Joachim will ever find out what happened to us."

Ridmark was silent for a moment. "The siege isn't over yet. A battle is not decided until it's finished."

"No," said Calliande, "but sometimes the outcome is clear before the swords are even drawn. Sometimes battles are decided before they even begin."

"Sometimes," agreed Ridmark. "But we don't yet know if this is one or not."

She laughed. "I'm not one of your soldiers. You don't have to keep my morale up."

"You're my wife. Keeping your morale up is more important."

"I'm glad you think so," said Calliande, taking another piece of bread.

"And maybe you're right," said Ridmark. "Maybe this is the end. You know I am not an optimistic man. But to lie down and wait for death...no, that is not in my nature." He looked at her. "If it was, I suppose I would have died years before I met you."

"And I would be the worse for it," said Calliande. She thought for a moment. "Dead, for that matter."

They ate and drank in silence for a while, passing the wineskin back and forth between them.

"Do you think we can win?" said Calliande at last.

Ridmark shook his head. "Probably not. There are just too many muridachs and too few gray elves. If we could find a way out of the city, I would take it. Better that than letting the Seven Swords fall into the hands of Nerzamdrathus. Though he can only wield one of the Seven at a time. The muridach horde would likely tear itself apart fighting over the three Swords, and they would never come anywhere near Owyllain itself. But Cathair Caedyn is probably going to fall."

"That is not cheering," said Calliande.

"No," said Ridmark. "But if Nerzamdrathus or Qazaldhar make a mistake, it could fall apart on them. You know what the muridachs are like. This horde is being held together by fear of the Great King and reverence for the prophet of the Lord of Carrion. If we can kill Nerzamdrathus, the muridach lords will likely tear each other apart before Qazaldhar can reestablish control. And if we can destroy Qazaldhar himself...I suspect he's the one keeping Nerzamdrathus on the throne of the Great King. Without the Maledictus of Death watching his back, one of the muridach lords might get ambitious and assassinate him, or Nerzamdrathus might make a mistake."

"I wish I had your confidence," said Calliande.

Ridmark shrugged. "It is a simple problem. Either we die fighting, or we win and see our sons again."

She nodded and then smiled. "It is simple when you put it that way." She paused. "I don't suppose Third knows anything new?"

"No," said Ridmark. "If she's destined to somehow save or destroy the gray elves, I can't see how. Perhaps the Augurs simply misinterpreted the vision." A dry note entered his voice. "You've met the High Augur. The woman would die before she admitted to making a mistake."

"Aye," said Calliande. It would have been easy to blame Athadira for the doom of the gray elves. But even if the High Augur had the battlefield skill of Alexander the Great, the wisdom of Solomon, and the courage of Arthur Pendragon, that still wouldn't have been enough.

She wondered what Kyralion felt as he watched the end of his people approach. Perhaps the Romans upon Old Earth had felt that way as they saw the barbarians march through the gates, or perhaps the knights of Arthur Pendragon had felt the same after the High King had fallen to his bastard son's treachery.

All Calliande felt was the overwhelming desire to see her sons once more.

But they were far away, and there was work to do.

"Thank you for bringing me food," said Calliande, finishing off the last of the bread.

Ridmark nodded. "If I didn't, you would neglect to eat and work yourself until you fell over."

"I would not," said Calliande.

He raised an eyebrow. "When was the last time you ate properly?"

"It was...ah..." She frowned. "We weren't yet inside Cathair Caedyn."

"My point exactly," said Ridmark. He got to his feet. "Ready?"

"Yes," said Calliande, rising. She hesitated. "Ridmark, if today doesn't go well, if the muridachs..."

"I know," said Ridmark, taking her hand.

She hugged him and rested her head against his shoulder for a moment, and then they left and walked to the walls.

"I THOUGHT WE WERE FINISHED," said the gray elven warrior, shaking his head. Beneath his winged helm, the face was pale and glistened with sweat, the black veins stark. Yet the gray elven warrior stood without trembling. "If you hadn't attacked those muridachs, I think we might have broken."

Kyralion shook his head. "You did well. My presence was merely fortunate."

Third watched Kyralion as he talked with the defenders manning the wall.

At the moment, the city was quiet, though that would not last for long. In the distance, she saw the muridachs swarming over another set of siege towers, heard the distant noises of hammering and sawing. Soon the muridachs would be ready to launch another assault. Probably in another two or three hours, unless Third missed her guess.

She had gone to the ramparts to watch for the inevitable attack and had come across Kyralion talking to the swordsmen and the archers. Third ought to have been watching for the muridachs. Instead, she listened to Kyralion, fascinated. She had never seen him quite like this. All the soldiers of Cathair Caedyn knew him, respected him. And he was lifting their spirits, she could tell. The Unity meant that the gray elven warriors knew each others' fears and doubts, and just looking over the battlements at the muridach horde was enough to inspire entirely rational fears and doubts.

But they couldn't read Kyralion's thoughts and emotions, and he projected confidence, talking to the men as if he was certain of victory.

And it worked.

The soldiers seemed more confident after he talked to them, and faced the battlements with new resolution. Third found herself following him, listening to his speeches.

About an hour later, they found themselves alone near the base of one of the towers.

"I have never heard you speak that way," said Third.

Kyralion sighed and leaned against the battlements, the weariness he had been hiding flashing across his face. "I usually do not. Only when I was with the scouts, when we led sorties against our enemies. Here in Cathair Caedyn, not being part of the Unity is a liability. But in the Illicaeryn Jungle, in the Takai Steppes, or the marshes of the xiatami, it does not matter. All that matters is the ability to fight and the skill to scout."

"And you are very good at both," said Third.

"Yes," said Kyralion. He shook his head and laughed a little. "When I was a child, I hated that I was not part of the Unity. All my life, I remained bitter over it."

"And you are not any longer," said Third.

"I am not."

"What changed?" said Third.

"The plague curse at first," said Kyralion. "All my kindred were affected, save for me. Then I found the Shield Knight and the Keeper, and my immunity to magic was useful several times." He let out a long breath. "And now at the end of the Liberated, it is useful again." He looked at Third. "Can you see how frightened they are?"

"Yes," said Third. "It is obvious."

"It is the Unity," said Kyralion. "It lets us...it lets them communicate so efficiently in battle, but it has liabilities, does it not?" Third nodded. "All their fear is communicated through the Unity. All the women who lost husbands and sons in the last three days? Their grief is communicated through the Unity. Fear is bad enough. Despair is worse."

"But they see you, and they cannot read your mind," said Third.

"And you are confident, and show no fear, and some of that is communicated to them and spreads through the Unity."

"It is as you say," said Kyralion. He shook his head. "Having the fear of thirty thousand gray elves inside your head must be a torment. Once I was jealous of my kindred. Now I pity them."

Third frowned. "Why did your ancestors create the Unity if it is such a liability?"

Kyralion shrugged. "It was not always so. When we fled to the Illicaeryn Jungle to escape the Sovereign's hosts, we were desperate. The Unity let us survive and withstand the Sovereign's armies." He shrugged again. "Or maybe the Augurs were wrong. Maybe the Sovereign did not need to bother with the last remnants of our kindred. It fell to the muridachs, the scavengers, to finish us off." He shook his head once more. "Perhaps we were desperate. Perhaps the Sylmarus took pity on us, the last shard of a civilization that once ruled an entire continent."

"Or maybe," said Third, "the first Augurs never thought that all your people would be gathered inside the walls of a single city, where their fears could feed endlessly upon each other."

"Maybe that was it," said Kyralion. "I suppose it does not matter now."

"No," said Third. "Why do you say the Sylmarus took pity upon the gray elves?"

"It is a living thing," said Kyralion. "With an ancient and powerful mind. Or so the Augurs say. I have never felt it myself. Yet I look at the Sylmarus, and I feel the age of it."

"I had the strangest feeling," said Third. "I looked at it, and I felt like it was looking back at me."

"Then you understand," said Kyralion.

"Are you confident?" said Third. "Do you think we can win this siege?"

"No," said Kyralion. "But neither do you."

"I do not," said Third. She hesitated. "I...am sorry."

Kyralion blinked. "Whatever for?"

"The Augurs sent you to find me, and you did," said Third. "They thought I could save the Unity, but they were wrong. I regret that you spent so much effort on something that was futile."

"No," said Kyralion. His golden eyes met hers. "I regret bringing you here. But I do not regret meeting you."

A shiver of tension went through her nerves.

"Nor do I regret meeting you," said Third.

He tried to smile. "Even if I was bold enough to kiss you in the jungle?" He shook his head. "That was inappropriate. It was not fair to you, or to..."

"Rilmeira?" said Third. He looked back at her. "Perhaps it does not matter. We are all about to die, most likely. Since we are speaking of regrets, perhaps it is better to be bold than to add to their numbers."

"Perhaps," said Kyralion.

They stood in silence for a while, watching the seething muridach host.

"I do not regret it," said Third. She took a deep breath. "No one... no one ever kissed me before, Kyralion. But...you did ask Rilmeira to marry you, did you not?"

"Twice," murmured Kyralion. "Once, years ago. Then right before I departed to find the Shield Knight and the Keeper."

"She was foolish to have refused you," said Third. Jealousy was a new emotion, and she did not care for it.

"She did not," said Kyralion. "Her mother did. As High Augur, she has the authority to adjudicate such things among us. She would not let her daughter marry the freak, and she said so to my face." Dismay went over his expression. "I wondered if Athadira lied about her vision from the Sylmarus to get rid of me. If so, then you have come to your death for no reason."

Third shook her head. "Lord Amruthyr spoke of the same vision in Cathair Selenias. He would not have lied about it. He said that the Augurs had lied to you when they failed to mention that you were also in the vision."

"As if I could save the Unity," said Kyralion. "I cannot even govern my own heart." He looked at her and sighed. "I find myself caught between two admirable women, and..."

"Kyralion," said Third. "Perhaps you are. But one of those women is far better suited to you than the other. Rilmeira could have your children, and she loves your people as you do. I can do neither."

"No," said Kyralion. "Athadira will never let Rilmeira marry as she chooses." He hesitated. "That was why I did what I did, in the jungle." The memory of his kiss flashed through her mind. "It seemed better to focus on what was in front of me than to cling to the memory of something that could never be. But you are right. It does not matter now. Almost certainly the muridachs will overcome us. All that remains, I expect, is to die well."

Third smiled at that.

Kyralion blinked. "You find that a cheering prospect?"

"Somewhat," said Third. "There were centuries where I dreamed of nothing but death. The prospect does not faze me. I have already lived too long and seen too much. But I wish things could have been different. I wish your people might have had a different fate." She gazed at him. "I wish..."

Distant drums boomed over the muridach host, and the shouts and cheers of the ratmen echoed over the city.

"They are coming again," said Kyralion. "More siege towers. And some kind of device I have not seen before."

"We had better join Lord Ridmark and the others," said Third.

Kyralion nodded, and together they jogged for the northern gate as the defenders rushed to take their posts.

15

THUNDERBOLTS

Ridmark and Calliande stepped out of the house and into the street near the northern gate, and he heard the distant booming of drums.

"Here they come again," said Ridmark.

Calliande nodded, and together they ran for the stairs to the ramparts. Already the city was echoing with the sound of muridach drums, the gray elves moving with their usual eerie coordination. Swordsmen and archers rushed to the walls, and Ridmark and Calliande ran through the northern square.

They reached the rampart over the gate to see that Lord Rhomathar and Rilmeira were already there.

"Shield Knight," said Rhomathar. "The Augurs are on their way. I have also sent messages to your companions to join us." He glanced to the west. "And Lord Kyralion and Lady Third are on their way."

"Good," said Ridmark, looking over the battlements. Already he saw another wave of siege towers rolling forward, nearly a score of them. The muridachs had been laboring through the night. And behind the towers came...

Ridmark blinked.

"What is that?" said Calliande.

In the center of the line of towers rolled a strange device that Ridmark did not recognize.

His first thought was that it was a siege tower, but it was at least four times higher than the other towers. Its base was set in a wooden frame with a dozen wheels, giving the unwieldy thing far greater stability than it would have had otherwise. Nearly three hundred undead muridachs pushed the thing, heaving it up the slope. The huge machine had to weigh a great deal, and even the strength of hundreds of undead muridachs only managed to move it forward a few feet at a time.

But the device kept rolling toward the gate.

"Some kind of ram?" said Rhomathar.

"No," said Ridmark. "No, it's too tall and cumbersome for that. I think it's a..."

"A ramp." Third approached with Kyralion, her eyes on the device. "You can see the hinges at the bottom." She pointed, and Ridmark saw the bronze mechanisms at the bottom of the machine. "When it gets close enough, the front will swing down and land on the battlements, and the back will collapse. The muridachs will charge up the ramp and onto the walls."

Ridmark turned as Tamlin and Tamara and the others joined them. Magatai was grinning as he held his bow. Likely the Takai looked forward to another long day of killing muridachs.

"That is a siege ramp, is it not?" said Krastikon.

"It is," said Ridmark. "Kalussa, can you destroy the wheels? If that thing gets close to the wall, we're going to have problems." If the broad ramp reached the battlements, the muridachs could swarm up to the ramparts in a mass. The gray elves might not be able to repulse an attack of that size.

Kalussa hesitated and then shook her head. "Not quite yet. It's still too far away. Once it gets a few hundred yards closer..."

There was a flare of blue light and a pulse of dark shadow near the siege ramp. Ridmark wondered if the muridach priests and Qazaldhar were about to launch a magical attack, but a dome of shadow and flickering blue light settled around the ramp.

"A warding spell," said Calliande. "A powerful one. Strong enough to block both magical attacks and catapult missiles."

Ridmark scowled. "That's it. They're centering their next attack around that damned ramp." He heard the rustle of robes as Athadira and the other Augurs joined them. "They'll use the siege towers to hold our attention, and once they're engaged, the main attack will come up the ramp." Already he saw columns of muridach infantry forming up behind the towers, shields held ready to deflect arrows.

Clangs echoed over the wall, and the gray elven catapults released. The stones soared over the hillside and smashed into the approaching siege towers. The catapult crews had refined their tactics since the first attack, adjusting their aim to target the top third of the towers. Most of the stones bounced away, but the tops of three towers exploded into a spray of splinters and twisted bronze. The rest continued their steady climb, pushed by the unwavering strength of the undead muridachs.

"Let us show them the folly of this plan," said Athadira, raising her hand as she cast a spell. Lightning snarled around her fingers.

"Wait!" said Calliande. "Don't…"

Athadira finished her spell, and a bolt of lightning screamed out of the sky towards the siege ramp. It struck the dome of shadow and blue light around the ramp and then rebounded with a thunderclap.

It hurtled right towards the rampart over the gate.

Calliande was already moving. She thrust out her hand, and a pale wall of light appeared before them. The lightning blast struck the ward and vanished with a spray of sparks, the wall of light winking out of existence a half-second later.

For the first time, Athadira looked taken aback.

"Don't," said Calliande again, letting out a long breath. "The ward will reflect any spell back at its caster."

"I see," said Athadira.

"I can probably work through it given enough time," said Calliande, "but the ramp will get to the wall long before that."

Arrows began hissing from the battlements as the archers

targeted the columns of muridach infantry behind the advancing towers.

"Maybe it would be better to let the ramp get here," said Tamlin. "With the Swords of Earth and Death and Air, we can cut it apart. It won't do the muridachs any good then."

"I don't see that we have any other choice," said Ridmark. He looked at Calliande and the others. "We ought to focus on destroying as many of the siege towers as we can. They'll get here before the ramp."

Krastikon nodded. "Most likely they want the towers to hold most of the defenders in place."

"Then let's spoil their plan," said Ridmark, lifting Oathshield. The blade flickered with white fire. "Come."

TAMLIN TOOK one last look at Tamara, and then followed Ridmark, Third, Calem, Krastikon, Kyralion, and Magatai as they headed west along the battlements, preparing to meet the siege towers as they drew nearer. Ridmark looked grim as always, and Third and Kyralion impassive. Magatai was humming to himself, but the mad halfling laughed as he fought. From what Tamlin had observed of the Takai halflings, they regarded cowardice as the worst of all sins, and glorious death in battle as the highest of virtues.

Tamlin supposed that the muridachs would give Magatai an ample chance for a glorious death.

They stopped a few hundred yards down the western side of the northern wall, watching as the towers and the huge ramp creaked closer. The catapults smashed several more towers, and the archers sent volleys of arrows into the advancing muridach soldiers. Both Magatai and Kyralion used their bows, sending arrows with unerring accuracy into the enemy. Dead muridachs tumbled down the slope of the hill. If this siege went on long enough, perhaps the muridachs could simply scale the walls upon a ramp built from their own dead. Knowing the muridachs, they would not scruple from such a tactic.

White fire, lightning, and elemental flame blazed from the ramparts over the gate as Calliande, Kalussa, and the Augurs unleashed their spells. Tamlin saw one of the towers wobble, fall to the side, and roll back down the hill, breaking into pieces as it did. Likely Kalussa had blasted away its wheels with the Staff of Blades. More catapult stones arced overhead. Some bounced away from the sides of the towers, but others punched through in explosions of splinters.

As before, about half the towers were destroyed before they reached the walls.

The other half drew ever closer, and Tamlin saw the bronze ramps start to shift.

"All right," said Ridmark. "Here they come. Remember, focus on the ramps. Third and Kyralion and Magatai and I will hold them back while the rest of you cut the ramps loose. Calem, if you want to do that trick with the wraithcloak, do it, but don't take unnecessary risks. If you get killed outside the walls, the muridachs will gain the Sword of Air, and we'll have to contend with that as well."

Calem nodded, bringing up the silvery blade of the Sword. "I will not take any unnecessary risks."

Krastikon snorted. "Yes, the necessary risks will take up all our time."

The nearest tower shuddered to a stop, and the bronze ramp swung down with a massive clang. As before, a mob of muridach berserkers charged out, war axes in hand. Tamlin cast a spell, a forked bolt of lightning bursting from his fingers. It struck the two berserkers in the lead, and the creatures stumbled, screaming as the lightning coiled around their bodies.

In their moment of hesitation, Ridmark and Third moved.

The Shield Knight attacked first, swinging Oathshield in a blur of white fire. His two-handed blow took off a muridach's head. Third moved like a serpent, her blue swords flashing, and the second stunned muridach collapsed dead, its throat torn open. Magatai and Kyralion released their arrows in unison. Magatai's shaft punched through the throat of a berserker, and Kyralion's arrow found the eye of another.

Tamlin charged a half-step behind Krastikon. Purple light flared around Krastikon's shield as he called on earth magic, and he stepped into the fray. The muridachs howled and focused on him, axes rising and falling as they attacked, but Krastikon's earth magic deflected their strikes. Tamlin took the opportunity of their distraction to attack, and the green blade of the Sword of Earth carved through two muridach berserkers. Next to him Calem struck, the Sword of Air slicing silvery arcs through the air.

Tamlin pushed through the charge, and he slashed at the bronze hooks holding the tower's ramp to the battlements. There were four hooks, and he cut through the first two. The ramp shifted with a metallic rasp, and a berserker leaped off the shifting ramp with a howl, axe raised to strike. Tamlin dodged around the first swing and snapped the Sword of Earth up to parry the second swing. The bronze axe shattered against the blade, and the berserker stumbled, a look of confusion on its rat-like face.

The confusion worsened as Magatai stepped up and plunged his lightning-wreathed sword into the muridach's chest. The creature gurgled and died, and Tamlin jumped past it, intending to sever the remaining hooks. But Krastikon beat him to it, and the Sword of Death rose and fell in two quick chops. The ramp shuddered again, and swung down to clang against the side of the tower, three more muridach berserkers falling to their deaths against the corpse-strewn ground below.

"Calem!" said Ridmark. "Wait a..."

Calem seized the battlements and vaulted over them.

Ridmark sighed.

A moment later the tower shuddered and fell over, and a heart-beat after that, Calem sprang back over the rampart, wraithcloak swirling around him.

"I told you not to take any unnecessary chances," said Ridmark.

"I did not, Lord Ridmark," said Calem. "There was no chance that the muridachs could catch me."

Magatai boomed a laugh. "Well-spoken."

"Then let's catch some more muridachs," said Ridmark, and Tamlin followed him as the Shield Knight led the way to a knot of gray elves struggling against muridach berserkers.

TAMARA WATCHED THE BATTLE, clutching Amruthyr's staff with both hands.

Exhaustion flickered through her, but she kept it at bay. She had joined her powers with Calliande several times, using the magic of elemental earth to turn the ground beneath the towers' wheels to thick, wet mud. That had been enough to tip over several of the siege towers, the engines falling to add their debris to the wreckage littering the hillside. They had also tried the same tactic on the siege ramp, but it had failed. The machine was simply too massive and had too many wheels attached, and the undead muridachs kept pushing it. The ramp rolled right through the pools of mud and kept going.

Fighting raged up and down the ramparts to the west and the east. The gray elves and the Shield Knight were destroying the towers one by one, the archers sending flights of arrows into the charging muridachs, the ballistae hurling steady volleys of bolts into the enemy. Yet to judge from the tense expressions of the Lord Marshal and the High Augur, the gray elves were losing too many warriors.

And there were not many reserves left to fight against the siege ramp as it crawled ever closer.

Kalussa cursed and threw a crystalline sphere from the Staff of Blades. It struck the shivering dome of blue light around the ramp and shattered into nothingness.

"Don't bother," said Calliande. "It looks like dozens of muridach priests combined their powers with Qazaldhar to create that ward. If I had more time, I could batter it down, but we do not."

"Any minute the ramp will fall," said Rhomathar. "It will probably impact there, between the western gate tower and the first watch tower. I will summon what reserves we have, and we shall try to hold until the Shield Knight and the bearers of the Swords can destroy the ramp."

"Perhaps our powers alone shall be sufficient, Lord Marshal," said the High Augur with a disdainful sniff. Tamara resisted the urge to roll her eyes. When the city fell, Athadira's final words to the muridach who killed her would likely be a lecture on how the creature failed to appreciate the honor of killing the High Augur of the Liberated.

"I doubt that very much, High Augur," said Rhomathar. "I..."

"The ramp is falling!" said Calliande.

Tamara looked up as the massive wooden ramp started to fall forward, and she noticed two things at once.

First, dozens of Throne Guards in their crimson armor clung to the wood. The berserkers were dangerous, but the Throne Guards were worse. They would make deadly shock troops, and they might carve a foothold onto the ramparts.

Second, the ramp was coming down at the wrong angle.

There was something wrong with the western hinge at the base of the ramp, and it was leaning in that direction as it fell. For a wild moment, Tamara wondered if the muridach engineers had made a mistake and the siege ramp would collapse under its immense weight. But while the engineers had erred, they hadn't erred that badly. The line of the ramp slid to the west as it came down, and...

Tamara realized that it was going to land right on top of her.

"Move!" shouted Calliande. "Move, move, move!"

Tamara threw herself to the left just in time. The huge ramp landed with a clang against the ramparts about two yards in front of her, the slab of wood and bronze striking with enough force to pulverize a portion of the battlements. The impact knocked Tamara from her feet, and she landed hard, the breath exploding from her lungs.

Dozens of Throne Guards leaped from the ramp, swords raised high, and Tamara realized that the ramp had cut her off from Calliande and the Augurs and the others.

Which meant that for at least a moment, she had to face dozens of Throne Guards by herself.

And if she did not move right now, she was going to die.

Tamara threw herself back to her feet, her back and knees throbbing from the effort. A dozen Throne Guards rushed towards her, howling for blood, and Tamara cast a spell. A wall of white mist erupted from her hands, and the muridachs screamed as the acidic mist washed over them. Yet with her power divided among so many, the mist did little harm, and the sigils of blood sorcery upon the crimson armor of the Guards blunted her power further.

The creatures stumbled for a step, and then came at her.

Tamara cast another spell, her staff glowing with purple light as she charged it with the essence of elemental earth. She swung the staff with both hands, and the nearest Throne Guard raised its blade in a parry, no doubt expecting the blow to rebound from its sword.

Instead, the strength of the blow shattered the sword and broke every bone in the muridach's right arm. The Throne Guard roared in sudden pain, and Tamara drove the end of her staff into its stomach. A dent the size of her head appeared in its crimson cuirass, and the creature doubled over. Another Throne Guard sprang at her, and Tamara thrust her staff. Her blow clipped the side of the muridach's head, and that was enough to bend the creature's neck to the right at a ninety-degree angle.

Yet the rest of Throne Guards came at her, and Tamara retreated, trying to hold the spell over her staff. There was no way she could fight them all, but they were wary of her now, too cunning to let their blades come in contact with her glowing staff. Any moment now they would rush her.

This, Tamara realized, was how she was going to die.

A strange sense of calm settled over her. She had already died so many times in her nightmares. But what would this do to Tamlin? He had already seen her die twice. Would he have to see her die a third time?

The muridachs started forward, and Tamara brought her glowing staff up.

~

THE DEAFENING CRASH of the falling ramp filled Tamlin's ears, and he risked a quick look to the east.

The siege ramp had reached the walls, and he saw that the ramp had fallen against the ramparts. A second ramp had been lowered to the ground behind the first, and a mob of muridachs sprinted towards it. They would charge up the ramp and swarm over the walls. The archers directed their fire towards the advancing muridachs, as did several of the ballistae, but it was like throwing a bucket of water into a forest fire. There were simply too many muridachs, and unless that ramp was destroyed soon, the muridachs would flood the walls of Cathair Caedyn. Or they would seize control of the gate, and once they did, the city would fall.

"Let's go!" shouted Ridmark. "Destroy that ramp!"

They ran along the ramparts to the east as dozens of Throne Guards boiled off the ramp, and Tamlin saw a sight that made his blood run cold.

Tamara was fighting them alone. The ramp had come down at an angle, cutting her off from any help, and the Throne Guards moved towards her. The golden staff glowed purple in her hands as she retreated, but the muridachs saw the danger of her weapon. Step by step they advanced, and once they were ready, they would overwhelm her and kill her.

Tamlin sprinted forward as fast as he could, heedless of the dead muridachs and gray elves underfoot.

He had seen her die twice before, once in Urd Maelwyn, and again in Trojas. He could not see her die again.

He could not lose her again, not now, not after he had found her.

Tamlin cast a spell as he ran, and he jumped, drawing as much of the magic of elemental air as his strength would allow. The spell picked him up and enhanced his leap, and Tamlin soared over the ramparts, over the top of Tamara's head, and he crashed into the muridachs.

His downward blow slashed through the neck of a Throne Guard, and the creature's headless corpse fell to the ramparts, spurting blood. Tamlin landed, his knees buckling to absorb the impact of his landing, and he stabbed the Sword of Earth in several rapid blows, killing two more Throne Guards.

The other muridachs struck back. An axe blow hit Tamlin in the chest. His gray elven armor deflected the sharp edge, but the Throne Guard was hideously strong, and the force of the impact knocked him back and probably cracked a rib in the process. The edge of another axe gashed his left forearm, and a third hit the crest of his helmet. His helmet held, but there was an explosion of white light behind his eyes, and Tamlin staggered back.

"Tamlin!" shouted Tamara.

He took the Sword of Earth in both hands and attacked, ignoring the pain and the dizziness. He had fought for his life countless times in the Ring of Blood while in pain and terrified, and this was no different.

No, it was different. Tamara was behind him, and if he failed, the Throne Guards would kill her.

Tamlin could not let that happen, no matter what the cost.

TAMLIN FELL into the muridachs like a thunderbolt, and he started killing with the Sword of Earth. Yet Tamara could see that he was overmatched, that the Throne Guards would kill him in a matter of seconds. She had no spell that could help him. If she tried to use her acidic mist, she would only hurt him, and the muridachs would finish him.

No! She had dreamed about him for years, and his face had been the only comforting thing in her nightmares. How could she lose him so quickly? She had never even kissed him. She had seen his face in the nightmare where she had been stabbed from behind, and in the more recent dream where she burned in the courtyard of the Blue Castra of Trojas.

That dream...she had been someone else in that dream. Tirdua, the adoptive daughter of Theseus of Trojas. A separate life, but through some mystery of magic the same woman. It wasn't possible, yet it had happened. Tirdua had lived an entirely different life than Tamara, had known things that Tamara had not, had possessed knowledge that she did not.

Including the magic of elemental air.

Tamara had always known how to use the magic of elemental earth. The knowledge had been in her head as if someone else had learned how to use it and put it there.

Or if she had learned and forgotten.

And in her horror and desperation as she saw the Throne Guards swarm towards her beloved, another thing that she knew without knowing how appeared in her mind.

Tamara cast a spell, snarling with rage and urgency, and the light around her staff changed from purple to silver as for the first time in her life, she drew upon the magic of elemental air instead of earth.

She thrust her staff, and a snarling coil of blue white-lighting leaped from the end and screamed forward. It slammed into the muridach nearest to Tamlin, and the lightning struck with enough force to kill the Throne Guard, stopping the creature's heart in its chest. The lightning bolt leaped from Throne Guard to Throne Guard, killing five of them before the power of the spell drained away.

Tamlin froze, glanced back at her in astonishment, and went on the attack.

Tamara tried to pull together magic for another spell, but utter exhaustion rolled through her. She had never cast such a powerful spell before, and it was all she could do to keep standing. More Throne Guards rushed from the ramp, and she saw muridach soldiers reaching the bottom and starting to ascend, shields raised to ward off arrows.

She needed to cast another spell, or she and Tamlin were going to die together.

Oddly, she found that thought less distressing than the prospect of them dying separately.

Then white fire flashed before her eyes, and the Shield Knight crashed into the Throne Guards. Ridmark Arban moved fast, so fast he had to be drawing upon his burning sword for speed, and two of the Throne Guards fell dead. Third, Calem, and Krastikon charged after him, and Kyralion and Magatai came to a stop next to her, bows coming up.

"Fear not, Tamara Earthcaller!" boomed Magatai, sending two arrows into the muridachs. "We shall righteously smite the muridachs and send them fleeing back to their stinking caves!"

One of the muridachs' heads exploded as a crystalline sphere shot through it, and Calliande and the Augurs broke through from the other side of the ramp. The Augurs called more lightning, their bolts killing the Throne Guards, and Calem and Krastikon rushed to the edge of the ramp. They started hacking while Ridmark and Third protected them, and soon their two Swords had sliced through the section of the ramp against the battlements. The entire pile of wood and bronze shifted, and with a terrible rasping sound, the ramp slid against the outer face of the wall and crashed to the ground, killing a score of Throne Guards in the process.

The gray elves rushed to repulse the remaining muridachs.

TAMLIN DROPPED TO ONE KNEE, breathing hard, sweat and blood trickling down his face.

He could not seem to get his breath back, and the ramparts were spinning around him. He had been wounded enough times in his life to realize that he probably had a concussion and a damaged rib that was pressing against one of his lungs. Probably his right lung, from the agony in his side. He really ought to get up and help the others deal with the remaining muridachs, but he could not quite get his feet underneath him.

Metal rasped against stone, and a dark staff appeared in his vision, held in the right hand of a scowling young woman with blond hair.

"For God's sake, Tamlin," said Kalussa. "You keep trying to get yourself killed. Hold still."

Tamlin could not quite get enough breath to answer, and Kalussa dropped to one knee before him, put her left hand on his right temple, and cast a spell. White light flared around her fingers, and an icy chill washed over Tamlin. Kalussa went rigid, her teeth clenched, the cords standing out in her neck. The chill intensified, and then faded away.

The pain in his head and his side vanished, as did the gash in his arm and a half-dozen other minor scrapes he had acquired without noticing.

"Huh," said Kalussa, shaking her head. "That does get easier after time. That must be why women can have more than one child."

"Thank you," said Tamlin, getting to his feet and trying to clear his spinning head. "I...Tamara, where's Tamara? She..."

He started to turn, and Tamara slammed into him, her arms wrapping around him, and Tamlin almost fell over.

"You're all right?" said Tamara, looking him over with her mismatched eyes. "You're all right." She looked at Kalussa. "Is he all right?"

"Yes," said Kalussa. She looked pleased with herself. "Thanks to my healing spell."

"Thank you," said Tamara. "Thank you, Lady Kalussa. I thought he was about to die."

Kalussa swallowed, looked at Calem, and then back at Tamlin. "That leap was either the most gallant or the most foolish thing I have ever seen in my life."

"Why couldn't it be both?" said Tamlin, grinning at her.

Kalussa rolled her eyes but smiled as Tamara stepped back.

"Tamara." Tamlin turned his head and saw Calliande hurrying over. "That lightning bolt. Was that you?"

"Yes," said Tamara. "I have no idea how I did it. The spell...the spell just appeared in my head. Like I had learned it before but had forgotten it."

"Tirdua could use air magic," said Calliande, "but not so powerfully. I wondered if you could regain memories or even skills from your other lives. It seems like you can. Maybe..." She shook her head. "We can worry about it later."

"Yes," said Third, pointing over the damaged battlements. "We are about to have more immediate problems."

Tamlin looked over the walls. Most of the siege towers had been destroyed or pushed back, though several were still against the walls, the muridachs being driven back step by step. Yet the second wave of siege towers was already rolling forward, and in their midst came a huge siege engine that looked like a barn on wheels. Another flickering blue haze surrounded it, and the thing jerked forward foot by foot, pushed by hundreds of undead muridachs.

He did not recognize the device at first, but then a chill washed through him.

"They have a ram," said Third.

16

THE WOMAN IN FLAMES

R idmark stared at the approaching ram.

The damned thing looked like a barn on wheels. But that was only the housing for the ram, built to shield the muridachs wielding the huge weapon from arrows and ballista bolts. Inside the housing, Ridmark saw dozens of thick bronze chains hanging from a wooden framework. A half-dozen enormous tree trunks had been bound with bronze bands to form the shaft of the ram, and the head was an massive ball of polished stone. Sigils of blood sorcery burned on the stone head and the shaft of the ram, no doubt to give the weapon greater strength and power. Within the housing were hundreds of undead muridachs, packed next to each other, and they pushed the weapon forward.

It wasn't moving fast. But it was already crawling up the hill, and in another few moments, it would reach the gates. Even as Ridmark looked, light and shadow snarled around the ram, encasing it in a dome of twisting blue light and darkness.

"They've warded it," said Calliande, blinking as she used the Sight. "And stronger than before." She shook her head. "That siege ramp was a test, I think. To make sure we couldn't penetrate the warding spells. Now that they know we can't breach that spell, they're going to throw the ram against the gates."

"If we use the catapults, perhaps, in a coordinated barrage," said Rhomathar, "we might be able to overcome the spell..."

Calliande shook her head. "The spell is strong enough to withstand it. If we throw any magic at it, it will reflect the spells back at us. If I try to use the mantle of the Keeper to break the spell, it will repair itself faster than I can do damage. There are too many muridach priests feeding power into the ward, and Qazaldhar's skill is controlling the power. If I had a few hours, perhaps, I might be able to prepare something to shatter the ward, but I don't."

And as Ridmark looked at the advancing ram, at the next wave of siege towers, he realized that Cathair Caedyn and the gray elves only had a few hours left.

Ridmark knew in his bones that this was the attack that was going to break Cathair Caedyn's defense.

"We do not have enough soldiers left to man the walls and to stop a breach in the gates," said Rhomathar. "The wall was the only thing that kept the muridachs from bringing their full numbers to bear against us. Once the gate is breached..."

"We should focus on destroying as many of the siege towers as we can," said Ridmark. "If we can keep most of the muridachs away from the walls, perhaps you can concentrate your soldiers in the northern square and hold the gate."

Even as he said it, he realized how unlikely that was.

"And it might be wise," said Calliande in a soft voice, "to prepare to flee the city. Or to have the women and children flee through the southern gate while we fight on the northern wall."

"But the muridach host surrounds the city entirely," said Rhomathar. "We cannot break through."

"Some might," said Calliande. "Because if they stay inside the walls, they're going to die."

"It hardly matters," said Athadira. "The Sylmarus is the heart of the Unity, and once the Maledictus of Death enters the city, he will finish his evil work and destroy the Sylmarus. The Unity will be shattered, and any gray elves who survive shall be broken wanderers. No. If the Liberated are to be overcome, it will be here."

Ridmark wanted to argue, but he didn't see the point. The odds of any gray elves getting past the muridach horde were slim to none. A few, perhaps? Maybe a handful. Perhaps they would live with hope for a few moments longer before they died.

As he had told Calliande, the battle wasn't over until it was over. Qazaldhar and Nerzamdrathus might yet make a mistake. If they did, the gray elves could turn the tide of the battle.

But the Maledictus and the Great King had not yet made any mistakes. They had tied a noose around Cathair Caedyn, and they were squeezing it tighter. Tens of thousands of muridachs had fallen in battle, but that hardly mattered. Nerzamdrathus could replace them twenty times over.

There seemed no way to stop the muridach horde.

$\sim$

THIRD GAZED at the approaching ram and siege towers, a cold sense of inevitability falling over her.

This, it seemed, was the end.

She saw no way to stop it. Third supposed if she got out of the city and away from the influence of the Seven Swords, she could use her power to travel and try to assassinate the Great King or the Maledictus of Death, but she doubted that even she could do it. The Throne Guards surrounded the Great King, along with the muridach priests, and Third did not think she could defeat one of the Maledicti on her own.

Or she could use her power to escape the Illicaeryn Jungle entirely.

No. Third would not abandon her friends. Mara and Arandar had sent her to find the Shield Knight and the Keeper. Third would not return to Andomhaim to tell them how she had abandoned her friends to their fate.

And death did not daunt her. Hadn't there been long centuries where she had yearned for death? Centuries where the only thing that she wanted more than death was to kill her father?

No. If this was where God ordained for her to die, and then she would die well, with a ring of muridach corpses around her before she fell.

She looked at Kyralion and felt a stab of regret. Which was strange, because she knew he was in love with Rilmeira, that he had only been drawn to her because Rilmeira was unavailable. Kyralion started to turn towards Third.

And then he stopped.

Third looked around, wondering what had caught his attention.

Except he stayed motionless.

And the siege towers and the ram had stopped. Had the muridachs given up? That didn't make any sense. If they stopped there, the catapults would take the towers apart.

Third looked to the defenders to see how they had reacted.

They, too, had gone motionless.

Third stared at them in confusion, and then she saw the light.

She raised her hands.

The veins were glowing with blue fire beneath her skin. They did that when she used her power to travel several times in rapid succession, when she drew on the fiery song that filled her blood, the song that had taken the place of the Traveler's will. She heard her song now, loud and strong, rising within her like a storm.

She also heard the song of the Sylmarus. Her mind interpreted the mighty tree's aura as a song of infinite beauty and terrible sadness, stronger than any dark elven lord's aura. It was powerful, but it was sick, and it was dying. The song had been in her mind constantly for the last few days of battle, and she had grown so used to its presence that she had forgotten it was there.

But she heard it now. Suddenly she couldn't think of anything else.

Third turned and stared at the Sylmarus.

The gentle green glow of the veins drew her attention, and she stared at them, staring past the branches, past the tumorous black growths, past the crumbling bark, to the light at the heart of the ancient tree.

The song swelled in her thoughts, and the notes melded together, becoming...

Words.

LOST CHILD.

The song thundered through her head.

"What?" said Third, astonished.

LOST CHILD.

"I am not a child," said Third, baffled. "I have not been a child for a very long time."

BY THE MEASURE OF THE HUMANS YOU ARE ANCIENT. BUT I AM AS OLD AS THIS WORLD.

The strange voice sounded so weary. A mountain that had seen epochs come and go might sound that way if it could speak.

"I suppose all the gray elves must seem as children to you," said Third.

I SAW THIS MOMENT IN THE TAPESTRY OF TIME. I SAW YOUR BIRTH FORETOLD. YOUR MOTHER, A SLAVE. YOUR FATHER, A DARK ELVEN LORD. I SAW YOUR PATH WOULD BRING YOU HERE, TO THIS MOMENT WHEN THE GRAY ELVES ARE ABOUT TO DIE. YOU WOULD BE THE WOMAN OF FLAMES, AND YOU WOULD STAND AT THIS JUNCTION IN TIME.

"Then help them," said Third. "If you are so powerful, then help them."

I CANNOT. I JOINED THE LIBERATED TO ME, AND THEY ARE BOUND TO MY AURA. THE MALEDICTUS HAS POISONED ME, AND I CANNOT FIGHT THE CONTAGION. IT SPREADS THROUGH ME, AND WHEN IT KILLS ME, THEY TO SHALL DIE. THAT IS WHY WE ARE ONLY SPEAKING NOW. IT HAS TAKEN ME THIS LONG TO GATHER THE STRENGTH.

Third frowned. "If it made the gray elves so vulnerable, then why did you let them create the Unity?"

BECAUSE I TOOK PITY ON THEM.

Third blinked.

Pity...

Forgiveness. A conversation about forgiveness flickered at the edge of her memory, but she could not quite recall it.

"Why?" said Third.

YOU DO NOT UNDERSTAND? YOU CROSSED HALF THE WORLD TO FIND YOUR FRIENDS.

"They were my friends," said Third. "I owed them. I would still be an urdhracos without Ridmark. You owed the gray elves nothing."

THEN YOU DO NOT KNOW WHAT IT IS TO TAKE PITY ON THE PAIN OF ANOTHER?

"Likely not," said Third. Another half-forgotten memory tugged at her mind. Something about pity... "But if you cannot help the gray elves, why are we having this exceedingly strange conversation?"

I CANNOT HELP THEM. YOU CAN.

"How?" said Third. "How can I possibly help them? I am just one woman. I can kill a thousand muridachs, fight until a ring of the slain lies at my feet, and it will still make no difference to the outcome."

YOU ARE UNIQUE.

"Perhaps," said Third, "but I am still just one woman."

YOU AND YOUR SISTER ARE UNIQUE. IN ALL THE LONG HISTORY OF THIS WORLD, IN ALL THE HISTORY OF THE ELVES, THERE HAVE NEVER BEEN DARK ELVEN HYBRIDS WHO HAVE NOT BEEN SLAVES. YOUR SISTER WAS THE FIRST, AND YOU WERE THE SECOND. YOU ALONE CAN SAVE THE GRAY ELVES, LOST CHILD.

"Then tell me how," said Third. "Who must I defeat?"

YOURSELF.

"That does not make any sense," said Third. "Do you mean I need to face myself, the dark elven half of my blood? I did that nine years ago."

NOW YOU MUST FACE YOUR ENTIRE SELF.

"Once again, that fails to make any sense," said Third.

ONLY BY SAVING YOURSELF CAN YOU SAVE OR DESTROY THE UNITY. YOU MUST FACE YOURSELF. YOU MUST FACE

WHAT YOU HATE MOST ABOUT YOURSELF. ONLY BY FACING THE SHADOW INSIDE YOURSELF CAN YOU ACT.

Third hesitated. This didn't make any sense at all, and the battle was about to begin. She didn't have time to waste in riddling talk with a giant tree. Ridmark and the others needed her help.

And yet...

They were going to lose the battle, weren't they?

That giant damned ram was going to smash the gates, and the muridachs would swarm into the city and annihilate the gray elves. The Sylmarus would likely die as well. Qazaldhar would go out of his way to destroy the ancient tree. If Third fought alongside Ridmark when the battle began, he would die, she would die, and everyone else would die.

If there was a chance, even the slightest chance, that she had a way to alter the outcome of the battle, she had no choice but to take it.

Third said a brief prayer in the silence of her mind. She did not pray often. Brother Caius had told her that the Dominus Christus forgave all sins. But Third wondered if her soul, tainted by dark elven blood and centuries of murder, was something she wanted to bring to the attention of God.

"What must I do?" said Third.

COME TO ME IN THE HEART OF THE CITY. YOU WILL THEN SEE WHAT YOU MUST DO.

The song grew fainter, and the world exploded back into motion around her. The siege towers and the great ram continued their slow advance. The defenders rushed to their positions on the walls. Calliande and the Augurs were discussing how best to use their spells to take down as many of the siege towers as possible. Third caught her breath, her heart racing in her chest.

Ridmark was staring at her.

He would have noticed if something was amiss. He knew her too well.

"Are you all right?" said Ridmark in a low voice.

"No," said Third. "No. I...do not know how to explain it. But I think the Sylmarus has summoned me. I do not know why."

"Is it anything I can help you with?" said Ridmark.

Third hesitated. "No. I do not know what it is. But I think I need to go alone."

Ridmark nodded. "We'll wait for you here, then." He tried to smile. "I'll save you a muridach or three."

Third was gripped by the sudden overwhelming feeling that she would never see him again.

"Maybe even four," said Third. "I will return as soon as I can."

"Good luck," said Ridmark.

Third took a deep breath, nodded, and left the ramparts before anyone noticed. She crossed through the square and headed for the street leading to the Court of the Sylmarus. The great tree filled her vision, and its song seemed to be somehow summoning her...

"Third!"

It was Kyralion's voice.

She turned and saw Kyralion and Rilmeira running towards her.

"I have to do this," said Third. "I do not know why, I do not understand why, but..."

"I know," said Kyralion.

"The Sylmarus spoke to me," said Rilmeira, her voice filled with wonder. "Through the Unity. It was as if time froze around me, and the Sylmarus spoke directly to me. It...it said I had to take Kyralion with me at once, that we had to accompany you. Or...or..."

"Or," said Kyralion, voice grim, "that you would die, and the Liberated would perish soon after."

"I do not understand what is happening," said Third, "but let us find out together."

Kyralion nodded, and the three of them walked down Cathair Caedyn's central street and came to the Court of the Sylmarus.

Third stepped off the flagstones and onto the grass, gazing up at the massive trunk of the Sylmarus. The Court was deserted, with all the gray elves either on the walls, attending to their duties elsewhere, or sitting in their homes and waiting for the end. The green glow beneath the bark held Third's attention, and the Sylmarus's song grew louder in her thoughts, more compelling.

She walked across the grass, past the gnarled roots thicker than a house, and headed for the base of the tree.

"Lady Third?" said Rilmeira, but she and Kyralion followed her.

At last, Third stopped at the foot of the tree, the green light flickering and dancing beneath the trunk. Driven by some suggestion of the song, she reached out and touched the bark. It felt warm beneath her hand, almost feverish.

And then it shivered beneath her fingers.

A hole appeared in the tree, opening like an iris, and expanded into a tunnel that led into the depths of the Sylmarus, glowing with a gentle green light.

"I never knew that was there," said Rilmeira, her voice stunned.

"Nor did I," said Kyralion.

The song pulsed in Third's head, inviting her onward.

"I do not think it existed until just now," said Third. She looked at the two gray elves. "If you desire to turn back…"

"No," said Kyralion. "You are the woman of flames from the Augurs' vision. I brought you here. This is my responsibility. And if Lord Amruthyr was right, then I must come with you."

"I will come with you," said Rilmeira. She looked at Kyralion. "This…this might be the end of all of us. If we are going to die, I want to do it standing at your side." She looked at Third as if pleading for permission. "Please. I…I need to do this."

Third nodded. "Then let us see the end of this."

She took a deep breath and walked into the tunnel, Kyralion and Rilmeira following her.

17

RUIN

The drums boomed over the city, growing louder as the siege towers and the ram drew closer.

And with them came the muridach host.

Calliande watched as the siege camps emptied, tens of thousands of muridach warriors forming up at the bottom of the hill. Their plan was obvious enough. The siege towers would reach the wall, and the muridach shock troops would hold the defenders in place. Then the ram would reach the gate and tear it open.

And once it did, the muridach horde would charge into Cathair Caedyn.

Calliande, Kalussa, and Tamara unleashed their magic, focusing their powers on the siege towers. As before, Calliande and Tamara used spells of elemental earth, turning the ground to mud and unbalancing the towers. In short order, they sent two towers tumbling down the slope, smashing to pieces as they rolled. Kalussa hurled volleys of crystalline spheres at the towers, blasting their wheels into splinters. With the full might of the muridach priests and the Maledictus of Death shielding the huge ram, the Augurs were free to turn their magic against the towers. They called blasts of magical lightning that splintered the towers like trees, or firestorms that consumed both the timbers of the towers and the undead muridachs pushing them. It helped that there were so many dead muridachs and so much wreckage left over from the previous assaults. The towers had to take a careful path, weaving their way around the smashed debris of earlier attacks.

Calliande and the others wiped out half of the towers before they reached the walls.

But the other half came to the ramparts nonetheless, lowering their bronze ramps onto the battlements with a crash.

And still the ram crawled ever closer to the wall.

RIDMARK CHARGED INTO THE FRAY, Oathshield drawn back to strike.

Tamlin, Calem, Krastikon, and Magatai followed him into the fighting. He keenly missed the presence of Third. Ridmark could always rely on her, and they had fought alongside each other so many times that they knew what the other was thinking without the need for speech.

He hoped the Sylmarus had a good reason for summoning her.

Ridmark also missed Kyralion's presence. The gray elf was an unfailingly accurate archer.

And there were no shortage of targets pouring from the siege towers.

A mob of muridach berserkers leaped from the nearest tower, swarming down the ramp and charging into the waiting gray elves. The golden steel of the gray elves clanged against the bronze axes of the muridachs, and in the initial crash of combat, Ridmark saw four muridach berserkers and two gray elven swordsmen fall, dead before they hit the ground.

He attacked, sweeping Oathshield around, and opened the throat of the nearest muridach berserker. The creature stiffened and collapsed to the ground, thrashing as it choked on its own blood, and Ridmark stepped past it to kill a second. A third muridach leaped at him, only for Magatai's arrow to land in its throat.

By then Tamlin, Calem, and Krastikon were past him. The three bearers of the Seven Swords ripped into the muridachs like a knife through butter. Krastikon went first, his shield flickering with purple light, and he deflected and avoided the strikes of the berserkers. Tamlin and Calem came next, moving with speed and skill, and the blurring blades of the Swords of Air and Earth left slain muridachs in their wake.

Then Ridmark broke through and stood at the base of the ramp. A pair of berserkers came at him, and Ridmark parried, deflecting the blows of their axes against Oathshield's blade. He sidestepped, dodged around another blow, and brought Oathshield hammering down, burying the soulblade in the nearest muridach's skull. Using the augmented strength the soulblade granted, Ridmark wrenched the blade free in a spray of blood and turned to face the second muridach.

The creature started to bellow, but then a green sword flashed and took off its head. Tamlin did not slow, and his second swing severed two of the four bronze hooks holding the ramp to the battlements. Calem got the other two, and the ramp fell back against the tower with a scream of stressed hinges.

"Good work!" said Ridmark, looking at the battles raging along the western side of the northern wall. A dozen more siege towers had made it to the ramparts, muridachs pouring down the ramp.

They had done well against the first tower, but there was far more to do.

And the ram crawled ever closer to the gate.

TAMARA THREW another sphere of lightning, aiming for the siege tower.

Or more specifically, at the bronze ramp attached to the tower.

A score of spells related to controlling the magic of elemental air had swum to the surface of her mind after the attack of the siege ramp, and Tamara used those spells now, throwing her powers into the battle against the muridach horde. With the staff of Lord Amruthyr, she could strengthen her attacks with magical lightning, and she had figured out a way to amplify her spells further.

Bronze conducted lightning quite well.

The whirling sphere of lightning struck the ramp and exploded into dozens of crawling fingers of blue-white light. The dozen muridachs packed onto the ramp thrashed and jerked as the lightning stabbed into them, and three of the creatures lost their balance and fell to their death.

A half-dozen more perished when the gray elven archers sent a volley of arrows into the muridachs at close range. Tamara was drawing together power to strike again when the Augurs cast their spell. A bolt of lightning screamed out of the sky and hit the tower, blasting its top third to smoking kindling. The bronze ramp went flying, spinning over and over, and landed with enough force to decapitate two muridachs running up the hill.

Hundreds more rushed past the decapitated ratmen, converging on the towers remaining against the wall.

Next to Tamara stood Calliande, both hands grasping her staff, purple fire playing along its length. The Keeper threw spells of elemental magic, far stronger than Tamara could manage even with the golden staff. She conjured sheets of sleeping mist that rolled over the muridachs on the ramps, and they fell unconscious to their deaths. Or Calliande cast spells of elemental fire that exploded across the tops of the siege towers, setting them ablaze. For all the time and effort that Calliande devoted to healing magic, she could cause a tremendous amount of destruction when she put her mind to it.

On Tamara's other side Kalussa used the Staff of Blades, sending a steady stream of crystalline spheres in all directions. Once the towers had reached the walls, she had changed her focus, attacking the individual muridachs instead of the towers themselves, and the crystal spheres punched through the creatures and their armor without slowing.

Any other army, Tamara thought, would have broken and fled under the force of the defense. The gray elves and their Augurs alone were formidable, and with the aid of the Shield Knight and the Keeper and their allies, they were devastating. How many muridachs lay slain outside the walls of Cathair Caedyn? Thirty thousand? Maybe even fifty thousand?

It hardly mattered. That was barely a tenth of Nerzamdrathus's army.

And the ram was almost to the gates.

The housing was so tall that it almost reached the battlements. Had Tamara wanted, she could have jumped from the ramparts and landed atop the thick, bronze-plated planks of the housing without injury. That would have been foolish. The hazy dome of shadow and blue light writhed and swirled around the ram, and Calliande said that jumping onto it would be like throwing yourself against a stone wall. A few of the archers had loosed arrows at it, only for the shafts to shatter. One of the bolder gray elven wizards had thrown a bolt of fire at it, only for the blast to hurtle back at him. The unfortunate wizard had barely gotten out of the way in time.

A shudder went through the rampart beneath Tamara's boots.

The ram's housing had crashed against the gate.

Another band of muridachs emerged from a nearby siege tower, and Tamara focused her attention on them, hurling another sphere of lightning that knocked the creatures from the ramp. She started to draw together power for another spell, focusing her will on the tower.

The ramparts heaved beneath her.

Tamara staggered forward a step, planting the end of her staff against the ground to keep her balance. A tremendous crashing noise filled her ears.

"What the devil was that?" said Tamara.

"I don't know," said Kalussa, looking around. "I think..."

There was another shuddering jolt, another ringing crash.

"That is the ram striking the gates," said Calliande. "They're about to break through."

～

Tamlin cut another muridach warrior in half and turned, intending to bring the Sword of Earth to bear against the bronze hooks of the ramp.

But he saw that there was no need. Krastikon and Calem were already there, slicing through the hooks with ease. The ramp shuddered and fell to slam against the side of the tower, and the gray elven swordsmen cut down the few remaining muridachs.

Tamlin stepped back to catch his breath, blinking the sweat from his eyes. Another tower, they needed to take down another tower. There were still too many of the damned things against the walls. Worse, the muridachs were starting to carve footholds into the ramparts. Too much longer, and they might be able to secure large sections of the wall. If that happened...

A booming clang rang over the city, and the wall shuddered beneath Tamlin.

"What was that?" said Calem, looking at the sky.

"The ram," said Ridmark, his voice grimmer than usual. "They're at the gates. We need to go to the northern square. If we're going to hold them off, we'll do it there."

Tamlin nodded and followed the Shield Knight as he ran along the ramparts.

A peculiar sort of icy calm settled over him.

Tamlin realized that he was almost certainly about to die. They were in a trap from which there was no escape. The fact did not daunt him, and he even felt at peace.

He had found Tysia again.

Tamlin just wished he could have unraveled the mystery of the New God, could have freed his mother and learned her secrets.

Perhaps he would have a shot at taking the head of that damned Great King or the wretched Qazaldhar before this was over.

Ridmark came to a stop in the northern square and saw that the defenders were already gathering behind the gates of golden metal.

The five Augurs were there, along with Lord Rhomathar and the most powerful wizards of the gray elves. All the reserves stood in lines through the square, swordsmen in front, archers behind. Calliande, Kalussa, and Tamara stood with the Augurs, staring at the gate. The doors themselves were dented from the hammering of the ram, and even as Ridmark looked, another boom rang out, another dent appearing in the reinforced doors.

They bulged open a crack, and through it, Ridmark saw muridach berserkers waiting to strike.

"Why are the Augurs here?" said Ridmark as he joined Calliande. "They should move to a safer location."

Athadira must have overheard him. "This is our home, Shield Knight. We shall not quail from its defense."

"The gates are about to break," said Calliande. "If our most powerful wizards strike when they do, we can hold the muridachs back for a little while longer." She hesitated. "Has Third…"

Ridmark shook his head. "The Sight has shown you nothing?"

"No," said Calliande. "I don't even know where she is."

Ridmark nodded as the ram boomed again. He supposed this was the end. Perhaps the Augurs and Lord Amruthyr both had misinterpreted their visions. It seemed that their visions had not shown the possible salvation of the Unity and the gray elves, but their final destruction. Maybe hope had infected their interpretation, hope beyond hope that somehow the tide would turn.

But it would not, and Ridmark and his wife and his friends would die here with the gray elves.

He looked at Calliande and saw the same realization in her eyes. Tamara reached out and took Tamlin's right hand. Kalussa and Calem were staring at each other. Ridmark regretted that he had brought them here, regretted that he had led them to their deaths, but he could not see what he could have done differently. Maybe nothing. Maybe everything.

The ram boomed, and the doors screeched.

"One more hit, I think," said Rhomathar, lifting his sword. "Be ready!"

Ridmark took a deep breath and raised Oathshield. When the fighting grew fiercest, when they were about to be overwhelmed, he would unlock the power of the Shield Knight. Perhaps Nerzamdrathus or Qazaldhar would be foolish enough to lead the assault in person, and Ridmark could cut them down, weakening the muridach host before it turned north to Owyllain.

The doors exploded open, and the muridachs charged screaming into the square.

The wizards answered at once, lightning and fire and ice screaming through the gate and into the charge. Hundreds of muridach warriors died in the blink of an eye, but hundreds more rushed forward. And as they did, Ridmark heard a distant roaring sound, a roar that was getting louder.

Tens of thousands of muridachs were cheering, and they were charging for the broken gate and the remaining siege towers. The final defense of Cathair Caedyn was about to be swept aside in a wave of muridach fury.

Ridmark charged to meet the enemy, Oathshield drawn back to strike.

18

BLOOD OF THE DARK ELVES

I t was like walking through an empty blood vessel.

The strange tunnel led deeper into the heart of the Sylmarus. Third walked in front, Kyralion and Rilmeira behind her. She felt an overwhelming urge to draw her swords, which was ridiculous. There couldn't possibly be any enemies inside the tree.

But the sense of danger would not leave her.

The tunnel's walls were smooth, unmarked living wood. It reminded Third of some of the natural caverns of the Deeps, tunnels created over the millennia by the flow of water. It was cool and dry within the tunnel, and in the distance, she heard a steady pulsing, drumming sound.

Like a heartbeat.

Veins and fingers of that gentle green light glowed in the walls and the ceilings, providing ample illumination as the tunnel turned and twisted deeper into the Sylmarus.

"Something is strange," said Rilmeira.

"Unquestionably," said Kyralion.

"No," said Rilmeira. "I mean...the Sylmarus is huge. But we've already walked much farther than should have been possible. At least a mile. The Sylmarus isn't that large."

"No," said Third. "Magic is at work here." She thought for a moment. "Rilmeira. When the Sylmarus summoned you, what did it say?"

"It just said that the time had come," said Rilmeira. "That I needed to find Kyralion and bring him to you. Ah...what did the Sylmarus say to you?"

Third shook her head. "Many things. I did not understand most of them. It said that the moment had come to save or destroy the gray elves, that I would have to face the darkness within myself. I do not know what that means. Presumably it thinks that I will need you both to help me."

"It is a great honor," said Rilmeira in a soft voice. "The Sylmarus has only ever spoken to the Augurs."

Third let out a breath. "Then perhaps the Sylmarus could have warned the Augurs about the muridachs sooner. Or about Qazaldhar and his plague curse."

"I suppose that is the entire reason I am here," said Rilmeira. "The Sylmarus could not speak directly to Kyralion, since he is not part of the Unity..."

KYRALION.

Third froze. It was the same voice as before, but far louder. For that matter, she heard it with her ears, not inside of her skull.

Kyralion looked around uncertainly. "Did...I just hear that?"

"I think we all did," said Third.

"It is the voice of the Sylmarus," said Rilmeira, fresh awe in her expression. She reached out a tentative hand and touched the smooth wall of the tunnel.

YES. I HAVE WAITED LONG FOR ONE LIKE YOU, KYRALION.

"Why?" said Kyralion. "I am not part of the Unity. I have always been outside of it."

BECAUSE AN OUTSIDER IS NECESSARY. THE UNITY HAS CRIPPLED YOUR PEOPLE. THEY CANNOT ACT OUTSIDE THE CONSENSUS OF THE UNITY. THEY LOOK NOT OUTSIDE THE BOUNDARIES OF THE ILLICAERYN JUNGLE. THE UNITY IS FLAWED, AND ITS FLAWS HAVE WEAKENED YOUR PEOPLE.

"If the Unity was flawed," said Third with some asperity, "then why did you create it?"

BECAUSE I KNEW NOT THAT IT WAS FLAWED. BECAUSE WITHOUT THE UNITY, THE SOVEREIGN WOULD HAVE DESTROYED THE LIBERATED LONG AGO. I KNEW THE WOMAN IN FLAMES WAS COMING. I KNEW SHE WOULD HAVE THE POWER TO SAVE OR DESTROY THE UNITY. BUT I KNEW SHE NEEDED A GUIDE. SHE NEEDED SOMEONE OUTSIDE THE UNITY, SOMEONE ABLE TO IGNORE ITS CONSENSUS.

"Me," said Kyralion. "Then what must we do?"

SOON YOU WILL COME TO THE HEART OF THE UNITY. THERE THE WOMAN OF FLAMES WILL DECIDE YOUR FATE. BUT FIRST, SHE MUST FACE HERSELF.

"Why?" said Third, irritated. "If you want to save the gray elves, then let me pass without the damned games."

I CANNOT. IT IS IN THE NATURE OF THE MAGIC AROUND THE HEART. YOU MUST FACE YOURSELF. I AM SORRY FOR THIS ORDEAL, BUT YOU MUST FACE IT.

"And what must I do?" said Kyralion.

YOU MUST SAVE HER.

Third waited, but there was no further speech from the Sylmarus.

"Riddling talk," she muttered. She gave an irritated shake of her head. "Let us keep going. If the Sylmarus can offer any aid against the muridachs, better to find it sooner rather than later."

She led the way forward, the tunnel twisting and turning through the great tree. The green lights in the walls grew brighter, and the strange sound of the heartbeat became louder. The heart of the Unity? What did that mean?

Third didn't know, but she suspected that she was about to find out.

The tunnel sloped downward, and then widened. It opened into a vast hall of living wood, the walls gnarled and knotted. Green light glimmered and shone within the wood, and Third looked around.

"If there was an empty space this large within the Sylmarus," said Third, "the tree would have collapsed long ago."

"The Sylmarus has great magic," said Rilmeira.

The heartbeat grew louder, sounding almost like the beat of the muridach war drums.

"Plainly," said Third. "We..."

Everything went black.

Third froze. Her first reaction was annoyance. Was the Sylmarus going to amuse itself by playing games with the lighting? Yet not everything had gone dark. Third lifted her hands and found that she could see herself just fine. She still felt the floor beneath her boots.

"Kyralion?" she said.

There was no answer in the darkness, the echoes of her voice fading away.

Third took a step forward, and another voice came from behind her.

"There is no one here to help you, daughter."

Every inch of Third's skin crawled with revulsion, and she whirled.

A dark elven lord stood a dozen yards behind her.

He was over seven feet tall, his face pale and stark, his eyes filled with a bottomless void. He wore blue dark elven armor, like Ridmark's, but far more ornate and adorned with silver reliefs. A winged helm of blue dark elven steel protected his head, and a black cloak had been flung back from his armored shoulders. A longsword of the same blue metal rested in his right hand, and shadows and blue fire twisted around the fingers of his left hand.

She knew him. She knew him as well as she knew herself, and the sight filled her with hatred as hot and searing as molten steel.

"Mara killed you," spat Third.

The dark elven lord who had once been known as the Traveler laughed at her. "Death has no hold over me, daughter. I am a god! And I am your lord and master!"

"You are not a god!" snarled Third. "You were a fool with delusions of grandeur and you are dead, you have been dead for ten years!"

This had to be a trick. Some damned trick of the Sylmarus. Yet it looked so real. And the hatred for the man who had tormented her for all those years exploded through Third's head like a storm.

The Traveler's mirth turned to rage faster than a sane mind could have managed. "You are mine, daughter. You were always mine! Now fall to your knees before your god!"

His song exploded through her thoughts. Her mind interpreted the aura of a powerful dark elven lord as a song, and the Traveler's song echoed through her, beautiful and horrible, wondrous and terrible.

And to her horror, Third felt it start to drown out the song of her own blood, felt her knees start to buckle.

No! This wasn't real. Her father was dead, her father had been dead for years, slain in Khald Azalar at Mara's hand...

Perhaps this was an illusion, but the hatred was real.

And the hatred gave her strength.

Third screamed and yanked her swords from their scabbards, her teeth bared in a snarl.

"I said to kneel!" thundered the Traveler. "I am your god, and I command you to kneel!"

"Come and make me," spat Third.

The Traveler's fury intensified, and then it turned back to mirth once more.

"Gladly!" he said, raising his longsword. "Then you have gotten ideas above yourself? You think you are anything more than my slave? I shall teach you otherwise."

He strode forward, and the dark cloak rippled behind him. Except it wasn't really a cloak, it was thousands of coils of shadow stretching off into the darkness. Like he was walking at the center of a vast, ambulatory web.

Third ran towards him, swords drawn back to strike, and the Traveler raised his left hand to cast a spell. She drew on her power, traveled, and reappeared behind him, both her swords stabbing for his back. The Traveler whirled, and her swords clanged against her father's blade. His face became a cold mask, and he stalked after her, his longsword rising and falling like a blacksmith's hammer. He was stronger than Third, quick as a serpent, and he had immense dark magic. But she was just as fast, and she could do something that he could not.

He lifted his left hand again, and Third traveled a half-second before the spell would have withered her to a lifeless husk. Again, she appeared behind him, but the Traveler had anticipated the movement, spinning around to parry her attacks. The coils of shadow behind him seemed to writhe and snap like ropes caught in a gale.

"You thought you knew pain before, daughter?" said the Traveler, laughing as he stalked after her. "It will be as nothing to what you will know now. You were foolish to have friends. I will kill them in front of you. Their deaths will take days. Do you wish to listen to the Keeper sob as her children beg for the mercy of death? Your precious sister will see all her work undone, her..."

Third snarled and went on the attack, her blades blurring around her. The Traveler's speech came to an abrupt end as he retreated, shifting his longsword to both hands to intercept her furious attacks. Cold amusement spread over that gaunt, terrifying face. He knew that he had provoked her to a furious rage, that when her momentum played out, he would have her.

But even in her rage, even gripped by hatred older than the realm of Owyllain itself, Third was too experienced to let her emotions govern her.

The Traveler jumped back, his left hand coming up to work a spell. As before, Third drew back her swords and used her power, traveling in a jump. The Traveler spun, raising his sword in guard.

Except this time Third reappeared on his right side, rather than behind him.

So it was easy, so easy, to step closer and plunge her swords into the gaps in his armor. Black blood splashed from the wounds, and the Traveler howled and twisted free, his sword driving for her head. Third ducked and rolled, calling upon her power as she did.

Her jump carried her behind the Traveler, and her father responded at once, turning to face her. Once again, Third's swords darted out and plunged through the gaps in his armor. The Traveler screamed and threw out his arms, and blue light and shadow exploded from him in all directions. The spell hit her with the force of a brick wall, and Third went flying, pain exploding through her body.

But the pain did not override her concentration, and she drew on her power and traveled again.

She reappeared right in front of the Traveler. Her father started to raise his sword, and Third brought one of her blades hammering down.

The sword sheared off his right hand at the wrist, black blood spurting from the wound. The armored hand hit the unseen floor with a clang, still clutching the blue sword. The Traveler stumbled back with a scream, his void-filled eyes wide with shock, the coils of shadow lashing and snarling around him. He looked too stunned to fight back, too shocked to do anything but stare at the stump that had been his right hand.

So Third chopped off his other hand.

The Traveler fell to his knees before her with a shriek, and a surge of vicious, burning satisfaction blazed through Third as if molten metal had been poured into her veins.

She kicked him in the face.

The Traveler's head snapped back with enough force that his helmet went clattering off into the darkness, and he fell upon his back with a grunt. Third leaped upon him and drove one of her swords into his chest, and the Traveler howled, blood bubbling from his lips.

Third seized the hilt of the sword and twisted, and his scream of agony was sweeter than any music than she had ever heard.

"Stop," he croaked, raising his ruined arms in a futile effort to ward her off. "Stop..."

"Stop?" said Third, her voice unrecognizable in her ears. "Stop? You want me to stop? You are asking me for mercy?" She kicked him in the face again, the coils of shadow thrashing around them. "When did you ever show mercy? When you killed my mother in front of me and transformed me into an urdhracos? When you forced me to kill your enemies, to slaughter villages of women and children? When you made me torture your prisoners? When you made me lie with them and kill them in the moment of their climax?"

She kicked him in the face again and again as she twisted the sword hilt, and his scream rose into something unrecognizable. Or was she screaming? She could not tell. Third's lips were peeled back from her teeth in a furious rictus, and the sight of watching the Traveler writhe in agony was more intoxicating than any pleasure she had ever experienced.

"Stop," he croaked.

Her next kick sent his teeth spattering across the floor.

Part of her mind, the increasingly small part of her mind that wasn't burning with hatred, noted that the Traveler should have died of blood loss already. That, and the sword through the heart. But she didn't care. Maybe he wouldn't die in this strange place. Maybe he would live no matter what Third did to him.

That thought filled her with glee. She hadn't died, either. She had suffered for years and years, for centuries, and she was going to repay him for every single moment. Third found herself trembling with reaction and rage and some emotion she could not identify.

Maybe this was what she had wanted all along. To be alone with her father, and to make him pay and pay and pay for what he had done to her.

Forever.

She started to twist her sword hilt again, and a distant, faraway voice came to her ears.

"Third!"

She blinked. That voice, she knew that voice. It was...

Kyralion. That was it.

"Whatever you are seeing, it is not real," said Kyralion.

She glared into the darkness. Maybe it was real, maybe it wasn't.

Did it matter? Her hatred was real. The satisfaction in seeing her father broken and bleeding was real.

"Rilmeira says the aura of the Sylmarus is reacting to your dark elven blood," said Kyralion's voice. "It is showing you something that is not real."

No. Her hatred was real. That was all she had ever wanted. To listen to her father scream in the darkness forever.

"Whatever you are seeing, it is not there," said Kyralion. His voice seemed louder, clearer. "Rilmeira thinks that it is showing you something within your own mind. But if you do not try to resist it, it will kill you."

"Why?" said Third. She forced the words through her throat. "My father is here. I want him to suffer for what he did to me."

"Is that all you want?" said Kyralion. "What about your sister? What about your mission from High King Arandar?"

Third blinked. Mara...Mara had asked her to find the Shield Knight and the Keeper and their children and bring them home. She hadn't yet fulfilled that mission. Third could not linger here.

She looked at the Traveler, the hate still burning in her veins. Didn't she deserve this? Didn't she deserve to repay him for centuries of torment? Didn't she have the right?

She was owed this.

Something caught her attention.

The Traveler's cloak, the coils of shadow, had wrapped around her arms.

They seemed to be pulling her further into the darkness.

If she continued, she could torment the Traveler forever.

But she would never see her sister again.

She would never see her friends again.

Ridmark and Calliande and the others would die fighting the muridachs.

Third closed her eyes and let out a ragged, painful breath.

She hated her father, but he was dead. Her friends were still alive. There were some things more important than her hatred.

Third opened her eyes and looked at the wretched mad tyrant who had been her father.

"I forgive you," said Third.

"What?" rasped the Traveler in bewilderment.

"I forgive you," said Third, and she ripped her sword free from his chest, "and I am done with you."

She turned and walked into the blackness.

"Weakling child!" screamed the Traveler after her. "Come back and finish your revenge. Come back. Come back! I command you to come back!" His voice rose to a pleading frenzy. "No! Come back, come back, I command you to come back now..."

The voice faded away.

The darkness snapped out of existence, and Third stumbled.

She found herself back in the strange hall within the heart of the Sylmarus. Her heart was a thunderous drum inside her chest, and sweat drenched her body. Third wavered on her feet, and Rilmeira grabbed her left arm and Kyralion her right.

"What happened?" whispered Third. Her mouth felt like dust, and she forced moisture back into it.

"You froze," said Kyralion, "and Rilmeira said you were having a vision."

"It was worse than that," said Rilmeira. "The Sylmarus said we were approaching the heart of the Unity. That power reacted to you. It wouldn't affect me because I'm part of the Unity, and Kyralion is immune to magic. But you..."

"It affected me," said Third, straightening up.

"I think it reached into your mind and showed you something within yourself," said Rilmeira. "Some weakness, maybe, or some horror from your past."

"I saw my father," said Third. "I..."

She shook her head and took a deep breath.

"He is dead," said Third. "It is the living who must concern us. Come."

She turned and kept walking, Kyralion and Rilmeira following her deeper into the Sylmarus.

19

SOMETHING NEW

The heartbeat grew louder with every step, and the song of the Sylmarus filled Third's thoughts, stronger and louder than her father's song had ever been.

Stronger and louder than her own.

But there was no malice within that song, no hatred. Only infinite weariness and sadness. And sickness, as well. The Sylmarus was dying, Qazaldhar's plague curse working through its limbs and roots. Even if the muridach horde had not been outside the walls, the curse would soon have killed the Sylmarus, and the gray elves would have died as well.

The song filled her thoughts and drew Third onward.

Another tunnel opened at the far end of the strange hall, winding deeper into the Sylmarus. The veins of green light shone brighter, pulsing in time to the sound of the heartbeat. The air crawled with magical force, strong and mighty.

"We are almost there," whispered Third. She had no logical basis for that. But she heard it in the song that filled her head.

The tunnel widened into a large round chamber grown from the living wood of the tree. It reminded Third of the domed churches of Owyllain, if churches had been grown from trees rather than built from masonry. Thousands of the green veins covered the walls and ceiling, joining together in the center of the chamber. There were also thousands of the black, tumor-like growths of Qazaldhar's plague curse, blighting the walls and the ceiling.

And there was the heart of the Unity, the heart of the Sylmarus itself.

It looked like an enormous seed the size of a house. It pulsed with the green light, and the heartbeat sound came from it. Third felt the power radiating from the heart, and the song in her head was coming from it. Black veins of corruption, dark and thick, threaded through its bulk, the plague curse slowly but surely killing off the heart.

"I have never seen anything like it," said Rilmeira. She closed her eyes, opened them again. "The Unity...it is overpoweringly strong here."

"This is the heart of the Unity," said Third.

IT IS.

The great voice of the Sylmarus came from every direction at once and filled both Third's ears and her thoughts.

"I did not know that trees could have hearts," said Kyralion.

ONCE THERE WERE MANY OF US ON THIS WORLD, AND WE CAST OUR SEEDS UPON THE WINDS OF THE COSMOS TO VISIT OTHER WORLDS. NOW I AM THE ONLY ONE THAT REMAINS. WOMAN OF FLAMES, THIS IS THE MOMENT THAT WAS FORETOLD. YOU SHALL DECIDE THE FATE OF THE UNITY. DESTROY IT OR SAVE IT AS YOU WILL.

"I understand," said Third, her voice soft.

She looked at Kyralion and Rilmeira. She remembered the scorn the High Augur had shown him, how the gray elves seemed enslaved to the consensus of their emotions. She remembered the gray elves falling dead of the plague, the black growths and tumors covering the bark of the Sylmarus.

Perhaps the destruction of the Unity was inevitable. Maybe it was her purpose to serve as the instrument of its destruction.

Inevitable...

It had been inevitable that Third would become an urdhracos, inevitable that she would remain an urdhracos until she died. It had been inevitable that Mara would transform and become an urdhracos.

It had been inevitable, right until it hadn't.

Third had transformed into something new, something the world had never seen before.

She had transformed. She had become something new.

Perhaps the gray elves could do likewise.

The song thundered inside her head, and Third knew what she must do.

"Come with me," she said, drawing a sword with her left hand.

Kyralion and Rilmeira followed as Third approached the great heart, the green light washing around them. Third stopped at the base of the heart and turned to face Kyralion and his beloved.

"Hold out your hands," she said.

"What are you going to do?" said Rilmeira, the fear plain on her face. "Are you going to destroy the Unity?"

The veins began to burn with blue fire beneath Third's skin.

"No," said Kyralion. There was understanding in his golden eyes. "No, she is not."

"I am not going to save the Unity," said Third. She shifted the sword to her right hand and slid the blade across her left forearm, the blood welling across the blade. Blue fire danced and burned in her blood. "I am not going to destroy the Unity. I need the blood of the dark elves." She stepped closer and slid the blade across Rilmeira's forearm. The gray elven woman only flinched a little. "I need the blood of a gray elf of the Unity." Third turned towards Kyralion. "And the blood of a gray elf not of the Unity."

He extended his forearm, and Third raked her blade across it.

The blood mixed together on the sword, all of it burning with blue fire.

Third turned and faced the heart of the Sylmarus.

"What are you doing?" said Rilmeira. "Are you..."

Third drew back the bloodied sword and plunged it to the hilt into the heart.

The heart looked as if it had been made of wood, but the steel of the dark elves sank into it with ease. The sword began to burn with a blue flame, and a shudder went through the enormous heart out of all proportion to the size of the wound.

"What did you do?" said Rilmeira.

"Something new," said Third.

All at once, the green light vanished from the heart and the walls, plunging the chamber into darkness. Rilmeira shrieked, and Third heard her stumble, heard Kyralion catch her.

"What is wrong?" said Kyralion.

"It's...it's gone..." said Rilmeira, her voice full of terror. "They're all gone. The Unity is gone."

Third said nothing, staring at the heart in the darkness.

Then blue fire blazed to life in the heart, and the thunder of the heartbeat filled the chamber anew.

20

BLUE FIRE

A nother pair of berserkers rushed at Ridmark, their axes drawn back to strike. He blinked the sweat from his eyes and rushed to meet their attack, Oathshield snarling with white fire in his fists. The first axe clanged off Oathshield's blade, and Ridmark twisted to the side and swung. His blade bit deep into the muridach's hip, and the creature snarled with rage and pain. Ridmark ripped Oathshield free, the soulblade's power driving his weary arms, and took off its head.

The second muridach chopped at him, and Ridmark dodged to the side, slashing Oathshield. The soulblade severed the muridach's right arm at the elbow, and the creature screamed as blood spurted from the stump. Ridmark opened its throat and stepped back.

A third muridach jumped at him, bronze sword drawn back to stab, and Ridmark tried to dodge.

He wasn't quite fast enough, and the bronze sword hammered into his chest, the edge clanging off his dark elven armor. The force of the impact knocked him off his feet, and Ridmark landed hard on his back. The muridach sprang after him, sword raised for the kill, and Ridmark got Oathshield up in time to deflect the stab that would have opened his throat. He drove his left foot into the muridach's right knee, and the heel of the boot landed with a crack. The muridach stumbled back, and Ridmark heaved himself to his feet and swung Oathshield. The soulblade punched through the muridach's leather armor and sank into its chest, and the creature staggered. Ridmark wrenched Oathshield loose and opened the muridach's throat.

The muridach collapsed in a heap, joining the dead carpeting the ground.

Ridmark took a quick step back and raised Oathshield in guard, risking a quick glance over the square.

The battle was not going well.

Truth be told, it was about to be lost.

The muridachs poured through the shattered gate in a horde, and Calliande and the Augurs and the other wizards unleashed their magic at the ruined gate. Fire and lightning and ice ripped into the muridachs, killing dozens of them. Kalussa hurled crystalline spheres with such force that they punched through multiple muridachs at once. Corpses carpeted the northern square, mostly muridachs, but with a growing number of gray elves.

A line of gray elven swordsmen struggled to hold against the muridachs pouring through the gate. They fought in perfect harmony, each swordsman covering the other, moving with perfect timing to avoid tripping each other, and they left slain muridachs heaped around them. Yet the sheer press of the muridachs forced the swordsmen back as more enemies swarmed through the gate.

The situation on the walls was just as bad. Ridmark saw that the muridachs had managed to clear two footholds on the ramparts, and more ratmen were swarming up the siege towers and onto the battlements. Some of them fought the defenders on the walls, but others descended from the ramparts and into the city's streets. If the muridach commanders had any wits, they would move through the streets and come at the defenders in the square from behind.

They needed a more defensible location, but there wasn't one. Cathair Caedyn had no citadel, relying upon its walls for protection.

Ridmark fought on, trying to keep the muridachs from reaching Calliande and the other wizards.

TAMARA DID NOT NEED to aim her spells.

There was no need. The enemy was everywhere. In every direction she looked, save for behind her, she saw muridachs pouring through the gate or scrambling over the walls. Tamara through lightning bolt after lightning bolt, leaving slain and stunned muridachs scattered across the ground.

Despite the danger, her eyes kept flicking to Tamlin.

He was a pillar of defense, laying around him with the Sword of Earth, killing muridachs with every blow. Krastikon and Calem fought with equal ferocity, their Swords slicing through armor and flesh. But the sheer weight of muridach numbers was pressing them back.

Calliande had suggested that some of the gray elves could flee through the southern gate and into the Illicaeryn Jungle, but Tamara now saw that was hopeless. If the defenders tried to flee, they would be overrun in a matter of moments.

A pair of Throne Guards rushed towards Tamlin, swords raised to strike, the blood sigils burning on their crimson armor. Tamara thrust her staff and cast a bolt of lightning, and her magic coiled around the two Guards, making them jerk and dance. The dark magic on their armor deflected her power, but it gave Tamlin the moment he needed to move. The Sword of Earth cut down both Throne Guards, their corpses falling to the ground.

Tamara started to pull together power for another spell, and she heard Calliande gasp.

She turned, fearing that the Keeper had been wounded, but Calliande looked fine, only exhausted. The Keeper was staring the to south, her blue eyes wide.

"What is it?" said Tamara.

"It's gone," said Calliande, astonished. "It's just gone."

The green glow under the bark of the Sylmarus winked out of existence.

Magic burned before Calliande's Sight, a storm of elemental and dark magic as the gray elven wizards and the muridach priests threw their spells into the fray. The competing powers seethed and snarled, battling each other with fierce violence.

And then, in the middle of the fighting, the aura of the Sylmarus vanished.

It just vanished, disappeared as if it had never existed.

"No," said Athadira, staring at the Sylmarus with wide, horrified eyes. "No, it cannot be."

"What happened?" said Calliande.

"She killed it," said Athadira. "She killed the Unity. Another moment and it will collapse."

And with that, Calliande realized that the battle was over.

When the Unity collapsed, the mental shock would stun or disable the gray elves. The muridachs would sweep the city in short order. Could Calliande and Ridmark and their friends escape? Perhaps, but she did not see how. The muridachs encircled the city. And Qazaldhar would make sure that Nerzamdrathus and the Throne Guards and the muridach priests came for them.

"Then this is the end of our people," said Athadira. "The Unity has failed, and..."

"Athadira, shut up," said Seruna. "Look. Look!"

Calliande stared at the Sylmarus and then saw what had caught Seruna's attention.

The base of the great tree's trunk was beginning to glow.

Not with green light, but with blue.

The blue light shot up the tree, spreading beneath its trunk, and soon it looked as if the Sylmarus was wreathed in harsh blue fire. The ghostly flames shone brighter and brighter, and it blazed brighter than the sun. A sudden pause came over the battle as both the muridachs and the gray elves gaped at the strange light. To Calliande's Sight, the Sylmarus's aura writhed with a power that she had never seen before.

Then the light exploded.

A wall of blue flame rushed out in all directions from the Sylmarus, a hundred feet tall, and surged forward with terrific speed. Calliande flinched and started to summon magic for a ward, but the blue fire moved too fast. It passed through her without harm, though she felt the sheer power of it. The muridachs cringed back as the fire shot through them, but it likewise did nothing to the ratmen.

It passed through the gray elves, and some of it settled on them, sinking into their flesh. All the gray elves had black veins visible beneath their skin, the marks of the plague curse, but now the veins glowed with blue fire.

Calliande looked around in surprise and saw that every single gray elf had gone motionless, their eyes and veins beginning to shine with blue flame.

21

ONE FINAL CHANCE

Ridmark looked around in confusion, unsure of what was happening.

The gray elves stood motionless, blue fire glowing beneath their skin. The muridachs had gone motionless as well, though from confusion, and growled questions at each other in their language.

"Calliande?" said Ridmark, his voice rough from exertion. He spotted her a dozen yards away, standing with Kalussa and Tamara and the Augurs.

"I don't know," said Calliande. "Something is happening to the Unity, I don't know what. But it's touching all of the gray elves at once."

And whatever it was, it held the gray elves enthralled, or perhaps paralyzed.

Which meant the muridachs had an excellent opportunity to finish them off.

A muridach berserker strode towards Lord Rhomathar, axe drawn back to strike, and the movement shook the other muridachs out their paralysis.

T<small>HIRD'S</small> <small>SWORD</small> burned in the heart of the Sylmarus, the ancient weapon of blue steel crumbling to ashes.

But with every beat of the heart, the blue fire shone brighter, the heartbeat growing louder and stronger. The blue fire spread through the veins of the wall, reaching higher and deeper into the living wood of the Sylmarus. Every time it touched one of the tumorous growths, the growth shriveled into nothingness, and the black veins had vanished from the heart.

Third looked at her forearm and saw that the gash she had cut there had already vanished, as had the cuts on Kyralion and Rilmeira.

"What is happening?" said Rilmeira. "I feel...the Unity..."

Third looked at her. Rilmeira's eyes glowed with blue fire, her veins shining with the same light. Kyralion looked the same, the golden hue of his eyes obscured by the azure flame.

"Third," said Kyralion, his burning eyes meeting hers. "What have we done?"

"I will show you," said Third. "Be ready to fight."

The song rose within her, the song of her blood. But she also heard the song of the Sylmarus inside of her head, and the two songs were in harmony. Third reached out and took both Kyralion's hand and Rilmeira's, and drew on her power to travel.

This time, the power of the Sylmarus answered her.

R<small>IDMARK</small> <small>SPRINTED</small> <small>FORWARD</small>, hoping to kill the muridach berserker before the creature took off Lord Rhomathar's head. As he took the first step, Ridmark knew he was going to be too late. Even Oathshield's speed would not let him cover the distance in time.

Then the Lord Marshal looked up, the blue fire shining brighter beneath his skin.

The axe blurred for his head, and Rhomathar vanished. The

muridach stumbled and overbalanced, bafflement going over its rat-like face.

Blue fire flashed, and Rhomathar reappeared behind the berserker. Before the creature could turn, Rhomathar drove his sword into its back. The creature gurgled and collapsed to the ground. A second muridach berserker came at Rhomathar, and he turned, parried, and vanished again, reappearing in a swirl of flame behind the berserker.

Just as Ridmark had seen Third and Mara do countless times before.

Rhomathar turned to face the muridachs, and they flinched from his gaze. The Augurs straightened up, the blue flames still dancing beneath their skin and in their eyes.

Then the plaza exploded in blue fire as every single gray elf vanished at once.

TAMARA FELT her jaw fall open in astonishment as the gray elves disappeared from the square and the walls. For a single hideous moment, it felt like she and Tamlin and their friends were alone in a city surrounded by tens of thousands of muridachs.

Then the gray elves reappeared, all of them, in swirls of blue flame. They were in different positions. It was just like Tamara had seen Third do, using the power of her blood to travel from place to place in the blink of an eye.

Except now all the gray elves could do it.

Tamara had seen them fight in fluid, graceful harmony, had seen their swordsmen move around each other with perfect timing, stepping with a half-second to spare to avoid their archers' arrows. It had been a wondrous and terrifying thing to behold, and that uncanny harmony was the reason the gray elves had held off the muridachs for so long.

And the gray elves showed the same deadly harmony as they flickered back and forth across the square and the rampart.

Blue fire flashed and flared, and the muridachs died. Every time a gray elf appeared, a muridach warrior perished, and the gray elves traveled away before their enemies could land a strike. Tamara lifted her staff, intending to throw her powers into the battle, but there was no need. In less than half a minute, the attack on the gate and the ramparts had collapsed, with most of the muridachs slain and the rest fleeing.

"How?" said Krastikon. "How are they doing that?"

"I have no idea," said Calliande. "The Sylmarus...the connection to the Unity has changed." Tamara looked back and saw the Sylmarus blazing like an azure torch, the veins seeming molten beneath its bark. To her astonishment, she saw that thousands of new leaves had bloomed on its branches, and the blue fire was burning away the tumorous growths while leaving the rest of the great tree untouched.

"The Unity," said Athadira, the haughtiness in her voice replaced by awe. "It has...it has changed. It is different. It is rejuvenated."

Calliande started to say something, and blue fire flashed near them.

Third, Kyralion, and Rilmeira appeared out of nothingness. Both Rilmeira and Kyralion had the glowing blue veins beneath their skin. The fire shone in Third's veins, and her eyes had turned to molten blue fire. It made her look beautiful and terrible. The ancient pagans on Old Earth had worshipped goddesses of war, Tamara knew, goddesses who strode among the battlefields with the blood of the slain dripping from their fingers.

If those goddesses could have seen Third, they would have fled in terror.

"Third?" said Ridmark. "Are you all right?"

"No," said Third. Her voice had a strange reverberation to it. "But there is a task to be done."

"What happened?" said Athadira.

"The blood of the dark elves," said Kyralion. "Liberated from its enslavement, as Third was liberated. The blood of the gray elves, joined to the Unity. We called ourselves the Liberated, but it was

Third who was truly liberated, for she knew enslavement more profound than any we shall ever experience. And it was she who has rejuvenated the Unity."

Athadira stared at them. For the first time, the High Augur seemed at a loss for words. Around them, the final few muridachs fled from the square, scrambling over each other to reach the ruined gate.

"What...what should we do now?" said Athadira.

"Perhaps we can hold here longer," said Rhomathar. "The muridachs are withdrawing to the base of the hill, and..."

"No," said Ridmark. "Now is the time to attack, right now."

"Attack?" said Athadira, aghast, but Rhomathar nodded. "They have hundreds of thousands, and we have barely four thousand still able to fight!"

"But those four thousand can transport themselves in the blink of an eye," said Ridmark. "The muridachs have never encountered anything like this before. They won't know how to handle it. If we hit them hard enough now, right now, before they can recover, we can break them." He looked at Rhomathar. "Tell your men to target the muridach captains, the lords, the priests, the leaders. An army without leaders is just a confused rabble."

"But the Maledictus..." started Athadira.

"We're going after him," said Ridmark. "Right now. If we can find Nerzamdrathus and Qazaldhar and kill them, we'll break the back of their army."

"We cannot kill the Maledictus of Death," said Athadira. "The Kratomachar gives him power. If you cut him down, his malevolent spirit will simply inhabit another corpse."

Something stirred in Tamara's mind, something from the same place that had held her knowledge of air magic.

Seven Swords. Seven spikes in the symbol of the New God.

The seven Maledicti...

"At the very least we can drive him off," said Ridmark. "We..."

"Wait!" said Tamara. "Wait!"

They all stared at her.

Tamara swallowed. "I know how we can stop Qazaldhar."

"How, girl?" demanded Athadira.

"Don't you see?" said Tamara. "There are Seven Swords, and seven high priests of the Maledicti...and their souls are bound to the Seven Swords. That's why they're immortal. That's why they keep coming back when they are slain. Their souls are drawn back to the Swords, and then to a new body. But if you cut down Qazaldhar with the Sword of Death itself..."

"He's the Maledictus of Death," said Tamlin with growing excitement, "and his soul would be bound within the Sword of Death until someone freed it."

Tamara nodded and looked at Calliande.

"Dear God," said Calliande. "I should have realized it sooner. I think she's right. Krastikon, if we can get close enough to Qazaldhar for you to use the Sword of Death to strike him...I think we can trap his spirit, keep him from taking a new body like Khurazalin did."

"But there are so many muridachs," said Athadira. "We cannot overcome them all."

"We don't need to overcome them all," said Ridmark. "We just need to kill their leaders. The gray elves can do that now. And if we kill Nerzamdrathus and Qazaldhar, the muridach host will turn on itself."

"Mother, he's right," said Rilmeira. "This is our very last chance. Lady Third and Kyralion have given it to us. We must not waste it."

Athadira stared at her daughter, terrible doubt on her face. Then her expression hardened, and she nodded.

"So be it," she said. "We shall decide our fate with one last battle. At least this way, if our kindred fall, we shall die fighting for victory, rather than waiting behind the walls for the end to claim us."

"Then let's move," said Ridmark.

22

THE LAST STAND OF THE GRAY ELVES

R idmark walked from beneath the ram's housing and looked down the slope towards the siege camps of the muridachs, the others following behind him.

The muridachs were ready for a fight.

They had poured forth from their camps and formed up at the base of the slope, ready to charge up the hill and through the broken gate. Yet Ridmark saw the ripples of uncertainty going through the muridach lines as the survivors of the attack on the walls retreated to join them. The muridachs so far had not suffered any serious setbacks in the siege of Cathair Caedyn. They had suffered tremendous casualties, yes, but the muridach leaders did not care about that.

But the muridach leaders had not yet seen one of their attacks repulsed so swiftly.

Now, Ridmark's instincts screamed. Now was the moment to strike. While the confusion and resultant demoralization worked their way through the muridach ranks. For all their viciousness and skill at combat, the muridachs were still scavengers. The gray elves had put up a ferocious fight, but they still had been weakened and dying, qualities the muridachs favored in their prey.

Whatever Third had done, the gray elves were no longer so weakened.

And it was obvious.

The remaining warriors of Cathair Caedyn had transported themselves outside the walls, halfway down the slope of the hill. The swordsmen had drawn up in front, and the archers loosed a steady stream of shafts at the muridachs. The ratmen had not yet brought any of their own archers forward, and the muridachs had raised their shields to ward off the missiles, though Ridmark saw muridach after muridach fall.

"There," said Calliande, pointing with her staff. "Nerzamdrathus and Qazaldhar are there."

In the middle of the muridach formation, Ridmark saw a crimson mass of Throne Guards, waiting for battle in their red armor. At this distance, Ridmark could not pick out the figures of the Great King and the Maledictus, but he knew they would be there.

"Then that's where we are going," said Ridmark.

He led the way down the hill, Oathshield burning with white fire in his right fist. Calliande came after him, staff glowing as she held the power of the Keeper ready to strike. Kalussa carried the Staff of Blades, and Tamara, the golden staff of Lord Amruthyr. Calem, Tamlin, and Krastikon had the Swords of Air, Earth, and Death ready. Magatai held his soulstone-empowered bronze sword, grinning like a madman, and Lord Rhomathar walked next to him. The Augurs came behind them, and Rilmeira stayed close to her mother, and Kyralion remained near her.

Third walked at Ridmark's side, her remaining short sword in hand. In her left hand, she carried a bronze war axe she had taken from one of the dead muridach berserkers. Ridmark wondered what had happened to her other sword. The gray elves now all had blue fire in their veins, but Third's burned the brightest, and her eyes were filled with the flames.

What had happened to her at the Sylmarus?

If they lived through this, there would be time to discuss it later.

They reached the back of the gray elven line, and the warriors began striding forward, keeping their formation. The archers advanced, still loosing shafts as they walked. The drums boomed from the muridach horde, and the ratmen let out a howling roar, striking spears and axes and swords against their shields.

Still the gray elves kept walking. The muridachs' taunts and shouts grew louder and more raucous, even as more of them fell to the arrows. The archers stopped releasing and slung their bows over their shoulders, drawing swords instead.

"The gray elves are about to attack," said Ridmark. "When they do, charge the Throne Guards."

"There are a few thousand muridach footmen between the Throne Guards and us," said Krastikon.

"It won't matter," said Ridmark. "The muridachs are about to get hit a lot harder than they expect, and when they do..."

The gray elven army disappeared in a single brilliant flash of blue light.

A heartbeat later, thousands of small flares of blue fire appeared throughout the muridach host.

A shocked ripple went through the muridachs as thousands of them died at once, stabbed or slashed by the gray elven warriors. The blue flares appeared and reappeared, scattering through the muridach lines, and the rippling in the muridach formations grew worse as the ratmen tried to deal with the elusive threat. No matter how experienced the muridachs were, no matter how brutal the iron discipline the Great King had imposed upon them, they weren't equipped to fight a foe that could travel from place to place in the blink of an eye.

The entire front rank of the muridach army dissolved into chaos, the flickers of blue fire dancing through them as the gray elves disappeared and reappeared, killing with every jump.

"Go!" said Ridmark.

He broke into a jog, Oathshield raised before him, and the others followed. The orderly lines of the muridachs had collapsed into a seething, panicked mob, and some of them turned towards Ridmark, seeing a foe they could fight.

He ran to meet them, and Calliande and Tamara unleashed their spells. The earth rippled like a banner caught in the wind, and dozens of muridachs fell. Ridmark charged into their midst and killed two before they could rise again. Blue fire flashed, and Third appeared behind a muridach soldier, driving her bronze axe into its neck. Before she had never been able to use her power within a hundred yards or so of one of the Seven Swords, but whatever had happened to her at the Sylmarus seemed to have removed that limitation. Two more muridachs turned towards her, and Third disappeared, reappeared behind them in a flash of blue fire, and killed them both.

Ridmark heard a booming laugh and saw Magatai dueling a pair of muridach warriors, his lightning-wreathed sword dancing in his hands. Every time his sword touched theirs, arcs of lightning leaped into the muridachs and stunned them. Tamlin, Krastikon, and Calem charged into the battle, Krastikon leading with his glowing shield and drawing the attention of the enemy, while Calem and Tamlin cut down the muridachs. More blue fire flashed before Ridmark, and Kyralion appeared out of nothingness, drove his golden longsword into a muridach, and disappeared in another flash of blue flame before the nearby creatures could focus on him.

Crystalline spheres shot past as Kalussa killed muridachs one by one, and the Augurs called their power, bolts of lightning falling from the sky to blast the ratmen. Ridmark wanted to tell them to save their power for the fight ahead. The Throne Guards and Qazaldhar would be far more challenging foes than the common muridach soldiers.

Ahead Ridmark saw a flash of crimson armor. Another three or four hundred yards and they would reach the Great King and his defenders. In every direction, Ridmark saw the blue flashes of the gray elves as they killed, but he did not see any near the Throne Guards.

Third appeared out of a swirl of blue fire next to him.

"There is a problem," she said, her cool voice a contrast to her burning eyes.

"Just one?" said Ridmark.

"A more serious one than the others," said Third. "Whatever happened in the Sylmarus allowed me to transport through the blocking effect created by the Seven Swords." Ridmark nodded. "There is a spell around the Throne Guards that is blocking my ability, and it will also block the ability of the gray elves."

"I can see it," said Calliande. "It's a ward, a powerful one. Qazaldhar must have cast it."

"Qazaldhar will rally the Throne Guards around the Great King," said Ridmark, "and to use the Throne Guards to rally the rest of the muridach host."

"Yes," said Third. "The logical course of action is to kill the Great King and the Maledictus."

"That's what we're here to do," said Ridmark.

He took a deep breath, trying to think. The muridach lines were collapsing as the gray elves tore through them. Yet the Throne Guards stood strong, protected by Qazaldhar's magic against the gray elves' newfound power to travel.

There was only one thing to do.

"We'll have to go right through them," said Ridmark, "and cut our way to Nerzamdrathus and Qazaldhar."

Tamara looked surprised. "Is that...is that wise, Lord Ridmark?"

"Probably not," said Ridmark.

"Do not worry, Tamara Earthcaller!" said Magatai, grinning as he lifted his lightning-wreathed sword. "Though our numbers are few, our valor shall give our blows the strength of ten men!"

"We also have three of the Seven Swords," said Tamlin, "and the Shield Knight, and the Keeper, and the five Augurs of the Liberated. It has to be us, or it's no one."

"Yes," said Ridmark, and he lifted Oathshield and concentrated on his link to the sword.

It was time.

One heartbeat passed, and then another, and another.

And then strength flooded through him as he unlocked the power of the Shield Knight.

Oathshield erupted with white flame, the fire pouring over his body. The flames hardened into plate armor the same color as the soulblade. The helmet covered Ridmark's head, though it did not impair his vision, and the armor felt like it weighed nothing, though it could deflect anything short of a ballista bolt. The armor made him faster and stronger and blocked magical attacks. With the power of the Shield Knight, Ridmark was nearly invincible.

Though against foes with the power of Nerzamdrathus and Qazaldhar, nearly invincible might not be enough.

And it would only last a short time. Ridmark could keep his grip upon that mighty power for a brief time, and when his grip failed, he could not call that power again for twenty-four hours. The exhaustion would have been crippling, if not for the magical bracer that Antenora had made him.

He only had a few minutes. Ridmark had to put them to good use.

"What did you do?" said Athadira, astonished.

"Straight through them until we reach the Great King and the Maledictus," said Ridmark.

He did not wait for an answer but sprinted forward, and he heard the others following him.

~

THE FINAL FEW muridach warriors melted away, and Calliande saw the Throne Guards.

There were hundreds of the hulking muridachs, and her Sight showed the corruptive blood sorcery on their crimson armor. Around them, she saw the dome of Qazaldhar's warding spell to block magical travel and the snarling locus of dark magic around the Maledictus himself. Calliande had fought Qazaldhar to a standstill in Cathair Valwyn and the Blue Castra of Trojas.

Perhaps the third battle would be decisive, one way or another.

But before they could reach the Maledictus, they had to go through the Throne Guards.

"Tamara," said Calliande, and Tamara nodded and began her spell. "When I give the word."

She watched as Ridmark shot towards the Throne Guards in a blur. Tamlin, Calem, and Krastikon were right behind him, and Third, Kyralion, and Magatai a half-step behind them. The air snarled with magical power around Third and Kyralion and Rilmeira.

"Now!" said Calliande.

She cast her spell, and Tamara did the same.

The earth folded and rippled, and a score of Throne Guards were knocked off their feet.

Ridmark crashed into them like a missile, moving so fast he became a blue blur in his armor. Tamlin, Krastikon, and Calem attacked then, aiming their blows at the joints in the Guards' spell-reinforced armor. Magatai loosed a wailing Takai war cry and charged, and Rilmeira and the Augurs cast spells. Blasts of lightning screamed down from the sky, knocking the Throne Guards from their feet. Kalussa began flinging crystalline spheres from the Staff of Blades. The sorcery-enhanced armor of the Throne Guards was strong enough to deflect the spheres, but the impact of Kalussa's attacks knocked the creatures from their feet, letting Ridmark or one of the others finish them off.

Calliande drew together power for another spell, and then dark magic surged before her Sight in a vicious torrent. Was Qazaldhar casting another spell? No, the surge came from many individual wizards working spells of dark magic.

The priests of the Lord of Carrion were about to join the battle.

"Athadira!" called Calliande, abandoning her spell of earth magic and summoning the power of the Well of Tarlion.

"We see them!" said Athadira, lightning snarling around her golden staff.

"Strike against them," said Calliande, her voice tight with strain and concentration as the magic burned through her. "I will defend…"

The dark magic reached a climax, and Calliande was out of time.

She cast her warding spell, and a dome of white light rose over them just in time to deflect a howling barrage of black flames. The muridach priests had not joined their power to cast a spell but had thrown dozens of individual attacks. Calliande gritted her teeth, her jaw flaring with pain as she deflected the volley of dark magic. She almost would have preferred a single massive attack rather than dozens of individual strikes. Perhaps the carrion priests thought to overwhelm her defense through sheer numbers.

But her ward held against the attack, and Athadira and the Augurs struck back. The High Augur raised her staff, and blasts of lightning fell from the sky, landing somewhere behind the struggling Throne Guards. Calliande saw several of the dark auras of the priests wink out as the elemental magic killed them.

But the other priests were casting spells, and Calliande forced more magic through her exhausted mind, preparing another ward.

THE THRONE GUARDS were far more disciplined and skilled fighters than the rest of the muridach soldiers, and Tamlin had to change his tactics. The Guards had realized the power of the Sword of Earth's deadly edge, and they spread out around him, giving each other enough room to maneuver. Under other circumstances, Tamlin would have hit them with lightning bolts, stunning them long enough to strike, but their spell-augmented armor let them shrug off elemental attacks.

But Tamlin had other tricks he had learned over the years.

He cast a spell of elemental air, one to use the wind to make himself faster, and with a surge of speed, he hurtled towards the nearest Throne Guard. The muridach's blade blurred towards his head, and Tamlin ducked, the sword missing the top of his helmet by about an inch. He stabbed the Sword of Earth with both hands as he ran, and the blade sheared through the gap in the armor below the muridach's arm.

The unfortunate muridach fell to the ground, the red armor clattering.

Tamlin turned, raced forward, and cast a variant on the same spell. He leaped, and the magic of elemental air lifted him. He shot over the heads of the Throne Guards, who looked at him in astonishment, and he landed next to Sir Calem, who battled three of the Guards. Tamlin landed and attacked from behind, cutting down one of the Throne Guards. Calem seized the opening and twisted to the side, the Sword of Air slicing through the neck of another Guard in a silvery blur. Next to him Krastikon raised his shield, caught the blow of a Guard's blade, and stabbed the Sword of Death into the muridach's face. He yanked the sword free as the Guard fell.

Tamlin tried to catch his breath, and another Throne Guard charged at him, sword raised for a strike. He started to step back, but the Throne Guard went rigid and jerked as Magatai appeared behind him, plunging his sword through a gap into the crimson armor. The armor deflected elemental magic, but it did no good once Magatai's blade was in the muridach's flesh, and the Throne Guard jerked as the sword lightning ripped into its heart.

The Sword of Earth took off the muridach's head with a single blow, and the creature collapsed.

"Thanks," said Tamlin.

Magatai grinned. "Tamara Earthcaller would be disappointed if you were killed."

There was another blast of blue fire across the sky, followed by a volley of lightning bolts. Tamlin looked to the south and saw Ridmark cut down three more Throne Guards. The Shield Knight moved in a blur of blue metal and white fire. Ridmark did not bother to block the blows of his enemies. They rebounded from that strange plate armor without leaving a scratch, and he cut down muridach after muridach.

Then Tamlin saw Nerzamdrathus and Qazaldhar.

The Great King strode towards the fighting, clad in his crimson armor. He was so much larger and wider than the other muridachs that he looked like an ambulatory metal boulder. That huge black sword waited in his right hand, a crimson haze snarling around the weapon. Next to him glided Qazaldhar, his face and his remaining hand hidden in the black cowl and sleeves of his robe. The Sign of the New God hung against his chest, glowing with blue fire. A shadow circled overhead, and Tamlin looked up to see the Scythe, her longsword of dark elven steel in her right hand, shadow and blue flame dancing around the talons of her left.

Throne Guards followed Nerzamdrathus, and Tamlin saw dozens of muridach priests behind Qazaldhar. All the carrion priests wore their crimson cowls and carried staffs adorned with the mummified heads of muridachs.

"That is a lot of Throne Guards," said Krastikon, the ward around his shield glowing with purple light.

"Excellent!" said Magatai. "That will make it harder to miss!"

White light caught the corner of Tamlin's eye, and he looked to the side as Ridmark joined him. Nerzamdrathus was huge, and while the Shield Knight was shorter, his blue armor had the same sort of solidity to it. Third and Kyralion came up behind him. Only a faint blue glow now came from Kyralion's veins, but Third's eyes still blazed with it.

"Calliande will deal with Qazaldhar," said Ridmark, his helm making his voice metallic. "It will be up to us to handle Nerzamdrathus. Krastikon, if you get close enough, try to take down Qazaldhar. If we can trap one of the Maledicti, it will be a heavy blow against the Masked One and the New God."

"If it can be done," said Krastikon, "I shall do it."

"Shield Knight!" called Qazaldhar, his rotting voice ringing over the melee. "Come to meet your end at last?"

"What do you think, Nerzamdrathus?" shouted Ridmark. "Do you believe that the Maledictus is a false prophet now? Else why would he have brought you to such ruin?"

"The battle is not over yet," said the Great King, his deep voice making Tamlin's teeth vibrate. The huge muridach raised his sword. "The Lord of Carrion rewards his faithful. When I crack your armor open and feast upon your flesh, think upon your folly. Take them!"

Nerzamdrathus roared and charged forward, flanked by his Throne Guards, and Qazaldhar and the muridach priests began casting spells.

"Stay close to me," said Calliande to the others. "My wards can hold back Qazaldhar, and I will hold his attention so Krastikon can attack him. Try to kill as many of the muridach priests as possible. The fewer of them hitting our defenses, the better."

For once, Athadira and the other Augurs did not argue. Perhaps they knew that Calliande's strategy was the best chance they had of winning this fight. Or maybe Athadira's Sight revealed the raw power of the Maledictus of Death. Then again, the gray elves had already seen Qazaldhar's might on the day that he had turned his magic against the Sylmarus and laid the plague curse on the Liberated. The Maledictus of Death was a foe with the power to shake even Athadira's invincible arrogance.

The Augurs, Kalussa, Rilmeira, and Tamara all began casting spells. The Augurs flung blasts of lighting into the muridach priests, as did Rilmeira, forcing the carrion priests to turn their attention to their defense. Tamara cast veils of acidic mist, stunning and burning the muridachs. Kalussa threw crystalline spheres wreathed in elemental flame, hammering at the warding spells around the priests.

Calliande focused on Qazaldhar, holding her power ready to attack or to defend as needed. The Maledictus drew together a vast current of necromantic power, the magic rotten and corrupt to Calliande's Sight. Qazaldhar's remaining hand shot forward, green light shining around his decaying fingers, and an enormous wall of rippling viridian mist erupted from the earth and rolled towards them.

She had seen this attack before. Qazaldhar had used it at both Cathair Valwyn and the Blue Castra. It was a spell of necromantic magic, a plague mist that would sicken and poison anyone it touched.

Once infected by the plague mist, a victim would be in too much pain to fight and would die in agony within a few moments.

White fire blazed along Calliande's staff, and she thrust the weapon before her. A wall of shimmering white light leaped up to meet Qazaldhar's attack, and the ward struck the billowing plague mist. There was a brilliant flash of white light, and both her ward and the necromantic spell collapsed, canceling each other out. Calliande started another spell, preparing to hit Qazaldhar as Kalussa and Tamara and the others dueled with muridach priests.

Then Qazaldhar cast a new spell, something that Calliande had never seen before.

The Maledictus seized the Sign of the New God that hung against his chest and raised the dark medallion high. The Sign burned with blood-colored fire, and the flames surrounded Qazaldhar.

Dark magic rushed out from him, and Calliande heard some muridachs screaming. She followed the currents of power and saw that five nearby muridach soldiers, fleeing from the gray elves, had gone motionless. Crimson fire played around the muridachs, and they shuddered, Qazaldhar's magic sinking its talons deeper into their flesh.

And then the muridachs exploded.

At least, that was what it looked like. Blood exploded from their eyes and mouths and nostrils and ears and sprayed out in a high crimson arc, drawn by Qazaldhar's power. The five muridachs fell dead, drained of every drop of blood, and the fluid hurtled towards Qazaldhar. Instead of striking him, it whirled around him in a crimson cloud, growing darker as his power charged it with malevolent force. The spell was a hideous, evil thing, a corruption of magic that Calliande had never seen before.

She hurled a shaft of white fire at Qazaldhar, hoping to disrupt him before he could finish his spell. The shaft of white flame stabbed into the snarling cloud, destroying a portion of it. More muridach soldiers screamed nearby, and more arcs of blood joined the cloud spinning around the Maledictus.

Qazaldhar gestured with the Sign of the New God, and a portion of the bloody mist exploded outward. It expanded into a curtain of rippling crimson mist, black flames dancing within its interior. The grass underfoot had already been trampled by the muridach host, but it withered and crumbled into ash as the bloody cloud passed over it. Calliande realized that the cloud was a spell of powerful necromantic magic, a plague so virulent and deadly that it would kill anything it touched.

She cast her warding spell again, and the bloody cloud pressed against it. Calliande gritted her teeth, trying to hold the ward in place, and her ward shattered against the power of Qazaldhar's blood spell. Yet it had also burned away a portion of the mist, and Calliande struck again at once. White fire burst from her staff and ripped through the bloody mist, burning it away.

But Qazaldhar was already casting again, killing more passing muridach soldiers and siphoning their blood into his whirling cloud, and Calliande summoned more power to fight him.

NERZAMDRATHUS THUNDERED TOWARDS RIDMARK, moving much faster than a creature his size should have been able to move. The spells on his armor must have made him faster, and no doubt they made him stronger. Ridmark started to raise Oathshield in guard, realized that a parry would be useless against a sword that large, and elected to dodge instead.

It was the only thing that saved his life.

Nerzamdrathus swept his black sword at Ridmark with a back-handed blow, and Ridmark avoided the blade. But the Great King stepped into the attack and punched with his armored left hand. It landed with the force of a catapult stone, and the impact picked Ridmark up and threw him backward a half-dozen yards. He landed with a clatter of armor. Without the armor of the Shield Knight, that blow would have collapsed his chest. Even with the armor of the Shield Knight, it had still knocked the wind from him.

The Great King sprang after him for the kill, and Ridmark rolled to the side, ignoring his pain and using the armor's power to get back on his feet. Nerzamdrathus started to straighten up, and Tamlin and Third reached him first. Third stabbed her remaining short sword into a gap in the armor, and Tamlin brought the Sword of Earth hammering down on the muridach's right wrist. Yet the Sword of Earth rebounded from the crimson metal of Nerzamdrathus's gauntlet. The blood sigils upon the armor were strong enough to deflect even the terrible power of the Sword of Earth.

Nerzamdrathus straightened with a roar, lashing his black sword at Tamlin. The younger knight had no choice but to duck and roll away, scrambling back to his feet. In the same motion, Nerzamdrathus drove his left fist at Third. She started to dodge, but the mighty blow clipped her left shoulder, and the impact spun her around and knocked her to the ground.

Ridmark charged and went into a furious attack, slashing Oathshield at the Great King with two-handed blows. The muridach held his ground, his black sword snapping back and forth to deflect Ridmark's attacks. At last Ridmark's momentum played out, and Nerzamdrathus went on the offensive. The black sword came up and fell in a massive blow, and Ridmark dodged, barely avoiding the sweep of the dark blade. He struck back and stabbed Oathshield, and the point of the soulblade skidded off Nerzamdrathus's cuirass. The tip slashed through two of the dozens of blood sigils on the armor, and they flickered, flared, and went dark.

And an idea came to Ridmark.

"Tamlin!" he shouted. "Keep the Throne Guards off me! I'll deal with Nerzamdrathus."

He saw Tamlin's dubious expression, but they had been through enough for the younger man to trust him. Tamlin ran to join Calem and Krastikon where the two men tried to cut their way through the Throne Guards to reach Qazaldhar, who stood wreathed in a swirling vortex of bloody light. Ridmark had never seen a spell like that, but he dared not take his attention from the Great King.

Nerzamdrathus's black sword blurred at him, and Ridmark dodged and attacked again, aiming his sword at the glowing symbols on the cuirass. Oathshield connected, and one of the sigils winked out, going dark beneath the fury of the soulblade's fire. Oathshield had been forged to destroy creatures and spells of dark magic, and the power on Nerzamdrathus's armor was surpassingly mighty, strong enough to resist even the edge of the Seven Swords themselves.

But nothing was invincible.

Nerzamdrathus recovered his balance and attacked, and Ridmark retreated, barely staying ahead of the Great King's sword. There was a flicker of dark armor and blue fire from the corner of his eye, and Third struck, slashing at the towering muridach's legs. Nerzamdrathus punched for her, but this time Third danced away, keeping out of the creature's reach.

"Third!" shouted Ridmark. "Blood sigils!"

Her burning eyes flicked over Nerzamdrathus's cuirass, noted the darkened sigils, and then widened with understanding. She attacked, and Nerzamdrathus whirled towards her, but Third jumped out of the way. Before Nerzamdrathus could turn back, Ridmark hit him again. Oathshield clanged off the crimson armor, quenching another of the blood sigils.

Then it was a race.

Could he break through Nerzamdrathus's armor before he lost his grip on the power of the Shield Knight?

Because if he lost his grip on the power before he had broken through the Great King's armor, Ridmark was going to die, and so was Third and anyone else Nerzamdrathus could reach.

CALLIANDE BATTLED against the clouds of plague blood that Qazaldhar hurled at her and the Augurs.

Somehow, Qazaldhar was getting stronger as the duel raged on, while Calliande felt exhaustion spreading through her limbs. The muridach army was collapsing around them, even as the Throne Guards and the priests fought on, and countless muridach soldiers were fleeing to escape from the fury of the gray elves and their newfound ability to travel in the blink of an eye.

Which meant Qazaldhar had countless victims to fuel his blood sorcery.

Most of the blood went to the hideous cloud of crimson mist that swirled around him, but some of it was converted to raw dark magic, adding its power to Qazaldhar's already potent strength. The Maledictus had been a match for Calliande, and now he was even stronger.

It took all Calliande's power to hold back the fury of the Maledictus and his plague mist.

Qazaldhar gestured with his amulet, and part of the cloud exploded out, rising up in a wall of crimson mist. Calliande's Sight showed her the dark power charging the mist. It rolled forward in a hideous crimson wave, killing any grass that it touched, or any unfortunate muridachs that blundered into its path. This time Calliande did not bother to ward against it. Instead, she went on the attack, sending a shaft of blazing white fire sweeping through the cloud. The magic of the Well of Tarlion disintegrated the walls of bloody mist and also destroyed a portion of the cloud swirling around Qazaldhar.

But it hardly mattered. The Maledictus of Death gestured with the Sign again, and more passing muridach soldiers died, blood exploding from their eyes and ears and mouths and noses. The blood arced across the battlefield to join the mist swirling around Qazaldhar, and to Calliande's Sight, the aura of dark magic around the undead wizard grew ever stronger.

Rilmeira shouted and flung a snarling globe of lightning into the cloud. That proved even less effective than Calliande's white fire. The cloud swallowed the lightning, and Qazaldhar began casting a new spell. Kalussa shot a crystalline sphere from the Staff of Blades into the mist, but that did little. It penetrated a yard into the crimson mist before it unraveled.

"He is too strong!" said Athadira. "Our magic is not enough to overcome him!"

"I know!" said Calliande. If they could not penetrate that cloud, the battle was over. She felt her strength wavering from the strain of both this fight and the last several days. Unless they found a way to punch through the cloud, Qazaldhar was going to kill them all in a few moments.

And without Calliande to distract him, Qazaldhar could kill Ridmark and Kyralion and Third and the others at his leisure...

She blinked as an idea came to her.

Kyralion was mostly immune to magic. The power of the Keeper's mantle could pierce his protection, as could the magic of the Seven Swords. Qazaldhar was linked to the Sword of Death if Tamara was right, but she didn't think Qazaldhar was drawing his power from the Sword.

Which meant Kyralion could walk unharmed through the cloud.

"Kyralion!" said Calliande, drawing power as Qazaldhar hurled another killing cloud at them. "Get Kyralion!"

Athadira scowled at her, but Rilmeira's eyes went wide.

"Yes," said Rilmeira. "Yes, of course!"

She ran to find Kyralion, ignoring her mother's cry.

THIRD WAS FASTER and stronger than a human, and she had centuries of experience with violence. She had fought nearly every kindred and every manner of dangerous creature to be found in Andomhaim, and she had won most of those fights.

But all of it, all her skill, experience, strength, and speed, was barely enough to keep her alive against the wrath of Nerzamdrathus.

The Great King of the muridachs was as large as a jotunmir but faster than Third. Worse, he was massively stronger than Third. If that black sword touched Third, there would likely be nothing left of her but blood and mangled meat.

But she fought on, heedless of the danger. The song of the Sylmarus filled her thoughts, but she ignored it. All around Third her friends fought for their lives against the Throne Guards, and that concerned her much more.

And the song of her own blood had changed, somehow, after the things she had faced within the Sylmarus. It had become louder and stronger, strong enough to let her transport through the aura surrounding the Seven Swords. Unfortunately, she still could not travel through the ward surrounding Qazaldhar. Though Third doubted it would have made a difference – if she transported behind Nerzamdrathus, her sword and axe could not have penetrated the crimson armor, and she did not have a weapon capable of destroying Qazaldhar.

So instead she attacked the Great King, drawing his attention as Ridmark hammered at him. The Shield Knight moved in a blur of blue metal, white fire trailing from Oathshield. Even a soulblade could not penetrate the crimson armor covering Nerzamdrathus. But every strike from Oathshield knocked out one of the dozens of crimson sigils covering the armor. Third guessed that those blood spells gave Nerzamdrathus his blurring speed and iron strength, and if Ridmark destroyed enough of them, the Great King would slow enough for Ridmark to land a killing strike.

Third dodged another blow of the huge black sword. The blade fell like a falling boulder and hammered into the earth, sinking a foot and a half into the ground. It should have gotten stuck, but Nerzamdrathus wrenched it free with ease, wheeling to follow Third and stepping back. Ridmark lunged at the Great King, and the muridach dodged, but not before Oathshield's burning blade struck Nerzamdrathus's hip.

Another blood sigil went dark.

Third attacked again, and Nerzamdrathus spun to meet her, his sword blurring towards her face. She dodged around the blow, launching a strike at his wrist with her bronze axe. It was a useless gesture. The axe blade struck the red bracer and rebounded without leaving a scratch. Third might as well have tried to penetrate the crimson armor with a slice of cheese.

But her attack distracted Nerzamdrathus long enough for Ridmark to strike, and Oathshield's tip quenched another of the bloody sigils.

Third leaped back, preparing to attack again, and a flicker of darkness caught her eye.

"Third!" shouted Ridmark.

She looked around but saw none of the Throne Guards or the muridach priests nearby. Come to think of it, nearly all the priests were dead, and there weren't that many of the Throne Guards left. The Augurs and Kalussa and Tamara had done a good job of battling the priests, and Third saw Tamlin and Calem and Krastikon and Kyralion carving their way through what remained of the Throne Guards. Save for Nerzamdrathus himself, there were no enemies left nearby.

No. Up, she needed to look up.

Third saw the dark shape of the Scythe plummeting towards her.

She threw herself to the side at the last possible instant, and the Scythe struck the ground, her sword plunging into the earth. Third started to attack, but the Scythe straightened up, and her wings flexed. Her right wing slammed across Third's body and chest, and it felt like she had just run at full speed into a wall. Third stumbled back, and the Scythe screamed in rage and leaped after her, longsword a blue blur.

"Together!" screamed the Scythe, her face twisted with rage and madness beneath her silver hair. "Why you should be free, and I am not? Together, we shall die together, and death is the only freedom!" She let out a wild, cackling laugh, but despite the blazing madness in her expression her sword work remained precise and controlled. Her attacks did not give Third even an instant to recover her footing, and Third had no choice but to retreat. "Let us drink from the cup of death together!"

Third stepped into the next swing, snapping up her bronze axe to deflect the Scythe's blade. The sword of dark elven steel sank into the axe, and the bronze blade shattered. Third cast aside the ruined weapon and went on the attack, slashing and stabbing with her remaining short sword. The Scythe snarled and retreated, parrying and dodging and ducking. Third dared not slow her attacks. The Scythe's blade had a far longer reach, to say nothing of her wings and talons. If Third faltered for even a second, she would never regain the initiative.

The Scythe's left hand came up, and shadows and blue fire exploded from her talons.

Third dodged the killing spell, but it still clipped her side. Pain exploded through her, and she spun around, stumbled, and fell on her back, the short sword tumbling from her grasp. The Scythe crowed in victory, seized the dropped sword, and raised it high.

She leaped forward, the short sword plunging towards Third's throat.

MAGIC BEYOND ANYTHING Tamara had ever imagined blazed back and forth around her.

The Keeper of Andomhaim and the Maledictus of Death remained locked in their ferocious duel, white fire battling against the deadly crimson fog. Tamara saw the strain on Calliande's features, saw the sweat pouring down the Keeper's face as white fire blazed up and down her staff. She looked like every fiber of her strength was going into the battle, and she was still only just holding Qazaldhar at bay.

And the undead Maledictus had no stamina to drain. Sooner or later Calliande's strength would fail, and Qazaldhar would kill them all.

Tamara desperately tried to think of something she could do to help, but no ideas came to her. She had thrown both spells of elemental earth and elemental air at the Maledictus, using her newfound knowledge to hurl volleys of lightning bolts at Qazaldhar. None of it had penetrated the vortex of bloody haze that snarled around the Maledictus. Even the Augurs' lightning and Kalussa's crystalline spheres had failed to do more than damage the barrier of bloody mist. As soon as the mist was weakened, Qazaldhar simply killed more muridachs to rebuild his barrier, and Tamara suspected Calliande and the Augurs would run out of strength long before Qazaldhar ran out of muridach soldiers to harvest.

Another volley of white fire slashed into the billowing crimson mist, and Tamara looked around, trying to find some way to help...

"Tamara Earthcaller!"

Tamara turned and saw Magatai running towards her, lightning snarling around his sword. Rilmeira ran after him, as did Kyralion and Krastikon. That was right – Calliande had sent Rilmeira to find Kyralion, and Magatai and Krastikon must have returned. Tamara still saw Tamlin and Calem slashing through Throne Guards.

"We must be ready to smite the Maledictus!" said Magatai.

"Yes," said Tamara. "But if you can think of a way to..."

"Kyralion," said Calliande through clenched teeth. "You might be immune to the necromantic mist. Can..."

"Tell me what I must do," said Kyralion.

Rilmeira gave him a stricken look, Athadira a neutral one, Seruna an approving nod.

Calliande cast a spell, and Kyralion's golden longsword began to shine with harsh white light. Tamara sensed the flow of power from Calliande that maintained the aura around the sword.

"That will wound Qazaldhar if you get close enough to him," said Calliande. "It will also damage the blood spell as you walk through it. If..."

She grimaced and sent another shaft of fire into the boiling clouds of bloody mist, driving them back.

"If you're ready," said Calliande, "it..."

Kyralion did not hesitate but sprinted forward, his glowing sword raised before him.

Tamara's heart rose into her throat as Kyralion raced into the bloody mist. It closed around him at once, and it swallowed the light of his sword. For an instant, nothing happened, and Tamara feared that the necromantic mist had killed him. Then a vicious ripple went through the mist, writhing as if it had been caught in a gale.

All at once the mist vanished, and Tamara saw Qazaldhar hurtling backward, the Maledictus gliding over the ground as

Kyralion raced after him. In a flash of insight, Tamara realized that Qazaldhar had to stand in one place to maintain the spell of poisoned mist around himself, and the Maledictus had been forced to flee before Kyralion struck him.

"Now!" shouted Calliande. "Now! Take him! This is our last chance!"

The five Augurs, Rilmeira, and Calliande all began casting spells. Kalussa leveled the Staff of Blades at the Maledictus. Kyralion kept pursuing Qazaldhar, and Tamara and Krastikon hurried towards him.

But the Maledictus stopped and lifted the Sign in his left hand, and shadows and blood-colored fire twisted around him.

THE SHORT SWORD stabbed towards Third's throat, and she raised her arms to block the blow.

Even as she did, Third knew it was futile. The Scythe's strike was perfect. There was no way Third could block it, no way Third could avoid it.

The song of her blood thundered through her mind, stronger than it had ever been. Her interaction with the Sylmarus seemed to have strengthened the song, charging it with new power, but that did Third little good. She could now travel through the blocking effect around the Seven Swords, but she still could not punch through the warding spell that Qazaldhar had raised.

But the song of her blood burned through her thoughts.

And then the song manifested a new melody.

The blue fire burned through the veins beneath the skin of her hands, as it did when she traveled.

But something else happened.

The power roared through her blood, and a sword of blue fire exploded from her right hand. It looked like a longsword wrought out of glowing azure flame, and Third reacted on instinct, rolling her wrist to intercept the descending blade.

The short sword struck the burning blade and shattered, fragments of dark elven steel raining around Third. The Scythe stumbled, her void-filled eyes going wide with surprise, and she overbalanced. Third kicked up, her left foot slamming into the Scythe's stomach, and the urdhracos jerked back with a wheeze, trying to recover her balance.

Third leaped to her feet and slashed with the burning sword. The Scythe jerked back, but the tip of the blade ripped across her chest and stomach, slicing through the armor plating as if it was not there. A sizzle filled Third's ears, accompanied by the smell of burning flesh, and the Scythe reared back with a shriek of pain, her sword coming up in guard.

They stared at each other, and then the Scythe leaped into the air, her wings beating as she turned and fled to the north.

Third ran to help Ridmark, the strange sword still burning in her right hand.

❧

CALLIANDE FINISHED HER WARDING SPELL, and Qazaldhar unleashed his dark magic in a storm.

Dozens of snarling coils of shadow leaped from his Sign of the New God, lashing and snapping like whips. Calliande called a ward of shimmering white light before them, and most of the coils struck the wall of light and rebounded from it. Yet several of them snarled past, and a tentacle of shadow struck one of the Augurs. It wrapped around her neck like a garrote, and before Calliande could do anything, the Augur fell dead to the ground, her life sucked away by the dark magic.

The Sight saw the slain Augur's stolen strength surging into Qazaldhar, fueling his sorcery.

Calliande struck with a blast of white fire, hoping to distract Qazaldhar as Kyralion, Magatai, and Krastikon closed on him. Her spell hit the Maledictus and knocked him back, the black robes billowing around him like a living shadow. Qazaldhar made a slashing motion with his left hand, and blue fire exploded from him in a ring. It struck Krastikon, Kyralion, and Magatai, throwing them to the ground, and Calliande could not tell if they were stunned or dead.

She started another spell, and Qazaldhar vanished in a swirl of blue fire and shadow. The Sight showed her the surge of power, and Calliande whirled as Qazaldhar reappeared twenty yards behind them, already casting another spell. She threw together another ward as swiftly as she could, and Qazaldhar struck. Blood-colored fire ripped from his Sign and snarled towards them, and Calliande cast her ward. The bloody fire snarled into it, and Qazaldhar shifted his aim. He killed another Augur, the lifeless body striking the ground. Calliande snarled and attacked with a lance of white fire, but again Qazaldhar traveled away, reappearing to her right.

Even without the crimson cloud of stolen blood, the Maledictus was a deadly foe, skilled in all manner of dark magic, and his power was augmented by the life force he had stolen from all those muridachs. If Calliande had been fresh and rested, she might have been able to take him, but with her mind exhausted and her reactions slowed, she was having a hard time holding her ground, let alone striking back...

"No!"

Rilmeira strode forward and thrust her hand out, and a ribbon of lightning leaped from her fingers and struck Qazaldhar. The Maledictus rocked back, the lightning snarling around him, and Calliande saw the strain in both Qazaldhar and Rilmeira as their wills strove against each other. The deaths of the two Augurs had enraged Rilmeira past reason, and her whole strength and will poured into the spell as she snarled.

"No more!" screamed Rilmeira. "No more will you torment our people! No more will you spill the blood of the innocent!"

Calliande added her own strength to the attack, as did Tamara and Kalussa and the surviving Augurs, but Qazaldhar's defenses held.

The Maledictus loosed his bubbling, wet laugh. "The Kratomachar rises! The New God comes! But you will not live to see it!"

He screamed and made a chopping motion with his hand, and crimson fire erupted from him in all directions with a tremendous surge of power. Calliande cast another ward, but the bloody fire smashed through it, and the impact knocked her over.

She hit the ground hard, rolled, and used her staff to force herself to one knee. Rilmeira had kept her feet and still flung her stream of lightning at the Maledictus. Qazaldhar gestured with the Sign, and Rilmeira went rigid with a scream, the lightning choking off. She floated a few inches into the air, and Qazaldhar laughed. Calliande saw the stirring of dark magic as the Maledictus prepared to kill Rilmeira as he had killed the muridach soldiers and harvested their lives.

"Daughter!" shrieked Athadira, and the High Augur stepped in front of Rilmeira, lightning leaping from her staff to stab at Qazaldhar.

The elemental magic failed to punch through the ward, and the killing spell that had been directed at Rilmeira struck the High Augur instead.

Blood exploded from Athadira's eyes and nose and mouth and ears, shooting in an arc toward Qazaldhar and spinning around him in a crimson haze. Athadira collapsed lifeless to the ground, and Rilmeira screamed again.

Magatai, Kyralion, and Krastikon closed on Qazaldhar from three different directions. The Maledictus glided backward, and Calliande saw the surge of dark magic as he prepared to transport himself away and attack from a different direction.

Then Magatai bellowed something in the Takai tongue and flung his sword.

The lightning-wreathed blade spun end over end and slammed into Qazaldhar's chest, the blade sinking a few inches into his torso. Qazaldhar rocked back, and his travel spell collapsed.

The lesser soulstone in Magatai's borrowed sword had pinned Qazaldhar in place.

The Maledictus reached for the hilt, intending to yank the weapon from his chest. But he had only one hand, and he could not relax his grip on the Sign of the New God. His fingers scrabbled against the hilt, and he wrenched the weapon free after a second.

But in that second, Krastikon closed with the Maledictus of Death.

The dark blade of the Sword of Death rose and fell, and Krastikon brought the Sword down in a diagonal cut through Qazaldhar's torso. Qazaldhar shrieked, and he fell in pieces to the ground, the blue fire in his eyes and around the Sign of the New God winking out. A hooded wraith of shadow and blue fire rose from the crumpled pile of robes and undead flesh. Qazaldhar's spirit, loosed from the undead shell.

But the Sword of Death glowed with blue fire, and the spirit was dragged towards the blade. It touched the Sword, and it seemed to shrink, drawn into the blade like water sinking into a sponge.

Then the blue fire faded away as the spirit disappeared into the Sword of Death.

RIDMARK FACED NERZAMDRATHUS ALONE.

He wasn't sure what had happened to Third. The Scythe had plunged towards her, and Third had been forced to fight the urdhracos. Ridmark wanted to aid her, but he dared not turn his attention from Nerzamdrathus for even a single instant. The Great King of the muridachs seemed untiring, his black sword weaving a net of metal before him.

Ridmark had no such luxury. He felt the fatigue dragging at him, felt it clouding his mind. The armor of the Shield Knight kept him moving with speed and strength, but his grip on that power was wavering. Any moment now he would lose his grip, and the power would leave him.

When it did, Nerzamdrathus was going to kill him.

Ridmark threw himself into the fight, hammering again and again at the huge muridach. The world shrank to his foe and the symbols of bloody fire shining upon Nerzamdrathus's crimson armor. Ridmark dodged around the attacks of the dark sword, and Oathshield stabbed out to quench the blood sigils. Ridmark destroyed sigil after sigil, and he felt his exhaustion building with every blow, while Nerzamdrathus never tired.

Then Ridmark struck another blood sigil, and the Great King stumbled.

There was a flash of crimson light from the armor, and a dozen sigils went dark. Nerzamdrathus stumbled with a bellow of frustration, fighting to keep his balance, his limbs trembling as if he suddenly had been burdened with a great weight.

Ridmark realized that the armor had to weigh a great deal. One of those spells must have eased the burden of all that metal, keeping it from dragging at Nerzamdrathus as he fought. But now the spell had been broken, and the Great King struggled to keep his balance, raising his sword with far less speed.

Oathshield burned in Ridmark's hands as he struck, and he surged inside Nerzamdrathus's guard before the muridach could react. He aimed for the right shoulder, and Oathshield bit into the gap in the armor there. Nerzamdrathus bellowed in pain and swept his blade out, but Ridmark dodged, ducking under the black sword. He sidestepped and swung Oathshield again, and this time the soulblade crunched into the back of Nerzamdrathus's right knee. The Great King roared, and Ridmark ripped the soulblade free, jumping back to keep out of reach of Nerzamdrathus's weapon.

The Great King charged after him, his sword rising high as he grasped the hilt with both hands for an overhanded blow.

Except the movement put too much stress on his wounded knee, and Nerzamdrathus staggered, his right leg buckling. The Great King came down on his right knee with a snarl of pain, and Ridmark seized the opening, all of the Shield Knight's power driving him forward.

Nerzamdrathus started to rise, but it was too late.

Oathshield plunged into the gap in Nerzamdrathus's armor above his cuirass, and the soulblade sank deep into his throat. The Great

King gurgled, blood spattering his chisel-like teeth, and Ridmark wrenched Oathshield free and started swinging.

On the third blow, Nerzamdrathus's head came off and rolled away. Ridmark jumped back as the armored body sagged and collapsed to the ground with a clang, the black sword bouncing away from Nerzamdrathus's limp hand.

He took a shuddering breath, and the power of the Shield Knight drained from him.

The blue armor dissolved into white flame and then vanished into nothingness, and the strength and speed disappeared with the armor. A wave of crushing exhaustion rolled through Ridmark, and he stumbled. Antenora's bracer weighed heavy upon his right forearm for a moment, taking the brunt of the fatigue that would have otherwise been crippling. After a moment Ridmark could keep his feet.

He was still bone tired.

Third ran towards him. She had lost her bronze axe and her remaining short sword of dark elven steel, and in her right hand she carried a sword that looked as if it had been fashioned from blue fire. The veins in her right hand burned, and it seemed like the fire was pouring from her arm and shaping itself into the sword.

Third came to a halt, looked at Ridmark, at Nerzamdrathus's headless corpse, and then back at Ridmark.

"You killed him," said Third.

"Aye," said Ridmark. He blew out a long breath and wiped the sweat from his eyes. "Suppose he missed his chance to feed on the women and children of Cathair Caedyn."

Third's lip twitched. "So he did."

"That sword," said Ridmark. "How...are you doing that?"

"I am not entirely certain," said Third. "We can ponder it later. The others will need our help."

"Yes," said Ridmark. "Yes, we should find them and..."

He trailed off as he looked around.

The muridach army had been shattered.

Everywhere Ridmark looked, he saw muridachs fleeing in terror to the jungle, saw gray elves flashing back and forth in pulses of blue fire to kill their foes. All the Throne Guards were dead. All the muridach priests were dead. The muridachs' siege engines and camps lay abandoned and broken. Further to the south Ridmark spotted Calliande, and there was no sign of Qazaldhar. Ridmark wondered if the Maledictus had fled, or if Tamara's idea to trap his spirit in the Sword of Death had worked.

But the muridach horde had been broken. The siege of Cathair Caedyn was over.

"Ridmark," said Third. There was an unsteady quaver in her voice.

He looked at her.

"Did we win?" she said. The blue sword unraveled in her grasp, the blue fire fading away, and the flames vanished within her black eyes.

"I'll be damned," said Ridmark. "I think we did."

∾

CALLIANDE LET out a long breath and looked around the battlefield.

"Is...is it over?" said Kalussa, leaning against the Staff of Blades in her exhaustion.

"For now," said Calliande, reaching for the Sight.

She needn't have bothered. Qazaldhar had been destroyed, Nerzamdrathus was dead, and most of the carrion priests had been slain by either the transporting gray elves or the furious lightning of the Augurs. Calliande's Sight spotted the dark auras of a few of them, but the survivors were fleeing into the jungles with the muridach soldiers.

The death of Nerzamdrathus and most of the muridach lords and priests had ripped the heart out of the muridach army. The mighty horde had fractured into a thousand mobs scrabbling over each other to escape from the victorious gray elves. The gray elven warriors kept transporting themselves in pursuit of their beaten enemies, cutting down as many as they could before the enemy escaped.

Even with the High Augur and two of the other Augurs dead, they kept fighting.

Kyralion was likely the reason for it.

"Keep after them," said Kyralion to Rhomathar. The Lord Marshal nodded. "The more of them we can take now, while they're running for their lives, the fewer who will return to fight us again."

"I doubt they will return for a long time," said Rhomathar, leaning on his sword, his golden armor spattered with muridach blood. "They took such appalling losses, and we killed nearly all of their lords and priests. Likely they will have a bloody civil war before they have a new Great King. Assuming a Great King can even take control, and the muridachs do not fracture back into warring cities once again."

"And the power is fading," said Seruna, her face lined with exhaustion as she leaned on her staff. "Whatever Lady Third did in the Sylmarus, it granted us the ability to travel as she does, but that strength is fading. The plague curse is gone, but the power to travel will not last for much longer."

"Nevertheless," said Kyralion. "The muridachs almost destroyed us. This is our chance to teach them a hard lesson. Let them never again travel to the Illicaeryn Jungle or think of the Liberated without fear."

"As you wish, then," said Rhomathar.

Kyralion stepped next to Rilmeira, who gazed at her mother's corpse with a stricken expression. Rilmeira hesitated, and then closed her eyes and rested her head against Kyralion's shoulder.

"Lady Calliande," said Kalussa. "Lord Ridmark. He's still alive."

Calliande turned, relief flooding through her as she saw Ridmark. He looked exhausted and battered, but he was walking under his own power, Oathshield in his right hand. Third came next to him, no weapons in her hands, the scabbards empty at her belt.

She faltered for a half-step when she saw Rilmeira leaning against Kyralion, then nodded to herself and kept walking.

"Ridmark," said Calliande. "Nerzamdrathus?"

"Dead," said Ridmark. He grimaced and rolled his shoulders. "Qazaldhar?"

"Destroyed," said Calliande. "Tamara was right." Tamara looked a little embarrassed. "When Krastikon cut Qazaldhar down with the Sword of Death, the Sword trapped his spirit. So long as Krastikon keeps the Sword, Qazaldhar will not be able to take another body."

"Good," said Ridmark. He looked around the battlefield. "I suppose we ought to..."

"Forgive me, Shield Knight," said Seruna. "But there is one thing we must attend to first."

Lord Rhomathar looked at Seruna and nodded in approval, and Rilmeira opened her eyes and straightened up.

"What is it?" said Ridmark.

"Lord Kyralion," said Seruna. "I regret I must ask this of you, but there is no one better suited to bear this responsibility."

Kyralion inclined his head.

"The Unity asks you to take the crown of the Liberated as our king," said Seruna.

Calliande felt her eyebrows climb halfway up her head.

"What? Why?" said Kyralion.

"Because you are the only one of the Liberated who is immune to the consensus of the Unity," said Seruna. She glanced at Third. "Lady Third has changed the Unity and the Liberated themselves in ways we do not yet understand. But for centuries, we were guided by the consensus of the Unity and the mind of the High Augur, and in the last twenty-five years, that brought us to disaster. I fear the High Augur refused to see the truth of the catastrophe that faced us, and because of that, we did not act as decisively as we could have."

"And what have I done to merit a crown?" said Kyralion, baffled.

"You took great risks on our behalf," said Rhomathar. "The High Augur sent you to find the woman in flames and bring her to us, and you did. If you had not, the Liberated would have been extinguished today."

"I loved my mother with all my heart," said Rilmeira, "but she was wrong about the muridachs, and she was wrong about you. She sent you to find the woman of flames in hopes that you would never return, but you did. You were the bravest of us, Kyralion. You were the only one able to defy the consensus of the Unity and the High Augur. None of the rest of us could."

"In ancient days, the Liberated had kings," said Seruna. "We thought the Unity had no need of kings, but this has proven us wrong. What we need is a king who can stand outside the Unity, who can ignore the consensus when it is wrong."

Kyralion took a deep breath and looked at Ridmark.

"Such a duty is a terrible burden," said Ridmark, his voice quiet, "but you are well suited for it, I fear."

Kyralion's golden eyes shifted to Third.

A strange expression, almost like longing, went over her tired face, but she nodded.

"Then so be it," said Kyralion. "I will accept this responsibility. I pray to God that I am equal to it."

23

FREEDOM

Three days later, Kyralion received the crown of Cathair Caedyn and married the Lady Rilmeira in the Court of the Sylmarus.

By necessity, it was a short ceremony.

There was so much work to be done. Calliande and Kalussa had labored for those three days, healing the wounded gray elves who could be saved. The gray elves had looted the camps of the muridachs, seizing vast quantities of supplies and enormous quantities of bronze. Cathair Caedyn would not lack for metals for years. The gray elves who had skill with elemental flame turned their attention to burning the countless thousands of muridach corpses that lay piled upon the battlefield. Best to burn them before a new plague spread among the gray elves.

Tamara assisted with the work where she could, using her earth magic to turn the ground to quicksand and letting it swallow the dead muridachs. The fields outside the walls of Cathair Caedyn would be a graveyard of slain muridachs, their bones bleaching in the sun for years to come. Tamara found herself unsympathetic. If the muridachs had stayed home rather than issuing forth to destroy a weakened and dying kindred, they would not have met their grim fates.

Especially when that weakened and dying prey was infused with unexpected new strength.

But work stopped for the coronation and the wedding. Tamara watched as Kyralion and Rilmeira pledged their troth to each other, and as Kyralion accepted the duties and responsibilities as the King of Cathair Caedyn. Of course, the rituals and ceremonies were conducted in the gray elven tongue, which Tamara did not understand.

She found both her mind and her eye turning towards where Tamlin stood next to Ridmark.

Tamara had almost seen Tamlin die during the battle. He had nearly seen her die, and if he had not leapt into the fray before her air magic manifested, she would have been slain. Tamlin would have seen her die for the third time. He could have lost her again.

She might have lost him before she had ever really gotten to know him.

But she did know him, didn't she? Her past lives had known him, even if she did not remember. A battle was a horrible thing, Tamara reflected, along with the attendant loss of life.

But it did have one great gift. A brush with death had made her consider what was important to her.

What mattered to her.

What she wanted.

Tamara wanted to know the truth about herself, about how she had been split into seven lives, but she found that she wanted something else just as much.

THIRD DID NOT GO to the wedding or the coronation, but instead stood on the battle-scarred wall of Cathair Caedyn, gazing to the north. The smell of ashes and soot and charred muridach flesh filled her nostrils, and her eyes wandered over the wreckage of the siege camps and the towers, across the distant green wall of the Illicaeryn Jungle.

She still heard the song of the Sylmarus inside her skull. It was different now, stronger, healthier, rejuvenated. And it also sounded familiar. Third supposed that was because she had left part of herself inside the Sylmarus and the Unity, even as the Sylmarus had left a piece of itself inside her blood.

Idly, she raised her right hand and drew on the power in her blood, calling the sword of blue fire. It appeared in her hand, the veins beneath her skin glowing, the blue light of the weapon falling over the white stone of the rampart. Calliande had said that the manifested sword could cut through nearly anything, much like the Seven Swords.

Third released the blade, and it vanished into nothingness. Summoning the weapon took at least as much effort as using her power to travel, and she could only use it for a short time. Still, it would be a highly useful ability.

Her journey to Owyllain had changed her in ways that she had not expected.

Which was why Third wanted to be alone with her thoughts.

A boot rasped against the ramparts, and she turned her head to see Ridmark climb up to join her.

Third wanted to be alone, but she was nonetheless glad that he was here.

He crossed to her side, and they stood together in companionable silence for a while, watching the jungle.

"We should leave tomorrow," said Third at last.

"Yes," said Ridmark. "I would have preferred to leave at once, but better to let the muridach survivors flee to the Deeps first."

"Perhaps you should carry Nerzamdrathus's head upon a lance," said Third. "It may scare the other muridachs away."

Ridmark looked at her.

"That was a joke," said Third. She considered. "Mostly. It would work."

Ridmark snorted. "Likely it would. But then we would have to smell rotting muridach all the way to the Monastery of St. James. I would be content if I can go the rest of my days without smelling muridach fur again."

Third smiled a little. "I am in full agreement."

"Will you come with us?" said Ridmark.

Third blinked in surprise. "Of course I shall. Why would I not?"

"Because you saved the gray elves," said Ridmark.

Third shook her head. "Kyralion saved the gray elves. He is the one they need, not me."

"You are the one who saved the gray elves," said Ridmark. "Kyralion found you, but you saved them. And you neither destroyed nor saved the Unity, but remade it. The gray elves have the power to travel as you do now, albeit only a few times a day, and they can disconnect or reconnect themselves to the Unity at will."

"I am glad of that," said Third. "Would not the Unity be hellish? To hear the thoughts and emotions of your neighbors at all times? The Unity is a great advantage in battle, yes. But to be joined in such a fashion for all your life...no. No. That is a form of slavery. Enslavement to the emotions of your neighbors."

"And you value freedom," said Ridmark.

She met his eyes. "I was a slave for longer than Owyllain has existed. No one values freedom as a freed slave does. Let the gray elves join the Unity as they will, and let them disconnect from it as they likewise wish."

"You gave them that," said Ridmark. "Do not mistake me, I am glad you are coming with us...but the gray elves would welcome you for as long as you might wish to stay."

"Yes," said Third, "but I am not a gray elf. My home is in Nightmane Forest with my sister." She blinked a few times. "And Kyralion's home is here."

Ridmark nodded.

"I am not a gray elf," said Third. "I might have saved the gray elves, but I am not one of them, nor will I ever be one. And Kyralion wed Rilmeira. That is as it should be."

"You didn't come to the wedding," said Ridmark.

"I did not wish to," said Third. "Rilmeira and Kyralion are suited to each other. She will be a good wife and a good Queen. She will give him children, something I would not have been able to do." She kept blinking. Her eyes felt strange for some reason. "I would not wish to settle here, and Kyralion would not want to leave his people. No. This is for the best. I would not...I would not..."

She could not seem to get the rest of the sentence out, and her eyes kept blurring.

"Third," said Ridmark, surprised. "You're crying."

"Am I?" She lifted a hand to her eyes and felt it come away wet. "I...I suppose I am, at that. What a very strange thing. I do not want to stay here, and yet..."

Ridmark hesitated, and then lifted his right arm and put it around her shoulders. Third flinched, then relaxed, rested her face against his shoulder, and cried in silence for a while.

Oddly, that made her feel better, and her roiling emotions settled.

"I still do not like to be touched," said Third at last.

"I know," said Ridmark. "If it helps, we're never doing this again."

Third laughed at that, but made no effort to move away.

"I forgave my father," she said.

"Your father?" said Ridmark, puzzled.

"Inside the Sylmarus," said Third. "The magic of the Sylmarus...I think it reflected my own mind back at me. And what it saw inside me was how much I hated my father. That is what the Sylmarus offered me. To stay in the darkness with my father and make him suffer forever."

"What changed your mind?" said Ridmark.

"You did," said Third. "Mara did. Jager did. Calliande did. Kyralion did. You and the others are more important to me than a man who has been dead for ten years."

"I'm glad," said Ridmark.

Third took a deep breath and straightened up, stepping away from Ridmark. "I am fine. Truly. I would not have wanted to stay here, and Kyralion and I would have been ill-suited to each other." She shook her head. "It is just that..."

Ridmark waited.

"I sometimes wish," said Third, "that I was something other than what I am."

"I wish you hadn't suffered as you did," said Ridmark, "but I've never wished for you to be someone other than who you are. Not ever."

"Ah," said Third, and she smiled. "You are going to make me cry again." She shook her head. "A thousand years old, and I am crying like a child."

"That is a good thing," said Ridmark. "Did the Traveler ever shed tears? Or the Warden? Or the Sovereign? No. A thousand years old... and you still have a heart and a conscience, Third."

"Maybe," said Third. "But...I do not want to stay here. I wish to finish my task from my sister and High King Arandar and return you and your family home to Andomhaim."

"Yes," said Ridmark. "We'll finish this together, and then return home."

AFTER THE CEREMONY WAS OVER, Tamlin found an empty house and sat on the floor, holding a cup of wine.

God and the saints, but he was tired. He couldn't complain, though. He had come through the battle unscathed, and they had won the fight. Even if Tamlin lived another hundred years, he would never forget the sight of the gray elves tearing through the muridachs in flashes of blue fire. He had thought the Battle of the Plains between King Hektor and King Justin had been the biggest fight he had ever seen, but Tamlin had been wrong.

Hopefully, he would not see another battle of that size.

He had looked for Tamara but hadn't been able to find her. Likely she was with Calliande and Kalussa. He would have thought she would be with Magatai, but the Takai halfling had been leading a group of gray elven warriors in toasts. Tamlin wondered if the sensation of a hangover spread through the Unity as emotions and feelings did and decided he would rather not know.

The gray elven wine burned against his tongue and made his head swim a little, but Tamlin would have only one cup. Tomorrow they would leave to continue their oft-interrupted journey to the Monastery of St. James, and Tamlin needed a clear head to protect Tamara from any dangers that might show themselves.

A pity that Aegeus wasn't here. Tamlin missed his friend. Aegeus had always fought hard and then celebrated just as hard once the battle was over. He would have loved the wine of the gray elves. They would have gotten drunk on it together, and then marched with hangovers the next day...

"Tamlin?"

Tamlin looked up, startled out of his thoughts, and saw Tamara standing in the doorway to the street.

"I didn't startle you, did I?" said Tamara.

"You did," said Tamlin, getting to his feet, "but that's all right. I was simply drinking by myself. Hardly a good habit, I'm afraid."

She hesitated. "Then you are alone?"

"Yes," said Tamlin. "I just wanted to sit and think for a while." He smiled at her. "But if you want to interrupt me, I won't mind."

"Good." Tamara closed the door behind her and propped her golden staff in the corner. "I...we almost died during the battle, Tamlin. Several times."

"Yes," said Tamlin.

She shrugged out of her long coat and put it on the floor next to her staff. It had to be heavy, but it never seemed to trouble her. Though removing her coat let Tamlin note how well her trousers fit her legs.

"That made me think," said Tamara. "About what was important to me. About what I would regret if I died."

Tamlin nodded. "I understand that. I have regrets, my lady."

"Yes," said Tamara. "I don't want to add to them. Or to mine." She took a deep breath, seeming suddenly nervous. "Which is why I want...I want to make sure there is one less thing to regret."

She slipped out of her vest of scutian hide. Tamlin's first thought was that she must have been warmer than he had thought, and then she grasped the hem of her shirt, lifted it over her head, and dropped it to the floor, and suddenly Tamlin couldn't think about anything else.

He stepped closer and took her hands. She looked up at him, her face flushed, her lips parted, her mismatched eyes enormous.

"Are you sure?" said Tamlin, his voice hoarse.

"Tamlin," she whispered. "You're my husband. I'm sure of that. Show me that you're sure, too."

He grasped the waist of her trousers and slid them down her legs, and she helped him out of his clothes. Tamlin supposed he ought to do more with the sheathed Sword of Earth than to drop it on the floor, but right now he didn't care. Soon they stood naked before each other, and Tamara looked...

He had never seen her naked before, but she looked just as he remembered.

Tamlin could hold himself back no longer, and he pulled her close and kissed her long and hard. She answered him with a moan, her arms wrapping around his back. A short time later he lowered her to the floor, his cloak serving as a blanket. The feel of her body was both new and familiar, and he both remembered and experienced anew the rapid draw of her breath, the touch of her fingers sliding against his back, the way her hips rolled to meet him. He remembered how her eyes popped open wide when she finished, and a few moments later every muscle in his body went rigid as stars exploded behind his eyes.

After, they lay in a tangled heap together. Tamlin's breathing slowed at last, and he pushed the sweaty hair from Tamara's face and kissed her.

"Yes. Yes, I'm sure," Tamlin said, and Tamara smiled at him.

24

QUEST

The next day, Ridmark and the others came to the Court of the Sylmarus one last time before departing for the ruins of the Monastery of St. James.

The Sylmarus looked different now. The green glow beneath its bark had been replaced by a blue one, the light the exact same color as the blue fire that swirled around Third when she used her power to transport herself. But the tree looked healthier now, the black tumors burned away by the transformation that Third had worked upon it.

Kyralion and his Queen awaited them at the base of the Sylmarus, along with Lord Rhomathar and the Augur Seruna. Both had taken up the role of advisors to the new King of Cathair Caedyn. Ridmark walked towards them, Calliande at his side. Third, Calem, Krastikon, Kalussa, Magatai, Tamlin and Tamara walked after them. Tamara and Tamlin walked hand in hand, and Tamara kept smiling at both Tamlin and at nothing as if she had a secret that pleased her.

"My friends," said Kyralion. "You are leaving today?"

"We are," said Ridmark. "You have your duty, and we have ours."

"Though I am pleased that our duties overlapped for a time," said Calliande, her expression the cool mien of the Keeper of

Andomhaim. "The New God and its Maledicti, it seems, are our mutual foes, and we dealt them a sharp defeat. Especially if we are correct and Qazaldhar cannot take a new body so long as Krastikon carries the Sword of Death."

"It was a great victory," said Seruna. "The Maledictus Qazaldhar caused great harm to the Liberated. To see him brought low was justice indeed."

"You are welcome to stay as long as you wish," said Rilmeira. She looked at Third. "All of you. For without you, the Liberated would have been destroyed, and Qazaldhar would have turned the muridach horde towards your homelands."

Third inclined her head in a slight nod.

"But you traveled with us long enough," said Ridmark, "to know the urgency of our mission. We have to speak with Cathala. She might have the knowledge we need to stop the Kratomachar and the Maledicti. For that matter, we have three of the Seven Swords. If we stay here with the Swords, that might put Cathair Caedyn in danger."

"I understand," said Kyralion, "and we shall give you all the supplies and equipment that we can. Is there anything you would ask of us? If not for you and Lady Third and the others, Cathair Caedyn would now be ashes, and the Liberated would be extinct."

"There is only one boon I would ask of you," said Ridmark. "And it is the same thing that I asked of the Windcallers and the Tumaks of the Takai."

Kyralion inclined his head in understanding.

"But what boon is that, Shield Knight?" said Rilmeira.

"We must be ready," said Kyralion, "to march when the hour comes."

"Yes," said Ridmark. "The Kratomachar is coming. You've seen that firsthand. Qazaldhar leveled the plague curse on you in the name of the New God, and he brought the muridach host here in the name of the New God."

"You speak wisdom, Shield Knight," said Seruna. "I fear Qazaldhar's crimes against us were intended to sweep the Liberated from the path of the Kratomachar. We opposed the Sovereign for fifteen thousand years," her mouth twisted, "though not with overwhelming success. Perhaps the Maledictus of Death feared that we would hinder the Kratomachar, and so sought to destroy us before his New God could arise."

"I agree," said Ridmark. "The war of the Seven Swords raged for twenty-five years, and in the past two months, Justin Cyros and the Necromancer have fallen, and we have found the bearer of the Sword of Air. One way or another, the war is approaching its end. I fear the Maledicti will try to summon the New God, and if we are to stop them, we shall need every ally we can find."

"The Liberated will come," said Kyralion. "When the Shield Knight and the Keeper call, the Liberated will come." He smiled. "For the Shield Knight and the Keeper brought the woman of flames to us, and she was the one who saved us."

"And because of that," said Rilmeira, "we wish to give you a gift."

Third blinked. "Me?"

"Yes," said Rilmeira. "You, my lady Third. You who remade the Unity and who cleansed the Sylmarus of its plague curse."

Third shook her head. "I have no need of boons or gifts."

Kyralion smiled. "No, but you do like swords."

Third blinked again. "Swords?"

Rilmeira turned as another gray elven woman approached, holding a bundle wrapped in gray cloth.

"The war with first the Sovereign and then the muridachs raged for so long," said Kyralion, "that we have more weapons stored than we have hands to wield them. We wish you to have these." Rilmeira took the bundle and stepped towards Third. "You will put them to good use."

Rilmeira unwrapped the bundle, and Ridmark saw that the gray cloth was a cloak identical to the one that he and the gray elves wore. Rilmeira took the cloak and swirled it around Third's shoulders, pinning it in place with a small brooch of golden metal. Inside the bundled cloak was a sword belt wrapped around two scabbarded longswords of gray elven steel.

"Those weapons are enspelled," said Calliande.

Third shook her head. "This is generous, but I cannot use an enspelled blade. A soulstone would block my ability to travel."

"Yes," said Kyralion, "which is why neither of those blades uses soulstones. Those weapons were unique in our armory."

"Several centuries ago," said Seruna, "a dwarven scholar named Irizidur visited Cathair Caedyn."

Ridmark saw Calliande stiffen. "A dwarven scholar?"

"Aye, Keeper," said Seruna. "He was a wanderer, seeking lost secrets, though he would not tell us what he sought."

Ridmark shared a look with Calliande. The Seven Swords were of dwarven design and had been forged of adamant steel, an alloy known only to the master smiths of the dwarves. But there were no dwarves in Owyllain, and Ridmark had not heard the slightest scrap of evidence that there had ever been any dwarves in this land.

Until now.

"What happened to Irizidur?" said Ridmark.

"It is not known to anyone within the Unity," said Seruna. "He departed Cathair Caedyn and was never again seen by any elf of the Liberated. But before he departed, he forged these weapons as a gift for us, in gratitude for our hospitality. My Queen?"

Rilmeira drew one of the swords, and Ridmark saw that the golden steel had been carved with dwarven glyphs. The Queen's brow furrowed with concentration, and the sword burst into snarling elemental flame. She dismissed the flames, sheathed the sword, and drew the second weapon. It was identical to the first, save that the dwarven glyphs glowed with a blue-white glow instead of a sullen orange-red one. Rilmeira concentrated again, and the blade shimmered with crackling elemental lightning.

"We hope you will accept these," said Rilmeira.

"You lost both of your swords fighting in defense of the Liberated," said Kyralion. "It seems only just that we supply you with replacements."

Third hesitated and glanced in Ridmark's direction.

"The cloak suits you," he said.

"I accept this gift," said Third. "Thank you." She took the sword belt, buckled it around her chest like a baldric, and hooked the scabbards to her back. "It is a kingly gift."

"Which, since you are a king now, seems only suitable," said Tamlin.

"Indeed," said Kyralion. "Once again, we thank you all. For as long as you shall live, you will be welcome at Cathair Caedyn."

"We shall remember that," said Ridmark. "And now..."

"But before you go, Lord Ridmark," said Seruna, "the Sylmarus has something for you."

"The Sylmarus?" said Ridmark.

"Aye," said Seruna. "Kyralion suggested it. Look down."

Ridmark followed the suggestion. He stood near one of the thick roots of the mighty tree, and as he looked, a patch of the bark shivered. A twig emerged from the root, which thickened into a stick, which rose higher until it was about his own height.

There was a snapping sound, and the long, straight branch fell from the root.

Ridmark reacted on instinct and caught the branch as it fell.

The staff thumped into his hand. It was rough-looking, rather like Calliande's staff, but seemed to adhere to his palm as if the weapon had been made for his grip. Ridmark stepped back, testing the weapon's weight. It seemed perfectly balanced, suited for both swings and thrusts.

"A stick?" said Magatai, baffled. "What warrior fights with a stick?"

Tamlin laughed. "You might be surprised."

"You seemed annoyed when the fire drakes burned your bamboo staff," said Kyralion, "so this seemed a suitable replacement."

"It is enspelled," said Calliande, gazing at the staff. "At least as strongly as Third's swords."

"It is," said Seruna. "It will wound and slay creatures of dark magic. Something, Shield Knight, that I imagine you will find most useful. Additionally, it has another useful property. Throw the staff upon the ground."

Ridmark nodded and tossed the staff away.

"Now concentrate," said Seruna, "and call it back to your hand."

Ridmark frowned, shrugged, and held out his hand, thinking about the staff.

To his surprise, it leaped from the ground and landed in his outstretched hand.

"The staff is now linked to you," said Seruna. "Only you may wield it, and it will obey only your hand. It is not alive as your soul-blade is, but it will nonetheless be a potent weapon. May it serve you well."

"I am certain that it shall," said Ridmark. "Thank you, King Kyralion." He smiled. "It is indeed a kingly gift."

"Farewell, my friends," said Kyralion, and he smiled back. "I would like to go with you, but my duties lie here. And I suspect we shall see each other again when all kingdoms and all nations must face the New God or perish..."

"Wait!" said Magatai, stepping forward. "Friend Kyralion, Magatai is still carrying your sword. It would be grievous to depart with it."

"I hope you will accept the sword as a gift," said Kyralion. "For you used it well indeed. It is always difficult to throw a sword, but you pinned Qazaldhar into place. Had you not done so, he would have escaped to work his evil elsewhere. And you helped avenge all the gray elves slain at the hands of his sorcery." He grinned, one of the few times Ridmark had seen him do that. "Besides, think of the tale you can tell when you return to your tribe with a sword that wounded both the Maledictus of Fire and the Maledictus of Death."

"Magatai had not considered that," Magatai said. "Yes, Magatai will carry your sword, and do many valiant deeds with it."

A HALF-HOUR later they crossed the damaged northern gate and headed towards the Illicaeryn Jungle.

Ridmark glanced back at the others. Calliande walked next to him, green cloak streaming from her shoulders, her golden armor glinting in the sun. Third followed her, expression calm, the hilts of her new swords rising over her shoulders. Kalussa walked with Calliande, the Staff of Blades in hand. Behind her came Tamara and Tamlin, and both of them kept smiling at each other. Magatai rode atop Northwind, and Krastikon and Calem brought up the back.

"Three," announced Magatai.

"Eh?" said Krastikon.

"Magatai has now fought three of the seven Maledicti," said Magatai. "The Maledicti of Air and Shadows at the Tower of Nightmares, and now the Maledictus of Death."

"Aye." Krastikon tapped the pommel of the Sword of Death. "Hopefully we won't see him again."

"Now we must seek out the remaining four Maledicti immediately," said Magatai.

Krastikon let out an incredulous laugh. "You are mad, aren't you?"

"Don't worry, Prince Krastikon," said Ridmark. "We don't have to seek anyone out. I suspect the Maledicti will come to us."

Against all odds, they had survived the siege of Cathair Caedyn and won a crushing victory over the muridachs and the Maledicti. But the siege had only been a skirmish in a far larger war, and the New God was still coming.

And Cathala might know the secret to stopping the New God.

"Then we shall be ready to smite them," said Magatai.

"Indeed," said Ridmark. "And we might find the answers we need at the Monastery of St. James."

"Assuming our journey is not interrupted yet again," said Tamlin.

"Oh, I don't know," said Tamara, and she grinned at him. "Some interruptions are more enjoyable than others."

Ridmark wondered what that meant, and decided that it wasn't any of his business.

"Onward, then," said Ridmark, and he led the way north, staff in hand.

EPILOGUE: MALEDICTI

Night fell over the crumbling ruins of the Monastery of St. James.

It had once been a strong castra, a fortress where monks could conduct the work of God in peace, but the power of the Sword of Earth in Justin Cyros's hand had proven stronger. The gate had been smashed to rubble, breaches torn in the curtain wall. The buildings were empty stone shells, gutted by long-quenched fires, and weeds forced their way through the gaps in the flagstones of the courtyard.

The Maledictus of Shadows glided through the gloom of the courtyard, making his way towards the broken doors of the central keep.

No one, save for the other Maledicti and their master the Masked One, knew that he was here. Nor would anyone know that he was here. Thanks to the power the New God had granted him, anyone who observed the Maledictus of Shadows would fail to see him. Anyone who had the strength of will to perceive him would immediately forget that he was there.

Even the mighty Sight of the Keeper of Andomhaim could not find the Maledictus of Shadows when he did not wish to be found.

Of course, that had done him little good at Kalimnos.

Just as Qazaldhar's blood sorcery had failed at Cathair Caedyn.

The Shield Knight and the Keeper had hindered the Maledicti again and again, and they threatened the advent of the New God. Even worse, they might be able to realize the truth, the ultimate secret at the heart of the Seven Swords. That, the Masked One could never allow, so he had dispatched the Maledicti to deal with his foes.

And they had failed, again and again.

Fortunately, the answer was at hand.

The Maledictus of Shadows gazed at the woman who would destroy the Shield Knight and the Keeper.

A statue of white stone stood before the steps to the keep, her hands outstretched, her face tight with concentration. Before Justin Cyros had turned her to stone, Cathala of the Order of the Arcanii had been a striking woman, at least by the standards of humans. Her hair had been a long mass of reddish-gold, her eyes like jade, her skin fair and clear, her body shapely and strong. Cathala had been fully aware of her beauty, and she had employed it as a weapon, drawing men to her like moths to a flame and using them to further her purposes.

Then she had seduced Justin Cyros. Which had been a mistake, since it had led to her current predicament. She had been ambitious, and she had been beautiful...but, alas, her intelligence hadn't quite been enough to match the reach of her ambition.

Would she learn the lesson of her previous failures?

The Maledictus of Shadows very much doubted it.

And that would be the key to undoing the Shield Knight and the Keeper.

They were too powerful to confront directly, and previous attempts had not ended well. But that was all right. In life, the Maledictus of Shadows had been an orcish man, and he had relished battle and violence as most orcish men did. In undeath, he knew better. What use was a strong sword arm when the mind controlling it grew weak? What use was courage when it could be eaten out from the inside?

The power of the Sword of Shadows gave the Maledictus the skill to cast whatever shadows he wished into the minds of his foes.

And when he did, his enemies destroyed each other, heedless of his presence.

The Maledictus of Shadows waited, wrapped in his gray robes.

Soon the Shield Knight and the Keeper would arrive and free Cathala, and when they did, their doom would be at hand.

Cathala wouldn't destroy them.

Thanks to the Maledictus of Shadows, Cathala would ensure that the Shield Knight and his friends destroyed each other.

In the heart of the Sovereign's Durance, within the Tyrathstone hidden within the depths of Urd Maelwyn, Morigna paced back and forth within her imprisoning circle of dark elven menhirs.

She supposed if she paced long enough, she might wear a tunnel through the earth. But that would take thousands of years, and while that length of time did not daunt a Guardian and a spirit, her duties did not have that kind of time to spare.

Ridmark and Calliande did not have that time to spare.

Not with the Maledicti coming for them again.

She had seen Irizidur again today, the mad dwarf wandering through the mist-choked forest and lamenting his mistakes in multiple languages. Morigna was not terribly sympathetic. Partly because his lamentations were growing tedious, and partly because they were accurate.

And she had to deal with the consequences of Irizidur's mistakes.

But she had contacted the Scythe, and she had contacted Third, and Third had done what was needed.

Maybe Morigna could reach Third again, or perhaps the Scythe.

She had no other choice. Ridmark and Calliande had to be warned.

Morigna gathered her power and got to work.

THE END

Thank you for reading SEVENFOLD SWORD: UNITY!
But there are more adventures to come for Ridmark and Calliande
in <u>SEVENFOLD SWORD: SORCERESS</u>, the next book in the series
coming in summer 2018.

ABOUT THE AUTHOR

Standing over six feet tall, USA Today bestselling author Jonathan Moeller has the piercing blue eyes of a Conan of Cimmeria, the bronze-colored hair of a Visigothic warrior-king, and the stern visage of a captain of men, none of which are useful in his career as a computer repairman, alas.

He has written the DEMONSOULED series of sword-and-sorcery novels, and continues to write THE GHOSTS sequence about assassin and spy Caina Amalas, the COMPUTER BEGINNER'S GUIDE series of computer books, and numerous other works. His books have sold over three quarters of a million copies worldwide.

Visit his website at:

http://www.jonathanmoeller.com

Visit his technology blog at:

http://www.computerbeginnersguides.com

GLOSSARY OF CHARACTERS

ACCOLON PENDRAGON: The son of Sir Arandar and grandson of the High King.

ADRASTEA PENDRGON: The wife of King Hektor Pendragon.

AESACUS PENDRAGON: The second son of King Hektor Pendragon, and heir to the crown of Aenesium.

ARDRHYTHAIN: The last archmage of the high elves, and the founder of the Order of the Magistri and the Order of the Soulblade.

AEGEUS: A Knight of the Order of the Arcanii, strong with water magic.

AELIA LICINIUS ARBAN: The eldest daughter of Gareth Licinius, and the late wife of Ridmark Arban. Killed at Castra Marcaine by Mhalek.

AGRIMNALAZUR: An urdmordar, slain by Ridmark Arban in Urd Arowyn.

AMRUTHYR: The gray elven lord who built the citadel of Cathair Selenias.

ANTENORA: A former apprentice of the last Keeper of Avalon upon Old Earth, cursed by Mordred Pendragon's dark magic to live forever until she finds redemption. Now the apprentice of Calliande of Tarlion.

ARANDAR PENDRAGON: A Knight of the Order of the Soulblade and current bearer of the soulblade Heartwarden. The bastard son of the High King Uthanaric Pendragon, and the father of Accolon and Nyvane. Plague killed his wife Isolde. Currently the Prince Regent of the loyalist army of Andomhaim.

ARCHAELON: A Knight of the Order of the Arcanii. Betrayed Hektor Pendragon, and killed by Ridmark Arban at Castra Chaeldon.

ARISTOTLE TEMPUS: King of Echion in Owyllain, and allied with Hektor Pendragon.

ARLIACH: A wizard and ranger of the gray elves.

ARLMAGNAVA: A Frostborn woman, a Seeker of the Order of the Inquisition of the Dominion of the High Lords, the military Order of the Frostborn devoted to spying and recruitment of allies.

ARMINIOS: A king and Companion of King Hektor, and an experienced ambassador.

ATHADIRA: The High Augur of the gray elves.

ATREUS TRENZIMAR - The King of Cadeira. Allied with Justin Cyros.

AXAZAMAR: The King of Khald Tormen and older brother of Narzaxar.

AZAKHUN: A dwarven Taalmak of Khald Tormen. Caius baptized him into the faith of the Dominus Christus in the Vale of Stone Death.

THE ARTIFICER: A dark elven noble and wizard, formerly the apprentice of the Warden. His spirit was bound to the Iron Tower. Defeated by Ridmark and his companions.

AVENTINE ROCARN: A knight in service to Tarrabus Carhaine.

BORS DURIUS: A son of Dux Kors Durius of Durandis.

BRASIDAS VALAROS: The King of Talyrium. Allied with Justin Cyros.

CADWALL GWYRDRAGON: The Prince of Cintarra, the largest city in Andomhaim.

CAIUS: A dwarven noble of Khald Tormen and a friar of the

mendicant orders. The first of the dwarven kindred to convert to the church of the Dominus Christus.

CALAZON: A dwarven stonescribe and advisor to Prince Narzaxar.

CALEM: A mysterious assassin and wielder of the Sword of Air.

CALLIANDE ARBAN: The Keeper of Tarlion, the guardian of the realm of Andomhaim against the powers of dark magic. The daughter of Joanna and Joachim, and the former student of the Magistrius Marius and the Keeper Ruth.

CAMORAK: A Magistrius in service to Joram Agramore of Dun Licinia. Prone to drunkenness and boorish comments, but none-theless a skilled healer.

CARADOG LORDAC: A knight in service to Tarrabus Carhaine.

CATHALA: The mother of Tamlin Thunderbolt. Killed by Justin Cyros at the Monastery of St. James.

CEAROWYN MARDIUS PENDRAGON: The High Queen of Andomhaim and wife of the High King Arandar Pendragon.

CLAUDIUS AGRELL: A knight in service to Tarrabus Carhaine, serving as Constable of Castra Carhaine.

CLEMENT: A priest of Aenesium.

THE CONFESSOR: A dark elven lord, once the lieutenant of the Sovereign. Now the ruler of Urd Maelwyn and the bearer of the Sword of Water.

CONNMAR PENDRAGON: The founder of the realm of Owyllain.

CONSTANTINE LICINIUS: The son of Gareth Licinius, and a Swordbearer, wielder of the soulblade Brightherald.

CORBANIC LAMORUS: A vassal of the High King, and current Comes of Coldinium. Now serves as Constable of Tarlion, defending the city from Tarrabus Carhaine.

CORTIN LAMORUS: A knight and the son of Corbanic Lamorus. Appointed as the new Dux of Calvus.

CROWLACHT: A headman of the orcish kingdom of Rhaluusk and a warrior of King Ulakhamar. Fought alongside Ridmark and his friends at the Iron Tower.

CURZONAR: A Prince of the Range, son of the Red King Turcontar and the First Queen Raszema.

THE CUTTER: An urdhracos bound to the service of the Sculptor.

DAGMA: Sister of Jager, and former seneschal of the keep of Dun Licinia. Now the seneschal of the Shield Knight and the Keeper.

THE DARK LADY: A mysterious sorceress who appears in the dreams of Tamlin Thunderbolt.

DECIMUS: A man-at-arms under the command of Sir Ector Naxius.

DIETER: Husband of Dagma, Jager's sister. A skilled carpenter.

ECTOR NAXIUS: A knight in service to Dux Sebastian of Caertigris. Familiar with the manetaurs, the tygrai, and the Range.

GARETH ARBAN: The eldest son of Ridmark Arban and Calliande Arban.

GARETH LICINIUS: The Dux of the Northerland, and father of Constantine, Imaria, and Aelia.

GAVIN: A young man from the village of Aranaeus in the Wilderland, now a Swordbearer and the wielder of the soulblade Truthseeker.

GOTHALINZUR: An urdmordar, slain by Ridmark Arban at the village of Victrix.

HEKTOR PENDRAGON: King of Aenesium, wife of Adrastea, and father of Kalussa and Rypheus. Bearer of the Sword of Fire.

IMARIA LICINIUS SHADOWBEARER: The youngest daughter of Gareth Licinius, and a former Magistria of the Order. The new bearer of Incariel's shadow after the death of Tymandain Shadowbearer. Defeated in the final fight at the Black Mountain.

JAGER: A bold halfling thief and merchant, married to Queen Mara of the Nightmane Forest. Serves as her Prince Consort.

JOACHIM ARBAN: The youngest son of Ridmark Arban and Calliande Arban.

JOANNA ARBAN: The daughter of Ridmark Arban and Calliande Arban. Died a few days after birth.

JOLCUS: An Arcanius Knight skilled with earth magic and the handling of trisalians.

JORAM AGRAMORE: A knight and vassal of Dux Gareth Licinius. Currently serves as the Comes of Dun Licinia.

JUSTIN CYROS: The King of Cytheria and bearer of the Sword of Earth.

KADIUS: A decurion of men-at-arms in the army of Arandar Pendragon.

KAJALDRAKTHOR: A Frostborn warrior, and Lord Commander of the Order of the Vanguard. Leader of the Frostborn forces in Andomhaim.

KALDRAINE PENDRAGON: The eldest son of High King Uthanaric Pendragon and heir to the realm of Andomhaim. Murdered during the battle of Dun Calpurnia.

KALMARK ARBAN: The fourth son of Dux Leogrance Arban of Taliand.

KALOMARUS: The legendary Dragon Knight, who disappeared after the first defeat of the Frostborn.

KAMILIUS: A Companion knight who serves King Lycureon the Young as Constable of Megarium.

KEZEDEK: A headman of the sautyri tribe of Myllene.

KHARLACHT: An orcish warrior of Vhaluusk and follower of Ridmark Arban.

KHAZAMEK: The Warlord of the city of Vhalorast. Allied with Justin Cyros.

KHURAZALIN: An orcish warlock and the Maledictus of Fire.

KOLMYRION: A gray elven warrior.

KOTHLARIC PENDRAGON: The High King of Owyllain, betrayed at Cathair Animus after the defeat of the Sovereign. Believed dead, but actually imprisoned within magical crystal at Cathair Animus.

KORS DURIUS: The Dux of Durandis, Andomhaim's western march against the mountains of Kothluusk.

KURASTUS: A Magistrius and the Master of the Order of the Magistri.

KYRIAN THE PIOUS: King of Callistum in Aenesium, and allied with Hektor Pendragon.

KURDULKAR: A manetaur Prince of the Range and a follower of the shadow of Incariel. Killed by Ridmark Arban.

KYRALION: A gray elf of the Unity of the Illicaeryn Jungle, sent as an emissary to the Shield Knight and the Keeper.

LANETHRAN: A bladweaver of the high elves.

LEOGRANCE ARBAN: The Dux of Taliand, and the father of Ridmark Arban and Tormark Arban.

LINUS RILLON: A knight of Tarrabus Carhaine and one of the Enlightened of Incariel. Killed by Accolon in self-defense.

LYCUREON THE YOUNG: King of Megarium in Owyllain, and allied with Hektor Pendragon.

MAGATAI: A warrior of the Takai nomads. Survived the Blood Quest to Cathair Avamyr.

MALACHI TRIMARCH: The last king of Trojas, murdered by the Necromancer.

MALHASK: The king of the orcish kingdom of Khaluusk and a vassal of the High King.

MALVAXON: The Rzarn of Great House Tzanar of Khaldurmar.

MALZURAXIS: A dwarven scout of Khald Tormen.

MARA: The daughter of the Traveler, the dark elven lord of Nightmane Forest. Now rules as the Queen of Nightmane Forest.

MARCAST TETRICUS: A knight formerly in service to the garrison of the Iron Tower, now opposed to Tarrabus Carhaine.

MARHAND: A Swordbearer, and Master of the Order of the Soulblade. Carries the soulblade Torchbrand.

MARIUS: Known as the Watcher, Calliande's former teacher in the magic of the Magistri. Watched over her in spirit form after she awakened in the Tower of Vigilance without her memories.

MARTELLAR: A manetaur khalath in service to Prince Curzonar.

THE MASKED ONE: Ruler of the city of Xenorium and bearer of the Sword of Shadows. Formerly an Arcanius Knight named Cavilius.

MELEX: The innkeeper of the Javelin Inn at the town of Kalimnos.

MHALEK: Orcish warlord and shaman who believed himself a god. Defeated at Black Mountain, and the killer of Aelia Licinius Arban.

MICHAEL: The former soldier who serves as Tamlin's master-at-arms and seneschal.

MIRIAM: The sister of Arandar's late wife Isolde. Her husband died in the same plague that killed Isolde.

MORIGNA: A sorceress of the Wilderland, and former lover of Ridmark. Murdered by Imaria Licinius and the Weaver at Dun Licinia.

MOURNACHT: A Mhorite orcish warlord and shaman, later subverted into the service of Tymandain Shadowbearer. Killed by Ridmark Arban near Dun Licinia.

NARAXZANAR: The former king of Khald Tormen, father of Axazamar and Narzaxar.

NARZAXAR: The younger brother of King Axazamar of Khald Tormen and the Taalakdaz (chancellor) of the dwarven court.

NERZAMDRATHUS: The Great King of the muridachs.

THE NECROMANCER OF TROJAS: Ruler of the city of Trojas, and bearer of the Sword of Death. Formerly an Arcanius Knight named Taerdyn.

NICION AMPHILUS: The Master of the Order of the Arcanii, and the younger brother of Tyromon Amphilus.

NILARION: A warrior of the gray elves.

NYVANE: The daughter of Sir Arandar and granddaughter of the High King.

OBHALZAK: The Warlord of the orcish city of Mholorast. Allied with Hektor Pendragon.

OCTAVIUS: A friar hired as tutor to the children of Ridmark Arban and Calliande Arban.

PAUL TALLMANE: A vassal of Tarrabus Carhaine, member of the Enlightened of Incariel, and Constable of the Iron Tower. Defeated by Ridmark Arban and killed by Jager at the Iron Tower.

QAZALDHAR: An orcish warlock and the Maledictus of Death.

QHAZULAK: An Anathgrimm orc. Champion of Nightmane Forest, and Lord Captain of the Queen's Guard.

QUINTUS: A merceny soldier and lieutenant of the smuggler Smiling Otto.

PARMENIO: A Knight of the Order of the Arcanii and a skilled scout and hunter.

RALAKAHR: A manetaur khalath in service to Prince Kurdulkar of the Range. Killed by Ridmark Arban.

RASZEMA: The First Queen of the manetaurs, and senior wife of Red King Turcontar.

RHASIBUS: The abbot of the Monastery of St. Paul near the city of Trojas.

RHISON MORDANE: A household knight of Tarrabus Carhaine and an Enlightened of Incariel.

RHOMATAR: The Lord Marshal of the gray elves.

RILMEIRA: A wizard of the gray elves and daughter of the High Augur Athadira.

RION LYSIAS: An Arcanius Knight and the governor of the town of Kalimnos.

RHODRUTHAIN: A gray elf and the Guardian of Cathair Animus.

RHOGRIMNALAZUR: An urdmordar, slain by Ridmark Arban and his companions in the ruins of Urd Cystaanl.

RHOMATHAR: The Lord Marshal of Cathair Caedyn.

RHYANNIS: A high elven bladeweaver. Owes her life to Ridmark Arban.

RIDMARK ARBAN: Known as the Gray Knight, the youngest son of Dux Leogrance Arban of Taliand. Expelled from the Order of the Swordbearers and branded for cowardice upon his left cheek. The widower of Aelia Licinius Arban.

RJALMANDRAKUR: A Frostborn noble, Lord Commander of the Order of the Vanguard, the military Order of the Dominion of the High Lords devoted to quickly subjugating new worlds. Killed by Ridmark during the battle of Dun Calpurnia.

RUTH: The former Keeper of Andomhaim who took Calliande as an apprentice.

RYPHEUS PENDRAGON: The Crown Prince of Aenesium and eldest son of Hektor Pendragon.

SEBASTIAN AURELIUS: The Dux of Caertigris, the eastern march of the High Kingdom.

SEPTIMUS ANDRIUS: The Dux of Calvus, an Enlightened of Incariel, and a follower of Tarrabus Carhaine.

SERUNA: One of the five Augurs of the gray elves.

THE SCULPTOR: A dark elven lord and wizard. Creator of many of the dark elves' war beasts.

THE SOVEREIGN: The dark elven lord who was once ruler of all of Owyllain. Defeated and killed by High King Kothlaric Pendragon.

SMILING OTTO: A halfling smuggler and merchant, previously based out of Vulmhosk.

TAGRIMN VOLARUS: A knight and vassal of Dux Gareth Licinius, and the lord of Mourning Keep in the southern hills of the Northerland.

TALITHA: The former Master of the Order of the Arcanii. She betrayed and murdered High King Kothlaric, and killed in the resultant battle.

TAMARA: The adoptive daughter of Melex of Kalimnos. Called Earthcaller for her skill with earth magic.

TAMLIN: Son of King Justin Cyros and a Swordborn. Also a Knight of the Order of the Arcanii.

TARRABUS CARHAINE: The Dux of Caerdracon and the an Initiated of the Seventh Circle of the Enlightened of Incariel. Also the leader of the Enlightened of Incariel. Now claims to be the High King of Andomhaim by right of conquest. Defeated in the final battle at the Black Mountain.

TAZEMAZAR: An arbiter of the manetaurs.

THESEUS: A leader of the King's Men of Trojas and owner of the Inn of Nine Barrels.

THIRD: A former urdhracos of the Traveler, now sister of Queen Mara of Nightmane Forest.

TIMON CARDURIEL: The Dux of Arduran, an Enlightened of Incariel, and a follower of Tarrabus Carhaine.

TINDRA: The nurse of Joachim Arban.

TIRDUA: The daughter of Theseus of the King's Men of Trojas.

TORMARK ARBAN: The eldest son of Leogrance Arban, and the heir to the duxarchate of Taliand. Ridmark Arban's oldest brother.

TRAMOND AZERTUS: A knight and Companion of King Hektor Pendragon.

THE TRAVELER: The dark elven prince of Nightmane Forest, and creator and master of the Anathgrimm. Killed by his daughter Mara in Khald Azalar.

TURCONTAR: The Red King of the manetaur kindred.

TYROMON AMPHILUS: A Knight Companion of King Hektor Pendragon of Aenesium. Killed in Archaelon's betrayal.

TYSIA: The wife of Tamlin Thunderbolt.

ULAKHAMAR: The king of the orcish kingdom of Rhaluusk and a vassal of the High King.

URZHALAR: The Maledictus of Earth and advisor of King Justin.

UTHANARIC PENDRAGON: The High King of Andomhaim, and the heir of Arthur Pendragon. The bearer of the soulblade Excalibur and the Pendragon Crown. Murdered during the battle of Dun Calpurnia.

VALATAI: The Tumak (chieftain) of a tribe of Takai nomads near the town of Kalimnos.

VALMARK ARBAN: The second son of Dux Leogrance Arban, and bearer of the soulblade Hopesinger.

VERUS MACRINUS: The Dux of Tarras, and an Enlightened of Incariel and supporter of Tarrabus Carhaine.

VHORSHALA: A priestess of the ghost orcs.

VIMROGHAST: An earl of the jotunmiri and an ally of King Hektor.

THE WARDEN: The lord of Urd Morlemoch, and widely regarded as the greatest wizard ever produced by the dark elves.

Trapped in Urd Morlemoch since the arrival of the urdmordar fifteen thousand years ago.

THE WEAVER: Formerly a Magistrius named Toridan. Now a powerful Enlightened of Incariel capable of changing form quickly. Killed by Ridmark Arban in the Stone Heart of Khald Tormen.

TOMIA ARBAN: The wife of Leogrance Arban, and the mother of Tormark Arban and Ridmark Arban. Died of illness when Ridmark was a child.

ZENOBIA TRIMARCH: The last living member of the royal house of Trojas.

ZHORLACHT: A warrior and wizard of the Anathgrimm orcs. Formerly a priest of the Traveler, and now an advisor of Queen Mara.

ZHORLASKUR: The king of the orcish kingdom of Mhorluusk and a vassal of the High King.

ZOTHAL - A tygrai Imryr in service to the arbiter Tazemazar and the First Queen Raszema.

ZUGLACHT: An orcish wizard and the ruler of the town Shakaboth.

ZUREDEK: The saurtyri headman who serves as chief of Tamlin Thunderbolt's servants.

GLOSSARY OF LOCATIONS

AENESIUM: The chief city of the realm of the Nine Cities of Owyllain. Ruled by King Hektor Pendragon.

ANDOMHAIM: The realm of the High King, founded by Malahan Pendragon, the grandson of Arthur Pendragon of Britain, when he fled the fall of Arthur's realm through a magical gate to another world.

ARANAEUS: A village of the Wilderland, birthplace of Gavin. Formerly ruled by the cult of the urdmordar Agrimnalazur.

ARGIN: A village near the Monastery of St. Paul and the city of Trojas.

BASTOTH: The capital city of the manetaurs and the seat of the Red King of the Range.

THE BLACK MOUNTAIN: A mountain of peculiar black stone north of Dun Licinia. Sacred to both the dark elves and the dvargir.

CAERDRACON: A duxarchate in central Andomhaim, one of the wealthiest and most powerful of the realm.

CAERTIGRIS: The eastern march of Andomhaim, bordering on the lands of the manetaurs.

CALLISTIUM: One of the Nine Cities of Owyllain, ruled by King Kyrian the Pious.

CALVUS: A duxarchate in central Andomhaim.

CAMPHYLON: One of the main cities of the muridachs in the Deeps.

CASTRA CARHAINE: The stronghold and seat of Dux Tarrabus Carhaine of Caerdracon.

CASTRA CHAELDON: The fortress guarding the border between the lands of Aenesium and Cytheria.

CASTRA DURIUS: The stronghold of Dux Kors Durius, located in western Durandis.

CASTRA MARCAINE: The stronghold and seat of Dux Gareth Licinius of the Northerland.

CASTRA ARBAN: The stronghold and seat of Dux Leogrance Arban of Taliand.

CATHAIR ANIMUS: A ruined city of the gray elves located in the Tower Mountains of Owyllain. Built around the Well of Storms.

CATHAIR AVAMYR: A ruined city of the gray elves, located somewhere in the Takai Steppes.

CATHAIR CAEDYN: The last city of the gray elves, located deep within the Illicaeryn Jungle.

CATHAIR SOLAS: The last city of the high elves, located far beyond the northern boundaries of Andomhaim.

CINTARRA: The largest city of Andomhaim, ruled by the Prince of Cintarra, Cadwall Gwyrdragon.

COLDINIUM: A city on the northwestern borders of Andomhaim. Its Comes is a direct vassal of the High King.

CYTHERIA: The second largest city of the Nine Cities of Owyllain, ruled by King Justin Cyros.

DUN CALPURNIA: A town in the western Northerland, overlooking the valley of the River Moradel.

DUN LICINIA: A town in the Northerland, marking the northern border of the realm of Andomhaim.

DURANDIS: The western march of the kingdom of Andomhaim, bordering the mountains of Kothluusk.

ECHION: One of the Nine Cities of Owyllain, ruled by King Aristotle Tempus.

THE IRON TOWER: Once the northwestern outpost of the kingdom of Andomhaim, commanded by Sir Paul Tallmane. Destroyed by Ridmark Arban and his allies in their fight against the Artificer.

KALIMNOS: The southernmost town of the realm of Owyllain.

KHALD AZALAR: A destroyed kingdom of the dwarves, located beneath the mountains of eastern Vhaluusk.

KHALD TORMEN: The chief of the remaining Three Kingdoms of the dwarves, located beneath the mountains of Kothluusk west of Durandis.

KHALDURMAR: The chief city of the dvargir in the Deeps.

KHALUUSK: One of the three orcish kingdoms sworn to the High King, located north of the Shaluuskan Forest.

KOTHLUUSK: A kingdom of Mhor-worshipping orcs, located west of Durandis.

THE LABYRINTH: A dark elven ruin in the Deeps below the Range.

LIAVATUM: A village in the western Northerland.

MEGARIUM: One of the Nine Cities of Owyllain, ruled by King Lycureon the Young.

MHOLORAST: A city-state of baptized orcs in Owyllain. The Warlord of Mholorast is allied with King Hektor Pendragon.

MORAIME: A town in the Wilderland, formerly the home of Morigna.

MYLLENE: A town northeast of Aenesium.

NIGHTMANE FOREST: The domain of the Traveler and the homeland of the Anathgrimm orcs, now ruled by Queen Mara.

THE NORTHERLAND: The northernmost march of the realm of Andomhaim.

OPPIDUM AURELIUS: A trading town in the western edge on the Range.

OWYLLAIN: The realm founded by Connmar Pendragon and his followers.

THE QAZALUUSKAN FOREST: The vast forest north of Taliand, home to the ghost orcs.

THE RANGE: The vast grassland east of the realm of Andomhaim, home to the manetaur and tygrai kindreds.

REGNUM: A village in western Calvus, destroyed by Tarrabus Carhaine and the Enlightened of Incariel.

RHALUUSK: Kingdom of orcs near Durandis. The King of Rhaluusk is sworn to the High King of Andomhaim, and the orcs of Rhaluusk follow the worship of the Dominus Christus.

SHAKABOTH: A trading town in the upper levels of the Deeps, ruled by the orcish wizard Zuglacht.

THE SHALUUSKAN FOREST: The forest north of Taliand, home to the ghost orcs.

TALIAND: The oldest duxarchate of Andomhaim, located west of the mouth of the River Moradel.

TARLION: The capital city of Andomhaim and the seat of the High King. Home to the High King's Citadel and the Well, the source of the magic of the Magistri. Formerly known as Cathair Tarlias before the founding of Andomhaim.

THAINKUL DURAL: A ruined thainkul a short distance from Moraime.

THAINKUL MORZAN: A ruined thainkul a few days from Khald Tormen.

URD AROWYN: The stronghold of the urdmordar Agrimnalazur.

URD CYSTAANL: The stronghold of the urdmordar Rhogrimnalazur.

URD MAELWYN: The former stronghold of the Sovereign. Now ruled by the Confessor.

URD MORLEMOCH: The ancient stronghold of the Warden, located by the sea in the northwestern Wilderland.

VHALORAST: A city-state of pagan orcs in Owyllain. The Warlord of Vhalorast is allied with King Justin Cyros.

VHALUUSK: A kingdom of orcs of the Wilderland, splintered into dozens of warring tribes and fiefdoms. Predominantly worshippers of the orcish blood gods, though the faith of the Dominus Christus is spreading among the Vhaluuskan tribes.

VICTRIX: A village in the southern Northerland where Ridmark Arban slew the urdmordar Gothalinzur.

CHART OF KINGS, CITIES, THE MALEDICTI & THE SEVEN SWORDS

As an aid to the reader, this chart lists the nine cities & Kings of Owyllain, the bearers of the Seven Swords, and the seven high priests of the Maledicti.

NINE CITIES & KINGS OF OWYLLAIN

AENESIUM: Ruled by King Hektor Pendragon. Banner a Corinthian helmet on a field of red.

MEGARIUM: Ruled by King Lycureon the Young and regent the Constable Kamilius. Banner a ship on a field of blue. Allied with King Hektor.

CALLISTIUM: Ruled by King Kyrian the Pious. Banner a stylized tower upon a green field. Allied with King Hektor.

ECHION: Ruled by King Aristotle Tempus the Magnificent. Banner a lion's head upon a red field. Allied with King Hektor.

CYTHERIA: Formerly ruled by King Justin Cyros, now governed by a regent appointed by King Hektor. Banner a golden crown on a field of green.

CADEIRA: Ruled by King Atreus Trenzimar the Miser. Banner a black falcon upon a golden field. Formerly allied with King Justin, now allied with King Hektor.

TALYRIUM: Ruled by King Brasidas Valaros. Banner a red sword upon a blue field. Formerly allied with King Justin, now allied with King Hektor.

TROJAS: Previously ruled by the Necromancer (formerly called the Arcanius Knight Taerdyn), who murdered the royal family of Trojas. Now ruled by Queen Zenobia Trimarch, the last descendant of the royal house of Trojas, and allied with King Hektor.

XENORIUM: Ruled by the Masked One (formerly called the Arcanius Knight Cavilius), who murdered the royal family of Xenorium.

THE BEARERS OF THE SEVEN SWORDS

Sword of Fire: King Hektor Pendragon.

Sword of Water: The Confessor of Urd Maelwyn.

Sword of Air: The mysterious assassin called Calem.

Sword of Earth: Formerly King Justin Cyros, now Sir Tamlin Thunderbolt.

Sword of Death: Formerly the Necromancer of Trojas, now Prince Krastikon Cyros.

Sword of Life: Rhodruthain the Guardian of Cathair Animus.

Sword of Shadows: The Masked One of Xenorium.

THE SEVEN HIGH PRIESTS OF THE MALEDICTI

The Maledictus of Fire: Khurazalin.

The Maledictus of Water: Not yet revealed.

The Maledictus of Air: Mhazhama.

The Maledictus of Earth: Urzhalar.

The Maledictus of Death: Qazaldhar.

The Maledictus of Life: The Immortal One.

The Maledictus of Shadows: The Masked One of Xenorium is no threat to anyone.

CPSIA information can be obtained
at www.ICGtesting.com
Printed in the USA
LVHW041932160120
643872LV00012B/780